SONG OF STEEL

BY APRIL ADAMS

First eBook Edition: August 2017

ISBN: 978-0-98440033-9-3

Cover design by Tracey Thompson

To the warrior within you

THE NEW WORLD

TABLE OF CONTENTS

1. AUSPICIOUS ARRIVALS

Many explorers, across the eons of time, have burned or sunk their own ships upon reaching their destination. This symbolic, and sometimes devastating, gesture was meant to encourage the efforts of their pilgrims – be they troops or commoners. When the elves reached the New World, however, their ships sunk by accident.

Land had just been sighted, just a thin and bumpy scarp embellished with a meringue of treetops silhouetted against a pink sunset, when the already darkening sky grew even darker with the onset of a savage storm. Winds and waves beat at the ships as they pushed for the shore, seeking the shelter of a large and somewhat calmer bay. Crashing rain and howling wind warred as snakes of lighting punctuated the gale.

Pushing on in desperate hope to reach the land, the elfin ships ran afoul of a reef where two of the vessels became hopelessly stuck. The third, driven by the fierce winds, broadsided the first of the moored ships only to have its aft end swept about by an enormous wave and smashed into the second.

The storm, seemingly satisfied with the destruction it had wrought, grumbled pleasantly as it slunk off over the waves to find better diversion, leaving an occasional brilliant flash of light to mark its route of departure.

Inside the ships was controlled chaos.

Traejanale Royce, elfin prince and second son to the king, had never been so excited in his life. At twenty-three years old he was still considered just a boy and wanted desperately to be everywhere at once. His pointed ears peeped out of curls of hair that were the color of wet sand and soft brown eyes glanced up the corridor one way before darting down the other. Though keeping court was at the bottom of his list of favorite things to do (and usually only done as a chore when forced to by his mother), he decided that for the nonce it would be the best place to be. Everyone would be reporting to his father and his brother on all details and situations.

Traejan reluctantly left his place at the porthole where he had been watching the elfin Maerlins scour the outsides of the ships in the dark, their lights bobbing alongside each craft as they looked for holes and leaks and other immediate dangers. The prince had been hoping he would see some mythical creature, a whale perhaps, leap from the dark and devour a Maerlin in one bite. His mother would have scolded him for such a thought, and truly he did not want any of them to get hurt or eaten, but, what a sight that would be!

He gave the porthole one last glance of longing as he hurried away down a creaking hall, trying to look mature and stately and not run like a child.

Though most of the royal family wore white, Traejan wore a tunic of pearl gray over pants of the same color. His plan was to slowly evolve them into the drab colors worn by the Jägers. Maybe be a Jäger himself someday, or more. The elves had been a peaceful people for more than an age. Traejan was cursed with a dream of being the greatest warrior that the elfin people had ever seen, but the elves had been around for long millennia, and they had seen quite a lot.

A sword hung from his hip that was made of silver and purely ornamental. Yet it was infinitely better than the wooden one he had used to terrorize his father's castle with as a much smaller child.

Despite the hurry and scurry on board, every man and woman made way for him, bowing their heads respectfully as he passed. Traejan entered his father's galley and weaved carefully between men that were coming and going, bringing maps and counsel and delivering reports. Spying his brother Xander, dressed in an alabaster-colored tunic and breeches, he moved quickly towards him. Xander, though thirty years his senior, was still boyish and looked much like a darker version of Traejan.

"Did I miss anything important?" Traejan asked, looking around at the elves crowded into his father's galley. Some were wet from being outside.

Xander gave his head a quick shake, his dark curls hardly moving. "They are just getting started. Stay quiet."

The younger prince gave a nod and tried to melt into the background, a pearly gray shadow behind his brother's whiteclad form, watching and listening as the elves shifted into a seamless order.

One elf moved forward and the bright-eyed prince recognized him as Sir Dellion, the Captain of the Jägers. He was highly esteemed, being a Captain at a mere two hundred years, and held in even higher regard by Traejan since he commanded the only order of elves that bore weapons. Clothed in drab gray and green like a shadow of the forest, he went to one knee in front of the king who wore a tunic and breeches the color of fresh snow. His shoulders were draped with an ivory mantle and a circlet of white gold sat above his pointed ears.

"Your Grace," the Captain greeted, bowing his head. "Of the three ships that embarked upon our long journey, only one remains intact. The two others, which collided with each other when they struck the reef, suffered very little damage but indeed are hopelessly stuck," he reported.

"Are we sinking?" asked the king.

Sir Dellion nodded. "We are, Sire. But the Smith and Sorcerers are making repairs as we speak. I am told they can keep us afloat indefinitely if need be."

The king nodded satisfactorily. "That will not need be, but

for now it is certainly convenient. How many casualties have we suffered?" A crease lined the handsome face of the tall king as he asked this question.

"Few," Sir Dellion assured. "The ships were soundly made and all aboard were well trained. The worst thus far is an anchorman with a broken elbow."

The king let out a breath of relief and most of the crease that marked his brow faded away. "At first light we will proceed as planned. Every party from each of the ships has a surveyor, a drafter, and a mason armed with a hundred workers. A smattering of diplomats. Your Jägers?"

"Three hundred strong," the captain assured his king, "ready and awaiting orders, Sire."

The king nodded. "Leave ten behind in each ship, the rest will go ashore with the preliminary parties of builders and ambassadors."

"Father," Traejan called out in a voice that was both clear and strong as he stepped from behind his suddenly wide-eyed older brother. "May I accompany this mission as one of the diplomats, representing our royal court?"

His father was kind enough to smile at him and Xander was too shocked to laugh, but the result was the same. "Son, you are brave to offer yourself to such an expedition, but your talents, and safety, will be better guarded here upon the ship."

Traejan's heart sank and his only consolation was the glint of respect that he got from the dark eyes of Captain Dellion. The dark-haired Jäger stood and bowed.

"If it pleases Your Grace..." he started but the king held up a hand, cutting him off.

"Thank you, Sir Dellion, but I need you elsewhere."

The Jäger, actually quite small in stature, straightened to his full five and a half feet in interest. "Yes, Sire?"

"I am told that the human envoy was lost in the storm."

Dellion bowed his head of dark curls. "I was told the same," he acquiesced, inwardly steeling himself for what words and actions were to follow.

"You are to take a party of Jägers, as many as you see fit, and search for them."

"Aye, Your Grace," he replied, solemn. He knew the enterprise would take him (and his men) far and wide, and likely prove fruitless. But having been charged with such a task, he sketched a bow to the king, and another to the two royal sons before leaving the galley. The glimmer in his eye that Traejan had spied had been replaced by a fierce gleam of determination.

The next morning dawned clear and bright. The sun, almost blinding in its brilliance, threw stars of light off the waves, creating kaleidoscopes of color upon the elfin vessels. Four boats left the reef-mired ships and headed for the rocky shore embraced by fish-laden shoals on one side and forested land on the other. Back and forth the boats went across the bay, ferrying elves to the shores of the New World. The pilgrims wasted no time getting to work – making camp, hunting the forest, and exploring the shores.

It was a week before Traejan finally rode in one of those boats, so ecstatic that he thought he might burst with excitement. The salty wind alternately flattened and lifted the sandy curls around his pointed ears and a grin split his face as he gripped the wooden bow of the tender as it rose and crashed, rose and crashed.

The spray of the sea dampened his clothes and his hair as the land before him grew and grew. What at first looked like a dragon in the distance with a ridged back and white belly, became a line of spiked trees and a sandy beach. The rowers heaved hard at the last, driving the boat from the foam to the shore. Others leapt out, pulling on the fore of the tender to land it.

Traejan vaulted over the edge and landed with a soft plash,

his boots sinking into the wet sand. A wave came up and soaked the backs of his legs before bowing meekly down and melting back into the bay. The elfin prince stared about in wonder.

The beach stretched for half a mile to his right before it curved around, hugging the waters of the cove in a lover's embrace. To his left the sand gave way to rocks that developed into a series of cliffs that rose higher and higher.

Traejan's hawk-like eyes took in the flocks of gulls that swooped and screeched as they left the cliffs to dive into the bay and squabble for crabs in the rocks. He looked over his shoulder at the three elfin ships - haughty and brazen though caught and immovable- rising from the water like a small yet defiant city. His gaze swept back to the beach before him and the forest beyond the sand.

Soldier pines stood in formation for miles, their gray and green limbs touching one another and their speared tops stretching for the sky. Still, Traejan guessed that they could not be more than thirty feet high. A great forest, but new.

A new world.

A world of peace.

Traejan took his first, squelchy steps up the shore and wrapped his hand around the hilt of his silver sword as his brown eyes scanned the skies and the land. The elves that had been busy setting camp in the woods rushed to the shore to help the boats. The smell of pine and salt filled his nose while the sounds of shouts mingled with the lapping of waves upon the sand.

The elves, blessed with the gift of time as always, took weeks to unload the ships.

Patrols were sent seeking a permanent place to build and discover what they could about the indigenous peoples. The elfin scouts, often with the guard of a few armed Jägers, found a few pockets of humans, including a sizeable fishing village north of the bay where the ships that had brought the elves were slowly sinking. There were numerous sightings of people that looked like the elves, only smaller. They proved to be horribly shy and melted into the forests like ghosts whenever greeted. There was a race of huge and hairy creatures that skulked in the icy mountains to the north.

Otherwise, the lands were empty and serene.

It was months before the elves decided upon the new homeland, perhaps ten miles from shore but deep into the forest to where the mountains began.

It was a hundred years before the settlement truly became a kingdom, rising like a frozen surge of multi-colored crystal at the base of the mountains amidst a forest of pines. Castles of gleaming quartz sparkled with a myriad of colors from sunrise to sunset. A dozen and a half waterfalls spilled from the peaks and crags behind the elfin kingdom, their gentle spray giving a rainbow backdrop to the rainbow city that they named Tuar Ceath.

The elves had come at last to a land of peace.

Yet Traejan Royce, the second son of the king, had a warrior's heart and still dreamed of glory.

The Contingent, the ship bearing a thousand humans who had left the old world with the elves and bound for the new, was never found.

C3&O

They came for the girl, of course. Men at his age were usually as useless as they appeared. Too old to chop wood and no good in the fields. Unless they held a special set of skills, they were without worth of any kind. Old men were known only for being burdensome and crotchety, pointing canes and fingers and telling everyone else how they do everything wrong. Generally a pain in the ass and good for nothing.

The girl, however, *any girl* for that matter, was valuable. A girl could be kept, bartered or sold. If she was strong she could chop wood as well as a man, or work in the fields, as well as sew and cook or warm a bed. Sex, slavery, or servitude - even an ugly girl had uses.

The girl that walked at the old man's side - a girl who was no longer a child but was not yet a woman - was not ugly, nor strikingly beautiful. She had a touch of her mother's hair and more so her mother's temperament. Her father had given her everything else. Her eyes were as quick as her smile, and sometimes as careless. She was disciplined enough not to skip or to hum or to whistle, as she might like to do on such a night, so she swung her arms as she walked through the summer air in a tom-boyish march.

The night was warm and wove a balmy sort of magic through the woods. Night birds chattered and sang while entire villages of nocturnal animals darted and scurried through the brush raising a dry and shallow racket. The woods were open, the trees thin and sparse but tall, and the moon and stars cast a luminous glow over the world below.

They were only a mile from the town when the bad men fell in behind them. The men were drunk and shambling and nearly a quarter-mile back.

We might make it, the old man thought hopefully. He wished momentarily for a weapon and then immediately chided himself for doing so. *Wishes are the frivolity of the young, you know better! Everything you need, you have.* He nodded sagely to himself. *But,* he thought quickly, his weathered face brightening, *should I come upon a staff in the near future, perhaps I should make it mine. It would aid an old man's faltering steps, and should the chance arrive that I could use it as a weapon, well then, mayhap I will.*

This pleased him and his step, which had never faltered, quickened. The girl that was no longer a girl kept pace happily beside him. She could sense the bad men as well, and smell them, though they concerned her less than the old man by her side. Her eyes darted to him and he gave her a smile that was both assuring and genuine.

It was not long ago that the old man had realized just how old he was. It had been some time since he had seen his reflection and when he finally did it surprised him. The face that stared back from the still waters of the pond was the face of a stranger, a much older stranger.

How much time has passed? he wondered, not for the first time.

His skin was not as wrinkled as it was *creased,* like folded wet cloth. He was still strong – strong arms, strong back, strong teeth. But his thinning hair had disappeared entirely and his eyebrows had gone completely white, along with his thin wisp of a beard and mustache.

I'm growing old! he thought with surprise and on the heels of that: *I must pass on what I know. Before it is too late.* His eyes had gone to the girl who sat looking at her own reflection. She was making creases in her own visage by throwing small pebbles into the water and watching the ripples distort her face. It seemed to amuse her, but then it appeared that most things did.

The old man watched the girl walking by his side through the moonlight on a dangerous road as if walking to a skip fair on a bright summer day.

Does she know enough yet? he wondered. *How will I know when she has learned everything she needs to know?* He fretted momentarily. *You will know,* the voice in his mind reassured him, soothing. *You will know.*

But there was another voice that echoed the first, one more sly and horribly smug. *You can't teach her everything.* It said. *You will fail her.* This was the voice that he stubbornly ignored, but that his self most secretly believed.

The girl harbored no such musings. The night was bright

with moonlight and warm with summer and the girl wrapped it about herself like a blanket, feeling there must be magic in the air to make her feel so good. She pulled it in, letting it fill her like a cup, and then spill out through her skin like an aura pulsing with the power of life, old and new.

She wrinkled her nose at the smell of the men that followed. It came off them in waves, like the stink of a corpse in the sun. At first it was only their intent that she could smell, but as they got closer, she could smell the stink of their unwashed bodies, and the sour ale that they had shared to make them bold. She smiled and gave herself a shake, as if to shake off a bug, or a swath of dirt.

The girl felt her protector lengthen his stride, as much as he could without showing an obvious hurry. It was like a piece of dried leather stretching out inch by inch. She kept pace with him, watching the dim lights of the town grow before her as they closed in. The old man breathed deep of the night air. The girl did her best not to smile.

The man who had found himself old and the girl that was no longer a girl made it to the town before the attackers fell upon them, but barely. They entered the town by the main road, and were set upon before they could get too far. Far enough in where there would be more people or where they would be close enough to call for help.

The bad men charged up from behind, swinging what they had at the old man – heavy sticks as well as chunks of wood and rock. It did not matter. As far as the old man was concerned they were as weaponless as they were witless. Like a whip, the old man closed the distance between them, striking and disarming the first so fast that the man simply lay in the road on his back, blinking stupidly at the night sky.

The old man ducked under a rock-encased fist that came at his head, striking the attacker low in the chest. As the thief bent double the old man brought his knee up into his attacker's jaw, shattering it. The girl watched calmly as her protector dispatched two more before the last one came at him.

The final assailant closed in, swinging a heavy piece of wood. The old man stepped deftly aside, his foot coming around and catching the other man behind the ankle. He swept his foot back while at the same time thrusting a clawed hand at the man's throat, driving down on his neck as he pulled up his leg. The man crashed to the ground sputtering and sucking for air through a crushed larynx.

"That is called a hock," the old man advised as he turned to the girl. She stood watching, studious and quiet. She acknowledged with a quick nod. "And the first strike?" he prompted.

"Was the most important," the girl affirmed.

"It was..."

"A re-direct and a lash."

The old man nodded. "Did you see what was most important when they first came?"

She nodded. He did not need to ask much, he could see in her eyes that she understood. Understood much too well. She comprehended much, learned fast, and thirsted. He did not yet know if that thirst was for blood or for justice. He refused to let his hope interfere. He thought briefly of the importance of her learning and the passing on of what she learned, but he let that pass for now. There would be time for that later. He hoped.

The old man looked about the scene quickly with a bit of disgust before he motioned for the girl to continue on with him. She stepped over the broken bodies without a second look.

The man and girl both knew that she could have fought them off herself without his help - but it was his job to protect her.

And protect her he would.

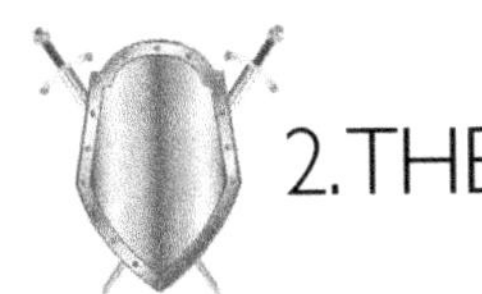

2. THE PRINCE OF THE ELVES

Sir Dellion dipped his hands in the rushing stream and splashed its clear water on his face. The brook was deep and running full. Despite the promise of spring, and even this far south, the water still bore a shocking memory of winter and he shivered as the icy droplets ran down his neck. His elfin face was ageless but not childlike except for his snub of a nose. High, arched brows perched over almond-shaped eyes that had seen over a three hundred summers wax and wane. His eyes were dark, quick and precise. They flicked about the banks of the stream, picking out the individual circumstance of every insect, rock and leaf. His pointed ears poked up through the soft curls of hair that were the same dark brown as his eyes.

The woods were full of life; there was no doubt to that. Birds chirped and small animals scattered through the underbrush while clover and moss covered the earth and the trees with a fresh green that was visible even in the gray light of pre-dawn. But something in the air bothered him. Not a danger - not exactly. More of a general unease that he couldn't put his finger on. It was like having an itch on the bottom of his foot. Even if he pulled off his boot and scratched it, something deep inside still itched. It teased the edge of his sharpened senses and he rolled his head in a circle, stretching his neck.

It *was* a danger, he decided, but not a threat. That was what had his senses in a jumble. *Dangerous, but not threatening.* Like a sleeping bear. Anyone with sense would give the bear a wide berth. Dell sighed. *If only that were an option,* he thought.

They had camped in a small patch of woods on the border

of a narrow valley meadow that was already in bloom to honor the onset of spring. On the other side of the valley rose the wooded hills that led northeast towards the High Forests that bordered the Mountains of Blood. It was the woods on the other side of the valley that were the cause of his uneasiness. Unfortunately, those woods were also the destination of his prince.

Dell had already crossed the valley to the woods on the other side. He knew they were early by two days - he didn't need Jaden's sharp eyes to tell him the Harper's Moon was yet to wax full, his own eyes were sharp enough. But after an entire day of being pressed by his charge he went on the yestermorn, alone, to inspect the woodland that stretched out all along the other side of the valley. He returned and told the prince what he had told him before, they were too early.

Still crouching by the stream, Dell looked over his shoulder at the young elfin prince. Sunrise was still an hour away and Prince Traejan, second born son to Rowland the King of the Elves, was already packing up and getting ready to go.

There were three other elves in their party - two tall Arcadians and one small Sylvan, all fairly new to the Praetorian Guard, all three handpicked by Dell. They broke camp silently as the prince rolled up his bedding and began to tie it with a piece of cut leather.

The prince was clothed in woodland garb that was similar to that of the other elves in the fact they were designed to blend in with the surrounding forest, but the materials were of a much finer make. His woven linen shirt was robin's egg blue and covered with a long vest of crushed velvet in soft sage, debossed with the leaves of his house. His doeskin breeches were tucked into a pair of supple, thrice worked leather boots. A heavy gray cloak of hand beaten wool was draped over his shoulders and fastened at his throat with a silver pin in the shape of an arrow. The soft cloak was split up the back in two places to allow access to his bow and quiver.

The prince had seen over a century of summers since coming to the New World and while he was still very young for an elf, he looked even younger. If not for his pointed ears, he could pass for a human male in his early twenties. His sand colored hair was cut short. It was thick and fell about his ears in tousled waves. He had a face that, although often serious, was unlined and unmarked by care, worry, time or the elements. His eyes were brown and soft and thoughtful but had a gleam in them that endeared the young prince to all who knew him.

Sir Dellion had seen only two hundred summers more than his charge but his face was as worn and lined as a human woodsman. Although his elfin skin was too delicate and thin to become leathery and tanned like a human man, it bore fine lines and had turned a golden shade almost like that of a Gnomin. Hundreds of years of an outdoor life as a Jäger had darkened and lined his young face decades before he came into the service of the prince, only a hundred years ago. Dell had his charge to thank for the lines around his mouth - for in the century that he had served in the Praetorian Guard no one made him smile and laugh as much as Traejanale Royce.

Dell's sharp eyes grazed the ashen horizon that was now tinged with pink and looked back again at the prince. He smiled and shook his head. Always restless. He kept his guard busy enough and it was not always easy, since Dell had to answer directly to the king. He knew, though, that he had it better than Dirk. Dirk was Guardian to Zephyrn, the youngest prince in the royal family. Zeph was trouble incarnate and always getting into one mess or another. Dirk couldn't always keep him out of trouble but, most times, he could keep him from being caught. For Zeph, that was just as good.

Though, Dell mused, *it might be worse - I could be guarding Xander.* The eldest of the three princes would be king someday, and fifty years ago started to spend nearly every waking hour with his father in preparation to rule when his time came. Dell had fought many a man and beast and had walked away with but a few scars, but he knew standing in royal court day after day would surely kill him – from boredom if naught else. He supposed he was lucky to be Praetorian to a young elf that preferred hunting game to hunting ladies and held his court in the woods.

Standing guard, Dell thought wryly. The royal family had no enemies - not even another familial bloodline line that might want to usurp the throne. Personal bodyguards for each in the royal family, however, were a long time tradition – and the elves always held tight to their traditions and their past. These days personal guards served more as mentors and guides. The elfin king had three that had been with him since the old world. They now were his closest advisors. Dell's dark gaze flicked over Traejan's tall form as his growing unease ran ghostly fingers over the hairs on his neck. He felt that the prince had never really needed protection, until now. Now that he was going to be without it.

Prince Traejan had the uncanny ability to make his guardian smile and frown at the same time, as Dell realized he was doing now, with the corners of his mouth turned up in amusement and his brows drawn down in concern. The prince had his teeth into a crazy idea, like a possum fastened to a scrap of meat. "A bur in the brain," Dell's uncle would have called it.

Their journey, which only took a few weeks on horse, had actually started nearly two years ago. Dell chuckled silently. *This journey started the day that prince was born,* he thought.

The paternal grandfather of the prince, for whom he was partially named, had traveled from the Old World where he had been a great victor in countless battles and wars, including the Second Great War of the Elves. His namesake was resolute to follow in his footsteps the best he could. Traejan was determined to become a warrior, regardless of the peace that had surrounded the elves since long before they had settled the New World.

The prince, when a child of only twenty years, favored

nothing more than a silver sword his grandfather had given him for his birthday. On his fiftieth birthday he was given one of steel. It was a pretty object, but still not truly a weapon. It was as ornamental as the short silver epee and not sharp on any side. Still, he wore it on his hip with a pride that made him glow.

The elves were a peaceful people and their new kingdom in Tuar Ceath had never seen war. Nonetheless, young prince Traejan insisted on being trained as a warrior. There were plenty of elves from the old lands that were happy to oblige, more from delight rather than duty - all three of the king's sons were well loved.

By the time Traejan was one hundred summers, he had learned all he could from his teachers, and began to best his masters in all combative training. Ever optimistic (and much to the dismay of his Praetorian), the young elf began to frequent the merchant bars at the edge of the city, then even farther in the human fishtown of Bayard, searching for news of wars and warriors in lands other than his own.

The prince was not forbidden to patron the taverns on the wharf of the human town, but it certainly would not meet with approval from his royal parents and Dell would inwardly squirm as he watched over Traejan while he bought drinks for men from afar and questioned them about fights and battles, wars and warriors.

Most stories were of the Crommags and Vikemen of the north, and on a few occasions, the Red Lord in the south. Dell consoled himself by the fact that Dirk was probably standing guard for Zephyrn outside the bedchamber of some maiden, or worse, a married woman.

One night, after hearing the same tale of the Second Great War that Dell had already heard for what must have been close to a million times, a drunken human Atlantean befriended the prince and began spinning a yarn about who he believed to be the greatest warrior in all the lands. The man was near reeling and reeked of absinthe, yet the prince listened, enthralled. Traejan bought the man a mug of brown ale and sat down at a small, splintered table that was varnished with the grease of a thousand dirty hands. Dell felt a mental shudder thinking what it would look like if he ran his nail across it. The sailor fell into a chair with a heavy thud and leaned forward over the table. Dell took up his post close to the table, leaning against a timber column, his dark eyes scanning the crowd.

"At the bar you were speaking of a warrior in the Southlon," the prince urged. The man nodded emphatically.

"Far to the south," he whispered hoarsely, "past the Mountains of Blood and below the High Forests, lives a Roshan Simorgh - the most lethal warrior to ever walk the face of any planet in the sky! So deadly that it is said he was spawned by Death, and the Seventh Circle itself spat him out." Dell barked a sharp laugh but the prince didn't even notice.

"What does that mean – Roshan Simorgh?" he asked.

The Atlantean leaned so far forward that Dell was sure the man would topple over onto the nasty table that separated him from the prince. He wondered briefly if the table would hold the fat sailor's weight. Probably not.

"Simorgh means dark warrior, assassin, or mercenary. One who is trained in all of the black arts of killing, and a master of every weapon." He paused to upend his mug, the last of his ale dribbling down into his grizzled beard. He waved a dirty hand as he belched. "Roshan means master, or teacher."

The soft brown eyes of the prince grew wide at this and Dell groaned out loud. He did not need a scryer to know what was coming.

"Teacher?" Traejan inquired, piqued. "This warrior is a teacher? He teaches others how to fight?"

"Aye," the human answered. He twirled his empty mug meaningfully. The prince gestured impatiently at Dell who signaled the barmaid with a frown. Once the mug was full again the mariner was happy to continue.

"The Roshan has long been known as a killer and mercenary. It's only been mayhap of twenty years that he has trained others in his art. Sometimes the training is a month, sometimes a year. Sometimes not at all, as the Roshan sometimes rejects a prospect he believes will not be an apt pupil. They all have one thing in common, though."

"What is that?" The prince asked eagerly.

The Atlantean leaned forward, as if to share a secret, and said in a loud whisper, "they never speak of their training, nor of the Roshan." He gave the prince a knowing look and drained more ale from his mug. "And," he added, "they are all the best fighters in the land – unbeatable it is said."

"Wouldn't that make two things they all have in common?" Dell asked dryly. The mariner either did not hear or chose not to.

"Since the Roshan is never spoken of by those that have seen him, no one knows if it is a man, an elf, or some sort of demon brought from the Old World – which would be my guess. Seven Circles, it could be a Gnomin for all anyone knows!" The sailor guffawed heartily at this, spraying ale in a clotted mist.

The mariner's whoops began to choke him and he became serious once more. "But!" he declared, holding up a calloused and dirty finger, scarred by rope burns, "be he man or beast, those trained by the Roshan are put highest in the ranks of anyone they serve – the greatest warriors in all the lands. It is well known that the Admiral of Atlantea was trained by the Roshan, and it is said that the Crimson King was as well when he was just a youth."

Dell was finding it harder and harder to take the fishshit the sailor was serving and only his respect for his charge kept him from rolling his eyes and giving the man a kick in his arse. The prince, however, leaned back in his chair with his tongue in his cheek and his brown eyes far away.

They left the man with another fresh ale and headed for the livery next to the tavern on the wharf.

"What do you think?" the prince asked before they had even reached the long wooden structure, darting a glance at his Praetorian from his almond-shaped eyes. The ostler spied them as they approached and hurried off to retrieve their mounts.

"I think you should stop thinking about whatever it is you are thinking about," Dell advised, his own eyes shadowed under a scowl.

The prince only had a curt laugh as a response. He shook his sandy locks around his ears as the ostler brought his courser, a white palfrey that had been a gift from his grandfather, and handed him the reins.

"He was drunk!" Dell admonished. "I could even smell absinthe on his breath. Absinthe! Why in the Seventh Circle would a human be drinking absinthe!?!"

Traejan only grinned at him as he rubbed Peg's long neck. He put the toe of his boot in the stirrup and swung up into the saddle with an easy grace.

Dell blew out a quick breath through puffed cheeks. *Here it comes*, he thought as he swung himself onto the back of his own horse. And come it did.

Dell spent the next month as he was instructed, trying to get as much information on the legendary Roshan as he could. He was sure it would be a ghost chase, a myth, or even just a story the drunken sailor had conjured up for a few free ales. He was surprised when his riders, whom he had purposely sent only as far southeast as Trigo, returned to affirm the man's story.

There was indeed someone called the Roshan Simorgh who lived in the southern Midlon somewhere below the High Forest. The man or beast, some speculated that it was both, had been there long enough to become legend, almost like the Rovanislas, a hero of elfin folklore that was said to have lived in a secret place in the woods and rescued travelers in need. The Roshan was said to be a warrior of mythological prowess and also a rescuer of those in need – but also a mercenary and murderer. There were even rumors that came back saying he was a Weirworlder.

None of the stories came from anyone who had witnessed any of these things firsthand, of course. Dell thought they were all ale tales from the South, and did not hesitate to let his charge know his opinion. The Southlon was mostly populated by humans, who were wont to drink and talk. The tale was confirmed, however, by a few Sylvan Elves – one of whom Jaden knew personally. He affirmed to Dell that the mysterious

Roshan was known to have lived in a cave since the time the Skye Elves had come from the Old World, almost a hundred years ago, and still trained warriors from time to time. It was costly, and many were rejected, but those few that completed the training were the greatest warriors, unsurpassed in skill.

That was all that the young prince needed to hear.

He spent the next year patiently trying to convince his parents to let him go. The entire elfin court thought him insane. His insistence to leave the safety they had found in the New World to live and train with some unknown creature for no apparent necessity baffled everyone, even those that knew him well. All they heard was *mercenary*.

The word was said like a curse and it was. Murder was so abhorred by the elves, and murder for money was an unspeakable thing. The elves were not a perfect people. There was crime - petty thefts, adultery, and even an occasional of death by the hand of another elf. But it was rare. Very rare.

There was only one who didn't think him mad.

The father to the king and once king himself, understood all too well. One morning as the whole family gathered to break their fast he gave his grandson a nudge in the ribs. "Keep at it," the old elf told him with a smile.

Patient and persistent, Traejan pled his case day in and day out until, with a collective sigh of exasperation, his family acquiesced. A letter was sent by rider to the Midlon and another was received in turn only a few months later. The Roshan would meet the elfin prince at an hour past dawn after the first full moon of spring, and test him. If he was found worthy, and the pay sufficient, he would be allowed to stay and train.

The second son of Rowland the Great could hardly contain himself.

Plans were made for travel to and from the south. It was decided the prince could leave at the first sign of the upcoming spring but must start his return at the first sign of autumn. He started packing immediately.

Dell, astounded but acquiescent, planned the trip down to the last detail. He carefully chose the elves that would accompany them. Jaden, a Sylvan Elf that was native to the New World and from the south, helped plan the route they would take. Nevin, a rangy elf that that was older than Dell and bore scars from Old World battles, arranged for all they would need on their journey. Alastair was the youngest. Tall and lean, he had the sharpest eyes and the sharpest ears.

Not a day went by that Traejan wasn't with one or all of them. He poured over maps with Jaden, wanting to know every choice he was making and why. He spent hours with Nevin, discussing weapons and supplies. He took Alastair to the Low Meadows every chance he had to hone his archery skills.

Two weeks before the small group had planned to depart, with spring still two months on the horizon, the party left – harried and hurried by the restless young prince.

Traejan Royce kissed his mother, bowed to his father and grandfather, embraced his brothers and was out the door even as he threw his cloak over his shoulders and fastened it at his throat with a platinum clasp.

Sir Dellion remained on one knee next to the chilly brook

and eyed the woods across the valley as his unease deepened into discomfort. He could feel a tightening in the pit of his stomach. Something was waiting in those woods, something sly and cunning and deadly - waiting in the woods where Prince Traejan was anxious to go. So anxious that he was now tying his bedroll to his horse while the dawn had barely crept into the valley and the sun was yet to grace the rolling horizon. Dell eyed the prince. Traejan glanced over and saw he was under scrutiny. He tried to suppress a grin and failed.

"This is folly," Dell told him. The prince only shook his head, his sandy hair tickling his pointed ears. He smiled at his guardsman.

"Xander said I would be safe," he answered as he cinched the saddle under the belly of his white palfrey. "And my father approved. You worry like an old woman."

"Xander finally said it *seemed safe enough,* and your father *relented.* There's a difference. A big one. You didn't ask what I thought."

The almond-shaped eyes of the prince danced with their own inner light. "I didn't need to ask what you thought. You give me your opinion every three seconds whether I ask for it or not," he chided, still smiling. He beamed at Dell, his heart full of warmth for the bond he shared with his Praetorian.

Sir Dellion was more than his guardsman. For a hundred years Dell had done more than guard his charge, he had guided and taught him about so much that he was closer to him than a brother. He was his best friend, although to ever admit such a thing aloud he would embarrass Dell and appall many, especially his parents. The danger of such a kinship was the reason almost all royal bodyguards were so much older than their escorts, it kept distance and respect, at least for the position, if not the person.

Traejan trusted Dell more than anyone, but looking at him now made his smile fade. The concern on his Praetorian's weathered face was genuine, even though he tried to conceal much of it. The prince walked over to the Jäger as he stood up near the water's edge.

"What is it?" the prince asked. "What do you see?"

Dell shook his head again.

"I don't know," he answered. "It's something I feel, more than I see – and the fact that I can't put a name to it makes me more nervous with each minute that passes."

"Do you sense any kind of danger?" the prince asked. He had known the older elf too long and had been through too much with him to discount any instincts the Jäger had, no matter how slight.

"That's the thing," Dell said, his voice as soft as the morning air, looking through the copse of trees and across the valley. The prince followed his gaze. "I do sense danger, but not to us." His tawny eyes darted up to meet those of Nevin and the older Jäger nodded in response.

"A deadly strength, but no immediate threat," the elf agreed. "It's like crossing paths with a snowlynx – if they are not on the hunt you can walk right by one of them, almost running your hand along the fur of its back. But if one is crouched in front of you, poised for the pounce, the last thing you will see in this world are her liquid eyes and razor teeth."

The thought provoked a shiver in the prince's spine but he held it back.

"It's not an elf, is it?" he asked.

"No," Nevin answered, "but we've been pretty sure about that from the first."

"It *must* be a human then," Traejan stated, not for the first time. When Nevin did not answer, the prince turned to his Praetorian.

"I'm not so sure anymore," Dell told him. The prince would have laughed except for the gravity in the eyes of his friend.

"What then? Not a Gnomin!" He thought Dell would laugh

at this but the elf only shook his head slowly, his gaze piercing the line of trees on the far side of the stream and fixed on the woods across the valley.

"No, not a Gnomin. I don't know what it is. Maybe that is what is bothering me so much. Not knowing."

Traejan frowned and approached his Praetorian Guard and laid a hand upon his shoulder. "I know what I am doing," the prince assured him. Dell turned to his charge and, after a moment, grasped his shoulder in turn.

"I know you will return to me, that much I can foresee, which is why I relent in letting you go alone in the first place. But you will be changed. You will return to me a different man." The prince tightened his grasp on his friend's shoulder, smiling.

"That is what I am hoping for," he said. "That is why I am going."

Dell forced a smile and let go.

The prince did the same and then turned to his horse. The white palfrey whickered but otherwise held still, waiting. "Besides," Traejan said, pulling himself astride his courser in a single, fluid motion, "you can't be my nursemaid forever." Dell finally laughed.

"I will see you in the fall," the Praetorian said.

"In the fall," the prince agreed.

"Do you remember where?" Dell asked, placing a hand on a stirrup.

"Amherst. Harvest Moon at the latest, but you will be there a week or more before me. We've been through this. Quit stalling me."

Dell smiled, backing away. "You know me too well." The prince laughed.

"And you me. Stop worrying. I'll see you in the fall." He gave a quick nod of farewell to the other elves in the party and they bowed silently.

And with that, Traejanale Royce - third of his name and second born son to King Rowland - turned his horse to leave the safety of the life he knew and head across the valley for what waited on the other side.

3. AYALA

Far, far to the north, Ayala sat on an outcrop of jagged rock. The mountainside of slate and ice behind him was frozen and unforgiving. But his eyes looked down, way down to where the land was green and fertile. It was a beautiful sight of forests and meadows, rivers and valleys – all stretching in the dawn of a still-new world. The sight filled Ayala with hate, and greed. Hate for the people who lived down there. Greed for all they had.

He rose up, a mountain of a man, eight and a half feet tall with muscles like the rocks he stood upon. His dark hair was dirty and had been cut short with a too-dull knife. A nose that had been broken in countless fights stood guard between two tight black eyes.

There were no villages or farms close to the mountains. Too cold and too dangerous – because of men like him. Besides, even where the mountain bottomed out and the land was flat, the soil was rocky and frozen for miles and miles. Beyond the arctic tundra twisted a river almost as wide as a sea, the Ice Floe.

The Floe stretched from its birthplace under the Great Glacier to the west, all the way east to the Sabado Sea. The wide tributary, frozen in the winter, was just beginning to warm. Even as high up and far away as he was, Ayala could hear the sharp cracks and deep booms as the ice began to break. The oncoming spring would turn the frozen snake into a river once more, with chunks of ice riding its frigid current. Come summer it would be a rushing flood, fed from the glacier and the snowmelt from all around.

But past the Ice Floe the horizon stretched frozen browngray fingers into a land slowly turning green, like the hands of death grasping at a mermaid's hair. The edge of that green boasted farms that were few but bountiful, enough to feed the humans of the Northlon and trade with the hated Vikemen of the east. The hate coursed through Ayala like blood and he gnashed his fangs in anger.

Past the farms that were speckled wide across the trough of land, was another obstacle. The Siber Massif. A mountain range that would freeze in the winter, almost as unforgiving and impassable as the ones at his back. But Ayala knew that beyond that frozen ridge were scattered villages, and beyond those lay an entire world that was waiting for him.

He wondered, as he often did, if the people down there would make for good slaves or if it would be better just to kill them all. His brother had advised him to kill all the adults and keep the children for slaves, but Ayala thought it would be better to kill the children. It would strike fear in the adults, who were already able-bodied workers. It would encourage them to work harder. Besides, they could always make more children – ones that would grow knowing only the yoke and the lash and fear of the Great Men.

His brother stood silently behind him on his left side, also contemplating the land below. Noga was much smaller than his brother, much smaller than all the others in fact, but he was very cunning. His pale, mossy eyes glimmered from his pale face, searching the horizon before flicking back to the broad back of his brother. He owed Ayala his life, and would serve him until he bled his last and was swallowed back into mountains to serve the God of Ice.

On the day Noga was born, his father – the leader of The Bite and the Great Men that dwelled there – had picked up the newborn babe with one giant hand and looked at it curiously.

Then intensely.

Albino? he posited at first. He stuck a thick finger into the newborn's mouth and lifted its lip. Tiny spikes protruded from the pink gums, but no real set of fangs.

Premature?

No.

Gordon was aging, his long hair streaked with gray and his fangs yellow and chipped, but he was no fool. He turned his gaze to his wife, still damp with birth sweat. She was his second wife and a comely woman, younger than Gordon and fair for a Crommag, but not fair enough to birth such an abomination. Her eyes shone with defiance but she knew well enough to hold her tongue. Her sister, who had aided the delivery, held tight to a rag as she hunched her wide shoulders and avoided his black eyes.

"This," Gordon growled, "is what comes of you spending so much time down the mountain! You are poisoned!"

He moved towards the door, intent upon hurling the thing from the cliff, and found young Ayala blocking his path.

The chief's son was not yet eight winters old, yet he was only a few inches shy of six feet tall. He had a wide square jaw, basing a head that diminished in size as it reached the crown of thick, black hair. He was broad of shoulder but still scrawny compared to his father and could easily be knocked aside.

"Move!" Gordon thundered.

Ayala shook his narrow head.

Gordon sighed, a mercy that he had only for his son. "It is a runt," he rumbled. "A mutant. It will not survive."

"Not if you throw it off the mountain." Ayala was slow, like all Crommags, but not stupid. Gordon found himself in a quandary.

"We do not forsake the strong for the weak!" he told his son. It was the Crommag way. "I will not take from what the tribe needs, to care for something that can give nothing in return!" Ayala, who shared his father's disgust for the weak, was still fascinated by the ball of white flesh in Gordon's giant hand.

"If it is weak, why does it not cry?"

Gordon's dilemma deepened. The babe must be cold, and hungry, yet it simply blinked its strange eyes that were the color of frozen leaves, and did not squall. "It is *too* weak," he offered as an explanation.

"I want it."

The chief's black eyes widened at the demand of his son. Gordon was filled with anger and hate, feelings that warred with the pride he felt for Ayala. The boy that stood before him was the biggest boy in the clan. The wad of transgression in his hand would be shamefully small, if it survived. Ayala was already a fighter, and fearless. He would easily follow his father to be chief of the Great Men. He would learn more to see his father hurl the abomination from the cliff.

"It doesn't even have teeth!"

Ayala frowned, puzzled at this last accusation. Crommags were all born with a full set of interlocking fangs. They gnawed on stew-bones for nourishment until able to properly chew meat. "I'll feed it something," he argued stubbornly.

Gordon's face screwed up into something terrible and frightening. "Bah!" he spat as he tossed the babe roughly to his son. "It is no better than a rodent! Keep it with your dogs if you want it!"

Ayala caught the tender package and cradled it against his broad chest as his father shouldered past him and threw open the door and stormed through it. His mother's sister finally turned, watching to see if the chief of the Great Men had truly departed. After a moment, she got up and hurried to the door and pulled it shut as Ayala marveled at the infant in his arms. It felt no heavier than a ball of snow.

His aunt lifted the babe long enough to wrap it in a snow rabbit pelt before tucking it back into his arms.

"Shelter him in the shed," she instructed. "Keep him dry

and warm. Feed him milk from the goat. We will help."

Ayala's black eyes rose to find those of his mother's sister. He noticed, for the first time, that they were the same light brown as his mother's, though most Crommags had eyes as dark as pitch. He looked to the bed in the corner and saw his mother's eyes and saw something else. Another first.

Pride.

She nodded at him, her light eyes full of tears – and pride.

Ayala looked down at the bundle in his arms and the mossy eyes that looked back at him. Babies were supposed to be born blind, like most animals, but he could tell that this babe could see him – clearly. Those eyes seemed to look right *into* him.

That stubborn boy was now a grown Crommag over eight feet tall and ruled The Bite as his father had done before him. He stood on the ridge between the lands where he had been born and the lands that he would conquer. The warm, heavy skin of a snowlynx draped his shoulders. He looked at Noga on his left. A similar skin draped the shoulders of his brother.

They had killed the cats together. The first kill for each of them.

Ayala had been fifteen. Noga, only seven. Ayala asked him who should take which pelt. "You're the bigger pussy," Noga had told his brother with a grin. "You get the bigger pussycat." Ayala had laughed and cuffed his brother hard enough to send him sprawling through a snowbank, also laughing.

They had skinned the great cats and taken the meat to the village and feasted. Ayala took his first woman that night.

The skins they wore, once pure white, had grayed and dinged a bit with time. Ayala noticed that his brother's hair was darker as well, either from time or what he rubbed in it to make himself look more like the other members of their tribe. Even wind burnt and sun ravaged, Noga's face was paler than most. But his eyes were the same color as winter lichen. They looked at his brother, and into him. The way he had done since he was a newborn babe.

On their right, a wide path curved around the mountainside, narrowing as it rose and lined with a hundred men. Ayala raised a hand and the first man was by his side. Ayala held up three fingers and then pointed west to a curl of smoke rising in the distance. The man nodded, signaled those behind him, and started down the mountain with thirty men behind him. Ayala sent his next leader south with fifty men and instructions to divide into groups of ten when they reached the forestlands. He watched their descent and felt an unfamiliar feeling in his chest. It seemed to expand and burn, but it was far from unpleasant. *Anticipation? Excitement? Pride?* He did not know – he would ask his brother later. All he knew was that it felt good. Good as a fire or a woman's bedfurs. He liked it. The wind whipped around him, smelling like snow and rattling pebbles along the path.

The giant Northman surveyed the lands laid out under his feet for a few moments more and then turned and headed back into the mountains for another path that would eventually take them east. The burning in his chest was like a star. His brother fell in beside him and the rest of the men followed. Noga would depart with more men ins few days. They had to meet with another tribe first.

But now, Ayala thought. *It begins now.*

The burning in his chest grew and grew.

4. SUNRISE AND SURPRISE

Traejan crossed the valley just as an arc of sun peeked over the horizon, flooding the valley with rose-colored light as it made its ascent. He crossed at the narrowest and lowest point of the valley, as had been instructed in the letter, breaching the woods on the far side. The trees were narrow at first, but soon gave way to thick oaks. Soon after, the woods opened up into a broad clearing, strewn with boulders and cut by a wide stream. A quick glance at his surroundings let him know he was in the right place. He had read the letter so many times the paper was now as soft as cloth and beginning to break apart. The meeting place was just as it had been described, and it fit the picture he had already made in his mind's eye.

Traejan swung down from his palfrey with the silence and grace of a Jäger. His mare, Peg, had been his grandfather's horse for centuries. She was an ancient, ageless courser, all white with deep brown eyes. The young prince had already been fond of her for years and had been deeply honored to be given such a companion. He led her through the break in the trees towards the stream bank.

The stream that cleaved the clearing was part of the Ravensbrook, the river that separated the Spawning from the Southlon. Trees of oak and sycamore mingled towards the waterway and the soft woodland floor was covered with the mulch of a thousand fallen leaves and their ancestral past lent a silent, spongy step under his soft boots. Two enormous ironwood trees guarded the far bank, their silvered limbs stretching above the others to reach the morning sky. He was in the right place.

Traejan looked around for the master of weapons and war whom he had sought for what seemed like his entire life. The deeper they had traveled into the Southlon the more they heard of the Roshan and the more excited he had become. Though he would never admit such to Dell, he too thought that the whole story might be human myth, legend, or straight bullshit. He knew he was young, but he was no woodland babe.

The brook was wide and shallow, no more than a few feet deep but at least thirty feet across. Huge boulders bordered the far side of the stream while smaller ones made paths across it and created hollows for pools to form on the bank closest to him. The water bubbled softly around the rocks. Morning sunlight danced with the last of the night shadows and the woods were full of birdsong. The Roshan had not yet come.

The legendary master, however, was close. Very close. Traejan could feel the heavy presence, just as Dell could. The aura was powerful and ominous, giving the oppressive feeling of swelling thunder. Like his Praetorian, he could tell that the master was definitely not elfin, and that something was a bit off. It was like a smell in the air that was familiar, but out of place, making it impossible to identify. It made the skin on his back and shoulders tingle, but it did not warn him of any danger. Peg snorted and shook her head.

Traejan rubbed her neck and whispered a few quiet words in his native tongue.

His calming, reassuring words were as much for himself as they were for Peg. He could feel the singular thud of each heartbeat against his ribcage and he could hear the sound of his own blood pulsing in his ears. He looked about anxiously, trying to control his excitement.

He approached the brook and knelt down and dipped a hand in the water. It was much warmer than its sister stream on the other side of the valley.

Roshan Simorgh, he thought. *A weapons master.* No more

fencing, or strawing, or childish games. *The real deal*, his brother Zephyrn would have said. He would to be a true warrior.

Traejan thought back to the last argument he had with his parents. The one that had finally decided the quest he had embarked upon. It was the week of the winter solstice and he had been conspicuously absent from all the celebrations. His parents had summoned him at the end of the week, just after another breakfast he had missed.

"Why do you do this?" the King had demanded. "Why do you *insist* on this? You are as stubborn as…"

"As me?" Acqtraejale, the aging father of the king, cocked his head in inquiry as he looked up at his son from his morning porridge. Every other family member had long since finished and had left or risen from the table.

"I was going to say as a goat," King Rowland told him, "but you are interchangeable in this case."

"Bah!" the Battle King spat, grinning in spite of the comment and returning to his porridge.

"I have to make a life for myself," Traejan interrupted, spurning further argument between the two. "I have to do *something*. Xander will be king and Zephyrn will be…well, Zephyrn. He is happy with where he is and what he is doing, I am not. What am I supposed to do?"

His mother came to him then, her long white hair flowing behind her, and clasped his hands in her own. "Come to court my son. There are so many lovely girls there. I am sure you would find one that you would love. My father's castle awaits you, you are the rightful lord there should you wish it. Maybe a family of your own is what your heart desires."

The queen had her eye on one girl in particular, and she planned to do what she could to see them together. The girl was lovely and compliant, and bore the same white hair and blue eyes that her own family had boasted for a millennium.

The queen intended on keeping as much of the Andromedan bloodline in her family that she could.

Traejan had pulled one hand free and placed it atop his mother's. "That is not what I am seeking," he told her softly.

"You cannot roam the forests all your life!" she scolded gently. She withdrew her hand and looked to his father for support, but he only drew a deep breath and sighed. It was Xander who spoke. Xander, the voice of reason.

"The elves of this land are not fighters, Traejan. Why do you pursue this?"

"We fought in the old lands."

"Which is why we left."

"What makes you think these lands will always remain the same?" Traejan asked, more sharply than he intended. Yet he did not miss the look that passed between his father and his brother. "I don't just want to do this," he said after neither one answered. "I *need* to do this. And not just for myself. I can feel it. I can't explain it, but I feel that this is what I am supposed to do."

His mother sighed as she turned away, defeated. His father, after a brief moment, let his shoulders drop and then looked to his oldest son. Traejan could sense something between his father and Xander. It was more than just a shared decision about the second royal prince. He squared his shoulders and met his brother's dark brown eyes with his own.

After what felt like an eternity but was more likely only a few seconds, Xander acquiesced with a short nod. Traejan looked hopefully at his father, who also gave him a curt nod.

"Make yourself ready," he commanded.

Traejan let out a deep breath that seemed to come all the way up from the toes of his boots.

"Thank you," he told his brother and father as he gave them a bow so low that it was almost ceremonial. He glanced at his grandfather who gave him a wink as he continued eating.

Unable to contain his elation any further, he strode quickly from the room. Dell had turned to follow his charge as always, but the king motioned for him to stay behind.

Prince Traejan's eyes grazed the tops of the trees and gauged the time by light and shadows.

I'm here, he thought. *Finally here. After all this time.*

Yes, it was time.

His grandfather had been a great warrior – the Battle King he was called. The old elf had fought every kind of evil creature to ever threaten the elfin kingdom of old and had led his people across the Starry Sea to the new land. He was the greatest fighter his people had ever known.

Until now, Traejan thought, his chest swelling. *I'll be better.* The whole prospect filled him with fire. He burned with it. Still crouched by the stream and lost for a moment in his memories and thoughts of glory, his sharp eyes caught movement on the edge of his vision. His head snapped up and all of the fire in his belly turned to ash.

An apparition in black robes and cowl rose twelve feet above the forest floor like the specter of death, silencing the woods with cold breath.

Instinctively, his hand went to his sword but before Traejan could free the weapon from its scabbard his elfin eyes separated shadows from truth and the woods rang with a laugh as light and quick as the babble of the stream.

Traejan felt his breath come out in a rush and watched wide-eyed as the specter pushed back its cowl just enough to reveal the face of a girl. *Not a girl*, Traejan corrected as his breath caught, *a woman. A human woman.* She was no giant, either – but merely standing atop a huge mountain rock, her dark cloak blending with the shadows of the boulder, making them seem as one.

"There is no need for your sword, elfling," she laughed. "I am not your enemy."

How did I not hear her approach? he wondered. *Was she here this whole time?* Her cloak was darkest gray, almost black, and was pinned at the shoulder, unlike the cloak he wore, which was pinned at the hollow of his throat. She jumped from the boulder she stood upon, holding the fabric of her wrap close about her as she leapt down. She landed easily on the forest floor and Traejan caught a glimpse of soft black riding boots as the bottom of the cloak swirled about her feet.

She landed softly, but her hood fell back to her shoulders, spilling her hair out into the morning light. Traejan felt the muscles in his jaw go slack and the next two minutes of his life streamed by, burning into his memory for all time.

It was her hair. The first shock was her hair.

Elfin women, of whom had filled his life since a child, had nothing like what he saw before him. Seleucian Elves had hair that was long and blonde and light as wisps of cloud. It fell past their waists in waves of golden light. Elfin women from the Sylvan Woods had hair the color of the tree bark and true Arcadian Elves had hair twice as dark and twice as long.

He had seen Gnomin women, with coarse blonde curls, and in his travels of late he had seen many human women. Women from Atlantea with fiery orange locks and Bohemian girls with ringlets as dark and soft as the earth of the woodlands. He had even seen a Keeper once, with rich brown hair laced with strands of emerald green. None were like the woman that stood before him now.

Her hair spilled out of her hood and pooled around her shoulders like blood. Dark auburn red, shot with gold, it looked like an autumn sunset through the Elfin Greatwood.

It looks like wine, Traejan thought, his breath stuck in his throat. *Like honeyed wine poured from a golden pitcher.* Try as he might, he could not tear his eyes away.

It did not fall down her back to delicate, wispy ends – the thick tresses came only a hand past her shoulders and were blunt, as if a blade had cut them. A small part fell forward, towards her face, but this too had been blunted by a blade and came only to her brow. Traejan had never seen anything like it. Her face was partially obscured by this strange thatch of locks that seemed to swing to the left, as if always brushed from her eyes.

As if to answer his thoughts her left hand came up and pushed the straying hair from her face. The locks fell back across her brow, only slightly more swayed to the left.

Garnet and gold, it shone like firestone in the fingers of the early morning sun and looked as soft as silk. Traejan felt hypnotized by it. He tried to focus on what was happening, on what she was saying, but he could not pull his eyes from the soft frame of her countenance. All he could think of was what it would be like to touch it. He felt compelled to touch it, run it through his hands, maybe hold it to his face.

His last thought was too much and his body gave a small shudder. She was smiling and talking as she made her way towards the stream. He realized he was still holding the hilt of his sword, half-pulled from its sheath. He slid it back into the scabbard without taking his eyes off her.

"I'm sorry if I startled you," she called to him across the water, "but you startled me as well."

"That makes us even, then," he responded, finding his voice. He smiled as easily as he could. His mind ran away like a beast unleashed.

What is she doing here? Could she be from Trimpe? It was the closest human town as far as he knew. *Why is she alone, and why for every goddess in the sky is she dressed that way?* He could see the top of her shirt along the edge of her dark cloak. It was a weave of black and gray, like ashes after a campfire. All of her clothes were dark. Black or near black.

Is she in mourning?

She did not seem to be grieving, though. Her smile was broad, if a bit crooked, and her eyes were bright. She was chatting merrily to him and hopping just as merrily from rock to rock as she began to cross the stream. He couldn't seem to hear her, though. All he could do was look at her hair, then her face, then at her lithe body and the way it moved, then back at her hair. He tried to slow his thoughts and concentrate on what she was saying.

"...still so cold..."

She did not seem surprised at all by his presence or wary of him in any way.

These woods must be well traveled, he thought, *and safe, for a young woman to be traveling alone and at ease.*

She hopped lightly, going from stone to stone across the broad shallows, holding her cloak close around her body to keep it from getting wet, closing the distance between them. He could hear her talking but found he could feel her words more than he could discern what she was saying. His sight seemed to be his only sense and he took in every detail of her face and the hair that framed it in an ethereal shroud of blood and gold.

"...I thought spring would *never* get here..."

Traejan guessed he must be a full head taller than her, but as to her age he could not tell. As she made it halfway across the brook, she shook her head and her hair obediently fell back to reveal more of her features. Although she was undoubtedly human, with a square-round face and strong straight nose, her eyes were almond-shaped, like an elf. She lacked the feminine roundness of a human woman but did not have the slight bone frame of an elfin woman either. Her voice was light, but warm and strong and Traejan brought all his will to bear so he might concentrate on what she was saying. Despite the fact she was almost across the brook, he still stood speechless. She was almost to him when he was able to focus on what she was saying.

"I've never seen someone in these woods so early before," she prattled, her smile never wavering as her eyes picked out her path across the water. "It's strange to see anything or anyone besides the deer out at this time."

Then she was there, right in front of him. Only one stone remained between her and the bank of the stream where Traejan stood, but she misjudged the distance. The toe of her outstretched boot scraped the slick surface of the flat rock and she slipped, plunging towards the water. Instinctively, Traejan reached out, his right boot coming down with a splash on the stone she was making for and catching her in his arms before she could fall into the swirling water.

He held her for a moment as she lay wide-eyed across his outstretched knee and he could see her eyes up close. They were bright brown, edged with black and shot with green and amber and gold.

Like jewels, he thought. *Unearthed by a storm.*

He held her in his arms, her face only inches from his own, and there *it* was - her hair, thick yet fine and shimmering and falling over his arm not an inch away from the water. Her eyes locked with his and he could feel her tremble in his grasp.

"It's a strange day in the woods," he said softly. She drew a deep breath and gathered herself, as he pulled her to her feet. Standing up next to him, she barely came up to his chin and looking down he could see nothing but the dark red waves of her silken hair. He held her for a moment, unsure of what to do or say.

She gently twisted out of his embrace and smiled at him. The pink of dawn made her face smooth and rosy, her eyes bright.

As he let her go he felt two things; that he wanted to hold her again, and that something was off.

He breathed deep before as she moved away, filling himself with her smell – warm hair, warm skin, leather, wild roses, and something else. A smell that was not quite right but he could not place what it was.

A smell that, for some reason, brought to him memories of his grandfather. And someplace hot. The memory was so distant and from so long ago that it seemed unimportant now.

It is important, his mind insisted.

"A strange day indeed," she agreed, still smiling. She stepped lightly away from him and gave her head a shake.

So light on her feet, Traejan admired as he tried to chase the memory of his grandfather. It tugged so insistently on his mind that he almost came to his senses. His real senses. Something was more than off, he realized at once, it was wrong.

That smell, his mind insisted. *And the way she moves. What is it?*

The young prince could not pin down what it was that suddenly bothered him. His senses were being pulled in too many directions. He was too distracted. One moment he was the honed hunter and tracker that Dell had schooled for over fifty years, the next he was like a dreamy schoolboy. Just when he thought he knew, he was consumed by her presence. Her closeness. Her smell. Her body so recently pressed against his.

I just held her in my arms, he thought with disbelief. *And she trembled. I could feel it! She trembled in my arms. Her hair fell over my arm and her face was so close to mine. Who is she?*He could still feel the warmth of her, along his left arm as it caught her, and the left side of his body and leg where her weight had rested for the longest and fastest four seconds of his life.

Where her weight had rested.

Her weight.

As she jumped lightly onto a pile of moss-covered stones and then jumped off, he knew that her weight was the one thing that was off the most. She had felt a bit heavy for someone so slight. More than a bit. Yet she skipped along like some woodland fairy. She walked and talked as if they were children on an outing in the woods. The memory of his grandfather pulled insistently at his brain *(what is that smell?)*

but he pushed it away to hear what she was saying.

"Strange enough day to meet an elf at the Ravensbrook," she was saying as she meandered downstream. Still farther away she sauntered and Traejan feared for a moment that she was going to disappear into the far side of the woods. Then she turned and smiled at him. Her eyes sparkled with merriment, teasing him. He couldn't help but smile back. She knelt and dipped a hand into the stream as if to check the temperature of the water. "Strange enough to meet a prince even," she called over shoulder through the thick gauze of her hair. His smile faltered and she stood and shook the water from her hand and their eyes locked for the second time. "Or even both," she finished, her eyes narrowing.

The smile on the prince vanished completely.

She knows who I am.

How?

She started back towards him, walking slowly, and Traejan recalled what Nevin had said not half an hour ago about being stalked by a snowlynx. She even looked like one, or the shadow of one, walking slowly, fluidly, and with lethal purpose, her eyes never leaving his own.

Traejan realized abruptly that her clothes were made much like the ones he wore – but where his were made to blend with the forest, hers were made to blend with the shadows. She looked now like a piece of night that had broken off to taunt the rise of the sun. He looked into her eyes and saw that they did not sparkle as he had thought. They glittered.

Only two things glitter, his mind whispered as he watched her, transfixed. *Diamonds, and death.*

But her eyes aren't black, he thought, feeling stupid. *They're like gemstones.*

Thoughts arrowed through his mind about witches and faeries and he speculated on how close he might actually be to the Spawning. He thought that she had perhaps caught him in some kind of spell. He tried to remember the tales he had heard of witches, both human and elfin, but his senses had deserted him. His limbs felt frozen in place and he could not find any words - he felt exposed, and completely helpless. Like the snowlynx, she stalked him on the feet of a cat, silent padded paws – lazy and languid on the surface but with a rolling power underneath, tense and ready to spring. Traejan felt his blood turn cold and was even more astounded to discover that he didn't care.

She reached behind her head and gathered her red tresses like a mortal coil, twisting them around her fist. She flicked a slim dagger from her cloak into her free hand and, holding her coiled hair near the crown of her head, she plunged the blade into her twisted locks. Whether the hair was to hold the dagger or the dagger to hold the hair, he didn't know.

Shadow and blood, she came at him like a ripple on water, each smooth step full of latent violence that was tightly held. He saw now that what he mistook for a trembling within his arms was a quiver that ran through her still, like a suppressed and barely controlled energy. She was like a bowstring pulled so taut that it must release or snap. She stopped when she was still a few feet away.

"I know who you are," she assured him. "And because I do, and since we have never met, you must know who I am as well." And with that the spell was broken.

The entire forest had gone still as he remembered suddenly where he was and why. Only one other person other than the ones he had left behind knew where he would be today, and with whom he would be meeting. He could not keep the look of shock from his face or from his voice.

"You can't be," he whispered hoarsely.

Her smile was so slight it was both seductive and lethal. "I can and I am."

The forge, his mind summoned from seemingly nowhere. *The blacksmith. It was the day grandfather took me to the blacksmith. It's iron. She smells like iron. Warm skin and smooth hair, leather and roses and iron.*

Traejan suppressed a shiver that wanted to shake his entire body and swallowed, hard. "You are the Roshan," he said at last.

"I am," she agreed, pleased. "And you are well met, Elfin Prince."

〇₰〇

Dell, as still as stone, felt his shoulders drop as his breath came rushing out. He had not even realized he had been holding it until now. Unlike his charge, he had no trouble identifying the Roshan. Unable to see through the trees across the valley, he had to rely on what he could smell, and hear, and feel. For the Northlon Elf even half a mile away there was no mistaking the smell of iron.

And whoever is wearing that much steel must be dressed for war, the Jäger thought. The smell was so heavy that it masked all others about the Roshan and he had no clue about the shock that Traejan was experiencing. All Dell knew was that the second son of Rowland the Great had finally met who he had traveled so far to find.

The tension in the air broke as sudden and as sure as the sunrise.

The arc of sunlight had become a full globe of molten gold that had breached the horizon and Dell's companions stood a few yards behind him, waiting. They were novice Jägers, even old Nevin, but they had learned much already. They kept perfectly still, holding the horses, until instructed to do otherwise. Dell waited just a little longer, watching the trees across the valley with the senses he had honed over many, many years.

The feeling of danger had passed and he knew the prince

was safe. He waited a minute longer, however, reluctant to leave. He heaved a sigh. There was nothing more to be done here. Traejan had made his decision long ago and his father had given not just his approval, but another task to Dell as well. The elf paused again, just a moment more, now that one job was done and another lay at his feet. He contemplated his new mission and what the implications were.

If King Rowland and Prince Xander were correct in their fears, it was the right thing to do – relenting to Traejan. They would need what he brought back.

The Praetorian motioned to his Jägers. Alastair handed him the reins to his mount and he swung up and into the saddle of his horse. His men mounted up as well, and followed him as he set their course. Not Northeast for home, but due North.

5. INTRODUCTIONS

Traejan bowed respectfully to the woman, if that's what she was, and noticed that she did not return the courtesy. Instead she walked right up to him, wearing a slight mocking smile that barely surfaced beneath her hard gaze. His courser, Peg, who had remained silent until now, snorted and nudged his backside as if to chastise him. He straightened, trying to keep the look of wonder from his eyes as he watched her extend a hand to him. He clutched it in the way of the humans, not knowing what to say.

He was not surprised that the Master of Weapons was human, he and Dell had suspected as much because of where the Roshan was rumored to live. Elves were not solitary creatures, and the only other civilizations this far west were either human or Gnomin. But he was awestruck that it was a woman, and completely astonished by her appearance.

"I am Ember donnis L'chiross," she said as she grasped his hand. Her grip was hard and he could feel a line of callous where her fingers met the palm of her hand. She held his own hand firmly for only a second as she looked into his face and then released it. "I will be your Roshan, and you can call me as such."

"Roshan," he said softly, though in his mind he whispered her name. *Ember donnis L'chiross.* He relived the second that she had grasped his hand, and wished he had more time to ponder it. Even more, to contemplate the way her hair had spilled out of her hood when he first saw her. She looked at him curiously, her smile again just taunting her lips.

"Why do you want to fight?" she asked bluntly.

"Elves believe that true victory goes to the one that has the grace to yield," he said firmly. She raised an eyebrow.

"Is this a belief of all elves?"

"There are different races of elves. But in general, yes."

"So why are *you* here?"

"When it comes to fighting, I don't believe in yielding."

The Roshan smiled. "That is something that we share. But I would think you could learn to fight almost anywhere, and have it within your power to do so. And I have met many elves before that are ready to fight, but you are the first one who has been interested in being a pupil of mine."

He could feel she wanted more of an answer from him but had no idea what it was and he was afraid to say the wrong thing.

"You have no need to do this," she said simply. "There are four elves in the woods across the valley who would lay down their lives for you."

Traejan bristled, a frown creasing his normally smooth brow. "And I would lay down my life for theirs. And, should that be the case, I do not want to fail them."

The Roshan regarded the prince with no small amount of surprise. Her brows finally dropped and she narrowed her eyes at the prince but he held his ground. She whistled and turned her face downstream. Traejan followed her line of sight and a few seconds later a giant shadow moved quietly out of the woods.

Peg immediately whinnied and shied away. Traejan caught her reins and soothed her, rubbing her neck and whispering words in elfin. The Roshan's sardonic smile resurfaced as she signaled her own mount to come closer. When Traejan saw what it was he recoiled in the same manner as his horse.

"Seven Hells!" he cursed before he could stop himself.

The horses that the elves rode and bred were slim and graceful. They were as lithe as their masters, treated gently and loved as if they were children. Traejan had seen the ones used by humans, mostly for plowing fields and pulling wagons, and they were much larger and more powerful than their elfin relations. This animal made even the largest farm horse look feeble.

Traejan stood over six feet tall but he knew that the top of his head would barely reach the shoulder of the beast, had he dared get that close – which he did not. The destrier was more than enormous and even blacker than his mistress. He was smooth and sleek – hairless except for a thick black mane and tail and wild black tufts of hair on the backs of his legs. His black eyes were ringed with red and, where any other horse had teeth, this beast had long and pointed fangs that dripped with bits of foam.

"You tamed a Night Colt?" he asked, amazed. The elf leaned back into his own horse to both give and receive a bit of comfort. And so he could lean back to look at the monster without falling backwards. "How is he so big?"

"A Night Stallion," the Roshan corrected. "And I didn't tame him, I saved him from a Mare before she could devour him. Twice."

The great beast whickered and jerked his head away sheepishly, as if embarrassed. Traejan eyed the creature's sharp teeth.

"Does he eat meat?" he asked.

The Roshan shrugged. "If you give it to him. Otherwise, he eats like a normal horse." She smiled wickedly. "Don't worry. I doubt he favors the taste of elf. He hasn't eaten one, yet. That I know of."

She turned towards her mount, unfastening her cloak and pulling it off as she did. Traejan tore his eyes from the creature to watch wide-eyed as she rolled her cloak and fastened it to her saddle. She had to reach high to do so.

Over her ash-colored garb she wore two curved short swords that crossed at the small of her back, a brace of knives in leather sheaths at her waist, and two huge daggers just below her hips. It was no wonder why she had felt heavy and smelled of a forge. He thought she might even have a few more in her arsenal that were still hidden. Then his eyes picked out a spot on her belt where two sheathes were empty. The dagger, too, on that hip seemed to be out of place. Pushed forward almost over her thigh. It all fell into place.

"You did not slip," he said. This time she did not fight her smile.

"I have not lost my footing in recent memory," she agreed, tightening the straps on her horse.

"You said in your letter that you would test me before accepting me as a pupil."

"I did."

"And that's what that was, when you fell."

"It was," she agreed.

"And that's it?"

"That's it for now," she said, turning to face him. Her demeanor was impatient and full of scorn. "You are soft. Soft of face and hands and heart." Traejan felt a flush creep up his cheeks but held his ground and lifted his chin. The Roshan nodded, but it was in approval and the look of scorn left her eyes. "I know what your reaction is to danger and how quick you are to react. I have a good gauge of your reflexes, strength, and merit. I know your motives, perhaps already better than you do, for coming here. I have all I need to know, for now. Do you?"

"Yes," he said softly, his cheeks burning. She gave him a twist of a smile.

"Do you still wish to go?" she asked.

"I do."

"Why do you want to learn to fight?" she demanded.

Traejan straightened, regaining his composure with a bloom of anger. The feeling was foreign but not unpleasant. "I don't want to learn to fight. I know how to fight. I want to learn how to win. Every battle, every time."

The Master of Weapons grinned at him. "You are learning already," she told him. She grabbed the strap of the girth and hauled herself way up and into the saddle. "Let's go."

ೞ

Miles to the north, past the High Forest were the Mountains of Blood, a volcanic range that was mostly dormant. Mostly. Despite that it was only an hour after dawn, the shouts of Gnomin voices filled the air.

"Komm zurück!"

"Komm zurück!"

For the Gnomin this phrase was war cry, motto, advice and warning. Translated to Anglicus, the common tongue, it meant get back. It was advice always well heeded and usually accompanied by a number of Gnomin running for their lives. This time was no different.

"Komm zurück!" voices shouted in a frenzied chorus as twenty Gnomin figuratively exploded from the mouth of the cave, pumping their short legs as fast and hard as they could before something literally exploded in the cave behind them.

Eighteen men and two women rode a wave of hot air, flying expertly before executing a roll as they landed, coming to a stop face down with their hands covering their heads. A boom echoed under the mountain and the hole, so recently exited by the Gnomin, belched a great cloud of black smoke that billowed and roiled as it rose into the bright morning sky.

Gunta turned his head, still carefully protected by his laced hands, towards Gerta. "Do you have plans for dinner tonight?" he asked.

Gerta shook her blond curls from under her own hands. A crash sounded from inside the cave and a second later another cloud came rolling out, though this time it was mostly rock and dust. Gerta waited for the noise to die down before responding.

"I was going to eat at home, but I'm not sure if I even have anything. What are you doing?"

Gunta did not answer right away since he was waiting for the second explosion. It resounded almost immediately, echoes rolling over the Gnomin laying in the meadow. "Some of us are going to the Wind Inn," he said. "My brother works in the kitchen. He said that they've invented a new potato pie machine."

"A new invention?" Gerta asked, her last word lost in the second crash. Gunta caught it anyway. He rose, along with the others, and held out a hand of stubby fingers to help Gerta to her feet.

"Yes," he said dusting himself off. "He claims it's spectacular."

"Well this I have to see."

The Gnomin were a people obsessed with inventions and Gerta was much more interested in the cooking device than the actual potato pie. Gunta shrugged with forced nonchalance. He liked Gerta. She could shoulder a heavy load as well as any man and carry it down a mineshaft with hardly a beam to light her way. And not only were her fingers nimble, able to wire and cross wire any explosive, but she had all ten.

"Come with me, then. I can get you into the kitchen."

Gerta was impressed. Though the kitchen at the Wind Inn (a massive room full of copper drums, kettles, igno-boxes and coils) was behind a great wall of glass so that any Gnomin may watch, it would be much better to actually get inside. She might be able to do some real crawling and poking around.

"It's a plan!" she announced.

Gnomin never dated, but they planned everything. She dusted off her own pants that were made of heavy leather and held up by suspenders over a red-checked shirt. The pants ended just below her knees where thick woolen socks disappeared into heavy work boots. The other Gnomin in the mining party were all dressed the same, the only variation being the colors of their checked shirts. The other common denominator among them was that they all wore a pair of heavy goggles made of brass ferrules and strap lugs with thick, dark glass lenses – though some wore them over their eyes and others had them pushed up onto their foreheads.

The group brushed themselves off and headed for the mineshaft to inspect the results of the explosion. They found that the blast had been a success and proceeded to congratulate each other, shaking hands and clapping backs, before they set themselves to removing the debris.

The Gnomin, as both a race and a culture, were questionable as to whether they were new or native to the New World. Either way, they were unquestionably advanced. Modestly, they would describe themselves as M&Ms – Miners and Makers.

They derived all sense of pleasure and purpose from these two fields. They had shaped a homeland in the Mountains of Blood. They mined what they found there and made what they could from those finds. It was a prestigious endeavor and they had barely scratched the surface (or the depths) of the great range.

Precious metals and gems were at first discarded. Then other races were discovered, meaning that other races discovered the Gnomin. As a people, they were not explorers unless it meant delving underground. They learned soon after that they could trade such items and get much more in return. So the jewels were tossed on the piles of soft, shiny metals, also favored by the other races, in hopes to trade for coal.

With water being a plentiful and renewable source, the Gnomin powered almost every invention with steam - and coal was the best way to make it.

Over the years the race of miners had unearthed much in the volcanic range in which they lived. Iron and tin and copper and zinc were the most vital and used to make bronze and brass – the most fundamental amalgam in the Gnomin culture.

The Gnomin had extensive knowledge of the properties of brass and its many uses. The alloy was an indispensable composite in anything where low friction was key, which meant pretty much the whole gamut in the field of invention. From locks and gears and casings (which included everything from zippers to plumbing valves), to the manufacture of their favorite musical instruments (all of which were horns). Most importantly, brass was crucial in tools that did not cause sparks next to explosive substances – another favorite and essential factor of Gnomin culture.

That night, Gerta did indeed get into the kitchen of the Wind Inn.

Gnomin hurried here in the kitchen the way they did everywhere – not manically but with great purpose and intensity.

The kitchen of one of the largest eateries in the Coil was a great gout of brass – boilers, wires, and gauges connected to pipes and ducts and vents. The fuel consumption for the machines was so considerable that it was not brought in by buckets or barrows, but by a conveyor belt.

Gerta crawled and poked, nothing that was considered unseemly by the Gnomin people and in truth was quite expected. She was careful not to get a steam burn anywhere, scars of which were worn by most of the kitchen staff.

Not only did she get a good look at the massive coal chamber and steam hammer, but Gunta's brother produced a double roller so they could take a closer look. Gunta and his date/planned companion for the dinner lay down upon it face up and slid backwards under the boiler.

"Look!" Gunta exclaimed, pointing with a stubby yet strong finger. "The steam is condensed and then pumped back into the boiler, instead of having to release it into the vents."

The ventilation system in the Coil was as extensive as its tunnels.

"Ohhh," Gerta breathed.

She counted the pistons and drivers and then slid out on the roller with Gunta to follow where they gave way to pumps and coils.

The two watched the machine in action and checked the pressure gauges as steam was built up and released, built up and released.

Their bright blue eyes, curious as always, followed the potatoes as they were dropped into a tank of boiling water. After exactly eight minutes, they were scooped out by a basket made of steel wire that hung on an automated brass arm. The arm waited five seconds for the potatoes to drain, then swung to the left where an attendant pulled a pin in the bottom of the basket, causing it to split open and spill its contents into an enormous funnel.

Gerta's eyes left the basket, where the attendant was fitting it back together, and went to the other side of the huge, many-armed monster of brass and copper and nickel. Another contraption was chopping blocks of cheese and feeding it into a tube. Gunta took her hand and led her to the other side, past a number of pumps that whistled and hissed, to where a steel belt came out bearing perfectly formed potato pies filled with cheese.

Workers wearing leather gloves transported the pies to trays. The trays were matched with orders and laden with steins of hard cider before being pushed through a window into the servers' station.

The restaurant was a great hall filled with wooden tables

and benches and Gnomin celebrating another day of work well done and well spent.

Gunta's brother had a spot saved for them at a long table so they would not have to wait. Gerta and her planned dinner companion then shared a potato pie while drinking ciders and talking excitedly about the Rankine cycle.

Later, Gunta walked Gerta to the entry of her tunnel where she rewarded him with a kiss on his round cheek and the promise of another plan for dinner.

6. THE HAUS

The elfin prince and the young woman rode the horses Southwest at an easy pace, taking them through the woods towards the mountains as the day grew bright around them. It was an open forest, with wide spaced oaks resplendent with morning light and life. The pair traveled down an avenue between the trees, the ground a spongy carpet of fallen leaves. The sun streamed through the woods and everywhere was a skittering and chirping of animals and birds.

Though the elf was a good foot taller than the Roshan, the beast upon which she rode more than made up for the difference and put her eyes level with his, maybe a tad higher. Traejan was filled with curiosity, and relief. A part of him had secretly harbored the fear that he would be turned away, for what reason he did not know, or that the legend would turn out to be a hoax. Even now he wondered, along with where they were headed, what they would be doing, and who the woman beside him really was.

Could she really be the Roshan Simorgh?

It seemed impossible. He briefly considered the possibility that someone was joking with him then dismissed it. Zephyrn was the only person who would do such a thing, but he lacked the patience for a jape so elaborate. Besides, just seeing the way she moved through the forest expelled any suspicions.

Still, Traejan recalled of all the stories he had heard of this person over the past two years. He could hardly believe the woman beside him was a warrior, much less a mercenary and a cold-blooded killer. It seemed ridiculous.

The prince watched her carefully without looking directly at her, mystified. She was slight of build, but carried the weight of her many weapons soundlessly, with a fearsome elegance. What her age was he could not even begin to guess. He had no experience judging the ages of humans. Dell had told him a rhyme once to help but he could only remember bits and pieces. It had to do with the straight lines at the corner of the eyes. *One for the raven, one for the crow,* and something about most being gone by a turn of the bow. He seemed to recall that each line marked a turn of the deca-harvest. Two faint creases feathered out from the corner of her left eye, and three from her right.

That would make her near fifty, Traejan thought frowning. *That cannot be right. That might be young for an elf, but I'm pretty sure it's not young for a human. By fifty years old humans are aging, some going gray. She looks no more than a girl. Except her eyes. Those eyes have seen more than one turn of the bow.*

The Roshan, he noticed, glanced at him openly – bereft of any elfin courtesy to observe him with averted eyes. She did not stare nor look at him for more than a second at a time, but the curiosity was plain upon her face. She seemed as confounded as he, but much less concerned.

She had seen Skye Elves before, but now realized that she had never actually met one, or seen one up close.

He is impossibly tall for an elf, the Roshan thought, *and broad as well.*

Every elf she had ever met was not just smaller, but actually *small*, with a slight build, almond eyes and high, arched eyebrows. His eyes were almond-shaped but his brows were not light nor arched – they were dark and ran straight across his brow, making him look serious and introspective. And he did not have an elf's snubbed little nose. It was straight and strong, like a man's – much like her own. His ears, however, were decidedly pointed at the tips - removing any possible doubt she might have regarding his race.

But he is so tall! How is that?

Something about him piqued her interest immediately. He had a quality that made her want to lean towards him – the way one would lean towards a tree for shade or support.

Why it that? she wondered. *How peculiar!*

What she found even more peculiar was the fact that it poked at some emotion in her.

It must be I am merely surprised by his height. The tallest elf she had ever met before was barely as tall as she. Traejanale Royce was at least a head taller than her and his shoulders and chest, while lean, were broad and a quiver of arrows was strapped to his back. His features were strong – straight brow, broad cheekbones, and sharp angled jaw line – yet he had a delicate beauty to him. Ember was very taken by his face and his hair, and it surprised her.

What had surprised her even more was his demeanor. She had expected a snotty, spoiled brat. So far, he was anything but. And his reaction to her prod about his guards. That was unexpected.

He's so tall! she thought again. *He looks almost as tall as Ryen - but that could not be!* Long and lean, he seemed larger than life to her. The feeling it gave her was surreal. *Even with me riding Coal, he is almost a height with me.* He rode quiet and smooth, like a shaft of sunlight making its way through the forest.

She found herself glancing at him again and gave her head a quick shake to clear it. Such musings were useless.

Traejan saw her looking him over and kept his eyes averted. He had seen the elves of the Southlon on his journey and knew he did not look like them. He could sense the questions rising in her mind like bubbles in ale. He contemplated his mixed heritage, not wondering what she would ask him, but when.

She startled him by asking instead, "Are elves immortal?"

His smile faltered as he looked into her eyes. They looked to him like strange jewels, hidden just beneath the surface, waiting to be unearthed. Traejan could tell by looking that everything that passed in front of them was taken, assessed, and stored away. Her eyes alone assured him that she would accept nothing but the truth.

"No," he told her quietly but earnestly. "It is a common misconception by humans, since we tend to outlive them by so many generations. But no, we are not immortal." She nodded, her lips pressed together and her brow furrowed, as if this was the answer she had suspected but did not expect him to affirm. He had a great many questions racing through his own mind about her, but not knowing what was proper, decided to remain silent on the subject. Instead, he inquired about her mount.

"How is it that you came to tame a Night Stallion?" Traejan ventured. A small smile crept onto her face. He liked the way it made her look.

"I was camping east of the Spawning, years ago. Ten years? Twenty? I do not know. His screams awoke me and I came running. It turned out to be screams of passion and, as it was, it saved his life. Had he been screaming in his death throes I would have been too late to save him.

"The Night Mare had gotten what she wanted, and was intent on killing him. She had already pinned him down, his right leg was bit deep and bleeding something awful. She was going for his throat when I surprised her from behind. If she had seen me coming it would have been a different story altogether. She was the meanest, toughest creature I have ever fought, and I have fought some real bastards. Even at the end, I was not able to kill her."

"I heard they could only be killed by other Night Mares," Traejan offered.

"That would not surprise me," the Roshan mused. "Anyway, after that he was bound to me. I patched him up and cared for him. He served me willingly but was sometimes difficult and strong headed. Then a few years back, we were on the southward plain when I awoke to the same sounds. He had caught the scent of a Night Mare nearby and snuck off - and again I came to his rescue. Since then he has been even more of a companion, and considerably more obedient. Maybe he was more grateful of the second rescue, though I think he was shamefaced that he could not help himself. Perhaps he knows it could happen again and I am the only one who will save his skin. Either way, I've come to be very fond of the mongrel."

"What do you call him?" Traejan asked.

"Coal," the Roshan replied. Traejan couldn't help but laugh.

"Crafty."

"I know," the Roshan agreed, chuckling. "I'm not the most creative."

Traejan watched her sharp eyes as they took everything in – including him.

They stopped at mid-day to rest, eat, and water the horses at a thin stream. The Roshan offered him some bread and cheese from her pack, and he shared some dried meat from his own. He watched to see if she would give some meat to her horse, but the beast seemed content to chew clover from the base of the tree. Peg still kept her distance from the strange animal and grazed with a wary eye fixed on him.

The Roshan watched Traejan as she ate. Though he wanted to shift about uncomfortably, he kept himself still under her gaze. After their short rest they continued on, riding till it was near sunset.

The sun had dipped to the tops of the trees when they came through the woods at the edge of the mountain's ridge into a clearing shaped like a horseshoe. The bend of it was to their left and was ringed in a half circle by the forest. To their right, the "open" end of the horseshoe, was a forested hill that terraced up until it became part of the mountains. The clearing in the middle was a scraggly patchwork of dirt and grass, dotted with boulders and tree stumps.

Halfway across the clearing on the right, was a small stone and timber cottage built into the hillside. Traejan guessed that it could be no more than one large room, with its back wall the hill itself.

A stream wound its way down from the hills to fall, turning a waterwheel next to the structure, before disappearing into the surrounding trees. All in all it was an idyllic, if small, settlement.

"My haus," the Roshan announced, dismounting.

She threw a sidelong glance at Traejan and continued across the clearing, leading her massive horse. He dismounted as well and followed, feeling his heart beat faster as he looked around.

She lives here, he thought, leading Peg. *I'm going to live here with her. Where she eats and sleeps and changes her clothes.*

He tried to fight the blush rising in his cheeks, feeling young and foolish.

When they reached the haus she pulled the bit and bridle from her destrier and tossed them into a weathered wooden bin next to the small structure. "Get your things," she told him. She took her own personal items, a leather satchel and a sheathed long sword, before unbuckling her saddle.

Traejan slung his bow over his shoulder and pulled his bedroll and saddlebags down off of Peg. Then he removed his tack and tossed it in the bin where the Roshan had left her own. A coarse and faded blanket hung on a nail driven into the wooden plank. She pulled it down and tossed it over the box to protect their gear from the elements.

"My horse?" he asked.

"Will be fine."

The Roshan went to Peg and cupped her hand under the horse's chin. To his amazement, Peg did not pull away but held still. The Roshan spoke in a language he did not recognize and moved away to give the courser a slap on the flank. Peg, although obviously reticent, did as she was told and followed the huge stallion as he walked from the clearing, towards the stream. She was still keeping a safe distance from the strange black creature.

"Do you have a special skill, or magic with animals?" Traejan asked, thinking of the special bond between the elves and their horses. The Roshan grinned and shook her head, a lock of her dark red hair escaping its capture by the dagger. She tucked it absently behind an ear.

"No. She just knows better than to disobey me." The Roshan gave him a knowing look as she shouldered the cloak and sword she had removed from Coal and headed for the door.

"Your house, you said?" Traejan asked. She shook her head and again had to tuck away an errant lock of hair.

"Haus."

"Haus," Traejan repeated. The word seemed both foreign and familiar. "Is that a Gnomin word?"

"Yes. Do speak Gnomin?" She cocked an auburn eyebrow at him but he shook his head in the negative. "You'll learn," she told him. "Some, at least. They helped make this place, you know."

Traejan did not know but kept silent as she pulled open the door. He was eager to see her dwelling, and where she had room for anything in so small a space. From the front it looked like it would barely have room to fit them both. He wondered if they would sleep on the floor and how close they would be to each other. The idea made his heart race so fast that he pushed it immediately from his mind.

The young prince walked into the dim room, pupils swelling as his elfin eyes adjusted almost instantly. He looked around in astonishment. The place was huge.

The haus that he saw from the front was indeed only one small room, but it served only as a mudroom – a place for boots and cloaks and gear. There were two windows with opaque glass that faced the clearing, letting in light but no view. Underneath the windows was a long bench. There were hooks on one wall for cloaks and an oblong wooden stand against the other that held a hodgepodge of small weaponry. A straight-backed wooden chair stood guard by the weapons and a lone pair of boots.

The true dwelling was built into the hill, and even further into the mountain itself if he guessed correctly. The mudroom opened into a great room carved into the earth, but it was by no means a cave. The plaster walls were straight and square, painted the color of pale butter and divided by polished wooden beams. The walls were hung with tapestries and ancient weapons. The floors were level and smooth and of cut and mortared stone, covered with thick rugs.

There were no windows, save the ones in the front, but there were panels of thick glass where the ceiling met the walls, thin as arrow slits, that seemed to let in natural light from somewhere. Sconces on the walls held flameless lamps that gave off a yellow glow.

Traejan surveyed the room, pleasantly surprised. It would never pass for a great hall in a castle, but it surpassed many hunting lodges in which he had stayed, which he preferred to castles anyway. There was a large living area on the left, with couches, stuffed chairs and small tables all turned towards a long fireplace along the wall. On the right was a kitchen of sorts.

There was a cooking area with sinks, iceboxes, and a pantry - but most interesting was how it was shaped. The only way to enter was from the direction he was facing. It was enclosed by a small L-shaped wall, nearly waist high, and topped with a counter of polished stone. Stools were pulled up to the nonkitchen side of the counter, like a tavern bar. On the far side of the split kitchen and living area was another greatroom with dining tables, chairs, and benches that could seat a good twenty men. Past the dining area was a wide hallway flanked by a closed door on either side. The hallway itself was deep, with two doors on the right side, two on the left side, and one at the very end.

"My room is at the end of the hall," the Roshan said, following his eyes as he took the place in. "You can put your things in the first room on the right."

"When will we start training?" Traejan asked.

The Roshan raised an eyebrow. "Are you that anxious?"

Traejan felt as if caught in a trap, but it was one he had set. He swallowed hard and nodded.

"Excellent!" the Roshan exclaimed. "Let's start now." She tossed her things down in the corner of the mudroom.

"Here?"

"Here." She pushed the wooden chair away with her foot. She was strapped with weapons but did not pull any out. Traejan glanced about, uncertain. "Come on," she said, circling around to stand in front of him. "Show me what you got." Her voice was deep and even. He was unsure of how to respond and mentally kicked himself for opening his mouth in the first place. "Draw your sword," she urged in hushed tones, as if helping him to cheat on a test. Traejan ignored the mockery in her voice and tossed his bedroll and pack aside and pulled his sword from the scabbard on his hip. His heart was pounding like mad but he took a deep breath and assumed a fighting stance in the small room.

The Roshan held his gaze for a moment, her face perfectly still and her eyes never leaving his. "Spend the rest of the evening unlearning everything you have been taught," she advised. She removed her cloak and hung it from a hook, then turned and walked towards the kitchen. "I'll start making supper," she called from over a small shoulder.

Traejan sheathed his sword, his face burning. He decided that from then on he was not going to open his mouth unless she asked him a question.

At least she didn't laugh at me, he thought, feeling grateful despite the humiliation. *I would have died with shame.*

The prince hung his own cloak and retrieved his other belongings. He walked through the great room and past the kitchen and into the dining area. There was a niche in each corner, each one holding a different suit of armor and lit from above. He entered the hallway and opened the door to his room, glancing first at the other doors. The ones set into the sides of the hall were of simple pine – ordinary house doors. The one at the end was larger, banded with iron and made of heavy oiled oak. His mind wanted to explore what might lie beyond, but he refused to let it.

He pushed his own door open and looked about the room. It had two slim beds with a carved wooden trunk at the foot of each. There was a small chest of drawers with a mirror on the wall above it, and a night table between the beds with an electric flambeau.

My new home, he thought, walking inside and dropping his things on a bed. *For the time being anyway.* He took a deep breath and let it out in a rush. *If I make it.*

The furniture was old and chipped and the mirror a poor quality, but there was a private bathroom for which he was grateful. It had a rain shower instead of a tub and, as he turned on the sink to wash the travel grime from his face, he discovered it had hot water – a luxury he had never seen outside of a castle.

He unpacked his things into one of the chests and ran his hand along the worn wood of the lid when it was closed. He wondered how many men before him had done the exact same thing, and what they had been like when that trunk was emptied. He straightened and looked into the mirror above the dresser and wondered if his reflection would be different in six months time.

Traejan ventured back into the common area of the haus in

anticipation of the promised supper. The afternoon meal had been small, and he had been too anxious to eat breakfast that morning, which already felt as if it had been a year past.

The Roshan was setting out steaming bowls of stew on one of the tables in the dining room and the smell of it made his mouth water. There was a small corner hearth in the room that he had missed seeing when he came in and a fire blossomed there, under a heavy iron kettle. The flames made even her bound hair glow with an unearthly light.

"Is there anything I can do?" he asked.

"Not unless you want something different to eat," she told him, favoring him with a smile. She pulled a cork from a dark green bottle and filled a glass with a deep red wine. "Would you like a glass?" she offered. Traejan shook his head.

"Water will be fine."

"In the kitchen," she directed. "And glasses are in that cupboard," she said pointing with the bottle. "I expect you to learn your way around the kitchen, shouldn't be hard." Traejan went to the kitchen and found a glass. He filled it from the tap and was surprised at how cold it was. He returned to the table and pulled out the chair opposite the Master of Weapons.

"I was not expecting you to wait on me," he told her. The Roshan grinned at him as he sat down.

"What did you expect?" she asked.

"Not you," he blurted before he could stop himself. The Roshan laughed heartily and he felt a flush sweep up his face.

"You are not quite what I expected either, Elfin Prince."

Indeed he was not. Southlon Elves were notoriously shy and the Northlon Elves were notoriously snobby. She had expected someone much more arrogant, haughty even. And smaller. She definitely expected someone smaller. Yet she was not displeased. Not in the least.

Traejan dug into his stew only because he feared what else he might say. He had never felt so nervous. He didn't know if it was because of the legend of the warrior who sat across from him and the training he was about to begin, or simply because of the attraction he felt to her.

Probably everything, he thought, spooning stew into his mouth. A part of him braced for the taste, not knowing what to expect but prepared to be polite at all costs. It was excellent. Thick chunks of tender meat with carrots and potatoes in a hearty gravy. There was a basket of warm biscuits and a small crock of butter. He finished two bowls and two biscuits with relish and relief.

The Roshan helped herself to seconds on the wine as she watched him eat his second bowl of stew.

"We'll start in the morning," she told him, "but before we do, there are some things we should talk about."

Traejan wiped his mouth on a napkin and nodded, not knowing what to say. The light of the flames danced upon her hair but a fiercer blaze burned within her eyes.

"What you are going to learn here, will serve you all your life – but it will take all that you have, maybe more than what you have. It will take self-sacrifice, and the knowledge that you can and will get hurt, possibly grievously. It will take a lot of nerve, resolve, and all the determination you have."

Traejan swallowed the piece of meat still in his mouth, unchewed. He felt a touch of fear, no more than a fingernail down the length of his spine, then swallowed it like his unmasticated food. Her words ignited a fire within him and it merely intensified the thrill he already felt. Moreover, he felt he had finally found what he had been searching for his whole life.

You do mean the training? his mind rustled at him, teasingly. *You found the training that you've been searching for your whole life, right?*

"You will have to fight fatigue and frustration," the Roshan continued, "and it will take the fortitude of your soul," she told him. "You must have humility, patience. For while you will learn to fight with great speed you will also learn to be still. I guarantee you this will be the most difficult thing you have ever done – the hardest thing you have even attempted, and the most worthwhile."

Traejan could feel his pulse quicken and his breath shorten. The Roshan put her wine glass down and leaned forward, resting her elbows on the table.

"When you are done," she told him, "you will have a greater responsibility than you have now. A warrior's responsibility. You learn to fight not just to defend yourself, but to protect those that are weaker than you."

Traejan started visibly. "I thought you," he started and then stopped just as suddenly. The Roshan did not miss a beat and her smile was immediate and mocking.

"You thought what?" she asked, her eyes narrowing. "That mercenary means merciless? That blood money means blood thirsty?" Traejan felt his whole body, not just his neck and face, flush with shame. He looked away, even though the Roshan seemed amused rather than angry. For that at least he was thankful.

The Roshan swirled the wine in her glass and took a sip. "We might not hold to the same gods," she told him, "but that does not mean I do not know right from wrong."

Traejan looked up, intrigued. "What gods do you hold to?"

The Roshan set her glass down, shaking her head. "My point is not the gods," she said. Traejan averted his brown eyes and she frowned, exhaling sharply. "I can see already that your mind is like a young frog, just gotten his legs. Jumping all over, splashing around - in the mud, on the rocks, in the water, over his head." She paused, as he looked away, her brow furrowing deeper. "And I don't like that I feel the urge to snap my fingers before your eyes to see if you are listening to me."

In truth she felt a bit like smacking him to bring his attention around, as he seemed reluctant to look her in the eyes when she spoke to him, but she felt it would not do to say so to the Prince of the Elves. Not on his first night, at least.

"I'm sorry," he apologized, forcing himself to make eye contact with her and holding it for the first time that night. It was so immediate a response to what she had been thinking that the Roshan feared for a second that he was reading her mind. She froze, startled, as he continued. "I will focus," he told her. "I'm just...just eager. To learn."

Eager to please you, was what he had thought, and was afraid he might say.

The Roshan relaxed, a little – though her gaze was as intense as ever. "Then get some sleep," she said, finally. "You have a lot of learning ahead of you." She jerked her head at the kitchen. "You can leave your dishes in the sink tonight."

Traejan bowed his dark blonde head, and rose, taking his dishes to the kitchen before retiring to his room.

The Roshan watched him go and then poured herself another glass. She sat quietly for a while, watching the flames die down under the kettle.

After washing up, Traejan climbed into one of the beds in his room. He wondered if all the beds in the haus were ever full. He wondered how many beds there were. He wondered what the morning would bring. He had so much going through his mind he didn't think he would ever get to sleep but, within a few short minutes, he was.

The Roshan was the foremost in his mind as sleep took him. The curve of her cheek and the smile she wore that seemed to mock his very existence. The fire in her eyes and the fire in her hair.

# 7. THE UNCARVED STONE

Ember donnis L'chiross poured leftover stew gravy over a biscuit and sat down on one of the stools at her kitchen counter. As she ate her breakfast she thought about one of her visits to the Americas. It was a world not far removed from the one she was in, and not even called the Americas, but it was what she had come to call it since the Americas was where she stayed most when she went weirworlding.

Her mind wandered to a time she did not visit the actual Americas, but another country on the other side of the same world. She had originally gone seeking a weapon of special importance, but ended up on another quest entirely. The weapon had been easier to find than she had anticipated, and she was able to acquire it without any bloodshed. Much to her surprise, she was able to simply walk away with the item - thinking it might not be missed for some time, if at all.

In the same town where the weapon was found, she happened upon a number of carvings done in marble. She was no lover of art, but the figures were too arresting for her eyes to ignore. The first few she noticed were at the church where she had appropriated the weapon she had been after.

Sculptures of men and women, children and beasts, fish and fowl, were carved into warm life from cold stone. She did not have words to describe them; they literally took her breath away. The young woman and her stolen weapon lingered among the statues, wide-eyed and enamored.

Some were sized true but others were of enormous proportions. Each one was so lifelike that they looked like actual beings frozen by a spell. Her gem-like eyes had flicked about; wondering if there was some sorcery at work and if she might not be the next piece mounted upon a block. The few people that were about at the early hour were men in brown robes with shaved heads. She cast another suspicious look about the brightening courtyard she was in but could not sense any danger.

Ember spent the rest of the day in town like a child on a treasure hunt. She inquired about the sculptures and was directed from one place to another, each time finding marble figures suspended in time like massive jewels hidden in plain view.

She found two in the village park and four in the fountain in the town square. She circled them slowly, and their eyes seemed to follow her as she moved. Each carved muscle seemed ready to flex and shift. The robes of the women were flowing and graceful. They seemed to stir in the same breeze that brushed Ember's face. Their expressions appeared as if the sculptor had caught them comfortably in mid-sentence. They glowed with life and whispered of magic.

At the hedgerow to the cattle fields that bordered the town she found another - a figure of a man, heavily muscled, holding back a massive bull. The bull stood with his head down, his nose sandwiched between the man's shoulder blades. The man stood with his feet digging into the ground, head thrown back, the cords in his neck standing out and every muscle bulging as he pushed back with all his might. The bull's great horns curved around the man's chest, almost touching. A blackened metal plate, fixed to a large stone nearby, bore the inscription *Battle of Will*.

The young Roshan had circled the sculpture over and over, marveling at it. Each time, she expected it might come to life, so real it was. She watched and waited for the bull to grunt and shift or for sweat to pour from the man's clenched brow.

Certain that there was some magic about and unable to find

a handy farmer or peasant, she returned to the town church and inquired of the artist. The old friar nodded as the sun began its decent in the west.

"He is from here," he told her proudly. "But there is much more to be found of him in the city to the north," he informed her. "The diocese there gave him a great commission for his work."

She thanked him and set off for the city, only to find disappointment.

It was dark when she arrived, so she lodged at a small inn, wondering what sort of chase she had set herself upon.

A quest within a quest, she had thought with a smile. She settled down into a strange bed under a strange moon, not for the first time in her life, and listened to the tolling of bells. She set out the next morning at daybreak.

The city did indeed have statues, almost everywhere it seemed, but none looked like the ones she had seen in the small town the day before. Every one of the carvings in the bustling city was massive and lifelike, but none held the quality of the previous works. They all looked like what they were made of – cold, lifeless, stone. They could not have been done by the same man.

The church in the city was colossal – a *cathedral* she had heard it called – and housed a number of the sculptures, inside and out. These were even worse. Angels and devils, women holding infants, men with wings and brandishing swords. The work was exceptional, yes. But the poses were rough and unnatural, their clothes gaudy, their expressions contrived.

Ember stopped an old monk crossing the church's gardens, hoping he was not vowed to silence.

"Were these done by Ethos?" she asked, gesturing to a trio of statues in the garden.

"Yes," the monk said, "those are Ethos." Ember frowned and shook her head, disappointed and frustrated.

"They can't be," she muttered, eyeing the carved figures.

The monk frowned in return. "Ask him if you don't believe me."

"He's alive?"

"Of course. He lives in the northeast end of the city, past the merchant shops in the workhouses."

"Are you serious?"

"I am a monk."

Ember laughed. "I don't know if that means I should trust you or not." The monk only smiled in answer and continued on his way. Ember adjusted the pack on her shoulder, pausing for only a moment to consider her errant mission, then headed north on foot.

The workhouses were just that. Quarters at the outermost edge of the city where people both worked and lived. The streets were not cobbled here, just hard packed dirt. It was dusty, hot, and had a distasteful smell that reminded Ember of a tannery. After much inquiry she finally found the place she was looking for.

It was the last dwelling on the street, and it looked more like a great gray barn than a house. Its windows were huge, but too filthy to see through. Next to the building were rocks and rubble in such great proportion that it gave the appearance that a landslide had come crashing down a nearby mountain only to stop just short of the structure. Inside, she could hear the clinks of hammer on chisel on stone - interrupted now and then by a great hacking cough.

Ember pounded a fist on the huge wood and metal door. The noise inside stopped abruptly and was punctuated by a great blowing of air, either in surprise or exasperation. She could hear the clunk of metal being dropped and the shuffling of feet towards the door. There was a squeak and a creak and it swung open to reveal a man well into the later years of his life, but still sturdy and strong. He was a bit wrinkled around the eyes, but his jaw was straight and his white hair and beard neatly trimmed. He stood tall and broad chested in a belted tunic and breeches that were covered with a powdery white dust. His eyes were bright blue chips of ice. The lines in his face were filled with the same white dust that covered his clothes. His eyes widened when he saw Ember.

"It's you!" he exclaimed.

"Excuse me?"

The old man bent and squinted his eyes as they adjusted better to the bright sunlight outside. Then he straightened and cleared his throat. "Forgive me, my dear. I'm just an old man, growing older. How can I help you?"

"Are you Ethos?"

"I am."

"I am sorry to disturb you, but if I could have a moment of your time, I would like to speak to you about your work." Ethos studied her for a moment, unsure. He eyed her thoughtfully but quickly, as if making a decision. He nodded curtly.

"I could use a break," he told her. "Would you like to come in?"

"Please."

She walked in as he opened the door for her and now it was her turn to squint as her eyes adjusted. It wasn't dark, but after the glare of the sun it took her a few seconds before she could understand what she was seeing. She stood in an enormous room with a single door in each wall. The floor was covered with almost as much rubble that guarded the side of the dwelling. Stone dust covered everything, including the walls and windows, and swirled in the air like flour at a bakery.

A massive chunk of marble dominated the center of the room, surrounded by piles of broken rock and discarded tools. Ethos closed the door and Ember noticed that the belt on his tunic was hung with pouches, most of them empty. He turned away with a clenched fist at his mouth, overcome by a fit of coughing.

"Forgive me," he said after a moment, waving a hand at the million motes that hung in the air, making them swirl and dance. "The dust has been making home and havoc in my lungs for many years now."

"Occupational hazard," Ember remarked. Ethos smiled and nodded.

"This way," he said, gesturing towards the door on the left. He led her through the opening into a kitchen of sorts with a nook that contained a finely set, if small, table. A pantry was half exposed by a thin curtain. "Can I offer you some tea?" he asked, "or coffee perhaps?" Ember smiled at the ruse.

"Coffee, please," she said, seating herself at the table and placing her pack carefully by her feet. He raised an eyebrow.

"How would you like it?"

"However you make it," she offered politely.

"Hmmph." He frowned and turned to a small stove to boil the water. "What brings you to Argos, business or pleasure?"

Ember laughed. "You can ask me where I am from," she told him. "I don't mind."

Ethos smiled as he seated himself. "But that would take all of the fun out of this."

"Very well. You brought me here."

"Me?"

"Yes. My actual destination was for Sparta. When I was done there, I came to see you."

"What on earth for?"

"If I told you, that would take all of the fun out of this."

"Ah." Ethos leaned back in his chair nodding and stroking his beard. Ember failed to suppress her grin. She had taking an instant liking to the man, something that very rarely happened. His blue eyes lit up and then narrowed. "Did you intend this visit before you left for Sparta?" he inquired.

"No."

"Then you must have seen my work there."

"Yes."

"Did you like it?"

"Very much."

"And you wanted to meet me because of it?"

"No," Ember confessed. "I didn't even know you were alive." Ethos frowned.

"Then you came here to see more work."

"Yes."

"What did you think?"

"It's terrible, by your own standards."

Ethos sighed. "I know."

"Why?"

Ethos pondered his response as he returned to the stove to finish making the coffee. He poured the thick dark liquid into two small cups and sat down again. Ember sipped hers and fought a grimace at the strong taste.

"I love stone," he confided. "Marble, granite, alabaster – even common rocks. When I look at stone, I believe I can see its true nature. There is always something in there, waiting to be freed. It has been this way since I was very young. My father cut millstones for his trade. I would use his tools and leftover stones to make cats, gophers, whatever I saw hiding in them. Back then it was a game. As I grew older and stronger, and my hand grew more sure, I found my own trade. I always loved what I did but I did not really see it as a gift until I had to deny it. When I came here. When I came to Argos."

"What happened? Why are the statues at the church so awful?"

"Because they are not what they were meant to be. They do not represent their true nature. The stone the diocese supplied was beautiful. I saw many things, but they were not to be."

Ethos sighed then smiled at her before his eyes drifted far away and a wistful smile played on his lips.

"In one I saw a great tree, bursting with leaves and birds on the fly. But the Bishop said, 'this is to be maidens being watched by angels.' In another I saw a great man, weeping on his knees. But the Bishop said, 'this is to be shepherd, tending his goats.' And so it went. Each time, I argued. I told him what the stone was meant to be, how it could be, and where it could be beautifully placed. Each time I was told no. If I could not make what they asked, they assured me, they would find someone else. I should have let them. I was experienced enough to produce what they asked for, but it was slow and painful."

Ember nodded, understanding. They drank their coffee in silence for another minute before Ethos shook off the gloom of memory and looked back at Ember.

"I like you, young lady. I don't know why, but I do," he told her.

"I like you, too," Ember said, smiling. "I feel as if I know you." She studied him, trying to remember if she had ever met him before. He studied her with the same intent, a suspicious smile on his lips. "Kindred spirits, perhaps?" she asked.

"Perhaps." He drummed his fingers softly on the table and she watched him curiously as he again struggled inwardly for a moment before he came to some sort of decision. "May I show you something?"

Ember gave him a nod and a smile and drank the last of the thick coffee in the small cup. Then the young Roshan rose and shouldered her pack. It was heavy and thumped on her backside as she followed him back into the stone-littered, dusty studio and through the door on the opposite side of the room.

This room, too, was large and full of stone, but these were all uncut. They stood side by side like monstrous sentinels. The smallest block stood eight feet tall and four feet wide. The largest was nearly twenty feet high and almost as wide. She wondered with half a smirk if he stood on ladders or if he just climbed the rocks at sat on them with chisel and hammer.

Ethos led the way through the room. As he passed each hunk of marble he touched it and quietly named what he saw in it. "Ares. Atlas. An archer. A trio of mermaids..." He guided Ember to the back corner where a dark swath of burgundy velvet was draped over a figure no less than eight feet tall. The velvet was old and dusty, but had a regal air in such a room. Ethos pulled it off with a flourish.

Underneath was a mass of white marble so pure that it seemed to glow with heavenly light, though it was rough and uncut. Ethos stared at it as if it were his greatest work. As far as Ember could tell, it hadn't been touched since it was dug out of the mountain that it came from. The dirt had been cleaned away, but that was all. It was a fine piece of rock, to be sure, but that was all she saw. Ember looked at Ethos, waiting.

"What is it?" she finally asked. He turned slowly, and looked right into her.

"It's you," he said, echoing the first words he had spoken to her. Ember, who was rarely surprised by anything, gaped at him.

"You see *me* in there?"

Ethos nodded. Ember leaned back and looked at the rough stone. All she saw was stone.

"You are a warrior," he said. It was not a question.

"Yes."

He nodded, pleased he had known all along.

"When I first saw this mass of marble, pulled from the quarry, it took my breath away. I saw you, sword drawn and prepared to enter a battle, the wind blowing back your cloak and your hair. I could see the image so clearly, it was like you were pulling against the chains that were dragging the stone from the excavation."

"When was that?"

"Twenty-five years ago."

Ember found herself taken aback for the second time in a matter of seconds. "Why haven't you carved it yet?"

Ethos pressed his lips together and his brows knitted in a frown. For a moment he sought to word his explanation and failed. He blew a burst of air from his nostrils, frustrated.

"For two reasons," he told her. "First, there is something magical in uncarved stone. Although its true nature is locked inside, it can still be anything. It is full of miraculous possibility. Its original simplicity contains the power of its true nature - which is often disfigured or lost when you try to change it. Does that make sense to you?"

Ember nodded, thinking of all the warriors she had trained over many years. So many came to her, so full of possibility. So few left shaped into the promise of what they could really become. Very few. She knew it all too well.

"What is the second reason?" she asked.

The artist looked wistfully at the stone and then reached out and touched it gently.

"I have done justice to most of my carvings," he told her, "other than the aberrations you saw at the cathedral, but sometimes even I do not have the power to unleash what is inside the stone. Sometimes I do not want to."

"Why would you not want to?"

"When I see something in a stone, a shape, a life – my tools seem to move with a will of their own. I free what is trapped inside. But with this stone, with you, I am afraid I would not be able to do you justice - and you do not seem to have the need to be freed."

〰

The Roshan had nearly finished her breakfast without even

tasting it, lost in her memory. She had meant to go back, to see the sculptor again someday, but never seemed to make it. She never saw him again, never knew if he had ever carved her likeness.

Traejan came out of his room bright and early, ready for his first day and nearly sick with nervous energy. The Roshan, dressed in all black, was sitting at the counter facing the kitchen, using the last bite of her biscuit to clean the plate of its gravy. He saw that her hair was tied tight against her head in a hasty bun, the ends tucked away and out of sight. She smiled wickedly at him.

"Good morning, Traejanalleh!" she chirruped.

He opened his mouth to correct her but then snapped it shut. He knew her mispronunciation of his name was deliberate. It changed the meaning of his name from "fighter" to "little fighter." Her smile broadened at his realization and he felt himself flush.

"So you do speak some Elfin," he said, putting a hand down on a stool.

"A little," she conceded. He felt too nervous to eat but she pushed a plate towards him. "I know you don't feel like it, but eat anyway. You'll need your strength today." She gave him an icy smile. "And every other day from now on." He nibbled the edge of a biscuit as she put her own plate in the sink. "There is cheese and fruit in the pantry," she said using a dagger to point to a cupboard, "and milk and juice in the coldbox. Eat, but don't dawdle." She wiped the dagger off with a cloth from the counter and went outside.

Traejan made an effort to consume a few bites but gave up soon after. He was afraid that anything he forced down might come back up. He left his dish in the sink and then grabbed his sword belt from the mudroom and buckled it on. He was glad that his silver sword had been replaced by one of steel. Even if it was just as ornamental, it wasn't as babyish.

He left the haus and walked into the bright morning light

in the clearing. The Roshan was sitting with her back against a cluster of giant rocks in the middle of the glen, sharpening her dagger on a whetstone. The elfin prince lifted his chin, forcing a confidence he did not feel.

The Roshan stopped what she was doing and watched him closely.

His walk was easy and smooth, almost confident. The sword at his side, however, looked ungainly – it banged against his thigh and seemed to throw his whole figure off balance.

The Roshan didn't like it.

She did not know if it was too heavy, or too big, or simply the way he wore it – but she didn't like it. It was not a good sign. She stood up as he approached her and the dagger disappeared.

The only weapons Traejan could see on her were the two short swords that crossed over the small of her back. He stopped in front of her, his heart thumping madly in his chest.

"Well," she said, "let's see what you have learned." A smile played at the edge of her lips but her eyes were hard.

Traejan stood still for just a moment and then reached down towards his sword. But instead of drawing his weapon, his hand grasped the buckle of the belt and with a quick yank he undid the clasp and pulled the belt off - sword, scabbard, and all. He tossed it aside and stood square in front of her, his arms at his sides, waiting. Her eyes glittered.

The uncarved stone, she thought.

8. IT BEGINS

The morning sun glinted off Traejan's dark eyes and through his sand-colored hair. The air was cool, even with his vest and tunic. His teacher, clothed and cloaked in black, looked no more than a shadow against the rocks.

"Why are you here?" the Roshan demanded.

"To learn to fight."

The Roshan frowned. "And win, so you told me. There is more."

"I..." Traejan stopped, trying to compose himself, to say the right thing. He gave up and blurted out, "The fight *will* come, I know it. And when it does, I want to be the last one standing." The Roshan's smile was slow and almost lecherous.

"Pay attention to what I teach you," she said, "and don't ever give up. I'll show you how." She pushed her body away from the rock and stood before him. "But before you learn how to run, you need to learn how to walk. And before you learn how to walk you must learn how to stand." She stepped closer to him, eyeing his feet.

Here, he thought, his heart picking up again and starting to hammer inside his chest. *Now. It begins now. I will never forget this moment.*

"Take a step forward with your left foot," she commanded. He did. "Now, without moving your feet, turn to the right so you are facing the woods." Traejan rotated his body at his hips a quarter turn so he was facing the woods. "Now turn your head, just your head, back towards me." Traejan did as she instructed. He was now facing her sideways, looking at her over his shoulder. "Now bring up your hands, like you are going to cuff me. Good. *This* is a fighting stance. When I tell you to assume a fighting stance, or to be on your guard, this is what I expect."

Traejan nodded, trying to burn his current position into his memory. *Left foot forward, body turned, face back. Got it.*

"Now, can you tell me why this is better stance than facing me squarely like you did yester eve?"

Traejan saw the logic immediately. "I am less of a target this way," he answered.

"Good!" The Roshan exclaimed, surprised. "That is exactly it. And if you are hit, it is not in your sword arm. Hopefully. Now, the hard part is done – the rest should be easy."

Traejan inwardly groaned and rejoiced, both fearing and eagerly anticipating what was to come. He felt at this point his greatest challenge would be to not stare at her face. Or her hair. It was tied into a nest at the back of her head but it still drew his eye. Almost painfully. He focused instead on what she was saying.

"You will learn the ten most basic moves in combat," she told him. "Five attacks and five checks. These will be the basis for your training this summer."

Traejan dropped his hands, astounded.

"That's it?" he asked, unable to help himself. "Five attacks and five checks? That's the secret of the greatest fighter living in all the lands?"

The Roshan's laugh was curt but genuine. "Do you want to pick up your sword and find out? Of course there is more - each attack, or strike, actually has ten variations, and each one of them has a hundred and fifty, but the five you will learn are the building blocks of close combat and all you will have time to master. It will be enough for you, and it will not be as easy as it sounds, not at first. But with time and practice you will be able to do them in your sleep. But, yes, that is it. Very simple. You will start using only your hands. Once you can kill with those, adding a sword only makes it easier. Well," she corrected, "maybe not easier, but it definitely gives you a better reach."

She smiled wickedly at her own humor. Traejan drew a shaky breath and squared his shoulders. Part of him blanched at how blithely she mentioned killing, while another part of himself was thrilled. He nodded for her to continue.

The Roshan began.

She started by showing him his greatest weapons, his hands. How to turn his hand into a blade, a claw, a fist, a ram, and a mace. Next she showed him strikes, and how each one could be used. Straight, back, up, sideways. She demonstrated where each strike should fall, explaining in detail the lethalness of each hit.

At one point Traejan nearly jumped when the Roshan reached out and touched him tenderly under the chin while she explained about the soft tissue around the neck. Her words became a blur of sound as two of her fingers traced down over his throat. His pulse quickened uncontrollably. She held up one hand with the fingers bent over at the second knuckle in what she called a "cat's paw" but he could not make sense of what she was saying. Time seemed to stop as the morning sun lit her hair and eyes with golden fire. She spoke and he heard nothing. His only sense was his sight – watching her lips as they formed words, the color in her eyes as she shifted them from her hand to his neck and back again.

Traejan struggled for control of his senses for what seemed like an eternity but in reality must have been mere seconds - for when he was able to distinguish one word from another she was still telling him how the throat could be struck or torn.

The Roshan dropped her hand away from him and Traejan drew in a slow shaky breath.

How am I going to learn anything this way? he thought

desperately.

She went on to show him how to use a fist like a hammer, and in a multitude of directions. She had names for every strike and they could all be combined in seemingly millions of ways. She explained in great length how to deliver each hit, and the importance of doing it correctly.

Finally, the Master of Weapons backed away and stood in front of the elfin prince. She began to demonstrate the hits slowly and had him mirror her movements. She was clucking her tongue and shaking her head only seconds later.

"The power in your assault does not come from your arm, or even from you," the Roshan told him. "It comes from the earth. You must learn to channel that power, and drive it," she instructed, motioning with her hands from the ground and up to her belly, "through your legs before you gather it into your core and thrust it through your opponent."

"That seems like a rather long process," Traejan remarked.

The Roshan nodded. "If you have to think about it to do it, you'll be dead before you can raise your arm. That is why we will practice until it is second nature. When you first learned to speak Anglicus, the human tongue, I'm sure it was much the same. You first thought of the word in Elfin, and then would mentally search for its human equivalent. Then you had to consider pronunciation, how to shape your mouth and move your tongue so the word would come out right. A lot to think to think about at first – but now, it is automatic."

Traejan shook his head, doubtful. "I don't think..."

"It is no different," the Roshan insisted, cutting him off. She turned at the waist and punched the air two feet in front of her. Traejan could feel the air sweep under his chin and the dark sleeve of her shirt gave a loud snap. She looked at him over her shoulder to see if he understood. He did. She nodded at him. "Now you."

The elfin prince did his best to replicate the blow.

"You are headed in the right direction," the Roshan encouraged, "if you are aiming for the chest. I want you to aim for the other side of it. Again."

Traejan punched the air again, this time driving his arm so far and so hard that he felt it might pop from his shoulder.

"Better," the Roshan said with a nod, though a deep frown creased her brows. "Sink down more." Her multi-colored eyes gauged and judged as he moved and adjusted. "There," she said. "Again."

Traejan threw punch after punch. Just when he thought his right arm might be working itself out of its socket, she had him change to the left.

If the Roshan was less than pleased with his right arm, she was outright disgusted with his left. She made no effort to hide it.

"It looks like repetition will be both friend and foe to you," she said, shaking her head. "Do it again. Ugh! Drive harder. Again. Aaahg! You hit the air like it is solid rock! It is air! Go *through* it! Again. Ugh!"

When he had what she said could pass for a left punch from a mutated Gnomin, she moved onto following a left strike with a right strike. It was equally arduous. Going from one punch to punch-punch was twice as hard.

The Roshan's commands were sometimes spoken, sometimes shouted. "Bend your knees, sink down. Again! Draw that power up through your legs. Again. Drive with your shoulder more! Again. Turn your hips more – you need to pull all your strength from there. Again. No! Turn your hips *as* you punch. Again. *Drive* with your hips. Seven Hells! Not both hips at the same time!" She shook her dark red crown in an equal mixture of disgust, amazement, and anger. Then she blew a burst of air through her nostrils, pulling her composure back together. "Right arm, right hip," she explained patiently and moving slowly as she pantomimed the strikes. "Left arm, left hip. Get it?"

The young prince nodded quickly, his already flushed face turning a darker shade of scarlet.

"Good. Then try it again. Bend your knees, it will steady you, give you more balance and control." The elf bent his knees. "More," she told him. He bent them a little more, but hated doing so. He felt like he was squatting. She laughed and he was sure it was because of how he looked. "I know how you feel," she said, reassuring him. "But you have very long legs, you are far from squatting." He looked at her surprised and she laughed again. "That's how it feels doesn't it?"

"Yes," he said, and then laughed a little as well. "That's exactly how it feels."

"Don't sound so surprised that I know. I had to learn and go through everything you are doing now. Or did you think I was born a warrior?"

"I think you must have been born a warrior," he said. They laughed together this time but she wasn't going to let him off the hook.

"Maybe I was, but I still had much to learn, as do you. Now bend your knees."

The elfin prince did as instructed, concentrating on the instructions he was given, not the instructor. The attraction he felt for her was more than a distraction. He found that instead of wanting to do well to become the warrior he had always dreamed of becoming, he wanted to do well to please her. It brought an intensity to the training that he had not foreseen.

On the side of the haus hung a small wooden bucket and the Roshan filled it with cold water from the stream. She would break off at times and take a drink from it, using a small copper cup. She offered some to Traejan each time, which he gratefully accepted. He was sweating freely, something he almost never did, both from what he was doing physically as well as the focus that it took. Even holding the fighting stance she wanted was enough to make his legs sore and his back ache as she circled him, making constant alterations to his feet, arms, hands, and elbows.

Just when his punches seemed to be getting straighter and more powerful (though his sleeve never snapped the way the Roshan's had done) she made him change the direction of his hand. She had him execute the same strike he had been doing, but with his fist upside down.

He threw punch after punch. When he had it down on his right side, she switched to the left. It proved to be as disappointing as the first set of strikes with his left arm. Still, she drove and corrected until he could do it in what she considered a passable manner. Then she had him combine the left and right strikes. Right, left, and again. Right, left, and again. Slow at first, then repetition giving him surety and speed.

Again, just as soon as he was getting the hang of it, she made him change the position of his hand. She had him drive with his fist coming down from over his head as if he were bringing down a hammer. Right, left, and again. Right, left, and again. Again and again.

Thoughts of her face and her hair finally fell away as he became more and more absorbed with what he was learning. He concentrated entirely on what he was being taught and how it would be applied. Her eyes, however, were inescapable and he quickly learned to read from them both approval and impatience. The latter he did all that he could to avoid. Not only did it make him contrite to displease her, but her impatience had a sharp edge to it that bespoke danger.

Hammer strike gave way to side strike.

Still, she drove him on. The morning passed quickly.

Three of the strikes he picked up almost immediately and only became easier with practice, the other two were difficult and felt clumsy. She made him do the difficult ones over and over until he reached a point that seemed to satisfy her. Despite any impatience in her glance, she always would repeat her directions or each move as slowly or as many times as she needed to help him. Her hands and voice were always correcting, gimlet eyes always darting.

When the sun reached its peak in the blue sky the Roshan called a halt for a quick lunch. Traejan's brown eyes scanned the sky, not realizing how much time had passed. His body, however, knew all too well.

The horses, which had been grazing at the edge of the glen all morning, sensed their intensity slackening and meandered over for a bit of attention. The Roshan rubbed her giant stallion vigorously on the sides of his lowered face and pushed him away. She frowned at the haus, thinking.

"I'll grab some food from inside," she said after a moment. "Let's eat out here. It's nice."

"Can I help?" Traejan offered as Peg nudged his shoulder. He put a hand against her velvety white nose, holding her back. The Roshan simply shook her head as she walked away and Traejan turned his attention to the palfrey. She appeared completely at ease now. "You seem to be doing well," he remarked, rubbing her long white neck and looking her over. The great black whickered as if to reprimand the prince, stomping an enormous hoof that churned the hard ground as if it were water. The elf regarded him warily. The beast still looked monstrous to him.

The Roshan returned with a loaf of bread in one hand, a wheel of cheese and two apples in the other.

"Take off my cloak," she instructed, holding her chin up, "and spread it on the ground." Traejan unfastened the clasp at her neck, the backs of his fingers touching the skin on her neck. It caused a ripple of feeling that went up his arm and over his shoulder. He pulled off her cloak and spread it out, following her lead to take a seat.

Grass was just starting to push green tips out of the earth, searching for the sunshine of spring. The breeze was cool, drying the sweat on Traejan's face and neck.

The Roshan tore the loaf of bread and handed him half, as well as one of the apples. She divided the cheese wheel with her dagger and gave him a ragged chunk before slicing up her own portion. Her apple she sliced up as well.

"Your people are called the Skye Elves," she remarked, "but I've also heard them called Arcadian, is that right?" she asked, topping a slice of apple with a slice of cheese before popping it into her mouth.

"Partly," the prince corrected. "The Arcadians were one of the races of elves that traveled to the New World. The Seleucians were the other."

"And which are you?" she asked, blunt.

"I am both," he said. "My father is Arcadian, darker of hair and eyes. My brother, Xander looks just like him. My mother is Seleucian, very slender and very fair. My brother, Zephyrn, looks just like her."

"And which one do you resemble?"

The elfin prince laughed around a piece of bread. He took a moment to chew and swallow it to give himself time to answer. "Both, I suppose."

"Then why did you laugh?"

"I guess because I always thought I looked like neither."

"A bit of dark, a bit of fair – I can see that," the Roshan remarked, appraising his dark eyes, fair skin, and sandy hair. "Which one do you resemble the most in temperament?"

Traejan laughed, harder this time. "Neither, for sure. If I resemble anyone, it would be my grandfather."

A quiet followed and Traejan longed to ask her about her parents, family, anything. How she got here and who she really was. Who taught her how to fight.

They finished the small meal and the Roshan was abruptly on her feet, brushing her hands on her pants.

"Back to work," she said.

Traejan tried to rise with as much rapid effortlessness but found his muscles had already stiffened. The Roshan gave him a slip of a smile as she shook out her cloak and tossed it onto a nearby boulder.

She eased him back into work by teaching him different ways to stand, how to turn, and where to draw the most power for each strike. She stopped often, showing him common applications of different hits, as well as when and where they would be used to be the most advantageous. She showed how different placement of the same hit would be the difference in rendering an enemy dazed, debilitated, or dead. He was amazed time and again by the logic of what she taught and by the dexterity with which she demonstrated her strikes. She was as light as an elf and quick as a snake in all her movements. Even when she moved slowly, she had the poise of a falcon.

The day wore on but the Roshan called a halt while the sun was still a ways above the tops of the trees. Spring was new and the day was already cooling.

Traejan, though he drank in what he was learning like a man dying of thirst, was too worn out to protest. He was sweaty and dusty and hurting from naught more than standing around and driving his fists into empty air. He knew he was doubly exhausted from taking in more information than he thought possible to store away in a single day.

The elfin prince walked on legs of lead into the haus in a near daze.

"It's going to be awhile before I can get dinner ready," the Roshan said. "Maybe an hour. Take your time."

By the time he had taken a long, hot shower and changed his clothes the Roshan was having her dinner in a stuffed chair across from the kitchen. A new fire roared in the long hearth.

"Help yourself," she instructed, gesturing with a knife towards the kitchen. Dinner consisted of fried steaks with peppers and peas along with rolls of crusty bread. Traejan piled some of everything onto a plate and sat in a soft chair next to the fire, opposite his teacher, and dug in to his meal with vigor.

"This is really good," he told her. He fought the urge to wolf his food, forcing himself to slow down. "I don't usually eat so much," he confessed between mouthfuls.

The Roshan, however, seemed amused by his appetite.

"You'll need it, now and in the days to come," she told him. "Drink lots of water. Get lots of rest, too, Traejanalleh. Today was only the prologue. Tomorrow the story begins."

Traejan was too damned hungry to worry about what she called him or what the next day would hold. For the moment, he only cared about how much his stomach would hold. He looked at his empty plate, the kitchen counter, then the Roshan. She smiled and nodded and he moved quickly to refill his plate. The master of weapons sat back, drinking wine the color of blood from a goblet made of heavy glass, watching him eat while the light of the fire painted the walls with an orange glow and cast flickering shadows in the recesses.

9. HUNTERS

Dell stood guard more from habit than from necessity. There was no settlement for miles and they were still far away from the dangers of the north. There were no other travelers that the Jägers could see or even sense and Dell did not expect to encounter any until they drew closer to the Slag. Still, it was a good habit to have and even better to instill into the younger elves, and Dell believed in leading by example.

They had camped close to the Doveline, a small waterway that they had followed north from the woods that encircled BirdRock. After the first day, the forest gave way to rolling hills and grasslands. The elves had made camp for the night in a sparsely wooded ridgeline that offered some cover and a good view in all directions.

Dell leaned against a tree and listened to the younger elves exchange stories of war and women. Dell chuckled occasionally, knowing they knew nothing of the first and not much more of the second. The tales grew with the night until they were fantastical, and even the normally stoic Nevin was laughing.

Nevin was an interesting elf. Two hundred years Dell's senior, though it was his first year as a Jäger. Not to say he was inexperienced. He had been a soldier in the Old World and was a veteran of two wars. He had seen five turns of the bow, the human equivalent of five centuries. He was still ruggedly handsome, if a bit rangy, when compared to the younger elves. His dark hair, with tendrils of a smoky gray creeping from his temples, fell to his shoulders. He was mostly quiet and introspective, and his dark brown eyes always carried something unspeakable from his past. Dell could only assume that it was all the killing that the older elf had seen.

He knew that Nevin regarded being a Jäger - an occupation that was demanding, sometimes dangerous and often lonely - as a sort of peaceful retirement.

Dell left his post overlooking the valley and strode towards the fire bringing instant, if not complete, composure to the others.

"Okay," he said, stifling a chuckle and kicking Alastair in the boot. "That's enough out of you. Take the next watch, wake Jaden at midnight."

"Yes, Sir." He quickly rose and took his post by the tree, throwing one last impish grin over his shoulder as he went. The others, including Dell, grinned back.

"Get some rest," Dell told the two others. "We leave at dawn, and we still have a good day of riding before us until we reach the Slag. It will probably take an entire day to cross all three rivers." He looked to Jaden for confirmation, who nodded.

Though Jaden was not the youngest, he looked it. He was a Sylvan Elf, the race of native elves that the Skye Elves had discovered when they reached the New World. He was not quite five feet tall, with a round, boyish face under his dark curls, and his ears were more sharply pointed than the others. Though he had grown up in the Midlon, between the Avian Ridge and the Sabado Sea, he had traveled extensively over all three lands. He was the first Sylvan Elf to be accepted to train as part of the elite force of elves called Jägers.

"There are two ferries at each river," he confirmed. "Unless you want to go east to Trigo, where we crossed on our way down to the Midlon, and cross all of them at once."

Dell shook his head. "Trigo would cost us a day's ride there and another to get back on course," he said. "Though we are not in a hurry, there is no need to waste time. Unless safety demands it, we take as straight a course as we can."

"Then the ferries will be our best bet," Jaden acknowledged.

"We should be on a direct course for the one that crosses the Slag," Dell mused aloud, looking out over the dark plain.

Jaden nodded. "If we don't run straight into it, it will be well within our sight when we get to the river."

Dell turned his face back towards the fire and nodded at Nevin. "Throw on a few more branches and get some rest." Then he looked at Jaden. "You, too," he instructed. "You have next watch. Wake Nevin at moonset."

The novice Jägers moved to do as he bid, and Dell settled himself against a tree to watch the land as it breathed softly under the cover of darkness and starlight.

The occupation of a Jäger, though the literal translation was hunter, was not quite what the name implied. Unlike human hunters, the elfin Jägers rarely tracked and killed game. They did, of course, when traveling for an extended amount of time and living off the land. It did not encompass their true occupation.

In truth, they were an elite group of elves, trained to fight and move in all manners of stealth. They were the only order of elves to carry weapons, armed with short swords and long knives, along with the usual forest accoutrement of hatchets and flint along with a bow and a quiver of arrows. Even the Praetorians, the Elfin Royal Guard, did not carry weapons unless they were escorting a royal subject out of the elfin city – and even then they typically wore something more ornamental than effective.

The remnants of an ancient order of elves from the Old World, the Jägers existed and operated at the whim of the King. They served in many ways – as escorts and patrols, spies and enforcers - whatever was needed in strength, skill and bravery. They were the ones called upon when something dangerous threatened, when someone or something needed to be silenced, sometimes forever.

More often than not, the Jägers hunted down information for the king – as Dell and his trainees had been sent out to do. First, Dell knew, they had to find a ferry to carry his Jägers and their horses over the three rivers that divided the Midlon from the Southlon.

こも

Far to the north, so far that it only touched the Northlon on the map, another group of men also sought a ferry. There were none, however, that would take this gruesome troop of huge and fearsome men – so they made their own. It was not easy finding trees to fell on the windward side of the Ice Floe, since nothing was hardy enough to grow tall or strong from the forbidding, frozen earth.

Noga had hoped the great river would still be solid enough to cross on foot, but he had not been that lucky. The water was still mostly ice, but it had broken. The river was slow, and sluggish, but moving and unstable. Right now he was trying to scrounge what he could to carry his two parties of warriors to the other side.

It took his motley group three days to find enough wood and two days more to build a suitable raft to carry them over the Floe. Noga gnashed his fangs in frustration at the time it consumed. This far north, spring was slow to arrive. But it was coming, and summer right behind her, as meager as the summers were in the height of the Northlon were. Still, time was a worry.

The Great Men were truly great. They feared no race, nor any animal. Their sheer size alone was enough to strike terror into the staunchest of humans. They conquered man and beast, even the harsh climate - but in this battle, time was their enemy. One they could not deny.

Great Men were often slow and sloppy, but Noga demanded from them a higher standard. He made them work carefully and meticulously and checked their work often. Despite his need for haste, he did not mean to start his great venture by losing a score of his best warriors on the first foray, or drown or freeze in the Ice Floe himself.

Noga checked their work and checked their weapons. His men were the hunters of traditional sort. They hunted animals for food and Gnomin for sport.

Soon, they would crush the race of elves to the south. The tiny natives as well as the soft and slender invaders that had come and claimed their land just as the world was changing for them, like a robber smashing a new wrought cradle made for an imperial babe. Then they would search out the Lesser Men – the humans. The whole of the world would belong to the Great Men as it was destined.

Noga looked north. His line of sight, of course, stopped at the first ridge of mountains - slate blue and covered with ice. The eyes of his mind, however, traveled far. Inside, he could imagine where his brother was, and wished he could be there with him. He was meeting with the other tribes of the Great Men; the tribes of Ice Combe and the Frozen Gorge, tribes from the Glacier and Berg and Swale Frost and more. For the first time all the tribes of the Great Men had been called, and all had answered.

Ayala was a great leader, fearsome and strong, but the advice of his younger brother was often more than a blessing. Noga had been his right hand for many years, even before Ayala had become the chief of their clan.

Noga knew that his advice was needed, but his presence on this undertaking was needed more. The brothers both knew that to conquer they must divide – at least for the time being. The cretins that accompanied Noga could not do what was needed on their own and meeting with the tribes could not wait. Noga wished he could be in both places, but saw it was impossible. Besides, he knew that Ayala was a mountain of a man. He commanded respect. He would manage without his brother.

Nonetheless, the younger Crommag gnashed his fangs and examined the work as it progressed. The rafts looked weak and feeble and he cursed the men. He did not have the respect that his brother commanded and evil looks followed in his wake. The pale and scrawny Crommag might be smart and cunning, but that counted little to Great Men. Size and strength were all they esteemed. The men in his party were not there because they revered him in any way. They respected and feared his brother and wanted the glory of the First Thrust. So they felled what trees they could scavenge from the barren and frost ravaged land and knitted them together like they were women making quilts.

Noga had even less respect for them. He had half a mind to take the better raft and leave the dim-witted rest to their fate, but even the better raft looked dicey.

Neither will float, he thought, angry. *Wood floats, but not all as well as some. What we have is already waterlogged with snowmelt. Soaked wood is not buoyant.*

He was the only Great Man that knew the term as well as the concept.

And spring, he thought, sniffing the air. *It's here.*

There were few visual signs, snow and ice still dominated as far as the eye could see in every direction. Anything of green was only to be imagined. What cried the season in this waste was that the lands were still frozen, but the river was not.

The mighty waterway that cut through the tundra and divided the Bitterlands from the rest of the Northlon, frozen into a bluish-white snake in the winter, had broken apart. The sluice of melting snow oozed eastward, burdened with chunks of ice – some as large as mammoths.

That slush means spring, Noga thought. *That, and the smell.* Even though the vapor from his breath still froze on his lips and nose, he could smell the change in the season.

The Great Man cursed again, his fangs almost cleaving his tongue in two as he brought them together in frustration. His pale moss-colored eyes cast about and fell upon the slaughterpile, festering with flies.

The twenty selected for the First Thrust had been encamped at the edge of the Ice Floe for five days and had killed a goat each night to roast and share along with the hunks of rechbread that the women had made and packed in abundance for the voyage. The carcasses, stripped of meat, had been thrown into a growing pile that was swarming with insectile scavengers strong enough to survive the cold.

Noga's mossy eyes traveled over what was left. Not much, under the scourge of frost flies, but heads and hooves and guts. Noga cocked his large head, suddenly able to discern which one had been killed the first night, and the second. They were bloating. Even in death they moved – distorted to gross proportions with air - like ballooned beans connected by bloated tubes, arching mournfully to the freezing sky.

He turned to Higa and caught the man's dark eyes. Noga jerked his head, summoning the man that might most resemble a second in command. The Great Man, seemingly dumb as the others, had a glint of evolution in his close-set eyes. He left his work of twining wood and edged closer to Noga, brother of Ayala, waiting.

Noga jerked his head at the carcasses of goat then looked at Higa. "Wash the intestines, fill them with more air, and tie the ends," he instructed. "Then tie them to the rafts, then tie the rafts together."

Higa eyed the undersized Crommag for a moment. Then he looked at the rafts, the carcasses, and then back at the small Crommag. Noga could see the slow works of the cretin's mind as it processed one thing at a time but he waited with the patience that was needed. Finally, Higa nodded and moved off to see that his instructions were carried out as given.

Noga breathed out through his fangs, the cold air turning to vapor in front of his strange, flat face.

Slow, he thought with a feeling of agony. *But sure*, he thought with an exultation of victory.

The next morning the Crommags launched a single but large ferry. Pushing and heaving with long poles of wood and wide paddles of bone in the freezing Floe, they made for the far bank. It took just shy of two hours and much of it was as grueling and as fearsome as the Great Men upon the rafts.

When they pulled themselves ashore, exhausted and shivering but not a single man missing, Higa's dark eyes sought out Noga and gave him a quick nod of acknowledgment, and respect.

Noga nodded back. He kept his face impassive but could not stop his chest from swelling with pride. He turned his countenance to the lands beyond the Floe. His men, and all the Great Men, were hunters in the true sense of the word. They had come to hunt indeed.

10. SORE TO THE TOUCH

And so it went, day after day, till his arms and shoulders and back and legs ached with the strain of exercise.

Traejan rose every morning to find his muscles sore and tight. Every inch of his body seemed to scream out at him as he pulled himself out of bed. He had never known the like, not in the hundred plus years of the life he had seen. Not until now. He groaned as moved about his room, dressing quickly and splashing some water on his face. It seemed the more he moved about the more parts he found that hurt like the Seventh Circle, and there were parts of him that simply did not want to work at all. He left his room in search of his teacher, and breakfast.

"Good morning Trae!" the Roshan exclaimed with wicked good cheer as he shambled awkwardly from his room.

Traejan could feel his face redden. His name had now been reduced from "little fighter" to "little one." An endearing name a mother might call her small child. He gave the Roshan a smile nonetheless.

"How are you feeling today?" she inquired from where she perched on a high stool at the kitchen counter.

She was up and dressed in what he now guessed must be her every day garb – black tunic over an ash-colored shirt that went to her wrists, charcoal pants tucked into black boots. Her brace of knives wrapped her waist like an assassin's corset and her dark auburn hair was balled into a nest on the back of her head.

"Hungry." He did not want to admit how he felt physically and felt he probably did not need to anyway. He was sure his movements spoke for him.

"Sore?" she asked, her small, square teeth visible as she leered at him.

He nodded, self-conscious to the point of embarrassment.

"Everywhere?"

Reluctantly, he nodded again.

"Good," the Roshan told him. "That means you are doing something right, or at least giving it your best attempt."

Traejan offered her part of a grin as she motioned him towards the kitchen to get going.

He broke his fast on cooked oats with butter and milk while the Roshan drank a strong-smelling coffee out of a clay mug. Traejan could feel her smile on him as he ate. He did not relish it. He finished as quickly as he could and washed his dish. The Roshan drained her mug and left it on the stone counter.

"Let's get to it," she said, gesturing to the door with a jerk of her head. She grabbed her belt that held the two curved short swords as she passed through the mudroom, buckling it on as she went.

Traejan followed her through the door and caught himself staring at where the short swords crossed at the small of her back and the way her swaying hips held the belt. He forced his eyes away and into the boulder-strewn glen as the sun threw the first of the morning rays over the mountains.

The young prince had found himself in a quandary. With each passing day he became more attracted to the Roshan. He equally became more anxious and sometimes afraid. At some times she could have tremendous patience, and other times she looked as if she would rather cut his throat and be done with him.

The elf gathered himself up, determination, trepidation, screaming muscles and all, and drew in a deep breath of the morning air. It was cool and clean, with a rich piney smell. He was ready for another day.

When they reached the middle of glen the Roshan squatted down and drew in the dirt with a handy stick. The prince went down on one knee, uncomfortable staring down at her. He watched her make a circle, then bisect it with a cross. At each of the four tips she wrote the letter that stood for the direction in which it pointed. She looked askance at her student with one arched brow.

"Do you know what this is?" she asked.

He knew, or thought he knew. It was so obvious that he thought she might be toying with him. She did that at times. But when he hesitated, unsure, he saw her jaw clench, and he spoke quickly.

"It's a mapstar," he told her.

"What is it used for?" she asked. Traejan shifted, uncomfortable, and the Roshan frowned. "Why do you hesitate in everything?" she demanded, angry.

"It's for showing direction," he blurted.

He cringed inwardly and waited for her wicked smile but she simply nodded.

"I thought you might have another name for it. It is also called a compass, but it is used for the same thing. The best fighting is done this way, like a mapstar, with the same circles and lines." She used the stick to trace the marks she had already made. "The circle is used to overcome the lines, and vice versa. I'll teach you more on that later, but I want you to keep this in mind as we train. Also, I've drawn it true. See how the left point of the star points east to the rising sun?"

"Yes."

"Does it give you a better sense of direction in the glen?"

Traejan was quick to nod this time, though he was already sure of his direction when he had first entered the glade, now six days past. Five days he had now spent, learning and practicing the different strikes.

"Good, because today we are going to be moving around. A lot. If I tell you north, you need to go north. If I tell you east, go east – and so on. You have a lot to learn, and only one summer to learn it."

"But it's not even summer yet!"

The Roshan laughed softly. "It will be before long – almost one week has already gone. And although you will have learned much, you will still have much to learn. I have nearly a lifetime of training behind me, you have only one mad season."

"Mad season?"

The Roshan nodded. "It's what the Gnomin call the summers here. The warm weather is usually early, making summer extra early and extra long. Or sometimes it's the fall that makes the summer longer. Sometimes it is both, and mad as a hatter. Either way, it's a long summer and the season before or after is practically nonexistent."

"It must be the cooler side of mad where I come from," Traejan said. "It gets cold in the winter, but the rest of the year is almost spring."

The Roshan laughed. "That is a mad season indeed. But at least it's spring. In the far north, it is winter that lasts most the year. In the south, it is always summer. The Gnomin call those seasons daft."

"I know of the north," Traejan said, "though I have only traveled as far as the Vikes. This is as far south as I have been."

The Roshan smiled as if this was common knowledge. "Are you ready?" she asked. Her tone was so soft it was frightening. Traejan nodded and felt his heart take off like a rabbit. "You know all the strikes now, at least the ones I am going to teach you. Do you remember all their names?"

He nodded again, frantically trying to bring them all to his mind's surface immediately. "Yes."

"Good. Today we will start combining them."

Traejan felt an odd mixture of elation and fear, an emotion that was becoming a common one for him.

The Roshan was kind enough to spend an entire minute reviewing the strikes he had learned over the past few days. The rest of the morning was spent on combining those strikes. The Roshan numbered each combination and the elfin prince labored to keep them in order, perform well, and please her.

He was frustrated immediately. The strikes that he felt he had almost mastered (at least in application) in the days before became gawky and slow as he sought to use them together. The Roshan was tolerant, unwearied, and only berated him for berating himself.

"You just learned the strikes," she told him. "Don't be so hard on yourself for not being able to incorporate and apply them so quickly. Let's try the first combination again. Forward straight fist to the chest, followed by an underhand hammer to the groin. Go slow. Speed comes with repetition."

The morning passed slowly and the afternoon was equally agonizing for the young elf. The prince was awake long after he went to bed that night, staring at the plaster ceiling and trying to mentally recall and rehearse what he had learned.

He finally consoled himself as the Roshan had done all day, telling himself that the more he learned and practiced – the easier it would be. But he was wrong. *She* was wrong. Horribly wrong.

The next day he tackled what she gave him with stout determination, but the more he learned the more confused he became.

But, like the day before, the Roshan drove him on. She did not seem to care if his strikes were slow, as long as they were done correctly. Again and again and again she made him repeat the combinations until he had them acceptable.

The next day she drove him to strike harder.

The day after she drove him to go faster.

Traejan found that speed and agility did not go hand in hand, and that he had little of either. He was sweating every day long before the morning air grew warm.

What made it worse was that just as he felt he was getting the hang of one move or another, she would move to the next combination. It was maddening.

"Not as easy as it sounded," she remarked with a smirk one day when they broke for their mid-day meal. "Is it?" She unfastened her cloak and pulled it from her shoulders. She was not nearly as warm as the elf. He did not even bother wearing a cloak out of the haus in the mornings anymore.

Traejan forced a smile as he wiped his brow with a sleeve and took a long drink of water. "When I started you told me five attacks, with variations. It did not sound easy, but overly simple. If you had said five attacks a thousand ways each, I would have been more afraid."

The Roshan laughed. She shook out her cloak and carried it to the edge of the glen so they could be in the shade. She arranged it on the ground under a spreading oak. Traejan noted how a few soft strands had come loose from her nest of hair and framed her face like a halo.

The elf was suddenly aware of eyes on him and he glanced about quickly, spotting Coal and Peg as they watched the prince and the Roshan from across the glen. Black and white, one monstrous and one delicate, they already seemed like old chums. They trotted together, in step, as they crossed the glade.

"You don't need to be afraid," she said as the horses joined them, bumping each other and nudging their masters for attention.

"But I am," Traejan admitted before he could stop himself. He frowned and looked away, embarrassed at his confession.

He reached out for Peg who obligingly put her nose in his hand.

The Roshan gave him a look of puzzlement as she shoved Coal's face away from her own. "Of what?"

Of displeasing you, Traejan thought without hesitation. This time, however, he chose his words. "Of failing," he told her, which was true. He looked over to meet her gaze. "I think everyone fears failing."

The Roshan thought silently for a moment, as if the idea of failure was something she herself had never considered.

"It's okay to be afraid," she told him. "Everyone has fear. Courage comes from learning how to use fear, instead of letting it use you."

"How do you use fear?" he asked.

"By knowing your body," she told him, "and knowing that it is trying to help you."

She reached out unexpectedly and placed her hand over the left side of his chest. He held back a gasp of surprise, but his heart took off uncontrollably.

"Your hearts starts beating faster," she said, though it was part of the lesson and not an observation. He hoped.

"Your blood vessels constrict," she continued, "and other functions, like digestion, stop altogether. Pain is lessened or blocked entirely, and your body is given a flood of energy."

She moved her hand to his arm, just below his shoulder and grasped it. Traejan fought to keep his breathing steady and even.

"The increased energy tenses your muscles and lends you more strength and speed than you normally would have."

The young elf nodded, mentally repeating her words and letting them sink in as every muscle in his body felt tense enough to burst – all the while hoping she would not stop touching him.

"The pupils of your eyes dilate, letting in more light, enhancing your vision." She paused here long enough to smirk at him. "Though your eyes seem that way often, must be an elfish thing."

"Must be," he agreed, his voice barely above a whisper. At that moment she was all he could see and hear, as if the rest of the world had fallen silently away.

"But," she warned, "it can also cause something called tunnel vision, which can be dangerous." She let go of his arm and he cursed inwardly. "It is good for focus, but not when you have more than one foe." Her smirk vanished and then reappeared. "And you should always expect there is more than one," she advised.

Traejan nodded, hoping there was more to the lesson and that she would touch him again. There was no enemy in sight at the moment, and he doubted what he felt was fear, despite her perfect depictions on what was afflicting him physically. Instead, the Roshan gave him a lopsided smile. "Come in and help me carry out lunch. I think you'll need more than bread and cheese today."

11. MINDFUL

The second week followed hard on the heels of this first, with the Roshan adding moves – little by little. First it was all the same strikes, but with different footwork. Then it was the same attacks, only turning around to attack from the other side.

At the end of the third week Traejan found he was getting better. He was less sore. He began falling into a rhythm with the strikes and combinations. So, of course, the Roshan began teaching him checks. She sometimes called it blocking or countering, but it all meant the same. More information, more learning, more movements that felt awkward, more aching muscles.

For seven days the young elfin prince learned how to defend against all the hits he had been taught, and some that he had not. He spent the whole week learning to bar a strike from every direction and then how to follow the blocks with a strike to start a counterattack.

All the while learning, learning, learning.

One of the first things he had learned, back in his first week, was that the Roshan was as mercurial as a wild stallion. She was often patient, but just as often she was shouting at him. She cursed at him in every tongue he knew and few that he did not. All the while giving him more to learn and pushing him to go faster.

Traejan collapsed on his bed one evening, wiped out from a day spent entirely on reviewing strikes. He lay on top of the coverlet, unbelievably exhausted from spending the day hitting nothing but air.

I would laugh at myself, he thought, *but it would hurt too much.*

He wanted to crawl under the sheet and go to sleep but he was filthy, and starving besides. Every muscle on his body ached. Muscles he did not even know that he had before today. Between the bones in his ribcage for instance.

How could there be muscles there? he wondered. He had no idea, never having noticed them before, not in the hundred and twenty five years of his life. He was sure of their existence now. Every deep breath sent small daggers of pain between his ribs. Gingerly, he felt his midsection with the fingers of his right hand, probing in between the bones. He winced at the pain and pulled his hand away.

Traejan sat up and groaned. His arms and shoulders were the worst. They felt like hot, heavy, lead. He could feel the nerves that ran between his muscles and they throbbed with fast angry pulses. The muscles in his back formed a stiff, grating V between his shoulder blades. He stripped off his clothes and climbed into the shower, eternally grateful for not just running water, but hot water to boot.

What will it be like doing this with a sword all day?

He had looked forward to that more than anything for what felt like his whole life, but now the thought of it made him want to cry like a child. A small laugh bubbled out of him. He closed his eyes and stood under the hot water, refusing to let his exhaustion turn him towards depression. After a few minutes his muscles began to relax and he scrubbed himself with soap. Just being clean made him feel better. He knew a meal would improve his condition even more.

He put on the cleanest shirt he could find and tried not to trudge as he made his way to the kitchen.

Every day of the week after that was spent on combining the attacks and checks. Just when he would get the hang of one thing (and his muscles become resilient to the use) she moved on to another. It was the one thing he could count on.

"I'm sore all over," Traejan confessed one morning as they ate. "And I'm not even using a weapon yet. I'm afraid I won't be able to lift a sword when the time comes."

The smile the Roshan gave him was uncharacteristically warm. "It's mostly just muscle tension from staying in positions you do not normally hold. You will get used to the moves and they will become easier, and smoother, but it will take a while. In the meantime, it is good conditioning."

The Roshan drilled him constantly on his attacks and his defensives, and all his combinations. She would call out numbers and circle him, correcting him with short, clipped commands.

"Widen your stance. Move your feet. Get your hands up higher. Widen your stance. Sink down more. Widen your stance."

One day she must have told him to widen his stance more times than she cared to. She stopped the training in an effort to be patient but her jaw was clenched and she had to speak through her teeth.

"If your legs are too close together," she explained, "you are about as stable as a one legged stool. Do you see what I mean?" The elf nodded. "You can narrow up your stance," she continued, "to make yourself less of a target, but you still need your feet at least shoulder width apart, preferably just a little bit farther, to keep your balance."

Not ten minutes later, as she circled him, he drew his stance in too close. Instead of stopping the lesson again, she simply came around to the front of him and before he could draw another breath she kicked him square in chest with the bottom of her boot. Traejan flew back and landed on his backside in the dirt.

"On your feet!" she commanded hoarsely. "And on your

guard."

The young prince scrambled to his feet and assumed his fighting stance, making sure his feet were wide apart and his knees were well bent. Before he could say anything she spun around and kicked him again. He staggered back, and his breath left his body in a painful rush, but he kept his feet.

"Do I need to explain it again?"

His voice was a haggard whisper. "No."

"Good. Show me drill number five."

Traejan drew a complete blank for two seconds before he pulled it together and showed her the combination of blocks and strikes she wanted. She nodded.

"Let's call it a day."

He called it a day – his backside aching almost as much as his pride.

The brutal physical toll the training took on his body always seemed to compete with the mental toll the instruction took on his mind.

During the middle of his third week, Traejan lay in bed one night thinking about his brother's wedding feast. What he remembered most was not the ceremony, the dancing, or the unearthly beauty of every soul in attendance. His keenest memory was of the food and how he felt afterwards – gorged to the point he thought he would split.

There had been so many rich foods and delicacies and Traejan, who had been in a rare and festive mood, decided to try some of everything.

There were meats of every kind. Beef and pork and lamb – broiled, roasted, braised, smoked, and pulled. Some rubbed with spices, others drowned in sauces and gravies. Roasted goose and duck and capon. Vegetables that had been steamed, sautéed and roasted. Creamy soups and heavy stews. Baked breads and crusty rolls and steamed dumplings. Pastries of every kind, some filled with meats and some with cream. Dried fruits and fresh fruits. Fruit gels, jams, jellies and marmalades. Toasted almonds and sugared pecans. Honeyed wine and plum port and wines of magnolia and sparkling pear. Chocolates and honeycombs, cakes and tarts and pies and puddings.

When the night finally drew to an end, Traejan's normally thin stomach felt stretched to burst. He and his younger brother Zephyrn had lurched to their rooms with their arms around each other's shoulders. Zephyrn was reeling, and demanding to go back and dance with the lovely girl that had been talking with him most the night, because he was drunk. Traejan staggered the same way, but only because he thought he might explode.

Laughing, even though it hurt, he pushed his younger brother into his chambers and pulled the door shut. Finally, he lay in his own bed, exhausted, and too full to sleep. He tried rubbing his stomach but that seemed to worsen it. He tried to get up and walk around but that brought no relief. In the nearby room he could hear Zephyrn getting sick. Traejan finally gave in to the inevitable and did the same.

As the young prince lay in his bed in the Roshan's haus, he thought that his brain was beginning to feel the same way his stomach had felt on that night. It was getting full. Gorged. When learning a new move, he only had to do it correct one time before the Roshan was teaching him something new. The combinations had all been learned, if not mastered, and the Roshan had quickly moved on to combining the combinations. It was fantastically horrifying.

She spent their lunch one day teaching him to count in Gnomin, and then began calling his numbered strikes in the new language.

Learning, learning, always learning. Always moving. Always something new. Always afraid of the disgrace of failure. He felt he was taking it all in faster than his brain could accommodate it. He feared it would stretch like a sack and then burst open like a rotted gourd. He wondered if his brain might throw it all up, the way his stomach had the night of his brother's wedding. Or if it was possible to actually digest it all. He doubted it.

The mental toll was killing him. At the end of his fourth week, physical toll was in the lead.

Traejan dressed quickly into the light garb he wore at night, mentally noting that he would have to do something soon about his clothing. He was in the habit of rinsing out his sweat–soaked shirt in his bathroom sink every evening after training and then hanging it in the closet to dry. He repeated this daily with the seven linen shirts he had brought, but they had all seen three rinsings and would need an actual wash with soap unless he wanted to end up smelling worse than the boots of Dell's stableman.

The thought of his guardsman made him straighten in surprise. Dell had been a constant companion for a hundred years, and yet this was the first he had thought of him since he had left him on the ridgeline.

I wonder where he is. And what he is up to. The only answer was an angry growl from his stomach. *Okay, okay. Let's see what we have for tonight.*

Traejan went into the living area and was not disappointed. The kitchen counter was laden with hot meat, fresh bread, and steamed roots with butter. The young elf had no idea when the Roshan had time to make such a meal and he didn't care. She was already sitting down eating – not at a table but in the stuffed chair by the fire – it seemed to be the usual place for her evening meal and the wine that always accompanied it.

Traejan fixed himself a plate and sat down in the chair opposite the Roshan. He ate his dinner, his eyes seemingly fixed on his plate, while in actuality he was watching his teacher. It was one practice he was getting quite well at doing without being noticed. She was so strange, so intense. Even when she was pleased he could see the cold calculation of her eye, watching and judging his every action. Even after four weeks, it made him nervous.

The knot of deep auburn hair, tied into a nest on the back of her head every morning, usually lost a number of strands during the day and formed a nimbus around her face every night that seemed to absorb the light of the fire.

Though Traejan had been there for a month, and had gleaned small bits of information about her from the few conversations they had, there were a million questions he wished he could ask her. The main ones consisted of; where had she come from? Who was she, really? How did she learn to fight? Why was she alone?

That night, though, as he drifted to off sleep, another thought occurred to Traejan.

Maybe she is not alone.

The thought was sparked by the feeling of being watched that overcame him in the glen that day. It was followed by the realization that it was not the first time in the past three weeks he had felt the same way. He always guessed it must be the eyes of the horses, since they were ever near. He was quite sure that Coal had made a sound now and then that sounded suspiciously like a laugh. The young prince was just always to distracted and busy to give it much consideration.

Even now, he was too damn dog-tired to think about it.

And, in the morning, he had forgotten.

12. THE ECHO SEA

As Traejan, the second son to Rowland the Great, was beginning his second month of training, the elfin party of Jägers who had escorted him from his New World homeland, came upon the place for which Sir Dellion had a mind to see. They had crossed the three great rivers of the Midlon and ridden north through the forests and into grassy hills and wild farmland. They had avoided all human settlements, but stopped at a small hamlet, inhabited by human and elfin traders, where Dell had Jaden ask an older Sylvan Elf about their next destination.

The smaller elf had nodded sagely and pointed the Jägers in the right direction. He also gave Dell a disturbing bit of news. News that Dell was seeking, but did not want to acknowledge, much less believe. The other Jägers listened, yet kept all need to shift with discomfort hidden deep inside.

The next morning found the party of elfin Jägers gazing down from green hills into a barren land. The stretch of terrain, called the Echo Sea, had slight rises and falls, and then seemed to split into small canyons on the far side. It was desolate, brown and dry and lacking vegetation, but not a desert. A small tributary from the north wound its way through a few of the canyons, and joined a wider, shallow stream that passed over the dun-colored land.

"Nothing grows here," Jaden mused softly from atop his mount. "Nothing ever has, though I never knew why. The area is huge and dry but it is surrounded by green, and there is no shortage of water."

Dell, who thought he knew, looked at Alastair and raised a dark, arched brow. He knew the younger elf had some knowledge of flora.

The youngest elf of the troop surveyed the lands with a keen eye, his horse shifting gently beneath his lean form. "Salt," he answered without hesitation. "There is too much salt in the ground there for anything to grow."

Jaden's brows went up over his bright eyes as his gaze traveled across the wide stretch of wasteland in an otherwise fertile plain. "That makes sense," he replied.

Nevin grunted in agreement and Dell nodded. He gigged his horse and urged it down the grassy hill and the others followed.

An hour later they had crossed over most of the bleak land and were guiding their horses through a high split and into a canyon, of sorts. The rock of the canyon walls, however, appeared strange now that they were up close. Instead of solid rock, the walls were porous with a million pocks and holes. They were thin and seemed to weft and weave with the wind, though they were solid and high. The porous walls were interspersed with what looked like leafless, thick-limbed trees made of stone, stretching upward towards the sky.

Dell climbed down from his horse and ran his hand across the ground. He pulled his fingers slowly through the dirt. It was like none he had ever seen. Most dirt was fine, gritty and when dry would stick to the moisture on the hand. This was a thick sand, but even more like billions of tiny rocks, the grains only slightly larger than those of sand, each worn smooth and slick as if by a millennia of moving water. He scooped up a handful and spread his fingers. It slid cleanly from his grasp. The Arcadian stood slowly, letting the rest of the tiny pebbles slip from his palm.

A river? he pondered, studying the landscape. *The ground is low, but not lower than the surrounding countryside. And the canyon is not cut from earth, only made by this strange formation of rocks. If that's what they are.*

"Sir Dellion!"

Dell turned sharply as Jaden approached, a rock in his hand. He handed the rock to his commander in silence. Dell turned the stone in his hands as the others looked on. One side was rough and porous, the other smooth - as if it had been cleaved in two. It was the smooth side that bore the imprint of a small fish, mostly by its bones. Dell looked at it for a long time without a word.

The fish stone, the smooth and glassy sand pebbles, the walls of stone kelp. There was only one explanation for what they saw – water. A lot of water, for a really long time. Dell looked to the north and the west. He could see for miles in both directions and knew what lay beyond his vision, blocked by the low canyon walls. There was no large body of water within sight. The small springs that wound their way through the desolate terrain could not have caused what he was seeing.

Only a great flood could bring water this high, and it would have to have lasted for eons to produce what he was looking at under his feet and which had created the thin walls around them before abandoning the land.

A flood, or the often-voiced belief of the fisher folk. The Atlanteans had always claimed that water once covered the entire world. But then again, Atlanteans were known for saying crazy things. The Sylvan Elves never denied nor affirmed this claim. But then again, the Sylvan Elves were known to hide from the rest of the world.

The place was called a sea, though there was no water. Just echoes of long ago. Dell grunted.

The seasoned Jäger looked at his men, seeing his own questions and realizations mirrored in their eyes.

"What is it?" Jaden asked Dell. "What disturbs you so?"

It was Nevin that answered. "What the elves dread most, but are always condemned to witness," he said. The others looked at him, their almond-shaped eyes growing wide and round.

"Change," Alastair whispered.

Dell had never before heard such gravity or wisdom in the young elf's voice, nor saw it reflected in the eyes of the other Jägers as he did now. Seeing the realization and the knowledge as it dawned upon them was terrible. Jaden was a native to the New World and Alastair had been born on the Great Journey. Neither knew the true horror of change firsthand, but as elves they could comprehend it, and it filled them with dread. The look on Nevin's face was what Dell found the worst – resignation.

The elves had come so far, so very far, in hopes that they could live in an unchanging world. The mission of the Jägers was to see if those hopes were to be dashed.

What they had seen made it seem inevitable.

"Let's get going," Dell told them. He put the fish-stone in a pouch behind his saddle and mounted his horse, turning him north. His men mounted their horses and followed without a word.

13. REDTOWN

Ryen gave a gentle tug on the reins and the khusar obediently leaned into a course-correction that was moderately more to the west. It was only late morning, and the Norseman rode under a canopy of leafy oaks, but it was already growing warm. Spring gave way to summer early in the Southlon it seemed.

The Norseman was from the Vikes, the frozen lands that spanned the north between the tail end of the Siber Massif and the Ice Ridge. Eyes like chips of blue ice peered out from under reddish-blonde hair. A short, downy beard of the same color covered his cheeks and chin and joined over his lip.

He draped the reins over the horn of the saddle and stripped off his cloak as he rode. The khusar, feeling the slack, picked up the pace as if suddenly freed.

"Fine, you ass!" Ryen chided the animal as he rolled his cloak and tucked it deftly into a leather loop above his right saddlebag. He held on tightly with his knees as the animal bounced him hard enough to make his teeth rattle. "Make good time, for once!"

The khusar, which was really more of a horse than an ass – and had to be to carry a rider the size of the Norseman - trotted merrily along. Ryen took the reins back up and the burdened beast gave a snort and slowed back down to a walk. Larger than a warhorse, the dappled grey gelding had been bred from the same icy steppes as the man who rode him.

Though Ryen hailed from the north, he had never settled there. He was content with a life of wandering, and roaming lands warmer than those from whence he came. He was familiar with the Gnomin and their Mountains of Blood, as well as the Sylvan Elves that bordered their land. He was acquainted with the Atlanteans as well as the Skye Elves - in the quietly austere fashion that they reserved for any race but their own.

He preferred roving the Midlon, with occasional forays into the Southlon.

The river lands stretched out west from the Sabado Sea and the human towns were awash with taverns and wenches. The Great Plains and Southlon forests sprawled like a slapped hand eastward across the continent and every hamlet and village was also replete with wenches and taverns.

"Warm lands and warmer beds, eh?" Ryen mused aloud. "But the heat here is ridiculous – it is not even half to summer!" The great grey snorted either to agree to his views on the weather or to remind his master that he had been gelded. Not that beds had held much meaning to him before his castration.

Ryen ran a hand over his face. The apprehension bothered him as much as the growing heat. Never before had the Norseman ventured this far south.

Few had.

The Redlands covered the southernmost part of the realm duly hailed as the Southlon, and were ruled by the Crimson King, often called the Red Lord or - just as often but in hushed tones as if the man could hear from miles away - the Mad King.

It was only during the past few years that the walled town had opened its gates and the citizens began to venture out, tentatively - mostly to trade with the villages deep within the Southlon.

"Stirrings in the North, stirrings in the South," Ryen told his courser. "That bodes no good, mark my words." The khusar ignored his words and kept plodding along on his southbound course.

At mid-day the horse and rider emerged from the forest of

low scrub oak into a field of red-tinged triticale. The still young grains atop their slender stalks undulated in the breeze for as far as Ryen's eyes could see, making the fields look like a sea of blood. His blue eyes widened at the sight, then widened more as he spied the town in the distance.

The fields dipped slightly over the course of a mile, and then rose again. On the ridge above the waving ocean of copper and claret grain was the biggest enclosed town he had ever seen.

A kingdom, his mind whispered. *That's no town or village; it is certainly not a ward. It's a kingdom.* Another word came to his mind, one he had heard from only one person but something he had never witnessed on his own. *City. It's a city.*

His own homeland was large. It was a network of loosely joined villages and boroughs that had been built up over the ages to form miles of connected townships. It sprawled across the frozen wasteland beneath the teeming mountainous teeth of ice that made up the lower Siber Massif. It was bordered on the west by the Great Cut and on the east by the Sliver, hemmed in on the south by the berg-ridden waters of the Sabado Sea.

The Vikemen were natives to the New World and had lived there for as long as the eldest elder could remember. The only other natives were the Atlanteans on the coast and the Sylvans in the woodlands. The Crommags to the north had always been considered more animal than man, so they did not count.

The newcomers were known as the Skye Elves and they had erected their delicate empire south of the Vikes – nestled between the Mountains of the Sun and the Mountains of the Moon. Airy castles and fine buildings of sparkling stone spread like jeweled fingers reaching daintily up the base of the ridge. It was the most impressive establishment built by hands that Ryen had ever seen, until now.

"What makes Redtown red?" Ryen had asked at the Chipped Plow, a tavern in Cillace, the most southern village in the Southlon.

"The reflection of the triticale," the barkeep said, wiping the polished oak of the bar with a rag.

"The lands of the Southlon are plagued with red clay," his wife said, voicing her own opinion. "It gets into and all over everything."

The wench that had been sitting on his lap leaned in close. Her dark hair fell down her back and covered the hand he had wrapped around her waist. "I am told that is from the blood of the slaves who built the castle," she whispered in his ear. "It is a dangerous place. You should stay here."

Ryen watched as she wet her lips and he considered the idea quickly before giving her a grin. "I'm sure I will be fine," he assured her, kissing her small but shapely ear. He also assured her that he would stop by on the way back to pay her a visit. It made her smile as he left, also smiling. Then an old drunk at a table by the door caught his sleeve.

"It is an aura," the old man rasped. "A foreboding of blood." Now, though he was out in broad daylight and far away from their dark whispers (from where he sat atop his giant horse), Ryen could believe them all.

The khusar must have felt the same for he jerked his head to the right as far as the reins would allow, attempting to turn around and go back into the forest.

"Stop it!" Ryen scolded, tugging the left rein and giving the khusar a kick in the flanks. "Get going! We have an appointment."

The khusar started forward, reluctant at first, then picking up speed until he was trotting happily in the sunshine.

Ryen's blue eyes were glued to Redtown and where it crouched like a scarlet dragon upon the distant hills. The buildings were all stone, some sort of ochre granite. They were almost all round, though of various sizes and heights, topped with conical roofs made of red clay tiles. It was the amount of edifices, however, that was flabbergasting.

Most villages had a saloon and a dry goods store. Some small shops – clothes for women or clothes for men. A tannery. A blacksmith with a common stable. A small number of eateries. Some villages had small houses on the outskirts but most residents lived above their place of business.

Trigo was larger, since it was built of a number of villages that had grown and eventually combined. The kingdoms of Atlantea and Tuar Ceath were of course considerably larger.

Redtown had more structures than the entire Northlon and Midlon combined. Though densely packed, it stretched out along the line of hills like a crimson tide cresting the ridge.

And around it all was a wall, so high and so long that Ryen thought there must not be a pebble of that ochre granite left in the Southlon. It made the city a vast fortress, an impregnable stronghold.

"Is that to keep people out, or keep people in?" he whispered nervously to the khusar. The massive horse shook his head, whipping its blue-gray mane. As the pair descended the gentle grade the wall seemed to grow and grow, until it was blotting out the sight of the buildings it guarded. They kept their slightly westward course and soon found a road that cut through the triticale fields, heading straight for the center of the walled city.

As they began to climb the opposite rise Ryen could make out the conical roofs again, many topped with red pennants that waved in a lazy manner with the gentle breeze.

"How could men build such a thing?" Ryen asked aloud as they neared the wall. Each great, rust-colored stone was four times the size of his khusar. "And how many did it take? How many are in there?" He voiced his questions to the fields of triticale, since the khusar never answered.

As they drew closer to the great red wall, Ryen saw that their path was leading to the only opening that was visible from the road – and even that was obstructed by a great portcullis made of blackened iron.

The sun inched upward above the horizon and the Vikeman and his giant mount, both damp with sweat, reached the gate and Ryen glanced around as his horse stamped its hooves and chewed at its bit. He truly did have an appointment, was there by invitation of the Crimson King himself, but it certainly felt like he was unexpected and unwelcome. And he knew he was being watched.

The promise of gold that had been made to him for this trip seemed suddenly hollow.

The Norseman did not consider himself a fighter, but he was unquestionably a survivor. His knees tightened around his courser as his right hand dropped to the hilt of his sword while his left reached for the shield that was slung behind his left knee.

"Halo!" a voice called, so abrupt and so loud that it made Ryen jerk his sword free before he could even see to whom the voice belonged. His horse whinnied and danced back as Ryen steadied the beast, squinting through the iron bars.

"Whoa!" the voice said again. "My apologies, I didn't mean to spook you."

"No worries," Ryen assured, which was not what he felt. "I did not expect the gate to be closed."

"You are Ryen Glace, then? Of the Northlon?"

"I am," Ryen agreed. "I am here by the invitation of the king."

There was a pained creak followed by a cheerful rattle of a chain as a winch turned and the portcullis began to rise. Ryen edged his mount a little closer and the blackened iron disappeared above, revealing a tall and comely youth with blonde hair and lively blue-green eyes.

"You are well met, Ryen Glace," the youth said with a sweeping bow. "Welcome to Redtown. I am Jack."

Ryen dismounted and bowed in return, but he could not resist a grin as he rose. "Well met indeed," he agreed, "but

Jack, you are too trusting. You are obviously wary of unwanted visitors," the Norseman said, looking around at the wall of stone and motioning to it with a finger. "How do you know I am who I say I am?"

Jack laughed and the sound was warm and comforting. "Because," he explained, his eyes full of mirth and mischief, "no one would claim to have an appointment with the king, who did not."

Ryen dipped his head in understanding, this time with a bit of curious trepidation.

"Whoa!" Jack exclaimed. "Is that a khusar?" he asked, leaning back so he could better see the great gray horse.

"It is," Ryen affirmed. "But be careful," he cautioned as Jack moved in for a closer inspection. "He is an unfriendly beast." The khusar nuzzled Jack on the back of his neck, making him laugh. He playfully pulled at the youth's hair with his velvety lips until Ryen pushed the great head away. The Vikeman gave the khusar a sour look.

"If you would like to remount," Jack offered, still tickled by the massive horse, "I will guide you to the castle."

Ryen shook his head and extended a long arm, inviting Jack to lead. "I have been riding all morning," he said. "If you don't mind, I would rather walk with you."

Jack laughed again and the sound filled Ryen with a strange sort of peace. "I don't mind at all," Jack assured him. "In fact," he confided in a low voice, leaning closer to the Vikeman as they left the gate and started down a wide street, "it will afford us better gossip!"

Ryen took an instant liking to Jack. He was bright and cheery, something odd for a boy that was on the brink of manhood. Most were sullen and self-conscious, unsure of the lives ahead of them.

Unless there's a pretty girl, Ryen thought with a smile.

But there was something else different about him. It only

took the Norseman a moment to figure out what it was.

It was his skin.

Jack had perfect skin for a young man so soon past his teen years. Ryen was likely more prone to notice because acne was the bane of young men and women in the Valley of Ice. It was Ryen's first whore that had aided in his own complexion.

"You need to use cream," the prostitute told him.

Ryen, thirteen years old and over six feet tall had pulled back, aghast. "Cream? On my face? Like a woman?"

The whore, ten years his senior and of much darker (but still ginger-colored) hair, nodded vigorously. "The air of our land is dry. When it dries your face, your skin makes extra oil to compensate. It raises the rash."

Young Ryen had run his thumb across her cheek. Her white skin was flawless.

"Can you get me some?" he asked. "I will add it to your... fee."

The whore had nodded and kissed him. "If you come to see me regularly, I will include it for free."

Ryen kissed her back, aroused again. "It's a deal," he had agreed.

"This way," Jack said, bringing him back to the present as he pointed down a street that led east, "is where the smithies are." He swept his arm to the left. "And down that way, are the stores and markets."

"What type of markets?" Ryen asked, his tone light.

Jack shrugged. "Fish, clams, meat. When trading is good, imports..."

"Imports?" Ryen asked, not knowing the word.

Jack grinned. "Imports, yes. Things we get from other colonies."

"Colonies?" Ryen asked, embarrassed that he was so unfamiliar with Southlon terminology.

Jack laughed lightly, shaking his head and suddenly aware of the culture gap. He made an effort to speak more simply without being condescending.

"Towns," Jack said. "Villages. People here trade with them, then sell their goods here in the city."

Ryen nodded, understanding. "Any pillow trade?" he asked, feigning nonchalance.

Jack opened his mouth to ask and then snapped it shut when he realized what Ryen was inquiring about. He nodded quickly and leaned closer to the Norseman. "Of course," he whispered, "but they are scattered, not all on one street." His blue-green eyes looked at the ice-blue eyes of the Vikeman as he drew back and stood straight as they walked. "I can recommend a good inn, should you wish to stay," he assured him.

Ryen grinned. "I would appreciate that," he remarked, looking around as they walked along. The quiet streets were not cobbled but paved with large, flat stones the same ochre color as the buildings and great wall that surrounded them.

The granite was a dark gold, swirled with caramel and crimson. Many of the storefronts had canopies and awnings of scarlet. *So it's not just the triticale that makes Redtown red,* Ryen thought.

Jack was full of chatter, pointing out one thing or another along the way. The shops had awnings over the doors, eateries had canopies as large as tents that covered patios of tables and chairs. City buildings and water towers were topped with red flags to make them easier to find. People were out, opening stores and doors in the late morning, but none were close enough for Ryen to catch more than a glimpse.

The women wore long, swirling skirts in bright colors and white blouses with puffed sleeves. Men wore pantaloons or riding pants, topped with crisp shirts and sometimes a vest. From his vantage it looked as normal as could be. Something about it all, however, made Ryen a shade uneasy as he led his horse along – who was chomping at his bit and stomping his hooves while he walked as if to voice his own discomfort.

The realization hit the Vikeman a second later like an unexpected pinch to his backside.

There are no children, Ryen thought with a shock. *That's why it's so quiet.* He looked around as discreetly as possible. *And no animals. No kids yelling, no dogs barking. No cats screeching as they dodge carts and feet. Seven Hells, there aren't any carts.*

The city was by no means silent. Ryen could hear adults calling to each other, the pounding of hammers, and the ring of steel upon steel from scattered forges and smithies through the part of the city that he and Jack were crossing. But the absence of screams, in both delight and terror, or the angst of a housewife shouting at her brood while flapping an apron to chase away pets, left a strange hole in the undercurrent of sound. It gave the Vikeman a chill.

Don't be such a goose, Ryen chided silently. He knew that elfin children spent their days being tutored. Gnomin children were much the same and were never out during the day – for fear of them being blown up or crushed in any number of accidents that happened on a regular basis.

"Right up here," Jack was saying, "is where most of the housing starts. Merchants and mercantile occupy most of the outer ring, then there is a ring of restaurants and, ahem, inns." Ryen caught his sidelong glance and gave him a nod. He also caught his first real look of a woman within the walled city.

She did not disappoint.

Ryen guessed she must be a merchant's wife, since she was toting bolts of red silk and laying them out on a table in front of a small corner shop. She wore an off-the-shoulder dress of crimson under a tight, black corset. The neckline was low and revealing but even more arresting was her face. It was narrow, with a pointed chin and high cheekbones. Her skin was dark brown, almost black, and framed by a mass of black hair that fell past her shoulders in tight curls. Her eyes were black and her full lips parted in a smile as she glanced up to find Ryen admiring more than her face.

Jack turned his blonde head in mid-sentence, following Ryen's stare and his own face split into a grin as he spied the woman.

"Hello, Ellie!" he called, cheerful.

"Hello, Jack," she murmured, eyeing Ryen.

"Good morning," Ryen said, pulling his eyes from the tops of her chestnut-colored breasts to her dark eyes.

Ellie's smile widened. "And who do we have here?" she asked.

"Ryen Glace, of the Northlon," Jack announced.

Ryen bowed as Ellie laughed in surprise.

"The Northlon?" she queried. "You are a long way from home!"

"Who is a long way from home?" a voice questioned as another woman emerged from the shop. She was dressed in the same manner as Ellie, but her corset was scarlet, and she was as fair as the other woman was dark. Large blue eyes peered from a round but stunning face, and hair almost as light a blonde as a Skye Elf cascaded over shoulders that were as smooth and white as milk. "Oh!" she remarked as she saw the Vikeman and his beast of a horse.

Ryen sketched another bow and the great, gray khusar whickered a hello to both women.

"Good Morn, Sedhi," Jack greeted.

"Good Morn, Jack," she replied politely before turning her attention back to Ryen. "You must be here to see the king," she stated.

"I am," Ryen confirmed.

"I hear you are a man who can get things," Ellie said with no small amount of admiration. It was both a compliment and a suggestion, one that usually suggested something more, and Ryen opened his mouth for what he deemed an equally suggestive response, but was distracted as Ellie slipped a dark arm around Sedhi's tiny waist. It could have been a show of sisterly affection, or simply friendship, but Ryen – who had a greater understanding (or so he had thought) about the body language of women - sensed something more. There was something about it that was gentle, yet oddly intimate.

"I am," he simply repeated, hoping he did not look as perplexed as he felt.

"Then see me on your way out of the city," Ellie told him, her smile revealing teeth that were white and perfect.

"I most certainly will," he assured, looking to Jack as both women gave them a respectful nod before returning to their business inside the shop.

Jack waved at them and they were on their way again, the gold and red stones of the road taking them on a slightly curved path as they wound their way up a gentle grade on the hill. Others called to Jack as they saw him and he always responded with a wave or jovial response.

Ryen was not so dim to notice that not just all of the women they met or saw were beautiful, but so were the men. He saw no cripples, no poor, no beggars, no drunks. And still, no children. Maybe he could find out more at a pillow house. The women who worked at such establishments were as often as ready with talk as they were with their bodies. Thinking of local women, his mind went to the two he had so recently met.

"Are Ellie and Sedhi married?" Ryen asked as casually as he could. A merchant woman usually meant a merchant husband.

Jack, though he seemed to know them well enough, took a moment to consider. "I don't think so," he said slowly. "But there is no law that says they should be."

"Law?" Ryen asked, puzzled, thinking about customs and traditions with young women in all the lands he had traveled.

"I wouldn't think there would be a law."

Jack shrugged. "The laws are made by the king," he said. "And unmade," he added in a quieter tone, leaning towards the Norseman. "Once," he continued, telling Ryen a tale of public drunkenness that made the Vikeman laugh almost all the way to the top of the hill. Ryen responded with a tale that made the young man blush as deep as his laughter.

Before Ryen knew it, they had reached another wall - the one that surrounded the castle. The great stones in this wall, like the buildings within, were more red than gold, and Ryen knew he was at the heart of the city. The portcullis here, however, was already raised. Four guards, two on each side, wearing crimson tunics and breeches and holding spears, flanked the wide entrance. As he and Jack passed through, one on each side fell in beside them.

Ryen realized that it was a curtain wall they had passed through and found himself crossing an outer bailey paved in the same flat stones, these even redder than the ones that paved the street. There were only smears of gold now within the rust-colored granite. They passed under another gate, this one smaller and cutting through the inner wall that surrounded the castle itself.

There seemed to be more hustle and bustle within the inner castle walls. Men shouted from the stables, women called from the kitchens, and the sound and smell of horses in their stalls filled the warming spring air, yet Ryen still found it eerily subdued. Red pennants topped the towers, snapping in the high breeze.

It's not just the quiet, he thought, *it's so clean.*

A groom came up to see to the khusar. A young man that looked much like Jack, except for the rust-colored livery coat he wore, bowed to Ryen. "I will see that he is fed and watered," he assured the Vikeman.

Ryen turned the reins of his khusar over to the groom

and the beast gave a snort of disdain at being left behind. Another young man, this one in a tunic of burgundy velvet over burgundy breeches, approached him and bowed deeply.

"Ryen Glace," Jack said with a flourish, "it was a pleasure to meet you."

"You're not coming in?" Ryen asked, surprised. What surprised him more was the look on Jack's face. It was forlorn, almost sad, and for the second time on this journey, Ryen became more than a bit uneasy.

Jack shook his head. "I will escort you from the city, when it is time for you to go," he stated.

Ryen had a fleeting thought that he might be leaving feetfirst in a box and hoped that it wasn't the type of escort that Jack was mentioning.

Don't be ridiculous, Ryen thought, chiding himself. *The king would not bring you all this way just to kill you.* The Norseman swallowed. *Unless...*

"Does the king have a queen?" Ryen asked. "Any daughters, perchance?"

Jack laughed and the sound was as warm as the sunshine, dispelling any temporary gloom. "No," he answered. "There are women in the castle, but you best let them alone. I'll find you an inn for tonight, should you wish to stay." Somewhat assured, Ryen stuck out a hand and Jack, delighted by the gesture, grasped it tightly and gave it a quick shake before letting it go. The Norseman, feeling little comfort over the fact that he towered over those around him, turned to the page in burgundy velvet and, escorted by the two guards from the gate, followed him across the inner bailey and into the crimson castle.

14. REST AND RESPITE

Traejan awoke one morning and, for the first time since his arrival, was not eager to train. Aches and frustration had gotten the better of him, and he was filled with an unsettling feeling that bordered on dread. He dressed listlessly and took a deep breath before opening his door. Despite what he felt, he was determined to keep it to himself. He knew he would get through it.

Maybe I will try a mug of coffee, he thought, trying to brighten his outlook.

The elfin prince squared his shoulders and came out of his room in time to see the Roshan strapping her brace of daggers around her waist, over her black jerkin. She stood next to one of the tables in dining room, her dark auburn hair seeming to absorb the light that seeped in from the skylights. She looked up immediately and spotted him in his doorway.

"No training today," she told him as she fastened the buckle and pulled it tight. "Do what you like, but stay out of trouble." She spared him a grin before returning her attention to her weapons. *As if you could get into trouble,* that smile said.

She donned the sword belt that held her two short swords and retrieved a longsword, sheathed and wrapped with a leather thong, from the table by her side. Without another word she turned and left, grabbing her cloak from the mudroom on the way out.

Traejan, slightly stunned and full of curiosity at the sudden turn of events, was subsequently filled with a relief so great he thought he might collapse. His shoulders slumped and he heaved a great sigh. Tears of gratitude burned behind the lids of his eyes and a small, almost delirious, chuckle escaped his lips as he pushed the door to his bedroom back open and fell on his bed.

He woke a few hours later, face down and fully dressed, his body stiff and aching but eternally grateful. He had needed the extra rest and despite his protesting muscles, the young prince felt worlds better as he got up and stretched. He poked his head out of the door to his room and looked around. No sign of the Roshan, or anything else for that matter.

Traejan ran a hand though the shag of his sand-colored hair, yawned and rubbed his eyes. The artificial light in the haus kept him from knowing what time of day it was, but his stomach was glad to fill in the gaps. He figured it must be close to half day.

He went to the kitchen and found cold meat in the icebox and heaped it on a plate along with some rolls of hard bread and a wedge of cheese. He couldn't believe how much meat he was consuming, or bread for that matter. He had always been a light eater, and was accustomed to eating while out on the trail with Dell, which meant a lot of dried meat and hard bread, and whatever small fruits or berries the land would give them.

Your body needs it, he thought, his mind echoing what he had heard the Roshan say more than once, as he took a pear from a basket in the pantry and balanced it on his plate. Something niggled at his mind as he closed the pantry door but he was too hungry to worry about it. He poured himself a mug of cold ale, not because it would make him feel anything, but because it sounded good with his cold lunch.

The Roshan doesn't seem to eat much, he mused as he sat at a table, nearly wolfing down his food. *A little something in the morning, sometimes just coffee. Nuts and cheese, and maybe a piece of fruit for lunch. Dinner is the only time she eats a real meal - meat, bread, roots or vegetables and, of course, a bottle of wine. Or two.*

Traejan washed down his meal with the ale and stood and stretched. He was still horribly stiff. He cleaned his plate and mug in the sink and went outside to check the time. As he had suspected, it was just about midday.

There was no one in sight or sound.

He considered exploring the woods, maybe whistling for Peg, then decided to explore the haus a little first. Considering he had lived there for nearly a month, he really knew nothing about it. He had done nothing more than glance around as he passed through it every day. His eyes were always intent on the queen of the castle, who (also after nearly a month), he knew almost nothing about.

The prince stopped at the kitchen where he opened and closed cupboards and drawers, harmlessly poking around for a few minutes before he opened the long pantry. Two double doors, slim but as tall as himself, opened onto the Roshan's larder. It was deep, with shelves only on the right side. The left was tall and empty, presumably for storing brooms or such but of cleaning tools he saw none.

He was not surprised at what he found on the shelves – it was part of their every day fare. Baskets of fruit and nuts and seeds, which the Roshan seemed to live off of during the day and the haus was always full of both. There were always bowls of them on the kitchen counter, on one of the dining tables, and on the table by the fire.

A middle shelf held neatly stacked green bottles, their tops sealed with wax – the Roshan's wine.

She's going to run out soon, he thought, counting the bottles.

Before Traejan closed the pantry door, he retrieved another pear. Something tugged at his mind again but now he was just sated enough not to worry about it. Instead, he marveled at his hunger.

Seven Circles, he thought. *Where does it all go?*

He walked through the living area, running his hand over the backs of chairs and couches, his eyes idly wandering over the tapestries that hung from the walls. The dining room was more interesting. Each corner had a small alcove that displayed a different suit or partial suit of armor along with a different weapon.

As he moved towards them he noticed his own body felt like armor. Old, rusty, armor that wanted to creak with every move. Every muscle from his ankles to his wrists moaned in protest as he crossed the room.

Maybe another nap will help.

Two suits, along with their weapons, he recognized immediately. They were from the Northlon, one set was that of a castellan and the other of a Vikien captain. The other two were foreign and unfamiliar. He could not tell what the armor had been made from and had no idea what the weapons were or how they could be used.

All four sets, however, did not seem to be old or outdated. They were clean and oiled, to the point that they could be taken down and worn.

Not by me, though. They would be too...

Realization dawned before his thought was even complete.

..small.

Hers, he thought. *These are hers.* He reached out a hand let his fingers slide delicately along the links of the mail shirt before him. He backed away and looked at the others again, as if seeing them for the first time.

Decoration? he pondered. *Gifts?*

No, she wore these.

Ceremonial, perhaps?

No.

His sharp brown eyes picked out what might be mistaken by some as imperfections in the armor but Traejan could see were repairs – hammered out dents and buffed out scratches in the plate, carefully mended pieces of hard leather, new and shining bits in the mail where links had been replaced.

She fought in these.

When? Why?

Traejan stared at the displays for long moments, wondering, then he gathered himself and remembered the pear in his hand. He rubbed it on the front of his shirt and pulled his attention from the armor.

He approached the doors that flanked the entrance to the hallway and reached out a hand, pausing for a second, feeling slightly guilty. He shrugged it off.

She told me to stay out of trouble, she never said to stay out of the other rooms.

It didn't matter. The door was locked, as was the one on the other side. The elfin prince leaned back and looked down the hall, trying to gauge the distance to the first set of doors and guess how big the locked rooms must be.

Maybe bedrooms, but small. Not as large as my room, though there would be plenty room for just a single bed and washtable.

Then why locked?

It's most likely they are storage rooms for weapons.

He ventured down the hallway to find the door next to his own as well as the ones on the opposite side of the hall unlocked, but also uninteresting. The other three rooms off the hallway mirrored his own.

Four rooms, other than her own of course. Eight beds. Are they ever full? How often does she train? Traejan wondered. *Who? How many?*

It seemed that the more the prince trained, the more confused he became. His mind was a jumbled mess of moves and numbers. Likewise, the longer he was with the Roshan, the more questions he seemed to have.

He was closing the door next to his own when something caught his eye. He pushed the door back open and stepped into the room.

The door that led from the bedroom and into its bathroom was partially open and, though the room was dim, the elf's eyes picked out a solid white claw on the floor. He crossed the room and pushed the bathroom door open all the way. An oversized, glazed white bathtub squatted on the slate.

Traejan had never been fond of baths. Sitting in a tepid pool of his own filth had somehow never appealed to him. Today his muscles said otherwise. He leaned down and turned on the water experimentally, full hot. It came out in a steaming rush. He turned it off only to stopper the tub and then turned it back on. He sat on the edge, watching greedily as it filled up, eating his pear. Juice ran down his chin and he wiped at it absently with the sleeve of his shirt.

When the tub was near full he shut off the water and cocked his head, for the first time listening to see if anyone was around or even approaching the haus. Nothing. Even the animals in the woods seemed to have taken the day off. He locked the door and quickly stripped off his clothes.

Traejan sank into the steaming water, closing his eyes, wondering if he had ever felt anything so exquisite.

After his bath, Traejan drained the tub and refilled it halfway with hot water. He gathered the dirty clothes from his room and proceeded to give them a good washing, with soap. After wringing them out he took them all (save for his smallclothes which he hung in his own bathroom) outside and draped them over the low branches of the trees in the glen.

Peg joined him, nudging him on the shoulder as he arranged his shirts in the sun.

"Lonely?" he asked, rubbing the sides of her long nose. "You seem to have become quite friendly with the Roshan's beast. Do you miss him?"

Peg whickered as if to reprimand him, or tell the elf it was none of his business.

"Alright, alright," he said by way of apology. "Stay here, I'll get you a carrot."

Traejan returned to the Roshan's larder for the third time that day, squatting down to where the carrots, onions, and potatoes were neatly separated in large, woven baskets. He selected a carrot and stood as he closed the doors to the pantry, and then looked at the closed doors with an odd suspicion.

The elf remembered that something had nagged at his mind here before, and now it was more pronounced. He opened the doors again abruptly, his brown eyes revisiting the dry goods he had just observed.

The nuts in the pantry were still in their shells. The ones placed in bowls about the haus were always shelled, though he had never seen the Roshan ever crack a nut. He reached out and gave an apple a gentle squeeze. Firm – fresh enough to have been picked yesterday. The thought of her picking apples almost made him laugh.

Where does the food come from? he thought suddenly. He was just as surprised that he never thought of it before. He took it for granted that there was always food, and he realized now that it was always fresh. Nuts and seeds seemed to be the Roshan's favorite staple during the day - she was like a squirrel the way she ate. And dinner was usually meat and wine. If there was no meat, it was cheese and bread, but when the meat *was* there it was always fresh, not dried.

Even if she had stocked the kitchen the day before I arrived, it would not have so much food, certainly not so fresh.

Where does it come from? he pondered again as he returned to the glen to give Peg her carrot. He rubbed her neck absently, trying to puzzle it out. As full as his mind was with his training, he guessed it was not too surprising that he had never considered how or when the Roshan had the time to run her household. She was as busy training as he was learning. *How then? Who?*

The Roshan returned at dusk to find Traejan preparing a dinner for them both. She dropped her things in the mudroom, hung her cloak, and came to the edge of the kitchen. She leaned back on the counter, crossing her arms.

"A domesticated elf?" she asked grinning.

Traejan grinned back, too rested and refreshed to let her remark make him flinch. He did refrain, however, from telling her he had also washed his clothes.

"It's just the rest of dinner from yesterday," he confessed. "Along with the small wheel of orange cheese."

"How are you feeling?"

"Like a new elf," he told her and she laughed.

"How did you know I'd be home for dinner?" she asked, indicating the two plates that had been laid out. She also noticed he had uncorked a bottle of red wine and set out a glass next to one of the plates.

"I heard you coming."

The Roshan's brows drew together, though she still smiled.

"From how far?"

Traejan shrugged and checked the meat in the oven. She watched him, intrigued. It felt good to come home to meal, even a leftover one.

"Do I have time to clean up?" she asked. Her face was streaked with dust and she felt generally grimy from riding most of the day. Her hair was in disarray, not just loose strands but stray locks had come free and lay this way and that around her head and shoulders. Traejan thought she looked beautiful.

"Of course. I'll keep it warm till you're ready."

The Roshan nodded and unbuckled her sword belt and pulled it from her waist. Traejan watched, transfixed for a moment, then quickly averted his eyes. It was too much like watching her undress.

She looked at him curiously for a moment as she threw the belt over her shoulder, the short curved swords still secure in their scabbards. Then she turned and headed for her room, grabbing the bottle and glass on her way.

The elfin prince blew out a great burst of air when she had gone into her chambers, closing the heavy door behind her.

They ate dinner by the fire, as they usually did, and Traejan realized that a day of rest had done more than replenish his tired muscles. Without his normal fatigue occupying his mind, and his brain racked by a day of training and memorization, he found himself even more enraptured by the woman across from him. The fire danced in her eyes and made the dark red of her hair glow with an eerie light.

He watched her discreetly and picked at his food as his mind turned over the questions that he always wanted to ask.

Who are you? Where did you come from? Who taught you to fight?

Though tonight, another question was added to the list.

Who does your shopping?

Traejan smiled, his breath just short of a chuckle. The Roshan, though she had not been looking at him, did not miss it. Her green-brown eyes glanced up, the bits of gold in them glinting red in the firelight.

"What is it?" she asked.

The elfin prince shook his head. "It's nothing," he said. "I just feel so different having some extra rest." Which was true.

The Roshan gave him a slight smile and took a drink from her glass.

As she did, the elfin prince watched her as intensely as he could without looking directly at her. Sometimes she would talk, and he would look right at her, but most times she was quiet. In that case he would feign looking at the fire, but really he would be watching the fire dance on her hair. Or, he would lean back and close his eyes nearly shut, while actually looking at her face.

His usual questions danced in his mind as he watched her. Traejan did not have to wonder long about his new question. It was answered the very next day.

15. THE MAD KING

The Vikeman Ryen Glace had actually known the Roshan for many years. He had even trained with her for a bit, on a whim, but gave it up having learned only the basics. After just a few weeks of training he knew that he wanted her more than he wanted any of her fighting skills. Though he was never able to get under her sword belt, they remained good friends. He saw her whenever he passed through the Midlon, and brought her a present every time. Now, as he followed the page through halls of red polished stone with the two crimson-clad guards escorting him, he strangely felt that she was there with him.

The feeling was so strong that he even glanced over his shoulder to make sure. She had an odd sense of humor and he could imagine her getting the drop on him as a joke. But there was no one there but his attendants.

He glanced over his other shoulder and noticed that the other guard was so similar to the one on his right that they could have been twins.

They must be twins, he thought.

All the guards he passed wore matching uniforms. That made it no different here than it was in any kingdom, human or elfin. But Ryen could have sworn that their faces looked exactly the same. Same shape of jaw and mouth and eyes that were the same exact shade of chocolate. Same chocolate-colored curls. Same complexion. Same straight nose. A perfect six feet tall, which made them an entire foot shorter than the Norseman but did nothing to assuage the growing apprehension he felt.

Something pinged inside his brain, warning him. As his icy

blue eyes darted about, he could imagine Ember's gimlet eyes darting about in an identical manner.

Then he heard her whisper in his ear and he almost jumped, realizing in the same second that the sound of her voice was only in his mind.

Nervous? she asked.

Yes.

Why?

Something is not right here.

What is it? she asked. *What do you see?*

There are no children, was his quick reply.

He could almost hear her sigh. *What would I see?*

My guards, he thought. *They are identical.*

He could hear her derisive laugh like a plume across his mind.

Brothers often take the same post and position, she told him. *Twins especially serve together. You know that. What else?*

Ryen glanced around as casually as he could. The castle was grand and palatial, that much was obvious at first blush. The stone inside was a deeper red, and polished to a high shine. The carpets were thick and soft and a deep garnet color. They ran the length of the hall, but only in the center. The floors to either side were the same polished stone as the walls.

Eyes like chips of blue ice traveled over the walls. Ryen had only been in a few castles, but all of them had one thing in common – the walls were hung with tapestries. In Atlantea the tapestries were woven in gorgeous colors with the images of fish and turtles and every other creature of the sea. The one elfin castle he had been in had tapestries that depicted scenes of the heavens and the stars.

The Vikemen had no castles, only keeps. But even those were hung with tapestries – an artistic element that insulated the walls and helped to keep back the cold.

Maybe they do not know the craft, Ryen thought. *Maybe they simply prefer other decoration.*

He heard the ghost of sardonic laugher in his mind. *Why do you make excuses for them? Are you that afraid? Do not quiet your fear, it exists only to save your skin.*

He did notice that the hall was hung with many mirrors, all finely made. He and his escorts passed an open door of red oak and Ryen looked in as he walked by. The room had superior furniture, nothing too large. Children would find it difficult to play Come Seek Me with such furniture – had there been any children in the castle.

The windows were breathtaking, made with colored glass. *No curtains.* Ryen realized as they walked along and the room was left behind. *No tapestries.*

He did not even need to hear the Roshan whisper the question in his ear. He knew the answer.

No place to hide.

The Vikeman's discomfort grew and then vanished like smoke in the wind as they approached a group of three women. They were clustered together, laughing and giggling like girls, but became silent and curious as Ryen passed by with his small entourage. It was not uncommon. With his reddish beard and towering height he often drew inquisitive looks, especially in the Southlon and even more so from women.

They wore no courtly dresses with wide skirts and plunging necklines, but to the fact they were courtly women there was no doubt. One had white-blonde hair pulled back into a simple horsetail. Two others had dark skin and dark hair cut short in a style Ryen had never seen before but discovered that he liked. All three wore riding leathers and scarlet silk shirts.

Ryen gave them a respectful nod that brought wide smiles and whispers in his wake. He was tempted to turn his head for another look but he had reached the end of the carpet and the boot heels of the page rang loudly on the polished stone before he stopped in front of a pair of doors, also of red oak, one of which stood open. Another pair of guards flanked the doorway. *And I'll be damned if they don't look identical to the guards escorting me,* the Norseman thought. *Quadruplets?* he mentally queried of his teacher from long ago. *Is that likely?*

Her answer was as curt as it was silent.

No.

The guard on the right side gave a nod to the page who stepped into the room beyond, glancing at Ryen to make sure he was following.

"Ryen Glace!" the page announced. "Vikeman of the Northlon!" He bowed and left the room, closing the heavy oak door as he departed.

Ryen's cold blue eyes took in everything at once.

The room was like the one he had seen off the hall, only much larger. Polished red stone was hung with polished mirrors framed in gold. A thick red carpet was laid under a desk of carved cherry wood and there was a smattering of more thick rugs, but most of the floor was polished red marble. There was a large chair padded with crimson velvet behind the desk and four smaller chairs facing it.

A regal figure turned from where he was gazing out of the windows and there was no doubt as to who it was. Ryen Glace stood before the man called the Mad Lord – the Crimson King himself.

The Vikeman found himself at a loss for what to do next. He knew that before Rowland, the elfin king, it was proper to sink to one knee, and not look him in the eye. For King Triton, it was custom to bow until recognized.

"I am sorry," he apologized, bowing at the waist. "I am not sure of your customs. Do I bow, or kneel perhaps?"

The Crimson King waved a hand. "If you feel you must, or if it is in accordance with your own customs. I require no such fawning." The man was tall, though not nearly as tall as the Norseman. His lean form was clothed in dark red riding leathers and a tunic the color of wine. A heavy scarlet cloak chased with gold draped his broad shoulders. He had a strikingly handsome face with dark eyes and a head of dark curls.

"I am Marco," he said, introducing himself bereft of fanfare. Ryen gave him a respectful nod as the man motioned with a hand to one of the chairs. "Please, sit down," he invited. "Are you tired, or hungry, after your journey? Would you like to rest and take refreshment before we speak?"

Ryen shook his head as he lowered his tall form into the chair. "I will enjoy a little of both, but after we have talked. I am quite curious to know why you wished to meet me, and would not feel comfortable nibbling before a king."

Marco, who had seemed on a nervous edge as he had introduced himself, laughed heartily and gave the Vikeman a respectful nod as he walked to the front of the wide desk. His boots, black leather with scarlet seams and chasings that looked like echoes of fire, rang upon the stone.

"And how is it," he asked as Ryen sat himself in one of the chairs, "that you act in front of your own king?" Marco leaned back against the heavy block of carved cherry wood and crossed his arms over his chest.

"The Vikemen do not have a king," Ryen informed the Red Lord. "We have a council of four Norsemen."

Marco raised a dark eyebrow. "The four Norsemen of the apocalypse?" he asked, his tone high, almost mocking. His lips pulled back in amusement, revealing square, white teeth.

Ryen frowned, confused. "Excuse me?" he asked.

Marco waved the question away and frowned as well.

"Forgive me. A word play on something I heard, once." His dark brows raised again. "You, I am sure, have questions?"

"Well," Ryen answered, "yes."

"First!" Marco exclaimed. "Payment." The desk upon which he leaned was topped with a blotter and parchment, a quill and inkpot, and a number of carved wooden boxes. He opened the box next to the inkpot and pulled out a small twill bag, tied at the top, and tossed it to the Norseman. "For your journey."

Ryen caught it deftly, instantly measured the gold by its weight, and made it disappear. It was not, however, the question foremost on his mind. He had come, after invitation by the king, curious to know two things – why was Redtown red, and was the man called the Mad King truly mad?

Like the elfin prince, training miles away from the Red Lands, the Norseman had more questions now than when he had started his current expedition.

Just then, a loud noise came from beyond the closed doors. A grating schreech that made the king jump as he turned towards the sound, his right hand falling to a box on the left corner of his desk. He eased the lid open, his dark eyes fixed upon the door.

"Not to worry, your majesty!" a voice called from the hall as the door was pushed open by a large, booted foot just enough to deliver a soothing assertion. "It is merely the wardrobe you wanted removed from your chambers."

The king dropped the lid to the box and waved a dismissive hand, though the movers in the hall could not see it. "Break it, burn it, give it to a flax-spinner's daughter, I care not! Just make sure it is out of the castle before dark!"

"Yes, sir," came a clipped call from beyond the door before it swung shut once again by the large boot.

The Red King heaved a sigh and turned to Ryen and motioned for him to continue the conversation they had started.

"You had questions," he reminded the Vikeman.

"Ah, yes!" Ryen agreed, cocking his head. "I know now what makes your city red, but not why. It must be more than just a plentiful supply of red-tinged granite."

Marco shrugged, his heavy cloak rising above strong shoulders. "I dream in blue. This way it is easy for me to distinguish what is real."

Well, Ryen thought, *that answers two questions.*

"And, well...I mean...I was curious..." the Norseman continued, though he left his sentence hanging in the air between him and Marco. The light coming through the stained glass of the windows began to catch the sun, giving it a red hue and staining their skin pink and bright.

"You want to know why you were the first person from the Northlon invited into Redtown?"

Ryen nodded. The Red King pushed away from the desk and paced to a window. Again his boots made a hollow ringing sound upon the stone floor. Ryen got the feeling that the man was never still for long. He had an air of restlessness about him.

"I heard you are a man who can get things," Marco mused aloud, gazing through the glass. His right thumb found his square chin while his forefinger touched his lips thoughtfully.

"Yes," Ryen agreed, guarded.

The king chuckled softly and turned his dark eyes on the Vikeman. "I also heard you are a pirate and a thief."

"I am a trader," Ryen corrected.

"What would inspire a man to such a trade?" the king asked. "Wealth?"

It was Ryen's turn to chuckle. "I doubt that what I do would make me a wealthy man." He considered stopping there, but knew that the king had been forthwith in the confession of his dreams, so he continued. "I am restless by nature and I am not comfortable staying in one place for too long. I like to see new things and new places, while visiting old favorites. In my journeys, I like to bring people things they thought they could never have. If I profit from it, it lends coin to my next adventure."

Marco chuckled again and slowly shook a finger at Ryen, as if he had been naughty. "You have a nobility, hidden within you," he teased.

Ryen gave him a shamefaced grin, his blue eyes sparkling. "Don't tell anybody."

Marco let his head of dark curls fall back as he laughed. "A noble thief," he chortled. "There are others like you, are there not?"

Ryen stroked his ginger beard. "Are you asking about pirates, thieves, or noble men?" he asked.

"I am asking after men like you," the king acquiesced, flashing a white smile. "Traders. Noble traders."

"There are other traders. Some more noble than I, some less."

"And yet it is you that I want," the king conceded. "You are the one who can acquire what I seek. Would you take gold as a trade?"

Ryen shifted in his seat, tempted, more curious than ever, and more than a tad nervous. "Usually. What is it that you are after?"

The Red King leaned back against the casement and regarded him with raised brows. "You do not know? Or have not guessed? You are a man who can get things, so you said. You also said that there are other men in your occupation. Therefore, you must be privy to something unique, something other men cannot deliver, or possibly even get close to."

Ryen sat up taller in his seat, his interest raised and his ginger brows drawn together. "What is it that you are after?" he asked again.

The Red King approached him and took his place once more before him, leaning back on the carved cherry wood desk and folding his arms over his broad chest. A small smile quirked the corners of his shapely mouth.

"I want the Roshan Simorgh."

Ryen almost laughed aloud in the midst of mirth and terror. And hard. Almost. Instead, he shifted his weight in his seat and fixed his bright blue eyes on the dark gaze of the king.

"It would cost a lot more gold than what you paid me just to visit," Ryen advised him. Marco bowed his head as if to say the Vikeman could name his price. "Considering," the Norseman continued, "that it might cost me an equal amount of blood. Or my life."

"Is that all?" the king asked, his dark brows up once again over his handsome face. "Gold?"

"And a present," Ryen added. "A really nice present."

"For you?"

Ryen shook his head.

The Red King seemed pleased by this and pushed away again from the desk as Ryen stood, so they might shake hands. With the deal made, the king clapped Ryen on the back, reaching up to do so.

"Join me for a lunch in the gardens," the king invited, "and we can discuss this...this...present. You must leave the castle by nightfall, but Jack can find you a room in the city if you wish to stay."

"I would like that very much," Ryen said amiably.

The king clapped his hands and called for Ryen's escort. The identical crimson-clad youths were instructed to take the towering Vikeman to a suite where he might clean up and refresh himself. The Red Lord gave further commands to have a table made ready in the gardens for their luncheon. He took his leave of the looming and ginger-haired man from the north and strode from the room ushered by his personal guard who, to Ryen, looked eerily identical to the ones that accompanied himself.

The mood of the Norseman, however, was already lightened by thinking about the pleasures and delights the new city might hold after suppertime. He tried to think about what the women of the city might have in store for him and tried not to consider what a certain woman (one that wore knives to bed rather than silks) might do to him, should she find out what service he had just agreed to deliver.

16. PINECONES AND PRIDE

Traejan left his room the morning that followed his day off of training feeling better than he had since the day he arrived at the haus. The extra sleep and clean clothes made him feel new again. He was ready to learn again, ready to fight.

He joined the Roshan at the kitchen counter where she sat on a stool, drinking a mug of coffee. She smiled at Traejan and the elfin prince thought he had never seen anything or anyone more beautiful. She glanced away, her gimlet eyes sly, and he followed her gaze to two wide, circlets of heavy leather. His head jerked back up. Behind her, against a chair, leaned a staff. It was by no means a sword but yet, even then, Traejan could hardly contain himself.

"Are we starting with weapons today?" he asked.

The Roshan laughed and the sound was not cheerful. "No. Make yourself something to eat and meet me outside."

She took the leather circles and the staff with her as she left. The elf was too nervous to eat a large meal so he tore a hunk of bread in half and gnawed at it as he pulled on his boots. He stuffed the last crusty chunk in his mouth as he left the haus and crossed the glen. It was not as bare as it had been when he had arrived a month ago. Instead of mostly dirt, it was mostly grass.

Spring was heaving her fertile sigh upon the earth for yet another year, and had touched everything, blessing every inch of the forest with warmth and water and light. Moss stretched up the trunks of trees that surrounded the glade, the border stream burbled louder than ever from unseen snowmelt, and wildflowers grew frequent and random.

The Roshan waited for him near the boulders and ironwood tree that had become their customary spot for training. The staff was leaning against a large stone, on top of which balanced a basket of pinecones. She picked up the leather circlets as he approached.

"Hold up your hands," she instructed.

Traejan held them up as if being threatened at sword point by a robber. The Roshan pressed her lips together tightly, thought whether in amusement or anger, the prince could not tell.

"Give me your right hand," she said, her tone patient.

Traejan held out his right hand and she fastened one of the circlets around his wrist and tied it again where it ended in a point towards his elbow.

"This is called a vambrace," the Roshan told him as she motioned for his other arm and fastened the second vambrace in a similar manner. "These will protect the lower part of your arms."

After she had fitted him with the armbands, his brown eyes full of hope and expectation, the prince spent the rest of the day in near humiliation. It started with her poking the staff at him, calling out every block he had learned, then the strikes, and then their combinations. She would thrust at him from every which way until she was satisfied he could defend and attack from all directions.

Then she picked up the basket of pinecones he had seen waiting on the boulder and started to lob them at him in the same manner. He knocked each one away as she hurled them, sometimes quite fast, obeying each command she called.

The Roshan was quiet when they broke for lunch, more quiet that usual anyway, and Traejan found he had nothing to offer. Every poke from the staff was a poke at his pride.

Missing a block on a pinecone and getting knocked in the head was no better. He ate little, in silence, and washed it down with cold water from the bucket.

After lunch came the rocks. The Roshan had a nice pile of them and he only had a brief moment to wonder when she had time to assemble them before they were coming at him, one after the other.

"Two!" she shouted, meaning his second combination of blocks, as a stone half the size of her fist came zinging towards his face.

His hand came up instinctively and the rock ricocheted off the heavy leather of the vambrace. Traejan had no time to think about it, for the next stone was already on its way.

"Five!" she called and his right hand was down in an instant, saving his hip from a nasty bruise.

"One and five!"

His right arm came up and his left came down as two rocks came at him in quick succession.

"Six and two! Two, three, four!"

Within less than five minutes he was pouring sweat. Not from the physical strain but from the mental concentration and worry that he might get pelted with a rock. As always, his fear of embarrassment was greater than any fear of pain. When the Roshan finally called a halt he heaved a great sigh of relief.

Throughout the course of the day the young elf had managed to knock away all but one pinecone and was only poked twice with the staff. He never got hit with a rock.

He cleaned up before dinner, examining the welt on his ribs where the Roshan had jabbed him with the blunted spear she passed off as a staff. She was gradually becoming faster and less gentle in her attacks as his training progressed. She had used a stick before to thrust at his blocking points, but never the staff. As much as he was looking forward to the day they started using steel, part of him was more than a little fearful.

Reminding himself that learning the sword was the entire reason for his presence there, the elfin prince walked out his bedroom door and found himself face to face, waist to face actually, with a Gnomin.

Traejan was so surprised that he could not yelp in astonishment nor stammer a hello. The Gnomin, a female with short, slightly graying blonde hair, gave him a smile (or a grimace, he could not be sure which) and went into the Roshan's bedroom and closed the door behind her. His shock was now amazement. He looked towards the kitchen to see the Roshan fixing herself a plate of food and then moving around the counter to head for her spot by the fire. She saw Traejan in the hallway and motioned to him.

"Come eat while it's still hot," she directed.

Traejan silently fixed himself a plate of hot meat and spiced carrots, glancing every few seconds at the heavy oak door at the end of the hall. There was a pot of white mush tonight and he put a spoonful on his plate to be polite. He sat down in his usual place by the fire and waited but the Roshan did not offer any explanation for the Gnomin. He had picked through half of his carrots before his curiosity got the better of his silence.

"Who was that?" he asked.

The Roshan looked up sharply.

"Who?" she asked. She seemed so surprised that Traejan wondered briefly if the Gnomin had snuck in unawares to the Roshan, or maybe that she had been a hallucination.

"The Gnomin," Traejan said. The Roshan looked bewildered for a second and then returned to her dinner.

"Oh," she said, a small smile at the corner of her mouth.

"That's Gatha."

"Gatha?"

"Yes. She comes here to help me out."

"Help you out?"

"Yes, she helps with almost everything around here. A sort of housekeeper, among other things I suppose. You've never seen her?" Now it was his turn to be startled. Had this Gnomin been here the entire time without him noticing? "I suppose you've always been asleep when she comes," the Roshan mused. "Or outside training."

The person of discussion came out of the Roshan's bedroom and headed for the kitchen. Traejan watched her, slightly amazed. She was tall enough that the top of her head was nearly chest high to Traejan, making her somewhat the size of a Sylvan Elf, though much more stout and stocky.

She wore rough leather trousers that stopped at the knee. Leather straps rose from her pants and went over her shoulders to cross in the back over a blue and white gingham shirt. The trousers ended at the knee and she wore thick socks and heavy, short boots.

"What does she help with?" he asked. He could not discern if she was a servant or a friend to the Roshan and he did not want to sound ignorant, though it seemed that he was always doomed to do just that. "What do you call her?" he whispered. The Roshan got his meaning easily enough and gave him a wicked grin.

"Gatha!" she called as she walked by on her way to the kitchen. "What would you call yourself? My squire? My guardian angel? My lady in waiting?" The last struck the Roshan as particularly funny and sent her into gales of laughter. Gatha favored her with a dour look and went about her business.

Traejan watched the exchange in silent amazement. His astonishment could not crowd out his curiosity, it seemed. He had always been too fearful to ask the Roshan any questions about herself but this subject seemed safe. Safe enough anyway.

"How did you," he stammered, "I mean, how is it that she came to be with you?"

The Roshan chewed thoughtfully for a moment. "Years ago," she told him, "I was traveling in the Northlon and found out that the Crommags had been coming down into the Gnomin Valley, and killing the Gnomin for sport." The Roshan let out a heavy sigh. "I stayed in the north of the valley for near six months, and hunted them in turn." She paused long enough to refill her wine glass. "The last raiding party I found was larger than any that came before, and even though none of them left alive, I suffered a ugly wound that left me in the Mountains of Blood for another two months. When I came back here, Gatha came with me. She doesn't always stay, but she always comes back."

Gatha kept about her business in the kitchen during the story. Her only commentary was the occasional bang of a cupboard door.

"Was her family killed in any of the raids?" Traejan asked.

"I don't know."

"Why did she come with you?"

"I don't know."

"Did she come voluntarily?"

The Roshan's auburn brows went up over her brown and green eyes and she washed down a mouthful of food with a swig of wine.

"Seven Circles, Traejan! Are you suggesting I took her prisoner?"

The elfin prince looked from the Roshan to the Gnomin who had stopped what she was doing and was staring at him over the counter with dark, steely blue eyes full of indignation and amusement.

"Ah, no. I mean, no. I'm just so surprised. And curious, I guess. In the elfin kingdom, people serve for many reasons – pay, loyalty..." Traejan trailed off as he gave the Gnomin woman a sheepish glance.

"Ah!" the Roshan exclaimed. "I see what you are getting at.

To look at her expression most times it would seem she is here to serve out some kind of punishment, but I'm pretty sure she likes me."

From the kitchen a shelled nut flew at the Roshan's head. The Roshan caught it smartly and broke the shell with her hand, shaking it away and devouring the small nugget of green meat inside - her eyes and smile never leaving the Gnomin woman.

Gatha piled a plate high with chunks of fresh bread still hot from the oven, and added a crock of butter. She brought it to the elf and placed it on the table in front of him.

"Thank you," Traejan told her as he picked up a slice of warm bread and watched her return to the kitchen.

Gatha held up a bottle of red wine but the elf shook his head.

"No thank you," he said. "A glass of water will be fine. I can get it myself."

The Gnomin ignored his offer as she grunted loudly, looking fiercely at the Roshan as she drew a glass of water and brought it to him.

"I can't hear you!" the Roshan called, not looking up as she ate. Then she laughed, putting a hand to her mouth so no food would come out.

The elfin prince, confused as ever, buttered a slice of bread and ate it without tasting it.

"She thinks I drink too much," the Roshan explained between mouthfuls. Another grunt was heard from the kitchen and the Roshan brought a fist to her mouth to again stifle her laugh.

Another nut came flying at her from the kitchen and this one the Roshan caught without looking and put it on the short table in front of her, next to her plate.

"Can she speak?" Traejan asked, his voice quiet. He put his napkin down on the same low table and sat back in his heavy chair across from his teacher.

The Roshan shrugged, chewing her food. She took a drink of wine and wiped her mouth with the cuff of her sleeve. "Either she can't or she won't. She's never spoken to me." She pointed to his plate with her fork. "Eat."

Traejan picked up his own fork to obey. "What's the white stuff?" he asked, his voice still low.

"Potatoes."

"Potatoes? They don't look like a potato."

"They've been boiled and mashed. Try them, they are really good."

Traejan took a small bite and found that she was right. They were delicious. He took a larger bite.

"Gatha must know a hundred ways to cook a potato," the Roshan told him as she ate. "The dumplings that we had with the chicken last week – those were made from potatoes, not bread dough."

"Really?" Traejan asked. He remembered the dumplings quite clearly. It did not occur to him that dumplings could be made from anything but bread dough, and that he never saw the Roshan cook.

You need to start opening your eyes, he told himself. *What else don't you see?*

After he had eaten a dinner that would choke a half-starved Jäger, and Gatha had disappeared behind one of the locked doors next to the dining hall, Traejan returned to his chair by the fire to secretly stare at the Roshan.

She balanced her wine glass on her knee and narrowed her eyes at him. "I think you and I need to talk about something," she said quietly.

Traejan felt his innards clench even as his head swiveled to face her. He forced a small smile and hoped beyond anything that his expression was casual and did not betray the fear that coursed through him.

Does she know? Do I look at her too much, or too long? Have my emotions betrayed me? Will she send me away?

"You are doing exceedingly well," she told him, staring at the wine in her glass, "and progressing quickly, but there is something within you that is keeping you from getter better."

Traejan let the air out of his lungs in a slow even breath. He was not out of the woods yet, but he felt the edge of his fear dull a bit.

"Your reflexes are fine, today showed that."

"Is that what today was?" Traejan asked, the humiliation of being a fixed target still fresh in his mind. The Roshan waved the question away.

"Of course that was what the day was for – to test your instincts and how they are meshing with your training. I'm not here to shame you."

Traejan's narrow face reddened, shamed by his own (and incorrect) suppositions.

"Your movements are becoming quicker, and more instinctive, which is good, but they are lacking a smoothness that I know you can perform. Your movements are too jerky, too forced. They need to be smoother. I know practice will bring about much of that, but there is something else. You need to have more confidence in what you are doing. You need to have more confidence in yourself."

Traejan took a deep breath and let it out in a rush, relieved that her discussion had nothing to do with her. But he knew exactly what she was talking about. He had felt it himself, had been feeling it for at least two weeks. He knew the basics of everything she had taught him but could see a glaring difference in the way she moved and the way he mimicked her movements. Even though there was hardly a pause in his movements, hardly a pause was far from no pause. Short moments of hesitation were still there. He felt unsure of himself and awkward in all that he did.

"I don't know what it is," he admitted. "But I know what you mean."

"Why don't you believe in yourself?" she asked.

Traejan sat back, surprised not by the bluntness of her question, but by the accuracy of it. "I don't know," he said softly. The Roshan picked up the wine bottle from the table and refilled her glass.

"Tell me about your family," she said.

"My family?"

"Yes."

Traejan laughed softly, his eyes growing distant. "They are like any family, I suppose." The Roshan echoed his laughter gently.

"I imagine they must be different from just any family, they are the royalty and rulers of the Skye Elves!"

Traejan shrugged and shook his dark blonde head. "The difference is merely one of occupation. The way the life of a miller's family would differ from the life of a merchant's family. They fight, they love. They have children, and weddings. They celebrate and grieve. The wife of a miller or merchant berates her husband for working too late, or too much, although it is done out of love for him. My mother does the same to my father."

The Roshan chuckled, understanding the concept.

"I see your point, though I am amazed you are so nonchalant about it. It must be different. Especially for you."

"Well, I don't have to work to earn a living," Traejan conceded. "But many elves born into wealthy families do not have to pursue occupation."

"But they probably do not feel the restlessness that you feel."

"Do you think I am restless?"

"Why else would you be here?"

Traejan sat back in his chair, astonished. Not because it was the truth, he knew it to be the truth, but because she knew it as well. He thought for a while before he spoke again.

"Do you know that the elves hold three to be a number of power?" he asked. The Roshan nodded. "It's more than that," he continued. "It is like some omnipresent obsession - like something that rises unspoken from the earth and permeates our very lives. It has no sense to it, and because it has no sense there is a part of me that tries to fight against it."

The Roshan cocked her head, intrigued. "Does it have to do with the Holy Trinity? The three gods – Peace, Honor, and Justice – that rule as one in the First Circle? That is what the elves believe, is it not?"

"It is. But it is something more than that, more than religion. Elfin cities are built with three chief corners, forming a triangle. Castles have three distinct sections, and when they are built they are grouped into threes. Each neighborhood has three boroughs. Every home is made of three structures. I don't understand it and can explain it even less, but it is something that has bothered me all my life."

"And you think this is what is holding you back in your fighting?"

Traejan chuckled softly, the firelight in his hair and his eyes. "No, I just think it has something to do with my restlessness."

"Why?"

"I don't know why. I guess if there is a reason, it is because there is no reason for it at all. Elves are a very balanced people, and strive for balance in all things. But three is both an unbalanced and an odd number. The world is not built on threes – it is built on twos. Black and white, day and night. A scale has two sides, and a coin, and a sword. For everything there is only two. I hate it when things don't make sense. There are two people in a marriage, but is considered very lucky to have three children. It makes no sense."

"There are three in your family as well, if I am not mistaken."

"Yes, my parents were blessed with three sons." "Ah!" the Roshan exclaimed.

Traejan shook his head, smiling. "I know what you are thinking and, no – I am not jealous of my brothers. I love them deeply and would not trade places with either of them for even an hour."

"Maybe you want what they have."

Traejan laughed. "My brother Xander will be king someday. He spends all his time learning to serve the people. My brother Zephyrn has no such compunction, and spends all day serving himself."

The Roshan lifted her chin. "And you? Who will you serve?"

You, Traejan thought. *If you would let me. I would serve you all my life.*

"I don't know," he answered quietly. "I've never thought about it before."

"Think about it now," she told him, and he did.

"Whoever needs me, I guess."

"Don't guess."

"Whoever needs me."

The Roshan smiled, the light and shadows of the fire playing upon her face. "Xander has purpose. Zephyrn is carefree and lets nothing bother him. You do not wish you could feel the same?"

The elfin prince stared at the fire. The revelation her words brought unraveled something in his mind and his memory.

It was a time when his grandfather had invited him out for a long ride. Xander had just begun to spend every waking hour in court and Zeph, only fifty years old, had already begun to run wild.

Traejan, always glad to be outside, felt even better spending time with his grandfather. They rode north, a winding trail up and into the mountain ridge that cradled the elfin city. The horses climbed carefully, picking their way along for an hour before his grandfather stopped his horse. The old warrior still rode Peg back then and his hair, as white as his robes and his courser, trailed behind his crown like a bridal veil.

The young prince turned his horse so that he could look down into the green valley that cupped Tuar Ceath like a multicolored jewel. His grandfather, however, turned his horse northwest, toward the first mountain in the chain that made up the Mountains of the Moon. Its top was kissed with snow and a lone cloud nudged its side. The river Lethe hugged its base and then rushed off, tumbling over jagged stones in a rush towards the far valley.

His grandfather pointed and spoke. "There is a river, a mountain, and a cloud."

Traejan nodded, knowing the preface to a lesson when he heard it.

"Is the mountain jealous of the river because he cannot flow?" the aged warrior asked his grandson. "Or the river jealous of the mountain because he cannot be still? Or the cloud jealous of both because he never knows the comfort of the land?"

Traejan considered the questions and made the associations quickly. Xander was the river. The source of so many things for so many people. Zephyrn was the cloud. Light and ethereal, floating aimlessly, blown in any direction by any whim of a wind. That left him as the mountain.

"No," he answered. "They need not be jealous for they all have their purpose, except for the mountain. The cloud has a purpose – to bring the rain. The river's purpose is to feed the land and people it touches. What is the purpose of the mountain – what is it supposed to do? It does nothing!"

His grandfather smiled. "You are right. But the mountain

does not need to do anything. It simply needs to be."

"Then what good is it?" Traejan demanded, his tone uncomfortably sullen.

"Well, that depends on who you ask."

Traejan's brown eyes flashed and the gray palfrey beneath him edged forward and back in a nervous manner. His grandfather held back a small laugh only to spare his grandson the possible anger. He could see the dark brows of the young elf drawn fiercely together.

So serious already, he thought. *So serious for one so young.* He stifled his mirth as best he could.

"For the bear," he instructed, "the mountain is shelter. For the tree, a home."

"What about people? What good is a mountain to people?"

Grandfather urged Peg close, right up next to the gray, and laid a hand on Traejan's knee. "The mountain often marks the line on the map that keeps the good people from the evil, and keeps them safe."

Traejan was oddly struck by this remark and, although a bit placated, was not entirely assured. "At least it's something," he finally conceded. Now his grandfather did laugh.

"It *is* something. And for now, my mountain of an elf, just try to be."

Traejan had bowed his head respectfully. His grandfather was everything he hoped he would be someday. A fearless fighter and an elf of great wisdom.

The memory came and went like a flicker of flame in the long fire, reflected in the Roshan's eyes.

"Why do you want to fight?" she asked like she so often did. But this time, he knew the answer.

"So I will have purpose."

The Roshan nodded. "And why did you want to learn from me?"

"So I would be the best."

The Roshan cocked her head, waiting for more.

"So I will never be beaten," Traejan continued, his voice quiet but strong.

The Roshan nodded sagely. "Good. Now, what are you most afraid of?"

Looking stupid in front of you, Traejan thought, but was not about to say. "Failing," he said, instead. It was true enough.

The Roshan frowned. "You have said so before. What makes you think you might fail?"

"Because that is the worst thing I can think of happening."

"Really?" The Roshan seemed genuinely surprised. "I can think of a hundred things worse than failing. But at least I think we are getting somewhere. For right now I want you to understand that failing is a part of learning. The day in the yard, when you failed to keep your feet apart and failed to keep your balance?"

Traejan could feel himself blush. "I remember."

"You haven't done that again, have you?"

"I suppose not."

The Roshan laughed. "You would know if you had. You haven't. And it was only that one time. You did not fail, you learned. There are some men I have trained, some that are great fighters now, who would end up in the dirt more than five times in a day, and on more than one day."

"Ouch."

"Yeah, ouch. Because you can believe that I kicked them harder each time." Traejan grimaced. He could believe that all too well. He had seen her temper. "But that is not here and that is not now," the Roshan continued. "Here and now, you need to have more confidence in yourself, and more than that, you need to know yourself. You need to know why you are here, and why you are doing this. Continuing your training at this point will be useless until you know."

"But," Traejan started. The Roshan held up a hand and he stopped.

"Have you ever heard that you can never truly love another, until you love yourself?" she asked. She did not expect that he had, but he nodded.

"Yes," he said softly, "but I've never believed it." *After all,* he thought, *I would lay down my life for you. I couldn't care less about myself.*

"It is true," she assured him. "The whole gamut. And until you know yourself, you cannot know others. And you have to accept yourself or you can never accept others. You have to accept that your training is just that, training. It is not the final judgment on your life. Take my instruction for what it is, instead of trying to control the outcome. You certainly cannot fight another until you stop fighting yourself."

Traejan felt her words seep into his soul, yet something inside still rebelled, making him felt petulant, like a child.

"And what if I can't do that?" he asked.

The Roshan lowered her chin, her gem-like eyes boring into him. "Then what you perceive as reality all around you is just an illusion."

She watched her words sink into him. It did not look like he was entirely comfortable. He turned his face away, towards the fire.

"And you are wrong about the twos," she told him.

Traejan looked back at his teacher, his brown eyes sharp and focused. "What do you mean?"

The Roshan blinked slowly, thoughtfully, before she answered. "There is not only the black and the white, there is the gray, from which spring all colors. There is day and night, but also the dusk – which is a time for magic, and the dawn, which is a time for miracles. A scale has two sides but it is the center that stays the balance, and only a whole coin has any value. A sword has two sides, but it is the edge that makes it sharp, and without the hilt you would be unable to wield it, and it would be utterly useless."

Traejan stared at her, lost for words. She smiled at him – not a cold or mocking smile that seemed so often her choice - but one that was warm and reassuring. His heart felt like a pat of butter left in the blazing sun.

The Roshan got up from her chair and he rose courteously.

"Good night, Trae," she told him.

"Good night," he said softly.

She smiled at him again, but already the scorn was creeping back to her lips. She picked up both her glass and the bottle and disappeared into her room.

17. THE KNIFE

The very next day it happened for Traejan, like a miracle. Suddenly, when the Roshan called out her countless numbers of strikes and blocks and their crazy combinations, he performed them all without hesitation. There they were - all numbered and ordered and structured in his head. His mind commanded and his body obeyed. It didn't matter the number she called out, the sequence she called it or any way she combined them. He could hardly believe it.

The Roshan encouraged him, pleased with his progress. Traejan tried to control his elation, feeling that he might lose his newfound ability at any time. He also knew that his increased aptitude would mean newer and more difficult lessons. He moved through the drill seamlessly and felt that he was ready to move on. He had no idea how difficult it was about to become.

Less than an hour into his practice, Traejan had gone through most of his numbered drills. The Roshan signaled for him to stop. The spring had waxed full and even the mornings were becoming warm and she had since stopped wearing her cloak. Now, she unbuttoned the black suede jerkin that she always wore and shrugged it off, leaving only the dark shirt underneath. It should not have surprised him. He had long since stopped wearing his own vest. Her charcoal-colored shirt buttoned up the front and came down to her wrists, but the material was thin, and clung to her body. For Traejan it was the equivalent of seeing her in her smallclothes.

Traejan was careful to keep his brown eyes fixed on hers

as she tossed the jerkin onto one of the boulders and moved towards him. His first instincts were to avert his eyes and back away but he held his ground.

"Ready to begin again?" the Roshan asked, her smile as wicked as ever. Traejan forced a nod.

The Roshan moved close and began throwing slow strikes and correcting his blocks by physically moving him. Her hand on his arm or his shoulder or (*my hip, my god she has her hand on my hip*) brought the feel of her skin into sharp relief and he found himself unable to concentrate wholly on what she was saying.

Then he found himself with his face next to hers. He could feel her breath on his neck and see the amber and gold flecks in the brown of her eyes. It was like seeing sunlight through the wing of a hawk. He knew she was talking but all he could hear was his own heartbeat pulsing hard on his eardrums. He felt strong fingers close around his wrist and move it above his head. She said something about a backfist and he must have responded with what she was looking for because she smiled and moved away. He thought she said something encouraging but he had no idea what it was.

You need to get yourself under control, he warned himself.

He pushed all thoughts of her skin and her smell from his mind, concentrated on what she was saying, and let the newly ingrained habitual movements of his training take over.

"I'm going to come at you with an overhead swing," she told him, "then a kick. I want to see maneuver number five."

Traejan nodded. *Number five,* he thought frantically. *It's an overhead block, a low block and then a strike to the side.* The Roshan watched him mentally process everything for a moment.

"I'll go slow to start with," she assured him. She moved her arm in an arc over her head, coming down on top of his own. He brought both his arms up, crossed between his elbows and his wrists, blocking her hand. Then she kicked at him, slowly as promised, and he swept his arm down, knocking her leg away. His other arm he brought around and mimed a strike to her ribcage.

The whole series was slow but smooth, rather than clumsy, and the Roshan was obviously pleased.

"Good!" she said. "Again."

This time she went a little faster and he was not quite fast enough. When he brought down his arm it was on top of her leg instead of blocking her kick. He blew out a sharp breath, frustrated.

"It's okay," she told him. "This is why we practice." She leveled her eyes at him. "Also, I don't want you afraid to go too fast or be afraid of hurting me. Uncertainty is the ruin of all action. Understood?"

Traejan swallowed and nodded. She repeated her movements and this time he blocked and struck as he was supposed to.

And so they went, going a little faster each time, building his speed and confidence with each successive block or blow. When she felt he had it down, she would make him do the same movements from different directions, or with her attacking him from different directions. Just before lunch she began the same with number six.

They broke for lunch and ate cold ham and cheese and bread in their spot under the oak tree. As usual, the horses would join them for some attention. Traejan had finally grown accustomed to Coal - his fire-rimmed eyes, foaming fangs and all.

Without having his morning training to focus on and berate himself with, Traejan found his eyes going over the curves of the Roshan's body under her thin shirt. If he looked away he was filled with thoughts of how it felt for her to be close to him and the smell of her skin. When she got up to refill the bucket from the stream he watched the way her hips moved as she walked. Coal, munching tufts of grass with Peg nearby, whickered. Traejan was sure the beast was laughing at him.

"At least I wouldn't chase a mate that wanted to kill me," the elf told the horse, his voice low.

Coal whickered again and Traejan made a sound that was half of a laugh and half of a sigh. "Yeah," he said. "I know. I should be so lucky."

After lunch he and the Roshan continued practicing all of the maneuvers he had now mastered.

Over the next few days she kept at him, changing the combinations or making him go faster.

Traejan could feel the confidence grow within him. The movements were becoming second nature to him now and he felt like he was really learning, and actually making progress. He only faltered at times when he would become acutely aware of her skin upon his own or the nearness of their bodies.

Or once, when she was trying to teach him how to avoid a blow by turning his body and drawing in, and then turning back and extending in a strike. After a few slow attempts she showed him how it should look at full speed. She spun so quickly that her hair came unbound. Half of it fell from the band that normally kept it tightly wound on the back of her neck.

The Roshan seemed to notice it only as a nuisance and pulled the band out and shook her hair while she kept talking about the move she was demonstrating. Loose, it poured from her head in a wave of red and gold.

Traejan felt his breath catch in his throat and he looked away. It was as bad or worse as the week past when she had stripped down to her shirt for the first time. The sight of that red veil unfurling around her smooth cheek and jaw gave him an almost uncontrollable urge to reach out and touch it.

Not knowing what to say or where to look, he mumbled

something about the heat and stumbled toward the stream. He walked away trying to compose himself, his mind replaying the way the sun streamed through the fine locks of darkest red.

At the stream he splashed water on his face and took a long drink. When he returned, her hair was restored to its usual twist on the back of her head. Her look was curious but hard.

"Are you okay?" she asked. He nodded.

"Just hot. And thirsty."

"We'll start taking more breaks. Believe it or not, summer has come. It's easy to get overheated when it gets warm like this and we are working this hard."

You have no idea, Traejan thought, but nodded instead.

ॐ

"Today," the Roshan announced over her steaming cup of coffee and with no small amount of satisfaction, "you should be pleased to know that we are going to start training with weapons."

Traejan nodded calmly as he sat down with his breakfast, but inside he felt he might explode. His breath came in short, shallow puffs and he could feel his blood pulse in his temples and his hands.

"We will start with the knife," she told him. "You will be able to see a more deadly use for what you have learned, along with the adjustments you will need to make that comes from having something in your hands."

Traejan chewed a strip of cold beef, thoughtful. It wasn't exactly everything he had been waiting for, but he was a step closer. A big step.

After breakfast he followed the Roshan into the practice yard. The air hummed and buzzed with the ripeness of summer. The morning was bright and wildflowers of many colors sat at the edge of the clearing, peeking from behind trees and waving, the only spectators to the day ahead. The horses were uncharacteristically absent, making Traejan oddly nervous.

For some reason he got the idea into his head that Coal had led Peg away somewhere so she would not see what was going to happen to her master.

Stop it! Traejan told himself. *This is what you have been waiting for.*

He followed the Roshan to their customary spot by the boulders and the tall stump of ironwood. The grass there, now growing tall everywhere else in the glade, was bent flat or gone altogether from the constant crush of their boots as they trained.

The Roshan turned to Traejan and handed him a carved piece of wood that only slightly resembled a cutting tool and not a knife at all. It had a thick handle and was roughly eight inches long and two inches wide. The edge of the "blade" side was barely thinner the opposite flat side and ended in a point that was about as sharp as one of his toes. He'd have a better chance at stabbing someone with his finger than the "knife" she had given him.

"Afraid I'm going to cut you?" he joked, trying to hide his disdain. She gave him a look that was half derision and half amusement.

"I'm afraid you are going to cut yourself."

"I'll try to be careful," he said in a mocking tone.

The Roshan grinned. It was his first use of open sarcasm – at least, the first time he had directed it at her.

She started with the different ways to hold the knife.

"This way," she said, holding the hilt with knife straight out in front of her, "is obviously better for stabbing and gives you the advantage of reach." She flipped the ersatz knife around so that it was upside down and backwards with the end of the hilt buried in her fist and the flat edge of the knife lying along her forearm. "This way gives you better concealment of your weapon, and is better for slashing. You can cut with it on an upswing, downswing, or across in any direction. You don't have as much reach but you have more options for an attack and less chance of being disarmed."

The Roshan motioned to him to wield the blade and he experimented holding it the different ways she had showed him. After she felt he had time enough to familiarize himself with the blunted weapon she moved into what he instantly recognized as her attack stance. He dropped back fluidly and went to his guard.

"We are going to start with number three," she instructed. She moved in on him, slowly, and mimed a stab to his chest. He blocked her thrust, but it was awkward and slow as he tried to think of what to do with the knife. Holding a weapon changed the fluidness he had acquired with the simplest defense he knew.

"It feels weird," he confessed.

"Don't think about it. You know all the moves you should make. Try to do what comes naturally. Instead of compensating for having something in your hand, use it. Let it make you better, not worse. It is there to help, not hinder. Adjust. Do the same motion, but instead of blocking with your fist, cut with the knife. Let's try again."

This time, when she moved at him, he slashed at her stabbing arm and then pivoted and thrust the blade behind himself at her ribcage.

"Very good!" The Roshan smiled, evidently impressed. She had never seen anyone catch on so fast. "Number four," she ordered.

He went slow but was less awkward this time. He blocked her overhead swing and came down with the blade across her neck. "Good," she said. "What else could you do?" He thought for a second and then pushed her over double and brought the blade down as if he were driving it through her spine. "Excellent!" she laughed, doubled over.

They spent the rest of the day practicing with the wooden blade. Going over each block, each strike and attack. When he had one down she would make him change hands, or change his grip. Traejan was so engrossed in combining what he already knew with what he was being taught that when the Roshan called a break for lunch he checked the position of the sun in disbelief. The morning had flown by.

The horses appeared from the forest for their midday considerations.

"There you are!" Traejan exclaimed as he gave Coal a vigorous rub on his long neck. "You had me worried."

The giant stallion gave the elf a playful shove with his nose that almost knocked him over. The young prince laughed and turned his attention to his own horse before following the Roshan into the haus to help her.

The afternoon was even better. The moves began to come naturally and he responded quicker and more fluidly to her attacks. For the elfin prince, it was the most enjoyable day he had had so far in his training. It also seemed like the fastest day of training he had ever had. The day was over before he knew it.

The Roshan was clearly pleased with his progress. She ended the day showing him a maneuver that was not numbered.

"Since you've done so well I'm going to show you something different," she told him. "Just for fun." Traejan snorted softly, considering her idea of fun. Then he realized his own idea of fun was probably the same. As long as he didn't embarrass himself. She shoved the wooden training weapon into her belt, leaving her hands empty and free.

"This move is used to counter an attack with a blade," she said. "Come at me with your knife."

Traejan poked the knife in her direction. The Roshan did not move, only looked at him as if she did not know whether to laugh or slap him. Traejan braced himself, hoping she would do neither.

"Is that how you would attack someone?" she asked, her voice icy. He shook his head quickly. "Do it again. And this time, come at me with that knife like you mean it, or you'll be eating it for dinner."

Traejan gritted his teeth and lunged at her as if to stab her dead center. The Roshan stepped deftly aside, grasping his arm and turning it down and back towards his own ribcage. She held him there with her arm locked over his. Her grip was firm and did not hurt, but he could tell that if either of them moved suddenly, his arm would break. He was astonished at how strong and temperate she could be at the same time.

"This is called 'Returning the Gift,'" she told him. He smiled, despite the predicament his arm was in.

"I like it," he breathed. "The move, I mean. And the name."

"Me too. Do you see how this allows me to both put the knife into your ribs and then break your arm?"

"All too well."

She smiled. "Then," she said, releasing his arm and moving up closer to his body, "I can bring my elbow up and break your nose, and then drive it back into your jaw." She mimed the motions slowly, carefully, gently. "See?"

Traejan nodded to show that he did indeed, see. She moved away from him.

"You know," he told her, "for a master of weapons, you seem to do just fine without any."

Indeed, he thought, *she could probably take down more men without a weapon in her hand than five soldiers with swords.*

The Roshan gave a slight nod to acknowledge the compliment and smiled knowingly at him. "To be sure, *you* are the greatest weapon *you* possess. If you can master it. I am no different."

Traejan sat by the fire that night to eat as was their custom. But before he dug into his meal he watched the Roshan move about the kitchen – fixing her plate, pouring her wine. She moved with as much grace and elegance as a lady at high court.

He tried to picture the Roshan at high court in a dress and holding a crystal glass and carrying on a conversation with a lord. He decided immediately that the Roshan would not likely be talking to any lord, unless she had her boot on his neck. And, rather than a dress, all that could conjure to mind was her in her black tunic and breeches. Instead of a crystal glass, he could only picture blood dripping from one of her daggers onto the white marble floor. And his mother fainting in the background. The whole idea made him laugh out loud.

The Roshan sat down in the chair facing him, placing her wine on the low table between them. Gatha had made the Roshan's favorite – rare roasted beef and Traejan's favorite -mashed potatoes covered with meat gravy.

"Why do I feel like that laugh was at my expense?" she asked.

Traejan shook his head. "It was my mother I was thinking about." It was the truth, if not all of it.

"What is she like?"

"Like most mothers I suppose. Overprotective, overbearing. I thought she was the most strong-willed and temperamental woman in the world – until I met you that was."

The Roshan laughed. She took a bite of food and washed it down with wine. "You've turned a corner," she remarked, eyeing him thoughtfully. "You have become less fearful in your fighting, and in your conversation."

"Then return the gift," he suggested. The Roshan's auburn brows went up as she chewed. "Tell me about your own mother," he ventured.

The Roshan shook her head as she took another drink of wine. "I never really knew my mother. She died when I was young. My father used to say I was so stubborn because he nursed me off the milk of a goat." Traejan could not help laughing at that. "I'm pretty sure I was past nursing, and that was just his idea of humor."

"Did he ever speak of your mother?"

"Very rarely. He told me that she was the most beautiful woman he had ever laid eyes upon. He said she undid everything he had worked for or ever believed in and, given the choice, he said he would do it all again."

The Roshan said no more, just chewed her food absently, staring into the fire. The elfin prince gazed at her, astounded to have such an insight into her past. He wanted to know more, but felt he had already pushed his luck.

"You did very well today," she told him after some time.

Traejan beamed. "Thank you. I actually enjoyed it."

"You did?"

"Yes. And this is the first time I've ended my day's lesson without cursing myself to pieces."

The Roshan laughed. "That is a good day indeed. And I think you did well enough that we can move on to another weapon tomorrow."

"Really? Already?"

The Roshan nodded, taking a sip from her wine. "The knife is usually just an opener to get the hang of fighting for the first time with something in your hand. You seemed to adjust quickly. We can always return to the knife later. It is a dependable weapon if used correctly. The best, besides your hands, for close and quiet work."

Work, he thought as he chewed a piece of meat. *And what would that be, the kind of employ that she mentioned so glibly?*

An assassination? Silencing a watchman or dispatching a guard in the night? Of course. What else?

He tensed the muscles in his back and shoulders to suppress the shudder that wanted to crawl up his spine. He looked at the slight frame and crooked smile of the woman seated near him and was almost unable to believe she was a merciless killer. She glanced up at him from under the thatch of red and gold hair that covered her brow. He looked into the warm eyes that he knew could make his blood run cold and did not doubt who or what she was for a second.

"Tomorrow we can take it up a notch if you like," she told him. "We can start with a short sword."

Traejan's chest swelled with breath. He felt for the first time since he had mastered his drills that he was really making progress. If the short sword was next, then the broadsword should be after. He hoped the short sword would be as easy as the knife.

It wasn't.

18. SETBACK

Traejan stood bent over in his bathroom, his forehead pressed against the cool porcelain of his sink. He had showered and washed away the dirt and sweat of the day but not the shame. In all his life he had never felt so discouraged. *It's just a setback,* he told himself. *Just a small setback. I should not have expected to do as well as I did yesterday with the knife. Yesterday I was just lucky. Or the knife is just easy. It certainly isn't a sword.*

That morning, Traejan had risen from bed as he had done since his training began. He washed his face and dressed as he had all spring and left his room for the kitchen. The Roshan stood at the counter sipping coffee from a steaming mug. Gatha bustled around the kitchen, taking stock of everything in the cupboard and not seeming to notice the presence of any other being in the room. It seemed like any other day at the Roshan Simorgh's Bed, Breakfast, and School for Warriors.

"Good morning, Trae," the Roshan had said with her usual sardonic charm.

"Good morning," he returned courteously. His elfin eyes spied a short sword, sheathed with the belt wrapped around it, leaning against the wall.

"Today is the day," the Roshan said, watching him with amusement. Traejan only nodded and fixed a small plate of cheese and fruit and tried not to look at the sword that was waiting for him. He ate little, just enough to give him the strength he knew he would need. After what seemed like an eternal breakfast he looked at the Roshan with the question only in his eyes. She nodded.

"Buckle it on. I'll meet you in the yard." She turned to speak to Gatha and he picked up the sword and left the haus, unrolling the belt as he went.

Traejan buckled the sword belt around his waist and looked around, knowing that today would be a day he would never forget. The morning air was warm and the earth breathed out life from every pore of her being. The consequences of spring and her marriage to summer burst from the earth and the air. The sky was a clear, cloudless blue and green covered the earth. Birds swooped through the air, darting out of the woods and then back in. Insects buzzed and flowers of every color shot up wherever they found space to root. The stream gurgled and danced among the rocks and turned the waterwheel with untiring motion. The façade of the haus against the wooded hill looked like something from a fairy tale.

The young prince pulled the sword from its scabbard and could not restrain his smile. It was a hideous weapon of untempered iron, heavy and blunt, obviously for training purposes only. It had all the care and craftsmanship of yesterday's knife. Traejan looked at it with the pride of a father looking upon his newborn son. He almost laughed at the foolishness of his emotion.

The elf shook his hair away from his face and lifted it to sun, letting the sword hang from his hand. His ears easily picked out the sound of the Roshan's approach, but it was not until she was almost upon him that his senses flared out and he spun, bringing up his sword defensively as her own cut through the air above his head.

The clash of the weapons jarred his bones and rattled his teeth as metal hit metal with a grating clang. He turned her sword as it cut towards his ribs and then again from the other side.

"Good!" the Roshan exclaimed, her sword still locked against his own. "I thought maybe you had fallen asleep standing up."

"Not sleeping," he replied, not letting his sword waver in the slightest, "just waiting."

The Roshan laughed and backed off. Traejan noted that her sword, too, was unforged iron. A practice sword, like his own. *It would have to be,* he thought. *Any good sword would be ruined after only a few strokes to this iron beast.*

"Before we begin I am going to tell you something now that will both blow your mind and yet seem like the most logical thing in the world."

The elf did not know what she meant by "blow your mind," but it didn't sound like fun. "Alright."

"Every block is a strike and every strike is a block."

Traejan stared at her as he turned this last nugget over in his mind. He nodded. "It is both astonishing and simple," he agreed.

"Good. Let's see if we can put it into practice." "I will try," he said.

She shook her head. "You will do. You will just do slowly, at first."

He wanted to repeat his last statement, it was so instinctive, but he nodded instead. "I will," he affirmed, bringing a small smile to the Roshan's small mouth.

"On your guard."

The words floated towards him, like a portentous warning carried on the morning breeze.

The elfin prince brought up his short sword and assumed a fighting stance, but not before the Roshan was already moving, coming at him.

Traejan stood up and looked in the mirror. He could hear the Roshan moving about in the kitchen. He knew he should join her even though he wasn't hungry. He knew she wanted to talk to him, hopefully not yell at him, and he knew he should not keep her waiting. He heaved a sigh and left his room.

The Roshan was leaving the kitchen with the bottle of wine she had opened the night before. She pulled out the half-stoppered cork with her teeth and spat it onto the counter. Traejan cringed inwardly and then straightened as he saw she had two glasses in her hand, curious. His brown eyes gave the room a quick sweep but there was no one else there.

The Roshan set the glasses on the table in front of the fire and filled them nearly to the top with the red. She set down the bottle and dropped heavily into her chair.

Traejan watched as Gatha pulled a plate from the cupboard and covered it with food and handed it to him over the counter. He gave her what smile he could muster and took it to his place by the fire.

The Roshan's eyes flicked up at him and he sank obediently into the chair across from her.

"What happened out there today?" she asked.

"I don't know," he answered honestly. She picked up her glass and motioned for him to take the other. He picked it up and took an experimental sip. It had a warm, earthy taste and he could feel it make its way towards his stomach. He did not exactly care for it but neither was it terrible. He risked a glance at his teacher who sat watching him with a double line between her eyebrows.

Not a frown, though, he thought. *She's not angry. Just trying to figure something out. Trying to figure me out.*

"You hit a wall," the Roshan told him.

Traejan was not sure what the actual translation of that was, but he got the general idea. The sword, though short, had thrown him entirely off-balance. He had flailed and he had failed, hacking about as if he had no training to speak of and had never learned a thing from his teacher.

The Roshan had been uncharacteristically patient while he was the one who grew more and more frustrated, almost to the point of fury. His first problem was that the sword felt clumsy, and trying to control it made *him* clumsy. All of the hits and all the blocks and all of the combinations he had worked he so hard to master and that were just coming together for him were lost amidst his aggravation. He had so little control that the Roshan called a halt far earlier than was normal. Traejan had almost thrown his sword in anger. He could not believe the magnitude of his own inability. It stung him just to think about it.

The Roshan seemed to be his exact opposite, almost jovial as she chewed a bite of corned beef. She washed it down with a mouthful of wine.

"Why are you so upset?" she asked.

Traejan gaped at her. "I was horrible out there today."

Now it was the Roshan's turn to look surprised. "Did you think it would be easy? That you would master the sword in one day?"

Traejan frowned, pushing a piece of potato around the edge of his plate with a biscuit. "I guess not," he said.

The Roshan took a sip of wine. "You guess not now," she said. "But you did before, didn't you?"

"Well, I didn't think I would master it," Traejan admitted. "But my fighting was just coming together, and I felt like I did well with the knife on my first day. I didn't think I would be so awful with the sword, especially a short one."

"You were not awful," the Roshan told him, "just awkward. No worse than your first week here. At least now you know how to move. Practice will help."

Traejan looked at her doubtfully and dug into his meal. The Roshan took a sip of wine and shrugged.

"You did look very natural with the knife," she told him in an effort to placate him, something she had never done. "Everyone has a weapon of choice. Maybe the knife will be yours."

Traejan finished chewing with a frown. "The knife is not an honorable weapon," he told her, his voice low. "It is the weapon of assassins." Once the words had left his mouth he was horrified. He looked at the Roshan, hoping the firelight concealed the blush that covered his face and ears. "I am so sorry," he said quickly.

The Roshan looked at him with her tongue in her cheek. "No offense taken," she assured him.

Traejan took a long drink of wine, wishing that it could make him feel more at ease. It didn't, but he felt that since he had plunged into the pond, he might as well swim. He took another long drink and spoke without looking up. "You have done that?" he asked. "Taken hire as an assassin?"

The Roshan grinned. "Many times." Traejan looked up at her and her grin widened. "I don't always have princes to train."

The elf, still blushing something fierce, took another long drink from his glass.

The Roshan redirected the subject to distract him. "Can you guess what my weapon of choice is?"

Traejan considered his answer. The sword would be his first guess but he held his tongue. The sword would be anyone's first guess. He thought of her height, stature, reach, and strength. He lifted his chin. "A staff," he told her.

She glanced up sharply, her brows raised. She did not expect him to guess right. Her smile started at the right corner of her mouth, pressing a soft cheek towards a glittering eye. It was not a smile of approval, but one of mocking derision.

"You are correct," she acquiesced with a slight dip of her head. "It gives me an equality with most of those I face. It might not always be the most lethal, but then I am not always out to be the Maidservant of Death." Her smile never waivered. It seemed to mock his very being. "Sometimes speed is the key to your fight, and with the staff you can fight more foes and bring them down just as quick. Whether they ever rise to see another day depends on your time, and if you care. Most assassins do not. Care, that is."

Traejan hid himself in his meal. His teacher finished her glass of wine and called something to Gatha in Gnomin. Gatha brought a new bottle from the kitchen and put it down on the low table with a flashing glare and an indignant grunt. The Roshan laughed.

"I don't drink that much," she informed the Gnomin.

The elfin prince finished chewing before he spoke. He thought she drank quite a bit, but did not know what too much might be and felt he had already outspoken his bounds for one evening.

The Roshan grasped the bottle of wine in one hand and a sharpened dirk in the other. Traejan watched as she twisted the dagger around the bottle's neck, breaking the wax seal. Then she edged the blade under the wax and flipped it off and into the air, catching it expertly with the same hand.

"You seem to enjoy the red wine," Traejan said in a tone he hoped was nonchalant. The Roshan looked at him with amusement, the light of the fire dancing on her hair and in her eyes.

"I do."

"Only reds?" he asked as he watched her twist an iron worm down to the cork and then ease it up before it gave a resounding pop.

It was a good sound and, in the Roshan's opinion, better than the wine deserved. All of her winter red was gone, and she was down to her Blackberry wine. She wasn't quite ready to start drinking the summer golds, though it was plenty warm enough, and also even though she knew that the Blackberry red would be sweeter than any of the golds she had in her larder.

"Mostly reds," she agreed, "although I do change it around from time to time. But I usually come back to the reds."

She filled her glass with the black-red liquid and took an experimental sip, grimacing at the sweetness. It didn't matter; she knew that after a glass or two she wouldn't notice. "And you, Trae?" she asked, her voice mocking. "What do you enjoy?"

"Honeyed red," he answered without hesitation. In truth, a few months ago he could take it or leave it. Now, there was a honey swirled red he would die to put his lips upon.

"I can't imagine enjoying a good meal without a good red wine," she confessed, "and it makes a meal out of what I am eating now. I like golden wine on occasion, but not usually until the fall. And it is harder to come by than the reds. The red is both plentiful, if you don't mind blackberry or plum when the grapes run short, and to my liking."

"After a few glasses, it changes you," he ventured cautiously. She smiled openly at him, curious.

"How does it change me?"

"I don't know exactly. You act the same on the outside - I think it just changes you inside. I can feel it."

"You can feel it?" she asked, intrigued. "A change in me?" Traejan nodded. "Can you tell *what* I'm feeling?"

He shook his head. "How does it make you feel?" he ventured. Her eyes grew somewhat distant as she thought about it. Then she looked at him as if discovering something for the first time.

"It makes me feel safe," she said quietly, almost surprised. "And vulnerable. At the same time. Two things I don't normally feel." She was thoughtful for a moment then looked up suddenly. "How does it make you feel?"

Traejan smiled. "Elves don't feel anything from wine, unless it is mixed with honey. Honeyed wine is a favorite amongst the nobility." It took everything he had not to look at her hair when he said it. Even though it was bound behind her head it was alive. It was color and movement restrained, like the deepest sunset, stretched and then coiled – ready to spring.

"And what do the common elves drink?

"Honeyed ale, or watered mead. Sometimes..." he trailed off. The Roshan's brows rose over eyes that sparkled with interest.

"Or sometimes what?"

"Sometimes absinthe," he said, almost embarrassed. "But not often and not much. It is more like a drug, it is so strong, and it is always watered down heavily." The Roshan's smile was wolfish and knowing.

"Have you tried it?"

"Once," he admitted, "with a group of Jägers." Traejan smiled but was unable to look at her. "They watered it down even more for me, and yet after even half a glass, I had to be carried home."

The Roshan laughed. "That's amazing! But nothing else has any effect on you? Not spirits or liquors, or wine or ale without honey?"

Traejan shook his head.

"Do you ever drink it, just for the taste?" she asked.

"Occasionally."

"I love it for both. It helps me relax."

"Why do you need to relax? Do you worry?"

She frowned. "Not about anything in particular. I think it is just in my blood to be on edge."

"The sword never sleeps," Traejan said, smiling.

She returned his smile and nodded. "I suppose that is it. Yet you seem more emboldened this evening. Is there anything else you wish to ask while you have the excuse of the wine?"

Seven Circles, where do I start? Traejan thought as the million questions he always carried about her blazed through his mind. But something else occurred to him.

"At our first meeting, you told me you knew my reason for

coming, perhaps better than I did."

The Roshan nodded slowly. "I remember."

"What did you mean by that? Why do you think I came?"

The Roshan answered as if she thought it was the most obvious thing in the world. "You want to live up to your name," she said.

Traejan sat back in his chair and, after a moment, picked up his glass. He rolled it between his palms as he had seen the Roshan do many times, warming it with his hands. He took a sip and stared into the fire.

How does she know me so well? he thought. *It is as if she can see into my heart yet, if she did she would see...*

The prince looked over and saw himself reflected in her eyes.

The Roshan was indeed looking at his face, noticing the contradiction of his features. His hard jaw was softened by his hesitant smile. His straight brow and sharp eyes diffused by his gentle gaze.

The young elf was aware of her sudden scrutiny and looked away hurriedly.

He ate everything on his plate and had another helping while the Roshan drank another glass of wine. Gatha seemed as pleased with his appetite as she was displeased with the Roshan's consumption of alcohol. She was still sipping on a glass when Traejan finally excused himself and went to his room for the night.

The Roshan stayed by the dying fire, watching as it gave way to her own namesake, then slowly sank into ash.

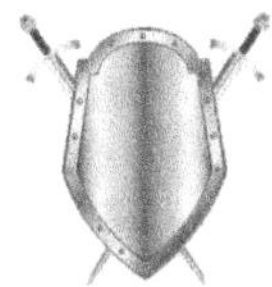

19. MASSACRE AT THE BARN

Dell surveyed the massacre from just inside the door of the barn. His heart felt like a lead weight in his chest and his stomach roiled. The place had been torn apart and the bodies of the farmer and his family had been decimated beyond recognition. It was not even possible to tell if they were human, though Dell had no doubt that they were.

The human villages he had passed through in the Northlon with his Jägers had been full of tales of monsters and demons, though some of the wiser ones knew them for what they were. Most of the attacks had been on the outlying farms of the vista delta, but even some of the villages had been attacked as well. Better armed and with more defenders, the villages were mostly able to rebuff the raiding parties that came through – the farms were not so lucky.

Some farmers had moved their families to the safety of town and left their fields even though they were close to harvest. Others pulled in an early harvest, working doggedly to set by young corn, apples, squashes and gourds, before common sense told them to take what they could and get away while they still had a chance. The elves had come across many farms with full barns and full larders, empty of people. The stubborn ones stayed where they were and farmed. And died.

The party of elfin Jägers had come upon the farm, still pushing north, and had thought it deserted like most of the others. A closer yet cautious inspection had brought them to the barn.

Dell watched his men for a moment, knowing this was probably the first time Alastair and Jaden had seen murder. Nevin had seen his share, old as he was, but it would not have been anything like this. Even Dell had never seen the like.

And this, this was not just murder, it was carnage.

The elves were obviously shaken, but holding together. Dell knew that the butchery itself was hard enough to stomach, but the flies made it worse. They buzzed everywhere and gathered in masses on the bloodied faces and wounds of the dead. Miraculously, none of his men had sicked up their lunch, and for that he felt a spark of pride for each one of them.

His dark eyes passed over the quiet farm outside and then back into the barn. The once dusty ground was now mud from the slaughter. What was once clean straw and sweet smelling hay that had been scattered on the floor of the barn was now soaked with blood that was starting to dry into a tacky glue. It had been a massacre.

The farmer, now no more than crushed pulp in overalls, and another, judging by his size and what was left of his sex to have been the oldest son, had managed to bring down one of their attackers. The monster lay in the bloodied barn with the murdered family, where they must have made their feeble stand. It had lost an arm to a scythe and had a hayfork plunged into its huge throat. It lay sprawled on its back, eyes locked into a stare that showed more confusion than surprise or pain.

What manner of creatures leave their dead? Dell thought. He thought he knew, but was not entirely sure. His eyes fell on the farmer and son, their bodies mangled and torn. The rest of the family lay tangled in a gory heap, as if they had been rag dolls that were beaten bloody and cast aside. He could see two of them had crushed skulls.

Dell looked away, sickened. Crommags. Only Crommags would do this. The wiser folks in the towns had agreed. Dell frowned at the creature with the hayfork in its neck. He had seen Crommags before, but they had looked much different.

That was over a hundred years ago, he told himself. *We had just gotten to the New World and I was on the foray that took us north as far as we dared.*

He thought back to that time when he had seen a Crommag and compared the image in his mind to the thing that lay on the blood soaked floor of the barn. Its body was huge, tall and covered with thick fat and heavy muscle. It had a neck like a boar and a square jaw that jutted out much too far. Dell could see lice popping around the patch of filthy hair that topped its large head. Beady eyes were set close to a great humped nose that rose over lips that were thick and pouty, the bottom one much larger than the top. The stench from the thing was awful.

Its massive chest had a pelt of hair that continued in a wide river of fur down into its roughspun trousers. Its belly rose in a huge curve, caked with grime and dried sweat. Arms like tree trunks ended in gnarled hands that were tipped with long yellow nails gorged with muck. Its feet were bare, covered with thick, hard yellow callous.

Dell looked it over, frowning. It was not as hair-covered as he recalled Crommags to be. And it was wearing clothes. Trousers and a vest too small and crudely made, but clothes nonetheless. He had only seen Crommags draped in skins and hides before. The brow was large, but not near as large as the great sloping forehead he remembered.

Dell hunkered down next to it and the young Jägers did the same, watching him. He waved away the flies that were gathered on its face and neck and they rose in an angry black cloud, some buzzing off for a quieter place, others simply settling back down to resume their meal. The thing was hideous, and smelled like the Seventh Circle, but different than what he remembered. He reached out a gloved hand and pushed up the creature's thick lip.

Its teeth were huge and yellowed and decayed, and some had rotted away. They all ended in sharp points. They were like the fangs of an animal, but flat in the front and back, rather than rounded. The top and bottom rows fit together like the teeth of metal gears when the mouth was closed.

"Crommag," Dell announced quietly. The Jägers exchanged glances. There was nothing to be unsure of any longer. Dell let go of the lip but it stayed where it was over the upper row of pointed teeth, giving the Crommag a frozen snarl. The elf stood up, absently wiping his gloved hand on his hip.

A hundred years, he mused. *Can the creatures change so much in so short a time?* he wondered. He thought it possible but not likely.

Elves change, he thought. But he knew it was mostly due to marrying other types of elves. The Arcadian Elves and Seleucian Elves were changing via their offspring – it came from a mixing of blood, it had nothing to do with time, Dell was fairly certain of that. But when elves lived for so long, it was hard to be sure.

Dell eyed the Crommag in disgust. Could time make such a difference in humans? He had no idea. Could Crommags be mixing with humans? Dell thought that idea appalling but possible. They could be carrying off women from their raids and enslaving them, breeding with them. The idea galled him and he was glad to dismiss it. If women were being carried off in any significant number, there would be war. They would have heard if anything like that was happening – all the way down to the Southlon. And besides, the women here had been left behind. Murdered, but not raped, Dell hoped, and not carried off.

Don't count the years, he thought suddenly, *count generations. One hundred years is nothing to an elf, but a generation marks a significant amount of time.*

Crommags lived to roundabouts twenty-five years he had been told by a Vikeman once. If that were true, that would mean the Crommags had gone through four generations since he had last seen one.

Would that make a difference? Would that make them

change?

Dell tried to imagine four generations of elves, but it would encompass such a large span of time that he had trouble getting his head around it. Instead, he tried to think ahead with what he knew of the elves now.

In the past few years, just the past few, some elves from the Old World that had moved south of the city had married Sylvan Elves. Certainly, in the generations to come, the elfin population would begin to look different.

But would they act differently, think differently, than the elves that he knew? Dell did not think so.

He considered what else could be driving the Crommags from the mountains. The most logical answer was food. He knew that their mainstay was yak meat and some rope-like roots that grew under the frozen ground. A Norseman once told Dell that the Crommags that lived near rivers would bust through the ice in the winter and snare steelhead trout and salmon.

Maybe their animals were wiped out from plague, Dell thought. *Or a shortage of fish or cattails is driving them with hunger. That would explain why they are raiding farms.*

A quick glimpse at the barn banished that theory. Plenty of food had been laid by – potatoes and pumpkins, yams and turnips, barrels of wheat and dried beans. Nothing had been touched, nothing had been taken. Four pigs grunted and squealed in a pen outside the barn and a number of chickens clucked and squawked in a coop next to the house. Even the animals had stockpiles of food in their pens. Dell cast his mind back to the other farms they had seen. All were the same.

Humans dead or gone. Provisions still there for the taking.

They weren't after the food.

Why then? Dell wondered, looking at the barn, the butchery, the blood and the flies. *Why do they do this?*

He looked at the fat lip caught in a snarl and the

interlocking teeth beneath them, filled with disgust.

"They're brutes," he said, answering himself out loud. "No matter how they look now, they are still animals." His charges looked at him and then glanced at each other. "Find some wood and pitch," he told them. "We cannot leave the bodies for the scavengers."

They moved off quietly to do as he bid, anxious to be done with the place. Nevin stopped short, bringing up an arm to halt the young Jäger on his right. Alastair looked at him in surprise before his eyes darted about, suspecting danger, but the older elf's eyes were on the ground.

"Sir Dellion!" Nevin called.

Dell was at his shoulder in an instant, peering around his form to see what had caused the elf to halt in his tracks. The Jäger had been too preoccupied with the display of brutality to notice it before, but now that it was pointed out, he could not miss it.

The signs of a struggle were clear. The way the hay and dirt had been kicked around left no doubt. But there was no body, human or Crommag. Only Crommag tracks leading out of the barn.

Dell swallowed the bile in his throat. He did not think he could feel more nauseous after what he had just seen, but he did now. He looked at Nevin and the old elf spoke as if reading his thoughts.

"They took a prisoner."

Dell nodded. "A man. Probably one of the farmer's sons, possibly a ranch hand."

There was a heavy pause as the elves considered this. Finally, Jaden spoke.

"Is this enough, Sir Dellion?" he asked. "Have we answered enough questions? Found what we are after?"

Dell shook his head.

"We still go north."

A grim dread settled over the party, but they nodded as one and moved again, eager to be done with the nasty task before them.

20. A WALK IN THE WOODS

Traejan rose and dressed, washed his face and left his room as he had done all spring. He tried to push away all thoughts of the day before and begin anew. It was a new season, after all. Summer had descended and laid warm hands upon the land. He looked to where the Roshan sat, drinking her coffee, and felt his heart skip a beat. That was nothing new. But when he saw what she was wearing his heart skipped again.

Her attire was the same as always for a day of training; loose but slim dark pants tucked into black boots, a belted full sleeve tunic with her usual arsenal strapped about her - but today, over her right shoulder he could see the hilt of her broadsword.

She wears it over her right shoulder so she can draw it with her right hand, he thought. *She is right-handed.*

He had wondered before if she was right or left-handed but could never tell as she seemed to use both with a natural ease when it came to holding anything from wineglasses to weapons.

"I am almost afraid to ask what you have planned for today." Traejan said as he joined her at the counter where Gatha placed a plate of food before him. The Roshan's look was sly and mocking. He had seen it too many times before. It made him squirm inwardly and he hated it, yet he could not help but smile back at her. "Feeding me to a dragon by the looks of it."

"There are no dragons," she informed him. "Not in this world, at least."

Traejan gave her a false grimace. "Then it must be worse."

The Roshan laughed. "You are developing quite the humor," she remarked as Gatha poured a glass of juice for the elf.

"Thank you, Gatha," he said, taking the glass and starting in on his breakfast.

"I thought we'd just take a walk today," the Roshan informed over her mug.

"A walk?"

"A walk. You are so focused on what you cannot do, what skills that are not inherit, that I thought we would spend a day on what you *can* do."

Traejan swallowed, understanding. "This is about my confidence," he said, sounding miles from confident. "You think my lack of it is what is holding me back."

The Roshan nodded. "It is. So today, you get to be *my* teacher."

Traejan almost laughed, but felt that he was already in a precarious situation.

The Roshan drained her mug and pushed it across the counter towards Gatha, who scooped it away. "Take your time, I will wait outside."

Traejan waited until she had reached the mudroom before he wolfed down what he could of his breakfast before pushing his plate towards Gatha who took it away, giving him a crooked smile. Traejan had little time to wonder what it meant since the Roshan called out to him, a dark silhouette in the doorway to the glen.

"Leave the sword," she instructed. "Bring your bow."

Traejan's heart thumped inside his chest as he returned to his room to retrieve the bow he had brought with him months ago. He slung it over his shoulder, along with his quiver. He left the haus expecting to find the Roshan waiting on the semicircle of boulders where they trained, but she was right there, outside the door.

"Close your eyes," she ordered. Traejan did as she bid. "What do you hear?"

"The stream," he said immediately. "Gatha washing dishes. Squirrels and birds."

"Can you tell what kind of birds?" the Roshan interrupted.

"A pair of thrushes," Traejan answered, his eyes still closed. Three or four jays. A single nightingale."

"Can you tell what the nightingale is singing?"

Traejan opened his brown eyes and looked at her quizzically. "Three short notes. I can't tell you which ones, I don't really know music."

The Roshan kept her gaze on him steady for a second, and then nodded. She had not much knowledge of music either, but she knew what the nightingale sang as if it were in plain Anglicus. *Time is short! Time is short!* the bird called. It sounded like a warning and the Roshan did not like it. She had never known the nightingale to be wrong.

"Anything else?" she asked.

Traejan cocked his head, listening.

"The horses."

"Can you tell where they are?" The question was offhanded. She did not expect him to actually know, but the prince nodded.

"Upstream, about half a mile. They are drinking from a pool where the stream curves and drops."

The Roshan stared at the elf. She knew the spot quite well, but did not think he had been up and into the hills to see it. "Have you been up there? Seen where the stream pools and then drops?"

The prince shook his head.

"Then how do you know?"

Traejan shrugged. "The quality of the water. It makes different sounds when it turns, drops, or gathers in a pool."

The Roshan stared at him for a moment and then began

walking across the glen, towards the stream, motioning for him to follow. The sun shone in his mass of hair, which was now thicker and longer, and quite golden in color.

"Your hair is getting lighter," she remarked as they walked. "From being outside so much in the sun I presume."

Yours is too, Traejan thought, seeing the shine of red from the corner of his eye. *When we met it was as dark as blood, and now it is like an autumn leaf.* He ran a hand through his locks, wishing he could touch hers.

"Long, too," he said. "I might have to cut it myself if we never visit a village this summer."

The Roshan smiled. "That's a good idea," she agreed, "visiting a village, that is. We should take a trip to Goldensword. See if they have any more winter red."

They reached the stream and the Roshan went right, walking downstream, away from the mountains and into the woods.

She motioned towards a path with one hand. "Take this path towards the river. I will walk alongside you, just a little to the south."

"We are really just going for a walk?" he asked.

She nodded, her eyes glittering.

"Just a walk." She turned and sauntered twenty feet away and then started into the woods.

Traejan turned and began walking through the woods. He watched the Roshan from the corner of his eye. She walked easily, though soundlessly. She glanced at him occasionally, but not often. Her crooked smile seemed to mock his very presence within her woods. His skin tingled and his nerves felt as if they were being stretched. He hated how she could make him feel like this. His senses called out ambush, but he could hardly believe she would attack him. He refused to look at her, but kept close watch with the side of his vision.

They walked along, with green leaves above and brown

ones underfoot. The trees here were many but had slim trunks, making her disappear and reappear constantly by obscuring his view of her for less than a second as they walked along.

Traejan quickly fell into an easy rhythm, seeing her come in and out of his sidelong vision. If felt good to be in the woods again. The smell of oak and occasional pine mingled with the now familiar scent of the Roshan. The leather of her clothes, the heavy steel she carried with ease, the wildrose that must have come from her bath. The more he was aware of her the more he seemed to see. He tried to look away but only saw more. The glint of the sun on her hair, the movement of her hip.

Seven Circles! he thought. *How her hips can still swing under the weight of her steel! She must...*

The elfin prince froze in his tracks. She was gone.

He turned to the last place he had seen her step between the trees but even the air there was still. It was if she had never been. The thought scared him. He closed his eyes and reassured himself of her presence. He could feel her smile more than anything. Sure and derisive. He gritted his teeth, fighting the heat that climbed his face.

She is not mocking you, he told himself. *She's testing you.*

He took a deep breath.

Cautiously, he walked to the place he had seen her last. Her smell was stronger here. She could not be far. He could even smell her skin. He pushed the thought from his mind and stretched out his other senses. He was very nearly convinced that she could not do magic, and the trees were too slender to hide behind, even for her. A quick glance at the ground showed no holes, the only place left was up. He looked up into the branches but they were empty save for the breeze.

Traejan could feel the tension, worse – the embarrassment – welling up inside.

Stop looking with your eyes, he told himself

He closed his lids and took a deep breath. Keeping his eyes shut, he walked ten paces forward into the woods and turned to his left, going back towards the stream. He took four more steps before he opened his eyes to see a gnarled oak tree right in front of his nose. His gaze went up the trunk to the lowest branch where the Roshan sat, a languid smile upon her lips.

"I have heard of 'elf eyes' but had never seen it for myself. How did you know where I was?"

"Once I relaxed, and I was able to see without seeing, I just knew."

"That doesn't make any sense. How can you see without seeing?"

Traejan looked away, searching for a way to explain. "I've seen you walk through the dark in your haus," he told her, "without bumping into walls, without seeing anything. You reach for the door to your room and do not miss the knob by even a hair." The elf laughed softly. "Seventh Circle! I've seen you pour yourself a glass of wine in darkness without missing the glass or spilling a drop. How do you explain that?"

The Roshan grinned at him from her perch. "It's different. It is my home. I know it intimately, in the light or dark. I have my memories, years of experience, and repetition to guide me. I know what is there, and where it is."

Traejan nodded, encouraging her line of thought. "It is the same with elves. We just don't need the experience, or the repetition. It is as if the memories are already there. It is called seeing without seeing. If we know what it is, we can see where it is. Or we can guess really well."

The Roshan laughed but bowed her head in acknowledgement, accepting his explanation. Traejan felt himself light up inside at her laughter. He wished he could make it happen at will. She jumped down from the branch and although she landed well on her feet he instinctively reached out to soften her fall. In a second he found himself within inches of her face with his hands on her hips.

"The more I learn about you the more amazed I am at how different we are and yet still how the same," she told him earnestly. She did not seem to be bothered by his proximity and her smile was genuine. But she did not linger in his touch. "Does that make any sense?" she asked as she moved away and headed towards the stream.

Traejan nodded dumbly, unable to speak. All he could think of was the way her body had felt under his hands. Her waist was so slim and his thumbs had wrapped around her hips as if they belonged there.

"Are you coming?"

Traejan's head snapped up, his gaze swinging around to find the Roshan crossing the stream over a series of stones. She was waiting, looking over her shoulder at him.

"Of course," he said, hurrying to keep up.

Farther downstream the waterway was joined by another and, now combined, they increased in speed and sound as they plunged ahead towards the river.

The woods opened up onto a shallow valley with more woodland on the other side. The elf followed the Roshan along the woodline, staying in the shade. The day was already warm. The Roshan stopped under a giant pine. From there, the trees across the valley were less than fifty yards away.

An easy shot, Traejan thought. *If that is what she intends.*

The Roshan motioned for him to hand over his quiver and he did so, watching as she went down to one knee and drew out a handful of arrows. She laid them down one at a time on the forest floor. "How do you aim?" she asked casually.

She knew that most humans aimed with their hands, looking down the arm that held the bow, sighting along the knuckle of their thumb. She had heard that elves aimed only with their eyes, but she suspected they merely sighted down the length of the arrow, the way humans did with the length of their arm. She laid the rest of the arrows neatly on the ground while he answered.

"I don't," he told her.

She looked up, surprised. "Pardon me?"

"I don't aim."

Her eyes narrowed and he had to force himself to stay still under the intensity of her gaze. The corner of her mouth drew up slightly. "How do you hit anything if you don't aim at it?" He shifted slightly, not sure what to say. She seemed to enjoy his unease and waited quietly, watching him.

"I don't know how to explain."

"Try."

Traejan remembered the first time he ever shot an arrow. He remembered trying to explain it then, too. He had been sitting in the shade along a woodline, much like where he was now, watching an Elfin Maester give six young elves their first formal archery lesson. Straw mats on sticks, painted with likeness of deer, were set up as targets in the low meadow and the young elves were being shown the proper way to hold a bow, as well as notch, draw, and release.

Archery was second nature to elves, and teaching was usually no more than space, practice, and a bit of advice from the Archery Maester. Teaching archery to elves was akin to merely giving a toddler the encouragement to take his first steps. But first steps are faltering ones and although the elfin boys shot easily enough, only a few of them hit their target. One arrow went terribly awry and went zinging by the Maester. Traejan, only twenty-five years old - old enough to sit a horse by himself but still too young to take up a bow, clapped a hand over his mouth as he snickered. The boys' sharp ears caught his laugh and they turned, more annoyed than angry.

Seeing the young prince watching at the edge of the woods they bowed respectfully. Traejan dipped his own head in acknowledgement.

"Do you think you could do better?"

Traejan had jumped, turning to the sound of the voice. It was his grandfather. "Grandda, you are as quiet as a Jäger!" he exclaimed. His grandfather, with white robes and white hair flowing behind his tall and slender form, merely smiled and repeated his question.

"Of course!" Traejan answered with the surety and quickness of the very young. His grandfather chuckled softly and motioned to the Archery Maester. The Maester bowed and herded his class off to see the Fletcher.

"Show me," he told Traejan.

They walked down to the low meadow where the other boys had been. Traejan eyed a bow with suspicion and longing. He looked at his grandfather.

"Is it alright?" he asked. Bows were weapons, and forbidden to those as young as himself. His father would skin him for even picking up an arrow. Xander did not have his first lesson until he was fifty summers.

"Only when you are with me."

Traejan didn't need to be told twice. He retrieved the closest bow, pulled an arrow from the bucket next to him and notched it to the bowstring and pulled it back to his cheek. He let it go and it flew to its mark, the target closest to him. The arrow quivered, stuck into antler of the deer that had been drawn there.

First timers luck, some would say, but his grandfather did not think so.

"Show me more," he urged.

Traejan did it again, this time hitting the next target. Dead center this time. He did it again, this time putting the arrow into the target farthest from them. Dead center again. He looked at his grandfather who smiled at him with pride.

"Very good," he told him. "How did you learn? Was it by watching the other boys?"

Traejan shook his head. "No. They were doing it wrong."

"What were they doing wrong?" he asked, curious. He watched his grandson furrow his brow, thinking deeply, and smiled. *So serious for one so young.*

"They were using their eyes instead of their heads." This time it was the older elf whose brow furrowed. "How do you know that?" he asked.

The young elf shrugged. "I just do."

The Roshan watched her student patiently, while he searched for the right answer. She could tell he was lost in a memory and was curious as to what it might be.

"I don't use my eyes," he said finally.

"Go on," she told him. He started to speak but then stopped, a faint flush creeping up his cheeks. "It's okay," she said, reassuring him. "Tell me." He took a deep breath.

"When I release the arrow I don't feel that is me using the arrow, but the arrow that is using me. That I am the means to *its* end, not the other way around." He waited for her to laugh but she didn't.

The Roshan sat back on her heels and looked at him. He felt her looking *into* him. His eyes and his heart. The corners of her mouth drew back slightly in wry amusement, but Traejan thought he saw approval there. There and in her eyes. He was sure he saw it in her eyes. A warmth spread through him and then she *did* smile.

She swept up the arrows with her hand, returned them to the quiver and stood in one fluid motion. Traejan watched her, nonplussed. She returned the quiver to his possession and began walking back the way they had come.

"What are you doing?" he asked. "Aren't we…"

She shook her head before he could finish and turned back to him. Her smile was gone but her derisive look of amusement was back.

"You have taught me enough for one day," she told him.

"Unless you need to impress me with a skill you already have." Traejan blushed. She gave a small sigh that was half a chuckle. "Go ahead and take a shot or two. I feel like you might burst if you don't." Traejan's flushed deepened.

"Is it that obvious?"

"It is." She jerked her head towards the trees on the far side of the narrow valley. "But you're fetching the arrows back."

Traejan unslung his bow and pulled two arrows from the quiver on his back, his gaze traveling over the mouth of the forest. Now, under her scrutiny, he was suddenly nervous. Especially as he thought of how humiliating it would be to miss.

Before he could lose his nerve, and almost faster than the Roshan could follow, he shot each arrow in quick succession. The first went into the high grass, the second went directly between two young pines.

His teacher was regarding him coolly with auburn eyebrows raised high.

Traejan gave her a sheepish smile. "Gatha left the haus on her donkey when we crossed the stream," he informed her. "Rabbit is the only thing I know how to cook."

The Roshan laughed. "Then fetch your quarry along with your quarrels." She cocked her head at the elf. "Are the horses far?"

The prince shook his head. "Not far. They followed us east but have stayed by the water."

The Roshan whistled and motioned for the elf to retrieve his game. By the time he was trotting back, his arrows cleaned and returned to their quiver and holding two fat cottontails by their hind feet, the horses had found them.

"Can you ride without a saddle?" the Roshan asked.

"Of course." He grabbed Peg's mane at the roots with his free hand and swung himself gracefully up and onto her back. He watched the Roshan, who could hardly reach the mane of the great stallion – much less where she could get a handhold.

There was no need.

The Roshan clucked her tongue and the beast lowered itself to one knee so that his mistress could climb easily onto his back. Then he stood and gave his head a good shake. The Roshan clucked her tongue again and he turned his long, narrow face towards the woods and began leading the way back home. Peg fell into step right next to him.

"There is nothing I can teach you with a bow," the Roshan told the young prince and he swelled with pride for the first time since meeting her. "I can't even tell you to practice. The only thing I can tell you is to experiment. Try shooting two arrows at the same time, or even three. Shoot running, riding, and falling. Shoot in the dark. Know that there are more targets than your enemy's heart. The vulnerable parts of the head – the eyes, the ears, the mouth, and of course the neck – will bring him down just as quick and are usually the least armored. Know that an arrow can be more than an arrow. It can be a knife, a dagger, a torch."

Traejan nodded, listening to her every word as butterflies swirled about where the sunshine streamed through the trees. A bird called in the distance. The Roshan was silent for a while, thoughtful. After the horses had crossed the stream, their hooves splashing through the shallows, she spoke again.

"I know that you want very badly to master the sword, but do not discount the skills you already possess. Not just your skill with the bow, but your aptitude as a woodsman as well." She gave him a sidelong glance from her gem-like eyes. "The way your senses are honed - I've never seen the like."

"Well," Traejan said, diffident under her gaze and her praise, "if I wanted to be a Master of Hearing, I could have stayed home."

The Roshan laughed. "Then tomorrow we will return to the sword. I just wanted you to get some perspective today. Some skills are learned, some are inherent. Do not minimize either one."

"I won't," he promised.

"I won't," he promised.

21. DANGEROUS ENGAGEMENTS

The summer air in the Gnomin Vale was redolent with the smell of grass and wildflowers. Butterflies flew low and lazy in the growing heat. Even the bees had slowed their normally manic buzz and high-speed brio across the meadows and instead were content with an indolent drone as they traveled from blossom to hive, engorged with nectar.

Raspberries and blackberries grew fat on the thorny bushes and vines that climbed the base of the mountains. Streams jumping with fish rushed through forests filled with game. Each breeze through the orchard brought with it the scent of ripe peaches and delicate apple blossoms.

Summer in the vale was idyllic – beautiful, peaceful, plentiful.

The Gnomin cared for none of these things.

For them, summer meant safety.

Safety meant a celebration - of work. Stubby hands were rubbed together in eager anticipation and greedy grins were not to be contained. It never bothered the race of Makers and Miners to live underground, but a season of planning was meant for a season of *doing.*

When summer came, the enormous Ice Floe melted and flooded, keeping the dreaded Crommags penned in their icy lands. It took the Gnomin a great many years to learn this, and a great many more to learn why. Once they had, life was good. Not just because they were safe, but because they could plan for it.

Spring could be dicey. If the weather was slow to warm the monsters could still cross the frozen river, but the Gnomin learned to post a watch on the most northern mountain that could send warning. That way, they could venture out –watchful and wary – to sow the seeds that would see them through another year. Besides, the Crommags themselves finally learned that a late crossing meant the ice could go at any time, trapping them on the wrong side of the river. They were as hated by the men and elves as they were the Gnomin, and stranded parties were usually hunted down by human Northlonders and never returned to the Ice Crags.

So the Gnomin, like most races, planted in the spring and harvested in the fall. During the winter they would stay beneath the Mountains of Blood, warm and safe and plot and plan.

But the summer was their favorite.

During the summer, Gnomin farmers were able to get outside and start constructing the new machines they had been devising and drawing while kept indoors all winter. Harvesters, pickers, balers, thrashers – some on wheels and some on spindly legs – all robotic contraptions of wood and brass. The vale would be thick with steam and smoke while small bodies wearing leather gloves and brass-rimmed goggles could be seen running here and there and everywhere from late spring till the middle of autumn.

More, summer meant that it was safe for mining teams to travel to other mountains in the chain. Even far from the safety of the Coil, Gnomin could set up camps in the warm valley and delve into new territory under the high range of soil and rock to discover the treasures buried there. If they were in luck, it was coal.

Coal. More useful than diamonds, more precious than rubies. Steam powered the Gnomin culture and coal powered steam.

Late that spring, Mining Team Number Twenty-Eight struck

the Gnomin equivalent of gold.

It happened on their first dig into the LonLine Mountain. The LonLine itself was actually an imaginary line that separated the Midlon from the Northlon. The LonLine Mountain, however, was quite real and discernible from the others in the Mountains of Blood because it was both the largest and the highest - located dead center in the volcanic chain. The Gnomin had explored farther north, all the way to the end of their mountains –they were nothing if not methodical - but so far and over all the ages they had been in the New World they had only mined as far as the center, and thus far only on one side. For the LonLine Mountain, it was time and turn.

Team Twenty-Eight was having a banner summer. On their very first explorative excavation of the LonLine they found a bed of *Braunkohle*, the brown lignite used for fuel and generating electric power. The enthusiasm of discovery only added to their efforts and soon they had broken into a vein of coal that was dark and dense and marked by bands that were alternately dull and bright. Even in the dim light of the mine, every blue eye shone with excitement. It was undoubtedly bituminous coal - the best source of energy for powering steam engines.

Before the dust had settled, the twenty-eight miners of Team Twenty-Eight met in the bright sunshine of late spring outside of the freshly dug cave. The tips of stubby fingers tapped each other in excitement, as if every Gnomin held an invisible ball between their hands.

What to do first? What was the plan?

Should they send for more donkeys? More miners? More equipment?

Each miner stood apart, each bringing the pads of his fingers together rapidly again and again, looking eagerly from one to the next as suggestions were made.

Finally, as a group, they prepared a plan.

The team would continue the excavation as originally designed. The original foursome that was set to transport the WeekLode to the Coil with the team's four donkeys would continue as planned. Depending on how much coal was exhumed in the next few days would determine if they should bring back more miners, more equipment and more donkeys.

It was a plan.

It was executed.

It was more than they could have imagined.

Team Twenty-Eight had found the largest lode of *Braunkole* that had ever been discovered. It was a small seam that became a bed the more they dug. And the vein of bituminous coal was only the tip. It widened and widened the further down they tunneled, a ripple of rich black within the earth.

Reinforcements were sent.

Miners, donkeys, equipment, and the resource staff to aid them all trundled eagerly to the LonLine. Tents for eating were erected in the Vale that had the atmosphere of a party. They were filled with long wooden tables and benches and a stage at one end for entertainment.

The miners spent their days as usual, digging, excavating and hauling. But in the evenings they went to the great tents that had spent the day roasting chickens and tapping kegs of beer just for them. Tuba bands honked and hooted. Steins clanked together to cheer their continuing accomplishment.

Midsummer came and passed. The weather in this part of the New World was unrivaled. Days were long - clear and sunny and warm. There was never too much heat, either above ground or below. When the sun finally set it was a stunning spectacle of bleeding red and plum and indigo over mountains of slate and volcanic ash that had sprouted a million wondrous trees of pine.

It was during one of these late and spectacular summer sunsets that two members of Team Twenty-Eight left one of the tents, the outer knuckles of their stubby pinky-fingers (hers on the right and his on the left) accidentally yet quite often brushing against one another.

"Gerta?"

The Gnomin woman cocked her head. She saw that her normally levelheaded teammate seemed a bit nervous, fidgety even. She stopped and faced him, worried.

"Yes, Gunta?" she asked.

Gunta, who could wire or cross-wire any explosive, architect a mine and backfill with front-lode or a booby trap, tapped the fingertips of one hand against the tips of the other and shuffled his feet. He had made a plan of what to say and what to do, but executing the plan was suddenly more fearsome than a thumb detonator.

He kneeled before Gerta, lost for words, and held out a small object that looked like the egg of a nightingale, made of polished brass with the numbers two and eight carved into the oblong sides. The oval top was hinged and Gerta lifted it gingerly to reveal the clock underneath.

The number signified, of course, their team and the way they had met and the way they had started. The egg was universal as the symbol of a beginning. The clock, carefully crafted was a pledge of time. For the Gnomin, the device in its entirety was a proposal. A plan. A plan for love and life and future.

Gerta held the brass egg against her heart. "Thank you, Gunta!" she exclaimed. "And, yes!"

Gunta rose and grasped her stubby hands within his own, pulling her close and planting a kiss upon her lips. When they broke apart Gerta practically squealed with delight and wrapped her arms around Gunta.

"What is your plan?" she asked, releasing him just enough to that she could see his wizened face, grinning from ear to ear.

"My plan," he told her, "is first to tell everyone. Then we can plan for the wedding. I would like for it to be here, on the day of Harvest Moon."

"That is a good plan!" Gerta agreed.

The day of Harvest Moon was the day before all mining parties throughout the vale packed up to leave their work for another season. Celebration tents were raised, kegs of beer and cider were tapped, and the sound of polka music filled the whole valley for nearly a week.

The northernmost mining team would spend a night in revelry, congratulating each other and sketching plans to meet during the winter, to plan some more. The next day they would travel south to the next mining team, where they could see the exploits of the other party's excavation and the night's festivities and merry-making would be double. The next day the teams would travel south together, the number of miners growing exponentially until they reached the Coil.

The welcome home party would be the most grand. Most every Gnomin over the age of twelve would be drunk. Some in celebration but most in sorrow that the working and building and discovering was through until summer came again. They would console one another that every invention began with a thought – something that often came in the quiet and the dark. Then, with arms around shoulders and swaying drunkenly, the Gnomin would stumble into the Coil and seal their entrance to the mountain until the winter had come and gone once again.

"Our Union Celebration will last a whole week!" Gerta exclaimed, clapping her hands. "And we won't have to pay for a hall, or the beer, or the food!"

Gunta smiled. He loved that she was as practical as she was beautiful. He watched the sun set through her golden curls, making it a halo of crimson.

"Can I wear my bridal wreath all week?" she asked.

"All week," he assured her.

Gerta grasped his hand. "Let's tell..." *everyone* she was

about to say, but everyone was suddenly coming at them in a flood. Some through the tent opening and some through the tent itself.

"Komm zurück!" came the cry.

"Komm zurück!" came the echo of many voices joined as one.

Gunta quickly pulled Gerta to the side, wrapping his arms around her protectively as his blue eyes looked hurriedly about and then scanned the lavender sky over the great tent of striped blue and white canvas.

"Fire," he murmured, seeing the twisting tail of smoke that rose from the back of the tent. "A flap or cord must have been blown too close to the chicken roaster. Odd though, it should have had a grill guard."

Gnomin came pouring out of the tent, but it was by no means a panic. As a people they were quite used to danger and their reactions and responses had been drilled into their psyche since they were very young. Already, four DCC's (those of Team Twenty Eight who were dedicated to Disaster Control and Containment) were detaching the parts of burning canvas even as they hosed it down.

Donkirk, the team leader of Mining Team Twenty-Eight held up his hands. "Not to worry," he assured. "I believe we only lost the back section. We can return to the..." his voice trailed off as his eyes followed a shadow, mounds of shadows actually, as they broke away from the line of sleeper tents to materialize as huge shapes that became more clear as they neared. "Komm zurück!" Donkirk shouted at the top of his lungs. "Crommags! "Komm zurück!"

The Gnomin scattered and this time it *was* panic.

Gunta grabbed Gerta's hand and ran with the others as they instinctively headed south. Many made it quite far, sprinting like the devil was after them. But most were still close enough to hear the commanding shout that went up behind them.

"Komm zurück!" a voice called, loud and clear and by no means Gnomin. Half of the fleeing troop stopped in their tracks and turned slowly, blue eyes wide.

The dozen invaders, despite that it was full summer, were indeed Crommags. One, however, was smaller than the others. Next to him, was a human man.

This was altogether new.

Humans and Crommags never traveled together. Never.

Forty workers, mostly miners but a number of support staff that had joined the excavation, had stopped mid-flight. They cocked their heads, falling prey to the greatest killer of the Gnomin people.

Curiosity.

It was the man that had yelled. He had scratches on his face and looked underfed, but then all humans looked underfed to the Gnomin. The small Crommag motioned to him and he shouted at them in the Gnomin tongue.

"You must come with us," he commanded with drawn brows. Then he added, softly but also in the Gnomin tongue, "I am sorry."

Dozens of blue eyes peered at him and Gunta squeezed Gerta's hand, ready again to flee. He turned slowly, only to find another line of Crommags at their backs.

They were trapped.

22. STORM AND SWORD

"You are literally fighting *with* that sword," the Roshan told him in exasperation. "By that I mean you are fighting against it!"

Traejan armed the sweat from his brow. The days were long and hot, the Roshan's temper short. The heat that day was oppressive and the humidity, usually never an issue, soared.

Their resident nightingale called from across the glen and the auburn-haired warrior whirled on it, furious.

"I know, I know!" she shouted. When she turned her face back to Traejan her eye caught on something over his shoulder. He swiveled around, following her gaze up and up. A triagle of white was peeking over the forested mountaintop. The Roshan regarded the puff of cloud for a moment then returned her attention to the task at hand.

"Let's go," she commanded.

The Roshan went on with the drills, but did not seem completely focused, even a little lost, perhaps. Her eye seemed constantly drawn to the cloud that was swelling over the mountain. By lunchtime it had become a cloud upon a cloud. White explosions over the peaks of the western horizon whose bottoms were dark gray edged with black were sneaking around the mountainsides. After lunch the Roshan's commands came quick and clipped as she glanced time and again at the now inevitable storm. What was more, she was hardly paying attention to him, not correcting him. She finally called a halt.

"That's enough for today," she told him, throwing a hurried

glance over his shoulder as she made for the haus.

The elf watched, amazed as she quickened her pace and practically darted through the door.

She couldn't possibly be afraid of the rain or the thunder, could she? Traejan wondered, doubtfully.

The young prince discarded the notion. Her furtive glances at the approaching clouds held excitement, not fear. Besides, he had a feeling there was nothing that she would not face head on.

"Gatha will see to dinner," she told him as he joined her inside. He could tell her mind was already far away as she motioned absently towards the kitchen on her way to her room. Gatha had already prepared an early dinner, as if she had somehow known the Roshan would call it an early day.

The Gnomin woman stood with her arms crossed over her chest as the weapons master passed. She looked more disgruntled than ever, angry even, with her graying brows knitted together over blue-gray eyes that bored into the Roshan's back and a wooden spoon clasped in a tight chubby fist.

Traejan got the feeling that Gatha knew about the upcoming storm and what it might portend. He washed up quickly in his bathroom and came back into the living area as the Roshan went by his door, pulling on a cloak and fastening it at the side of her throat. His sharp eyes caught a glimpse of the brace of daggers she often wore, as well as the short curved swords.

"Be ready in the morning," she told him. It was the only thing she said before she stopped in the mudroom to gather her long sword, adding it to her personal arsenal. Gatha stamped a booted foot and shook her wooden spoon at the Roshan as she slung the heavy blade over a slim shoulder and buckled the strap. Then she gave the small woman a grin and disappeared through the door.

Outside, they heard her whistle for Coal.

"What was that all about?" Traejan asked Gatha. Gatha only stamped and shook her spoon at him in response, more in exasperation than in anger. Then she pointed a finger at the prince, as if to accuse him that he had some part in this.

"What did I do?" he asked, surprised. Gatha only gave a series of annoyed huffs and then she stomped into the kitchen to fix him a plate of food. He was left to wonder about what was going on. He tried asking Gatha but only received responses similar to the ones she had already given him.

He ate his dinner slowly, listening to the storm build and then break outside. Thunder crashed and then a sound came like that of an approaching tidal wave. The mudroom gave a slight tremor as rain poured down in a wet roar. Traejan finished his meal and then stalled for as long as he could – washing his plate, having a glass of water in the kitchen, a piece of cheese. He even poured himself a measure of red wine and sipped it by the long fireplace that had not seen a fire in a month. It was too damn hot, even at night.

Finally, boredom got the better of his curiosity and he gave up and went to bed.

At some time in the early hours of the morning the elfin prince awoke to sounds in the hall. He sat up straight in bed, his head cocked, pointed ears listening. He could hear soft, angry stamps that could only be Gatha, and an exhausted chuckle that could only come from the Roshan.

"I know, I know," the Roshan whispered hoarsely. It was followed by more soft stamps and rustles and then an almost silent drunken cackle. Traejan's ears followed the sound down the hall. He could picture Gatha roughly undressing the Roshan and admonishing her with her silent fury. He stayed that way, motionless, for a long while before laying back down.

What in the Seventh Circle?

He tried to hear more but they were beyond the heavy oak of her door. He finally closed his eyes and went to sleep.

Despite the nocturnal disturbances, Traejan was up early the next morning and fixing a cold breakfast in eager anticipation of finding out what had happened. He finished eating and cleaning up and there was still no sound from anywhere else in the haus. He had decided to make some coffee when the door to the Roshan's room opened and she came out.

She was dressed in ash and black as always but looked even darker for some reason. Traejan thought that it might be the bluish half-moons under her eyes that had a bruise-like quality.

She moved slowly, obviously sore from whatever the night before had given her. She was even limping. Traejan watched with his almond-shaped eyes wide as she sat stiffly on a stool at the counter. She saw what he was doing and heaved a great sigh. Her eyes were thick, heavy slits in the top of her face.

"Thank the First Circle," she groaned.

He boiled the water, wondering if she had been drunk, or in a battle, or both. Her body was rigid and her entire demeanor was torpid. She seemed to have no desire to speak or stir, the only will to live held together by the promise of the coffee that now boiled on the stove.

As Traejan turned for the pot he bumped her waiting mug on the counter with his sleeve, sending it tumbling. Before he could even jerk in response her hand shot out (her body following automatically) and grabbed the mug while it was still a few inches off the floor. She pulled herself upright with a groan and put it back on the counter, her eyes barely open.

Traejan tried to keep his hands as steady as hers while he poured the black liquid into her cup. A small sigh escaped her lips and her auburn brows went up the slightest bit. Traejan knew what they asked.

Any milk?

He nodded quickly and pulled the glass bottle from the icebox and handed it to her. As she poured some into the mug he found the sugar bowl and spooned out a brownish lump and plopped it into her mug as well. She managed a slip of a smile in gratitude and sighed again.

The elf watched her and the mug as if he were some young Gnomin conducting his first science experiment. The Roshan stirred her coffee and than drank it all down at once like a sailor quaffing a mug of ale. She put her cup on the counter and heaved another sigh, this one more contented.

"Let's go," she said. She stood up and walked towards the door. Traejan followed wordlessly, stopping with her in the mudroom as she gathered up two things that were not there the day before – a pair of heavy broadswords. She handed one to the elf and opened the door, squinting at the glare.

Within the hour she was her same old self again, cursing at Traejan in every language he knew and a few where he had learned only a few words – none of them polite.

"Spin tighter!" the Roshan shouted. "Get your elbow down, this isn't a tea party!" Traejan spun, bringing his sword up to block her next blow.

"Back!" she commanded. He spun the other way, striking at her. She parried his blow effortlessly.

"Faster!" she shouted. He did it again, quicker this time.

"Keep your elbows down!"

He pulled his elbows down closer to his body but it made him feel constrained, cutting his reach practically in half. It felt unnatural to pull them in, and she moved so quickly, always just out of his reach.

The Roshan cursed at him and though he did not know all of the words, he knew it was Gnomin.

"Elbows!" she shouted at him in Anglicus, and then again in elfin on his next strike, as if he would understand it better. He made the correction every time, yet they seemed to rise out a little farther on their own with each turn. Each time, the Roshan lost a little more patience.

"Gods be damned and yourself as well!" she hollered at last, her sword dropping to hang by her side as she ranted at him. "I'll not waste my time training you so you can have both your arms cut off by the first drunkard that raises a sword against you!" The elfin prince took the rebuke in silence. His teacher fumed for a few seconds before regaining her poise. "On your guard."

Traejan brought up his sword, his elbows pointing down. He didn't feel balanced, but he did it anyway. The Roshan came at him instantly. He parried each blow she threw, but still she kept coming.

It was not a combination of strikes and blocks. It wasn't a drill. It was a fight.

The realization made him pour sweat more than the exertion of wielding the sword. She hammered at him for thirty seconds, and then a minute had passed. She did not stop and she did not slow. After two minutes his strength flagged. The spar didn't seem to faze her in the slightest. Instinctively, he began to reach out more with each strike, pulling his arms back less each time, putting a greater distance between them and giving himself the advantage of the reach.

The Roshan backed away and advanced again without delay. Traejan swung his sword and she turned it easily. Then she fell two swift strokes, one to each arm.

The young prince backpedaled, his sleeves severed at the elbows, hanging off his arms in tatters. She stood back from him.

"Next time it won't be your sleeves," she warned. His face burned from his neck to the tips of his ears. She brought up her sword as if she meant to attack again, and then lowered it, changing her mind.

"Get some lunch," she instructed before she turned and headed for the haus.

Traejan went inside and washed his face and changed his

shirt. The broadsword was much heavier than the short sword and his hands were already aching. He flexed them to keep them from stiffening.

He ate a piece of dried beef, alone at the kitchen counter and washed it down with cold ale. Twenty minutes later the Roshan emerged from her room. She paused in front of Traejan, as if she were going to say something, then shook her head and continued towards the front door, motioning for him to follow.

The afternoon was wordless. There was no instruction save for an occasional word and Traejan heeded each one well. He could feel his hands swelling with the effort of the heavier weapon and blisters rose in the crease where his palm met his fingers. Before long the blisters on his hands burst and ran. Like his teacher, he never stopped and never slowed.

When the Roshan was satisfied with their day of work they returned to the haus and both went to their rooms to clean up. Traejan went straight to his bath chamber and ran cold water over his hands until his wounds were clean. He showered and left his room to find the Roshan already in the kitchen putting out their dinner. By the time they were done eating, the pads of flesh at the base of his fingers were seeping clear fluid. He winced as he picked up his dish and carried it to the kitchen. The Roshan's eyes were like arrows.

"What is it?" she asked.

"Nothing, a little sore is all."

"Let me see your hands," she said putting down her bread. He walked over and showed her his hands. She reached out and grabbed a wrist, turning his hand so she could see his palm. "Oh, Traejan," she admonished. "Sit down." She put her wine glass aside and went quickly to her room.

The young prince sat down in a chair next to the empty fireplace, watching her go. It was the first time she had really said his name since they met. She returned with a small bowl that had a lid screwed on, a roll of cloth strips, and a small towel.

"Stay there," she told him as he started to rise. He sat back down and she knelt in front of him. She put the cloth strips on the low table, the towel across her knees, and took the lid off the bowl. It was nearly full of a thick, yellow salve. She gently took one of his hands in her own and dipped her fingers in the ointment. She dabbed it on every open cut and the pain vanished. Traejan hardly noticed.

All he could see was *her*. Kneeling before him, holding his hand. The light from the kitchen created a flaming halo around her head and turned her hair into a live thing. The red and gold in her hair took the place of the flames in the empty fireplace. Her touch was as gentle as a lover's caress. His breath quickened and it took a conscious effort to slow it and compose himself.

"You should have told me," she said softly. He smiled.

"I did not want to stop the lesson."

"You should have told me anyway," she rebuked, now smiling as well.

"Told you what?" he asked. "That after almost two seasons of fighting I still have soft hands?"

The Roshan snorted. "Do not mistake vulnerability for weakness or any weakness for vulnerability," she told him. "Your greatest weakness can be your most powerful weapon. Take me, for instance. My greatest weakness was once my size. Although I am not small for a woman, I have rarely fought a man, or any other creature for that matter, that was my size. Now I know how to use my build for speed and agility. I do not have need to fall flat on the ground to avoid the swing of most swords. A shift in weight and a simple lean in the right direction will take me out of the reach of most any man and afford me the opportunity to take him out before he can recover. At the very least I can usually take out his legs."

Traejan laughed softly, shaking his blonde curls. "And what strength can a man find in having soft hands?"

"Soft hands have a better touch, and a better grip. Swords tend to slip more in a calloused hand. It takes a soft hand to turn a sword, wield a knife, and notch an arrow. Which you do quite well." He beamed quietly at her praise, noticing for the first time how soft her hands were as well. "Your hands were not used to such abuse, from now on we will wrap them until they are. Once they are healed, that is."

She finished with the salve and unwound a cloth strip from the roll and began wrapping it around his hand. When it was done she lifted his other hand and began to repeat the process. Traejan thought it was the sweetest thing he had ever known. He watched the light of the sconces dance off her hair. Her face was both intent and caring. She glanced up at him as she was finishing his left hand and saw the softness in his eyes. She smiled at his expression.

"What is it?"

"I don't know," he said, smiling. "You can be so hard, and yet so tender." She snorted and tucked the end of the strip under the rest of the bandage.

"I'm about as tender as an old boot," she said looking back up at him. Her eyes widened suddenly and she sat back, hard. She dropped his hand and pushed herself back with her feet, away from him in a single fluid motion.

"What is it?" he asked.

"Your eyes," she whispered.

"My eyes?"

"They're blue," she told him.

Traejan blinked in surprise then quickly looked away. "It is an elfish thing," he told her.

"To change from brown to blue?"

"Sometimes."

Could it be? he wondered. And then, *does she know?*

The young prince tried to smile as if it were nothing and glanced at her cautiously, only for a second before looking away. The Roshan eyed him warily for a long moment and then replaced the lid on the bowl and stood up.

"Well, it's been quite the day," she said at last. "I think I'll turn in." He risked another glance at her but she was already up and moving away, her wine glass in one hand and the salve bowl in the other. She stopped in the kitchen to refill her glass and looked back at him. "I don't know if it is my knowledge of elves I have misjudged, or my perception of you. Hmm. Either way, I'm going to bed. I'm tired. How about you?"

"I'm exhausted," he admitted. "I'll turn in – in a minute. I'm going to finish my ale." She nodded and walked to her room. She turned and looked back up the hallway when she reached the door as if to tell him something, then shook her head and went in, closing the door behind her. He sat in the armchair and stared at the clean and cold fireplace thinking about his brother, Zephyrn.

"Your eyes will never bend the blue," his younger brother had said once, teasing, his own eyes blue and bright.

"I hope not!" Traejan laughed, ruffling his brother's hair. "Not if it makes me as wild as you!" Zeph had laughed.

There were a few in his family that thought it curious that Traejanale's eyes had never bent blue. Traejan had never really cared. He knew everyone was different, and his own peculiarities did not interest him. The blue was a gift from the Seleucian Elves. All Seleucian

Elves had blue eyes, and when they joined with the brown-eyed Arcadian Elves of the Wood, or Woodland Elves as they called themselves back then, the eyes of most elfin offspring were brown. Most of the time. In times of passion, however, - be it rage, fear, or (most often) love - their eyes would turn blue.

Bending the blue they called it.

The young prince took a swallow of ale and thought of how his brother Xander's eyes had bent blue on the day he met the lovely elf maid that would one day be his wife. Even still, they would bend blue every time she was near him. And his brother Zephyrn. So vibrant and full of life. Always intense, always full of passion, always in trouble. His eyes had been blue when he was born and .had been the same ever since.

Traejan - so calm, so composed, so even keel – had never bent the blue. Until now. It was her. She had done it to him. He had suspected that he had fallen in love with her the first time he saw her. Now he knew for sure.

Once the dam breaks, the floods will come with every rain.

It was something his grandfather had said. Like so many other things, the young elf did not understand what he meant by it at the time. He understood now. He also feared that this would not be the only thing that the Roshan would break inside of him.

23. FRIGHTENING FLOWERS

Alastair was the son a florist. It was where he had acquired his extensive knowledge of flora. His father owned a flower shop that had been *his* father's before him. One, or more, of his father's children would take over the shop one day. Both of Alastair's sisters had already offered to do so, and gladly. Alastair supposed that he was the apple that fell far from the tree.

It wasn't that he did not love the shop. On the contrary - it was often his favorite place to be. He loved that no matter how hot and dusty it might be outside, the shop was always cool and clean and crisp, with moisture that clung to his skin like morning dew. It was full of smells comforting and exotic and all of which were always fresh. He would sometimes go into the shop after playing with friends when he was younger or after a hard ride when he was older. His skin would drink in the air and he would feel reborn.

The shop carried a variety of plants and flowers year-round. From simple pine boughs to freshen a house, to rare ocean lilies from Atlantea that had to be frozen after they were picked to keep them whole. While Alastair never planned to take over the shop, he did learn much about flowers and plants over many decades.

That was why while out riding north of the Siber Massif that summer with his fellow Jägers, he was the first to notice the hydrangeas. His aunt Lily was his father's sister and was named after *their* father's favorite flower. His father was named Dougilas, after the dogwood tree. Alastair was lucky enough to escape being named for a flower or a tree, unlike his sisters Rosealea and Hyacinth. He did, however, pick up the nickname of "Thorn" quickly enough from his Aunt Lily. Like a true thorn, it stuck – at least within his family.

Aunt Lily was plump, especially for an elf, and always seemed to find her towheaded nephew under foot. "You'll be a thorn in my foot till I'm old and gray!" she would chide Alastair, not unkindly, before chasing him out of the shop with a daisy cracker. Oddly enough to the young elf, his aunt did not like lilies. *Her* favorite flower was the hydrangea, and she grew them for the shop.

Alastair always thought they were interesting flowers -ten to fifty small blooms packed together on a single head at the end of a long stem. His aunt Lily thought they were more than just interesting, she was wild about them, and grew all types. She had hydrangeas that flowered on vines, trees, and bushes - and in all colors. She would bring in cut blooms of different varietals every week. Blue-bud, Lace Cap, Ladies Pink, you name it, she grew every kind of hydrangea that there was.

"The trick in the colors," she told him one day, "is the soil. An alkaline soil will give you pink flowers, while an acidic soil will give you blue. But if you can get a perfectly neutral soil... ahhh," she said, producing a bouquet of Ladies Lace with a flourish like a wizard with his hat and wand, "you get a perfect cream color."

Alastair noticed the hydrangea bushes as they rode into the steppes at the foot of the hills that rose into the Trough. They were great green beasts, both woody and leafy, looming in groups at the base of the hills. They were covered with huge clusters of blooms.

Aunt Lil would be amazed at the size of these flowers, he thought, *but not the color. She would not like the color.* Come to think of it, he didn't like the color himself. No delicate shades here - the flowers on these bushes were purple. Not royal or lavender, but a dark, sick purple, like the color of a bruise.

A bruise is just blood pooled under the skin, his father told him once. The thought did not make him feel any better.

The air this far north was perfect. Even though it was summer, it was far from hot. They had crossed the Siber Massif through Tannlinn's Pass weeks ago. There was still snow on the mountaintops and come winter the entire Massif would be packed with snow, making even Tannlinn's Pass impassable.

They had left the horrors of the farmlands behind. Alastair and the other Jägers had burned more bodies than the young elf ever thought he would see. For a score of days now they had been riding through cool, sunny grasslands. They took turns scouting but stayed close, though there was no need. It was as if they had the entire Northlon to themselves.

Yet the farther they rode the more uneasy he began to feel. The day was bright and warm and there was no danger within sight or sound but those sickly purple buds were beginning to give Alastair a horrible feeling.

There is something wrong with those flowers, he thought.

As they rode along, the giant clusters seemed to nod at him as if agreeing with his thoughts. His horse could feel his nerves grow taught and gave a snort and danced sideways for a few steps. In any other riding party it would have gone unnoticed, but this was not just any party of riders. Dell's head snapped around immediately and he peered at the younger elf with raised brows. Alastair frowned and shook his head.

What was he supposed to do? Tell his commander that he was afraid of the flowers?

Jaden saved him the embarrassment.

"Those flowers give are giving me the creeps," the Sylvan announced quietly. Everyone in their small party had been quiet over the last few days.

"Do you smell it?" Nevin asked, looking at Dell, who nodded. He had been smelling it for a mile or more.

"Yes. And it's not coming from the flowers."

Alastair nodded in agreement. Hydrangeas, even ones as ugly as these, did not give off a rank odor. The great blooms nodded their agreement.

The land began to rise gently and the hideous bushes became more frequent, and closer together. Within a few minutes they were riding the horses between them, and they came upon the first body.

It was a Crommag. The size of the huge and rotting form left no doubt, but other than that it had decayed beyond recognition.

Dell, knowing they were utterly alone, stayed on his horse as his dark eyes flicked about. There was no sign of a struggle, not even an old one. The others looked at him but their question was mirrored on his own face.

What in the Seventh Circle?

He put his heels to his mount and urged him on, motioning with two fingers towards the east, telling his riders to fan out. A few minutes took them to the next body, not quite in the stage of decomposition as the first, but it was close. After that they found another, and another.

Carrion birds flapped on the ground between the bushes now, too gorged to take wing. Flies and maggots were also feasting here.

The corpses were obviously getting fresher and fresher and Jaden, who was already spooked but would die before he said so, was waiting to come upon one that was just *playing* dead.

The number of Crommag carcasses increased (Alastair had counted ten) and with them the stench and the scavengers. The bruise-colored hydrangeas nodding at them in their eternal and putrefying sleep.

A plague? Dell wondered as he searched for an answer, *some sort of sickness? Then what in the Seventh Circle are they all doing out here?*

Nevin gave a low, whistling call and Dell urged his horse

closer. Nevin pointed at a corpse not a week dead by Dell's guess, with a dagger between his ribs. On this one the cause of death was plain, but a quick glance around showed no splashes of blood on the leaves of the bushes or even the ground by the body.

"He was dumped here," Dell stated, matter of fact. His quick brown eyes swept the fields of Hydrangeas, littered with death and decay, and were filled with realization. "They all were."

Alastair drew a breath to ask a question and gagged on it. He turned his head to the side and coughed violently.

You will not be sick, he told himself fervently. *You will not!*

He cleared his throat and looked back at Dell. "But why?" he asked. When he did not answer, Alastair looked at Nevin who shrugged.

"They don't bury their dead," he said with open disgust. "They must still know, however, that a corpse will bring disease. Or even they cannot stomach the smell. So they drag them out here, and leave them."

"We're nearing their camp," Dell said, his eyes on the horizon that disappeared over a ridge as his horse danced nervously under him.

"They are getting lazier each time," Jaden noted aloud, looking at the bodies, awash with horror. "Not dragging them as far."

Dell looked at him and nodded. "Can you hear them yet?"

Jaden's eyes searched the small hills just to the north, as if he were looking through them. "Yes. We have these hills and a ridge between them and us - but I can hear them. It must be a very large camp."

Sir Dellion put his knees to his horse, urging him up the hill, and the others followed.

The Crommag camp must be more than large, Alastair figured. All the elves could hear it and smell it once the field of corpses was in their wake. Dell led them west, away from the noise and smells. They dismounted at the ridgeline and led the horses into a small copse of trees and waited for dusk. They knew they should eat, but no one even suggested it. Even the hardened Nevin had little appetite after seeing the abandoned bodies of the Crommags that had been left to rot.

When the light finally began to change, Dell looked at Alastair. "Stay here," he ordered, "but keep an ear out, we might need you to bring the horses. Possibly as fast and quietly as you can."

Alastair nodded. He planned on keeping both ears out. For anything.

The other three Jägers crept along the ridgeline; the yet unseen camp getting louder and smellier, but still did not come into view. Finally, Dell signaled a detour that would take them up a wide, flat hill so they could see farther as dusk began to shadow the land.

They crawled up the hill like ants, creeping to the top and catching sight of the other side with the last fading light of the day. All three were rendered speechless and motionless for a long time.

The Ice Floe had broken with spring and now rushed with summer – a great blue snake roiling with chunks of ice the size of horses as it wound its way across the plains. On the south side of the river, just down the hill from where the Jägers crouched against the setting sun, was a large camp of Crommags. One hundred or more enormous hairy bodies grunted or yelled or squatted as they built their fires for the evening. One tall but rickety looking tent erected with sticks and covered with animal skins was surrounded by smaller, even shabbier looking structures.

On the far, northern side of the river their numbers were exponential.

It wasn't a camp. It was a populace.

Shelters as crude as their owners littered the valley from

one side to the other and for as far as even their elfin eyes could see. Crommag men, women, children, along with their beasts of burden and fodder moved in and out and between tents and lean-tos.

Dell, his brown eyes wide, looked at Jaden first. "Count," he commanded and then glanced at Nevin before looking back at the valley. The sheer enormity of the camp drew his stare like a magnet to iron. "A migration?" he asked.

"Crommags don't migrate," Nevin said, then shook his head, his graying hair dusting his shoulders. "At least they haven't before. I don't know."

"That explains the bodies," Dell said softly. "They simply drag the dead away from the camp to keep away scavengers and disease. Instead of burning or burying them, they just dump them."

"Jaden was right," Nevin noted. "They are getting lazier. That's why the more decomposed ones were farther away. Now they're just tossing corpses over the hill." The older elf grimaced in disgust.

"Do you see..." Dell began to ask but then he saw for himself even as Nevin was nodding to his question. The seasoned Jägers knew to look for a center to the encampment, one that would point to a leader. It would help answer the question if what they were seeing was indeed a population turned nomad, or an army.

The activity of the Crommags seemed endless, but was obviously more focused at the center of the valley. The concentration of bodies there was greater, and the pace there was much quicker, movements more purposeful. Dell and Nevin could see the tents there were larger and better built than the others that spiraled out towards the edges. Also, those tents had guards.

"An army," Nevin whispered.

Jaden turned to Dell, his eyes bright even as the lands

succumbed to darkness.

"A thousand tents," he reported, "at least twice as many men, plus their families." The young Sylvan swallowed and licked his lips, excited. "And more are arriving at the other end of the valley even as we speak. Droves of them."

"And look!" Nevin exclaimed, keeping his voice low though there was no need. Not as far as they were from the camp and their sounds covered by the din and clamor below.

Dell followed the direction of his finger, though with descent of darkness he would have seen it on his own only a second later. Dotted around the thousand tents on the north side of the Ice Floe were a thousand cook fires and none were any different than their fellows. But on the south side of the river, on the far side of the camp just below where the Jägers watched, the fires were larger and more dense though there were less Crommags.

"Work fires," Nevin said. "Forges."

Dell's dark eyes picked out the figures that hurried between those larger fires, and they were not Crommag.

"Gnomin," he whispered, and did his own count. There were at least thirty and those that were not working were tied down. Crommags bellowed at those working, making them scurry as they poured, forged, and hammered metal.

Even Jaden, a young elf and native to the New World who had never seen war, knew what they were about.

"They're making weapons," he said softly, almost as if he could not believe his own words.

Dell had finally seen enough. He motioned at the two elves on either side of him and, after scooching backwards from the top, descended the hill in a running crouch. When he got to the bottom he paused just long enough to whistle softly for Alastair to bring the horses. Then he kept on again at a low run, trying to put as much distance as he could between the elfin party and the camp of monsters. Alastair met them more than halfway within moments, leading the well-trained mounts in a silent gallop. Dell motioned for him to dismount and he squatted down to confer with him and the others.

Nevin recounted to Alastair what they had just seen. Wide-eyed, he listened. When Nevin finished, Dell looked at his novice Jägers in turn.

"Do you see what they are about?" he asked.

"War," Alastair whispered.

Jaden nodded, his small form no more than a shadow in the darkness. "Thousands of Crommags and more arriving by the hundreds."

Nevin rubbed his chin. "Three thousand elves came over from the Old World, including women and children."

Dell shook his head. "Which means only about a thousand men."

"I was born here," Alastair said. "So were others."

Dell nodded, a frown creasing his brow. "True, but only a hundred or so for the first two decades. Anyone after that would be too young to fight."

"Do Crommag women fight?"

"It does not matter," Nevin said, "elfin women do not."

"Are you certain they are not simply moving their homeland?" Alastair asked, his young voice mournfully hopeful.

Jaden shook his head. "They would not be making weapons en masse if they were just trying to sneak into warmer lands."

"And they were smart enough to trap a number of Gnomin to make the weapons for them," Nevin mused aloud. "They want good quality."

"Then they will get it," Alastair said, despondent yet already resolute. "No race is more skilled in working ore."

"They intend to descend on us," Dell affirmed, looking around the small group to see what else they could surmise on their own.

Nevin nodded sagely and continued in more detail, his words mirroring the ones in Dell's mind. "They will wait for winter – for the river to freeze so they can all cross safely and together."

"But," Jaden argued, "if they wait for winter, they would still be trapped by the Siber Massif. It will be full of snow. There will be no way through until spring. Most game will be in hibernation and it did not look like they had enough supplies to last more than a few months, taking them perhaps through the fall. How will they make it through the winter?"

"The farms," Alastair said, feeling sick. "They weren't raiding those farms, they were simply driving the farmers off. Those empty farms will provide extra shelter, and are stocked with provisions, not to mention what is still growing in the fields and orchards."

Dell nodded at him, pleased with them all. They were good Jägers. He could see that they were sickened by the outcome of events and the prospect of the future, but were staunch and determined. They all turned their eyes to him, but it was Alastair that posed the question in those eyes.

"Now, Sir Dellion?" he asked. "Have you found what you were after?"

Dell nodded. "I have. It was not what I wanted, of course, but what the King had feared. Now we must return and tell him his fears were grounded."

"And help our people prepare," Nevin added, his voice grim.

"How?" Jaden asked. "How can people such as ours stand against such monsters, and so outnumbered?"

Alastair laid a hand on the smaller elf's shoulder and managed a reassuring smile. "We will find a way."

Dell smiled at him, proud, and motioned for them all to mount up.

One hundred years of peace, he thought, turning his horse south. *Such a small amount of time to an elf.*

He thought of all the hardships his people had faced to get to the New World. All for a short hundred years.

But, if we vanquish the brutes, the next peace could be longer. Maybe forever.

Dell wanted to hope for that outcome more than anything, but he knew - possibly more than anyone - how ill prepared the elves were for such an onslaught. In that, he was as full of trepidation as the small Sylvan.

Still, he thought, *we have time. Spring comes late to the Northlon, and the Crommags will have to wait for the snow to melt in the passes of the Siber Massif. After that, they will be on the move. It gives us time. Not a lot, but maybe enough.*

Thinking of time, the Jäger's gaze scanned the sky as he rode along. It was dark now and the stars were out in a brilliant display across the heavens. To the west, he could see the Reaper's Scythe rising over the mountains. Pretty soon that sliver of moon would become the Reaper's Grin, wide and greedy. Dell judged that they had three weeks, maybe a few days more, before the Grin became the Scream – otherwise known as the Harvest Moon.

24. FIELD TRIP

The elfin prince rose to find the Roshan already outside and pulling their riding gear from the tack box by the haus. The horses stood nearby, munching grass and waiting patiently.

"Let me help," he offered but the Roshan shook her head.

"Don't be ridiculous," she said, motioning with her chin to his bandaged hands. "Have you had breakfast yet?" Traejan shook his head. "We are going on a little trip," she informed him. "Get some fuel in your body."

"I can have a piece of bread while we ride," he offered, "or skip it altogether, if you want to leave sooner than later."

The Roshan balanced Coal's massive saddle on her knee while she checked the straps. "No," she said. "Eat. I still need to pack provisions. Afterwards, get your bedroll and anything else you might need for the next few days."

"Is everything okay?" he asked.

The Roshan gave him a wry smile. "I thought we'd get you that haircut," she said. "Unless you'd like me to give you one?" The prince returned her wry look of amusement. "I have the feeling you wouldn't use scissors."

The Roshan grinned and shook her head emphatically.

"A little trip sounds good then," Traejan chirped.

The Roshan laughed and turned her attention back to the tack. She finished checking their equipment and then followed him inside.

Traejan ate a quick breakfast while the Roshan filled a

leather sack with apples, hard bread, and dried meat. She held a small wheel of cheese for a moment, considering how well it would last in the heat, then tucked it in as well. It would be good for a day. She filled another, smaller pouch with shelled nuts. The auburn-haired warrior found a double mess kit in one cupboard and a small cast-iron pot for traveling in another. She filled a burlap sack with small, red-skinned potatoes as the young prince hurried to his room for his things.

She paused her work for a moment, watching him head down the hall. She bit her lip and frowned. She knew it was no time to be taking a vacation. He still had far to go and time was running short. She had been up half the night trying to decide what to do.

Well, she thought, *I certainly can't have him wielding a sword with his hands the way they are. A few days to heal won't hurt. Then we can be back at it, with a lighter sword next time. And a leather grip.*

It was a concession she had never made for a student before.

Time was never a constraint before, she conceded mentally. She gave her head a shake and finished her preparations.

When they had saddled and packed the horses, the elf and his teacher mounted up and headed south. Along with his bedroll, a tightly folded cloak and a change of clothes, he had brought his bow and quiver as well as his sword. He doubted he could wield it well with his hands in their current state, but he had a feeling that he could fight with it better in his existing condition than he could have only a few months ago. It was a good feeling.

They rode the entire day, pausing to rest and water the horses when they needed it, always staying within the shade of the woods. One of the stops they made was at a brook in a glade that bore a strong resemblance to the one where they first met. The young prince sat on a rock, eating bread and cheese and unable to keep the smile from his face. The Roshan did not miss it.

"Care to share?" she asked.

Traejan's smile widened. "I was just thinking about the first time we met."

The Roshan smiled as the memory was brought to her mind as well. "You have learned much since then," she said.

"It seems so long ago," he mused aloud, "yet also like it could have been just a few days past."

"Time can be that way," the Roshan said, her gem-like eyes growing distant as they focused on what was clearly another memory.

The elf watched her closely, wanting so badly to ask about her own thoughts and what made her face go so still – almost sad.

They rode south for the remainder of the day, following the brook, and Traejan could tell they were also angling east. He noticed as well that the trees were changing. The pines had long since disappeared and even the oaks were giving way to black walnut trees that were huge and spreading with dense tufts of small leaves. The tufts, however, sprouted in irregular places and their shade became more sporadic. The air warmed as they went further into the Southlon and Traejan was glad that the sun was almost down.

They stopped for the night and he saw to the horses while the Roshan gathered a stockpile of branches and made a small fire. She produced the small pot she had taken from the haus and covered the bottom with a layer of the small, red-skinned potatoes and some of the dried meat. Then she filled it half full of water from the brook, stirred in a pinch of powder from a tiny pouch, and put it on the low-burning branches at the edge of the fire.

Traejan brought their bedrolls and unrolled the Roshan's first as she stoked the fire.

"I can do that," she said over her shoulder as he shook out

the thick blanket.

"So can I," he told her. "I'm not completely useless."

The Roshan snorted as she stirred the pot, which was beginning to boil. Traejan straightened with a frown and stared at her auburn head, made red and orange by the light of the fire.

"Is that because you think I am?" he asked.

The Roshan turned her face to look up at him, surprised by his tone. A slow smile spread across her features. "It's because I think you are anything but," she told him. "Useless, that is."

The elfin prince fought the blush that wanted to rise in his cheeks and stood his ground. "Then would you care to share what *you* are smiling about?" he asked, employing the phrase the Roshan often used.

Her smile widened into a grin. "It is because you are finally growing a bit a nerve with me."

Now he did blush. "I am sorry," he apologized, moving quickly to shake out his own bedroll. The Roshan laughed.

"There is no need to apologize," she assured the elf. "I am just surprised that it took so long. Many that I trained have found themselves with enough audacity to question me within a week or two. Some in even less time than that, a day or two maybe. A few show up already that bold, or downright defiant."

Traejan sat down on his blanket and stared at her from over the low fire, his arms draped loosely around his knees. "What happened to them?"

The Roshan's grin widened even further. "What do you think happened to them?" she asked.

"I guess it depends on how angry you were."

Now the Roshan laughed. Traejan smiled, the sound of it warming him. "I wasn't ever angry. Well," she admitted, laughing again, "maybe once."

"And?"

The Roshan shrugged, ash-clad shoulders rising up. "If I thought they showed any sort of promise, I was patient. If not, I sent them packing." The elfin prince stared at her, waiting with his brows raised high. "Alright, alright," she confessed. "Maybe I sent a few packing with their bodies as bruised as their pride."

Traejan laughed. "I thought as much."

The Roshan shrugged again and this time it was much more exaggerated. "I have a reputation to protect."

Traejan laughed again as his teacher ladled the camp stew into the bowls she had brought and handed him one, along with a spoon. Of all of the dinnertime discussions they had shared over his months of training, this one somehow seemed the most personal. She dug a couple rolls of bread from her sack that were getting a bit hard and tossed one to him.

He took a bite of potato and after he had chewed and swallowed, ventured a question. "How do I compare against the others you have trained?"

The Roshan wiped her mouth with the cuff of her sleeve and peered at him from over the low flames. "You are not the best fighter that I have trained, though we still have some time left. You are certainly not the worst. Definitely the easiest."

Traejan, though he knew he wasn't the best fighter, darkened at her first remark, then brightened again at the next two.

"The easiest?" he asked. "How is that?"

"Because you listen to me," the Roshan shared between bites. She thought for a few seconds before she spoke again. "I am sure it has something to do with the boldness you are now showing." She cocked her head at him. "Do you think that comes from having more confidence in your fighting skills?"

The elf chuckled softly. "Definitely not." He ate a bit more stew as he thought. "Is that so bold," he asked finally, "asking what you are smiling about?"

The Roshan smiled and shook her head. "Definitely not," she told the prince, echoing his own words. "Just bold for you. When we first met, you were like a mouse."

Traejan's brows furrowed, though a smile creased the corners of his mouth. "And now?" he asked.

The Roshan chuckled around a bite of potato. "Now you are like a rabbit. A very fierce and determined rabbit," she added, laughing, as she saw the crease between his brows deepen. Traejan finally laughed as well.

"Thanks," he said, "though I doubt that is a compliment."

"It is," the Roshan assured. "I expected you to be the exact opposite – brash and haughty."

"Why?"

His question was so genuine that the Roshan almost wanted to shift in her seat but, as always, she was as steady as her gaze and thought carefully as she chose her words. "I don't know many Skye Elves, but they do have a reputation to be...a proud people. I expected the prince of such people to be...excessively so."

The young elf nodded, understanding. "It is a human assessment," he told her, "that comes from a difference in cultures." The prince sighed. "But is probably accurate, knowing my people."

"Then what makes you different?"

"You," Traejan answered before he could stop himself. The Roshan cocked her head at him again, curious, but he spoke again before she could say anything. "I doubt you have trained any Skye Elves before," he said quickly, knowing all too well that she had not. She shook her head and he continued. "We may, as a whole, be a bit arrogant. But respect is very important to us. Any elf would be a fool to think he could outmatch you in a fight and would respect that."

The Roshan smiled at his opinion and they finished their dinner in companionable silence. Traejan moved to collect their bowls but she waved him away and took them up herself.

"Keep those bandages dry if you can," she advised, taking the bowls and spoons to the brook to clean them. "And leave the pot. We'll have the rest for breakfast."

The young elf sat back down. He expected to feel uneasy at her taking care of things but instead he felt strangely comforted. He got up to check the horses and make sure they were settled for the night, suddenly aware that they would be going to sleep soon.

He wondered how the Roshan looked when she slept, feeling his heart rate quicken. It was not the first time he had speculated on that subject but he knew that he was finally going to find out.

Does she ever really rest? Is she ever at peace?

Traejan sat back down on his bedding as she returned from the brook and laid their mess kits by the dying fire to dry.

"Well," he said, "the rabbit, however fierce he may be, is tired."

The Roshan laughed, bringing a smile to his lips. "I hope that was not too offensive," she offered.

The prince held up his hands in mock surrender. "Truth be told, I compared you as an animal as well, the first time we met. Though I thought of you as a snowlynx."

She laughed again as she kicked open her blankets and crawled into them. "I'll take that as a compliment," she said, bunching her cloak under her head as a pillow.

"A rabbit and a snowlynx," Traejan remarked with mock despondency. "Could any two animals be more different?"

"They both make good coats," the Roshan said.

The elf and the warrior both laughed.

Traejan cast his soft brown eyes about their campsite, as far as the fire cast a glow and somewhat beyond. "Should we take turns sleeping?" he asked.

The Roshan shook her head. "There is no need. Crommags do not come this far south, and few humans venture far from the townships, even the bad ones. I doubt we need worry about elves," she added with raised brows. Traejan shook his blonde curls. "I didn't think so. Besides," she said, jerking her chin towards the horses, "Coal will let me know if anything comes too close."

The elfin prince nodded in understanding and took a last look at her face as the flames threw lights and shadows across her recumbent form before he lay down and pulled his blanket over him. He had forgotten how peaceful it was to sleep outside and before long he was drowsy. He was acutely aware, however, that the woman he loved was laying just a few feet away from him.

He closed his lids but kept his elf-eyes open. He slowed his breath and his heartbeat, picturing everything around him as if he were sitting up in broad daylight. It was a skill Dell had taught him decades ago that any elf could hone but that every Jäger must master. When he knew the Roshan's eyes had been shut continuously for at least ten minutes, and her respiration came slow and soft, Traejan opened his real eyes and peered at her through the dying flames of their fire.

The embers, however, obscured her face as they slowly expired into a measured and deliberate heap of coal and ash.

The elfin prince counted out ten more minutes, then lifted himself up just enough to see her. He put his elbow to the ground and propped his chin in his hand but had only a second to admire her smooth cheek and softened brow before her eyes popped open, looking directly into his own.

Traejan pushed himself all the way up and added a few short branches to bank the dying coals in an effort cover his nocturnal spying. His teacher watched him through narrowed lids until he lay back down and closed his own eyes, and kept them shut.

His heart was beating so fast that he thought he might

never sleep, but it overcame him with a quick and unexpected sureness.

The elf awoke the next day to find the Roshan sitting on top of her bedroll, tying her hair into a knot at the back of her head and fastening it with a band. He made a face, knowing that it must have been down only seconds before. Dawn was still fresh, reaching pinkish fingers of light into the woods.

"Good morning," she remarked with a slip of a smile.

"Good morning."

"Were you cold last night?" she asked, her smile widening.

"Not too much," Traejan said, "but I forgot to ask you something," he continued, changing the subject. The Roshan cocked her head, curious. Traejan cleared his throat. "How close are we to the Spawning?"

"Ah!" the Roshan exclaimed, as if he had answered a question instead of asking one. She poked at the remains of the fire, getting it going again under the pot. "Not far. Three miles, perhaps."

"Does that ever bother you?"

The Roshan shook her head. "The creatures that live there rarely venture out." The elf raised his brows and looked pointedly at Coal, the monstrous and fanged Night Stallion that stood close to his own mount, almost dwarfing her. The Roshan laughed. "He is the exception, rather than the rule."

Traejan harrumphed as he stood up, making her laugh again. He smiled at the sound of it as he went to the stream to wash his face while the Roshan stirred the pot. She took the last two rolls of bread, now quite hard, and tore them into chunks before lobbing the pieces into the warming stew.

They ate in silence, washed their dishes and then saddled their mounts, watering them again at the brook before dousing the fire and heading out. The Roshan led them directly east and within minutes they were leaving the woods.

"We'll cross the valley while it's still cool," she said from atop the giant Night Stallion. The sun was rising over woods on the other side of the basin and they angled slightly south to keep from staring into it. The warrior and the prince rode over grass that had long gone to seed and turned to gold in the summer heat.

It's a perfect summer day, the young elf decided. *Even this far south it is not too hot. No hotter than wielding a sword in the sun for six hours at a time.*

In less than an hour, however, the temperature had increased significantly. When they began their ascent on the far side of the valley the riders were damp with sweat, the horses doubly so. The rising sun began to beat down and the horses pressed hard to gain the hill. Minutes later they were entering the woods on the far side of the valley, enveloped in shade once again.

They stood in a gap of trees, too small to be a glade or a glen, more like a hollow. The woods on this side were denser, more of a forest. The Roshan immediately called a stop to rest the horses. "We won't hit the Talon for maybe an hour," the Roshan said, sliding down off Coal's massive back and then reaching up to retrieve a small pack full of apples that was tied to her saddle. She offered one to Traejan who declined politely. "Then feed it to Peg," she advised, handing it to the elf. "It should keep her until we hit the stream. There's plenty of grazing, but no water until then."

She took another apple and tossed it to Coal, who caught in smartly in his fangs and disposed of it in a single chomp. Traejan, whose head was close to said fangs, lurched away, startled. He threw the Roshan a look as he fed Peg, who munched on her fruit in a much more lady-like fashion. The Roshan grinned and sat down, leaning her back against a tree with a small apple of her own. She shined the fruit on her sleeve for a few seconds before biting into it.

Though the Talon was over a mile away, its presence throughout the Eaglewood and the cover of the trees had kept summer at bay. In sharp contrast to the dry and golden valley, shades of green burst from every inch of the forest. Ferns dipped and fanned the mossy trunks of the trees. Button willows gorged with new leaves bowed low to the ground. Cloverleaf grew in scattered patches and fawngrass sprouted out of every nook and cranny. The prince put his back against a sapling a few yards away, watching and listening.

"How are your hands?" the Roshan asked.

"Much better. Even before I slept last night they were better, and almost healed it seemed by this morning." He closed his hands into fists and opened them again, showing her. She smiled.

"Well, I doubt they're healed completely. Gatha's ointment can work wonders, but I've never seen it work miracles."

"I don't know," Traejan said, "that salve might have worked its way up my sword arm. I may be ready for my first battle."

The Roshan laughed. It was good to see him with both nerve and humor. "Well then, it has not worked its way up to your head. You can hardly hold a sword, much less wield one."

"That's not fair," the prince reproached, unable to hide his smile at the sound of her laugh.

"You are right," she agreed. "You are making great progress. You fight well enough, and you know all your defensive moves as well as the best attacks. The way you wield a sword, however, still bothers me - as if it is your enemy, rather than your friend. Like you are wielding a snake." The Roshan shrugged. "It might simply be that the broadsword is not your weapon," she said dismissively.

Traejan recoiled with an obvious jolt and the Roshan regretted her choice of words.

"Don't be discouraged," she soothed. "I'm just saying that it will possibly not be your weapon of choice. I am more than skilled with a sword and it is hardly ever my first choice." The prince nodded, his dismay still apparent. "And I'm not reducing you so quickly to something as dishonorable as the knife." This got a smile from the elf. "Your skill with the bow is like nothing I have ever seen," she told him. "But perhaps we must find something else you are comfortable with, the short sword perhaps."

Traejan beamed under her praise despite himself. "But it is the broadsword that I really wanted to master." In Traejan's mind, warriors always brandished huge and gleaming swords.

"You will master it enough before you return home," she assured him. "Like I said, you are getting good with everything else, you just don't seem to be comfortable with the sword. Maybe we can try a slimmer one, and one that is only a hand's length more than the knife. You were excellent with the knife and making progress on the short sword. Maybe it will just be a matter of more practice. It all came together for you one day before we even started with weapons. The same might happen with the sword."

Traejan sighed, hopeful yet doubtful. He pulled the sword he wore from the scabbard on his belt. He knew exactly what she meant, for he felt it himself. No matter which way he turned it or gripped it, it felt stiff and unwieldy in his grasp - as if it were an unforged chunk of iron instead of a finely wrought blade. Despairingly, he did not think changing swords would help. He had carried and practiced with the one in his hand for over fifty years. It felt a part of him, but not natural. Like a prosthetic limb carried over from childhood.

"I just can't figure out why I can't get a good feel for it. I want it to feel natural, like the way it feels when I pick up a bow." He turned it this way and that then shook his head. "Even after all this time, it still seems so foreign."

"You're trying too hard," the auburn-haired warrior told him. "Try to relax." The prince made his body go limp, his shoulders slumped. The Roshan laughed. "Not everywhere, just your arm. Relax your arm, your wrist, your grip." His arm lowered slightly. She shook her head and got up, placing her half-eaten apple carefully on a rock. He felt his pulse quicken, they way it always did, as she approached him. "Loosen your grip," she commanded. "You hold it as if someone is going to try to wrest it away from you."

Traejan smiled. "My arm, my wrist, my grasp, my stance. There is twice as much to think about as when I started training. I thought adding a weapon would just make it easier. In fact, I think I heard that somewhere before."

The Roshan gave him a sour look, though it was feigned. Coal snorted and stamped an enormous hoof, tearing up the earth.

"You're thinking about it *too* much. That's why it feels so uncomfortable. When you pick up your bow you don't think at all, you just *do* – you said so yourself. It has to be the same with the sword. Be with your opponent and be totally aware of your surroundings. Your training and practice will take over from there." She walked around behind him. His brown eyes widened in shock as he felt her press her body right up to his. She put her right arm down the length of his own and grasped his wrist, turning it. "This way," she said, showing him. "And then like this."

Traejan barely heard her. His heart was pounding madly in his chest. He leaned back into her, feeling her nearness, taking in every sensation of her touch. He could feel his breath come faster and made a conscious effort to slow it.

"That's much better!" the Roshan exclaimed.

The elfin prince was too far-gone mentally to appreciate the irony. He had spent so much time making an effort not to think about how he held his sword, to let it be natural. Yet now - try as he might - the sword was the last thing he could think about, or wanted to. His mind was focused only on the strength of the arm along his own. Her lanky muscles were like small ropes bound together by the smooth skin under her thin shirt. The feel of her fingers grasping his wrist was like iron wrapped in soft leather. Her entire being was a system of contradictions.

He leaned back into her as much as he dared. Her left thigh was pressed against the back of his own, and her left hand rested on his hip to keep them both steady. He closed his eyes, unable to make sense of what she was saying, and then opened them wide as she slipped around his body to face him, bringing his arm down gently. She wedged a finger between his bandaged hand and the hilt of his sword.

"That's even better. How does that feel?" she asked, looking up at him. He inhaled slowly and deeply. He could smell her skin, warmed by the morning sun, edged with leather and steel. Her hair smelled like rose and lavender.

The prince lowered his sword arm and let his other hand drop to her hip. He slid his hand around to the small of her back and drew her close. The Roshan looked up at him, nonplussed.

"Traejan?"

The young elf leaned closer, unable to stop himself.

25. RYEN AND THE ROSHAN

Traejan's lips parted, so close to the Roshan's that he could feel her breath like a whisper through the wood. His mouth grazed her cheek and he pressed her body close to his, relishing every second. "Someone has come into the forest," he said softly into her ear. He felt her whole body tense as every muscle wound tight and ready to spring, but she did not break the embrace.

"Where?" she whispered.

"On the southeast side of the tree line."

Like a wisp of smoke, her lithe form slipped from his arms and she took a few soft steps with her head cocked, listening. Then she stepped back, putting herself between him and the south, her hand on the hilt of the long sword at her hip as she peered into the woods.

He wanted to so badly to pull her back against him, yet the way she stood in front of his body, protecting it with her own small form, made his heart swell till he thought it would crush against his ribcage. She listened intently, but heard nothing save the sound of the forest.

"How many?" she whispered.

"Only one. A man. He has a horse but is walking, not riding." The elf was quiet for a moment, his own head cocked a little to one side. "He's whistling." The Roshan turned around and looked at him.

"Whistling?"

The prince nodded. She laughed and let go of her sword hilt. She walked back to where she had left her apple, picked it up and sat down on the rock. She glared at Coal but the Night Stallion snorted at her as if to say he had tried to warn her. She looked back at the elf. "Is he coming this way? Along the tree line?" Traejan nodded again.

"Keeping to the shade," she said. "Like we are."

She smiled and resumed eating. She did not look in the direction of where the stranger was reported to be, only munched on her apple, glancing curiously at the prince from time to time.

The young elf shifted uncomfortably under her gaze and put his sword back into the scabbard on his hip, more confused than ever. His heart raced and he fought to get it under control. He might have deceived her, but there was no deceiving himself. He had almost kissed her. He couldn't believe it.

She didn't pull away from me, he thought, elated. Then gave his head a quick shake. *She was just confused. That's all. If I had kissed her she probably would have killed me. But the way she stood in front of me...*

He decided not to think about it, not now anyway. But he knew that the feel of her body pressed again his own would fill his dreams for weeks to come. At this point, he thought it better to consider who might be coming towards them. Someone the Roshan most likely knew, or knew of, or at least did not fear. That much was obvious. The young elf crossed his arms in front of his lean form and took a step back, waiting, becoming a part of the forest. The Roshan finished her apple and grew still as well, suddenly part of the shadows.

The whistling, which had also become clear to the Roshan, grew louder with each passing moment. The breath and stamp of a horse was unmistakable, even as their own mounts grew silent and tense.

A moment later a man entered the hollow leading an enormous dappled gray horse. Though the huge khusar was nowhere close to the size of the Night Stallion, the man was very tall. He stood a good foot taller than the six-foot tall prince, with reddish-blond hair on his head as well as a light fringe along his lip and jaw. His eyes were like two bright blue chips of ice.

He must have sensed that something was afoot because he stopped, his whistle fading from his lips. He peered around the hollow but before he could tell elf from tree or woman from shadow, the Roshan whipped her apple core at him. He jerked his head instinctively, the projectile just barely missing his ear. The Roshan's laughter filled the air before he could get his sword from his belt and his anger vanished as quickly as it had come.

"Dammit, Em! You scared the hell out of me!"

The Roshan laughed harder. "You should have seen the look on your face!"

The man frowned, then chuckled, and then laughed, and then stopped as he noticed Traejan.

"Who else is here with you?" he asked, looking around the hollow, another chuckle bubbling to the surface. "For all the Circles! I thought you were Aiden! Only a Wildboy would be so bold as to throw fruit at me." He gathered his manners and walked to the elfin prince and extended his hand. "I am Ryen," he said, politely introducing himself since the Roshan did not seem inclined to do so.

"I am Traejan," the elf said, grasping the man's hand in greeting. It was a human custom, but one that he liked.

"Ah!" Ryen exclaimed. "I thought you looked familiar."

Traejan cocked his head, curious. "Do I know you?"

"No, but I have been to your city many times. I have seen you once or twice."

"Ryen is a pirate," the Roshan announced. The Norseman had the audacity to look shocked.

"I am a merchant sailor," he assured her.

"You are a thief."

"A trader."

"The only thing you have ever traded is a knife in the throat or a cloak in the night for whatever takes your fancy, including other men's wives."

"She is greatly exaggerating," Ryen assured Traejan. "I've never –oof!" The Roshan had jumped from the rock she had been sitting on and bounded into Ryen's arms. He hugged her enthusiastically, lifting her body a foot or more off of the ground. He set her down and kissed her cheek, beaming at her with his bright blue eyes. "Now *that* is the welcome I was expecting!"

The elf watched the exchange, amazed. He had not imagined the Roshan to have any friends, much less any affection in her. It was so unlike her, as far as he had known. The Norseman, however, glanced over the Roshan's auburn head and did not miss the expression on the face of the young prince – the surprise and, though it was subtle and mostly hidden, the longing.

That's curious, the Vikeman thought.

The Roshan moved away to retrieve her pack but Ryen watched Traejan and the way the elf's eyes followed her.

He's just encountered an armed man he has never met, the Vikeman thought, *and yet it is her that he watches closely. Curiouser and curiouser.*

"So, what brings you into such mixed company?" Ryen asked the prince.

"Learning to fight," he said automatically.

The smile on the Norseman was broad and genuine. "Well, you've come to the right place, or person, I should say. She has fought and taught the best of them," he said, nodding towards the Roshan.

The young elf smiled. "That's what I've heard."

Ryen laughed. "Heard? Wait till you've seen!" He looked closely at the prince. "She hasn't been mistreating you, I hope?"

he asked, indicating the bandages Traejan wore on his hands, but the elf shook his head.

"Hazard of hard training."

Ryen gave him a wicked smile. "I hope that is the only placed you're bandaged." Traejan looked back at him, confused.

"Ryen!" the Roshan hissed, knowing all too well what he was implying.

"And you!" he accused, turning to her with an appraising eye. "It's awfully warm for a long shirt isn't it? You're not hiding bandages somewhere are you?"

"You'll be wearing one around the side of your head if you don't watch yourself," she warned in a low voice, though she wore half a smile.

Ryen bowed respectfully and turned back to Traejan.

"And how does your training go?"

"Hard, and sometimes painful. But worth every bit of it."

"You'll be the best in your land when she's done with you."

Traejan smiled. "I hope so." He liked Ryen. He had the confidence and swagger that only human men seemed to possess, and his relationship with the Roshan seemed close, but not too close. His smile was warm and his blue eyes sparkled with a merriment that was contagious.

"Where are you two headed?" he asked them.

"The Dagger," the Roshan answered. Coal stepped from the shadows, Peg right behind him. The khusar whickered a tentative greeting. "And you?" she asked.

"I was coming to see you, of course. Did you think I was on my way to the Gnomin Vale, maybe to carry off some of their women?"

The Roshan snorted. "I wouldn't put it past you."

"You really give me no credit. And I was coming to give you a present."

"A present?" she asked, brightening. "For me?"

"Not anymore."

"Oooohh," she exclaimed, her hands folded tightly together. "What it is it? Can I have it?" She shifted from one foot to the other. "Please?"

Traejan watched her, astounded. She seemed almost childlike, nothing he had ever seen or imagined. Not even remotely close.

"Well, alright," Ryen relented. "But no more fruit at my head."

"Never," she promised.

Ryen reached into a saddlebag and produced a slim dagger with a handle that looked like carved ivory. "Here," he said, handing it to the Roshan, hilt first. It was plain and unadorned, but beautiful and elegant in its simplicity. "It's made from dragon bone," he told her. "Even the blade – it was dipped in molten steel which was forged around the hilt. It will never break."

"There are no such things as dragons," the Roshan said, matter of fact, her eyes never leaving the blade. She reached out, almost afraid to touch it at first, then snatched it from Ryen's outstretched hand. Expertly, she held up the weapon, stared down the edge with narrowed eyes, felt the weight, balance, and made it disappear. She hugged Ryen and stood on her toes to kiss him lightly on his bearded cheek – though he had to lean down for her to do so. "Thank you!" she told him.

"And thank you," he said, "for meeting me halfway. You've saved me a day's journey, and now can travel with me. You said you are headed for the Dagger?"

"We are. You as well?"

Ryen nodded, his face uncharacteristically serious. "I need to hire a messenger."

"Where to?"

"The Vikes."

The Roshan regarded him with auburn brows raised over her gimlet eyes. "Why not go yourself?" she asked. "You have not been home in years, and the weather is fairly nice this time of year."

The Norseman wrinkled his nose in distaste. "Still too cold," he told her. "And too far. I have unfinished business in the Southlon."

The Roshan shook her head, smiling as she readied her horse. She took Coal by the reins and began walking, leading him east. Ryen walked next to her, leading his khusar. Traejan walked on her other side, but was blocked from view by Coal's enormous girth. Also, the forest was thick here, and he sometimes had to skirt around a huge old oak. He had to content himself with elf eyes and elf ears.

"Coming to see me?" the Roshan asked the Norseman. "Just to give me a present? Or something more?" She gave him a sidelong glance and a wry smile. "What news of the Southlon? Did you truly go visit the Mad King?"

The Vikeman frowned at her, but there was no anger in it. "How did you know that?" The Roshan only smiled in answer and Ryen pursed his lips. "Has that nightingale been spilling my secrets?"

The Roshan shrugged, her smile widening.

"Bah! What else did he tell you?"

The Roshan chuckled silently. "Is the Mad King truly mad?"

"Why don't you ask your bird?" Ryen advised, disgruntled.

This time the Roshan laughed aloud. "He is all advice and warnings. He never answers questions."

The Norseman, never one to sulk for long, shrugged. "I wouldn't say mad. Paranoid for certain, but not quite mad."

"And why did you go see him?"

"Believe it or not, he wanted to see me."

The Roshan looked surprised. "Whatever for?"

"What do people ever want me for?" the Norseman asked. "Besides my charm and good looks?"

"To get things," the Roshan answered immediately. She looked at Ryen and the Norseman looked down at her slender face and black-clad form, his own face solemn once again, and nodded slowly. "What?" she asked. "What did he ask you to get?"

"You."

Traejan gaped at the Norseman, though he could not see him. The elf thought maybe he had misunderstood. He stared at Coal's immense flank, picturing the two that walked on the other side of the massive beast.

The Roshan was staring at the Vikeman, surprised.

"Me?"

The Norseman nodded, his eyes never leaving hers.

"Whatever for?" she demanded.

Now it was Ryen's turn to chuckle. "Not for your charm and good looks," he assured her.

The Roshan turned her face so that she was looking straight ahead again, and the answer came to her in an instant. "Like you," she said, "for what I can do." Ryen nodded and she turned her face back to him. A small line creased her auburn brows. "The Red King wants me to teach him to fight?" she asked doubtfully.

Ryen shook his head. "Not him. His men." The warrior's auburn brows went up again over her gem-like eyes.

"His men? How many?"

Ryen paused before he answered. "Several hundred."

The Roshan gaped at him again and Traejan gasped, engrossed in their exchange. "Several *hundred*?" she repeated.

Ryen smiled and his ginger brows rose up high over his blue eyes. "The pay would be...substantial."

"I am sure." The Roshan was quiet for a moment,

thoughtful. "I've never trained so many at one time."

Ryen shrugged. "How different could it be?" he asked. "You would just have to yell louder, something I doubt you would have trouble with."

Traejan bit his lip and the Roshan shot the Norseman a look of warning before she looked away again while she did what she excelled at most – deliberated all possibilities with uncanny speed.

It was mere seconds before she spoke. "There is only one reason to train so many," she said softly. "He wants an army." After a moment, Ryen nodded reluctantly.

"But why?" she asked and then shook her head. "I will not help him start a war," she said earnestly, looking at the Norseman. "Is that what he wants?" she asked, frowning. "To expand his domain?"

Ryen shook his head. "I do not think so, truly. Like I said, he seems more paranoid than mad. I think he wants an army to protect his city."

"From what? No one in the Southlon would charge the Red City. Why would anyone want to? The Midlon, as well, would not want anything from the South." She looked questioningly to her right where all she could see was Coal's massive shoulder as it flexed and moved under his smooth black skin. But on the other side of the beast the prince was leading his white palfrey. "The elves?" she asked.

Traejan drew back, shocked, and shook his thick, sandy hair. "The elves would not make war," he assured them from the other side of the Night Stallion. "They are not fighters."

"Why are you here, again?" Ryen asked, peering at the elf over the top of Coal's wide back with a crooked grin. Traejan blushed under his curls.

"I'm not like other elves," he confessed.

Ryen chuckled. "Well," he said, looking back at the Roshan, "consider the offer."

The auburn-haired warrior gave him a sidelong glance, her eyes first darting towards a bulging leather bag that hung from the saddle of the khusar. "And how much were you paid to bring this...offer?"

This time the Norseman tipped back his head and laughed. He did not answer but finally gave the Roshan a guilty shrug.

"And none for me?" she demanded, smiling.

"You got the dagger," he reminded her.

"Bah!" the Roshan cursed.

The Norseman's blue eyes became serious once more as he considered his next piece of information. He almost held it back, then charged ahead.

"The Red King himself gave me that dagger, and assured me that it is truly made of dragon bone."

"Bah," the Roshan repeated, softer this time and not looking at the giant of a man looming by her side. "There are no dragons."

"And he assured me of something else," he continued as if not interrupted. He paused and the Roshan looked at him, curious. The Norseman swallowed and again plunged ahead. "That he knew your parents."

The Roshan recoiled as if he had struck her across the face. Traejan tried to catch a glimpse of her over Coal's broad back, but all he could see was the top of her head. It was seconds later before she regained her composure. The elf thought she would be full of questions at this piece of news, he certainly was, but the warrior changed tack as easily as she shifted a weapon from one hand to the other.

"I heard that the miller's wife in Goldensword gave birth to twins this spring," she remarked casually. The Norseman pursed his lips thoughtfully but did not answer, so she continued. "Ginger and fair, though both the miller and his wife are dark-haired."

"Hmmm," Ryen remarked. "How interesting. I shall send

them a gift when we reach town."

"Discreetly, I am sure," the Roshan said, "and avoid the mill district altogether."

The Norseman grunted in response.

They walked the rest of the day, the Roshan and the Vikeman talking mostly about people they both knew and local events to expect at the late summer harvest. Ryen would ask Traejan an occasional question or two, but it seemed to be more out of courtesy than curiosity.

When the summer sun began to make its descent, the three travelers had cleared the Cassowary. The land began to rise on either side, golden hills spotted with scattered oaks. The small company kept to the low land, where the trees were more dense and the air a bit cooler. They mounted their horses for an hour ride as they angled up into the eastern hills. The hills gradually became a small mountain chain called Morningtop and the oak trees gave way to pines. They stopped when they were still an hour ride away from their destination to set up camp in a clearing of fir trees.

"The best way to see Goldensword," Ryen told Traejan as they unsaddled the horses, "is when you can see how she got her name. The town is at the crossing of two rivers, the Cimarone, and the Gehr. The Gehr widens for about half a mile, where it crosses the Cimarone, and makes the 'handguard.' The Cimarone is wide, and flat, and makes the 'hilt' on the north of the Gehr, and then the 'blade' on the south side where it narrows into a point as it passes into the Mandolin Hills. In the morning, the rising sun shines on the rivers and together they look like a great golden sword."

The prince smiled as he pulled his gear off of Peg. "I love to hear about how places are named, especially when they have a tale behind them. Are there any tales behind Goldensword?"

Ryen flashed a smile at him and pulled his own gear from the back of the khusar. "Only the tales they have about me!" Traejan laughed as the Vikeman jerked his chin towards the

Roshan. "But you have the best guide there is," he continued. "Em has an extensive knowledge of the entire Southlon and its history, not to mention the western mountains that she haunts." Traejan looked at the Roshan as she reached up high to untie the gear behind her saddle.

"I've lived here a long time," she said, pulling out her bedroll without so much as a glance in their direction. Traejan moved to her side and unsaddled Coal for her without being asked. Ryen watched without comment. The red-haired fighter tossed her bedroll down and threw her cloak on top of it.

The elfin prince leaned Coal's saddle against a tree and put his bedroll down not far from the Roshan's. He glanced up and saw Ryen watching him with interest. He looked away as Ryen gave him a knowing grin but then found himself staring at the Roshan as she unbuckled the belt of her longsword. He turned his flushed face towards the woods as she lay her sword and belt against Coal's saddle.

"Traejan?" Ryen called, jovial. "There's a brook at the edge of the copse. Would you please water the horses? Em and I can fill the water skins upstream."

Traejan nodded as Ember took his waterskin from Peg and retrieved her own. She walked by Ryen, heading uphill towards the tributary they could hear cutting through the woods of Morningtop. Ryen watched the prince a moment more and then turned and followed her.

They were almost to the brook when he finally spoke.

"How goes it with this elf?" he asked pointedly. The Roshan frowned at him and shook her head, still walking towards the stream. A burst of air came from between the teeth of the Norseman and he started to speak again but the Roshan's face snapped around before he could utter a word.

"Shhh!" she hissed.

"Why? He can't hear us up here."

"Actually," she said softly, "I think he can." She pointed to an area further upstream where the water bubbled over and between the small boulders in its path and walked towards it.

Traejan, who *could* hear them, and quite well, froze in his tracks. He had walked in the opposite direction, going downstream, and the horses were drinking noisily from the rushing water but it did not keep their words from being clear in his ears.

"He's doing well," the Roshan told the Vikeman quietly as she stooped to fill Traejan's waterskin. "He has a ways to go with the sword, but hand to hand he is where he should be and..."

"That's not what I mean," Ryen interrupted, filling his own skin.

The Roshan screwed the cap onto Traejan's waterskin and slung it over her shoulder. Ryen stood up and shook water from his hands. After a period of silence, the Roshan humored him.

"What *do* you mean?" she asked, mockingly defiant and demure. He walked up close to her and she had to tilt her head back to see his face. He pursed his lips, unsure of how to tell her, so he just came out with it.

"That boy is in love with you."

The Roshan stepped back, looking at the Norseman as if he had turned into a snake. "Don't be ridiculous!" she whispered hoarsely, a frown creasing her auburn brows as she looked quickly downstream before turning back to Ryen. "And he is not a boy – he's over a hundred years old."

"For an elf he is still a boy. And in love with you."

"That's crazy!"

"Is it? Do you not see the way he hangs on your every word, and watches your every move?"

The Roshan waved his words away but still kept her voice low. "He is an apt pupil, that is all. He wants very badly to do well. He's been that way since the first I met him."

"Then he has loved you since first he met you! He reveres you as a teacher, yes – but there is something much more. How can you not see it?"

The Roshan stood thoughtful for a moment before she spoke. "I'll admit that he is different – he is certainly quieter than most. But he is the first Northlonder I have met that isn't a Vikeman or a Gnomin, and he is a Skye Elf as well. You don't know that many yourself."

"I know enough."

She knelt to fill her own waterskin from the stream and then rose again, her brows knit together as she fastened the cap. "You think he is so different?"

Ryen took a step closer and laid a hand on her shoulder. "I can see it in the way he looks at you. I looked at you the same way, once."

The Roshan turned her face away.

"The whole idea is crazy," she finally whispered. "I am a human mercenary, he is an elfin prince!"

Ryen nodded. "That is what makes it so dangerous. You are comfortable with him because you think there is no chance of intimacy. It gives you a false sense of security. You need to be careful."

"You talk as if he is an assassin."

"He is more dangerous than that. An assassin you would spot in an instant and dispose of even quicker."

"You're talking nonsense."

"I am not. You don't see the way he looks at you. The way *he looks* when he looks at you. A blind man could see it, Em!"

"You're insane. The whole idea is insane!"

"Is it?"

The Roshan peered at the trees towards their camp and took a moment to consider Ryen's words. "I don't know," she said.

"What don't you know?"

"I still think you're crazy, but..."

"But what?"

The Roshan shook her head in answer, thinking back only a few hours, when she and Traejan were alone in the hollow at the edge of the woods. How he had put his arm around her and pulled her close. At first she was confused, and then she thought he was simply trying to be quiet, to warn her of the other presence in the wood. But there was a moment in between when she thought something else, if only for a fleeting second. And she thought back to how it had made her feel.

"Can I ask you something?" Ryen inquired.

The Roshan flashed him a look of irritation. "Can I stop you?"

The Norseman gave her a wry smile. "Have you taken any of your meals with him?"

The Roshan flushed. "Dammit!" she cursed. "Why do you always have to complicate things!" It was an accusation rather than a question.

"Me?"

"Yes, you! I'm going back! Don't you say a word about this!" She stomped past the man looming over her, heading back towards camp, but he caught her by the wrist and held her. He was almost certainly the only man in existence that could do such a thing and not lose the emboldened hand.

"What color are his eyes?" the Vikeman asked as if it was simply a curious question and part of their conversation. Thrown off by such nonchalance, the Roshan stopped in her tracks and answered him plainly.

"Brown."

Ryen's lightly bearded chin, already over a foot above her head, lifted. "Always?" he asked.

The furrow returned to her brow with ferocity and Ryen

took the look for an answer, which only angered her more.

She jerked her wrist free from the Norseman's hand. "You are being crazy!" she hissed once again before she stomped off through the trees.

The Roshan's mind ran untamed with possibility in the way that it always did, but Ryen's suggestions did not seem possible to her in any way.

Yet what he said about Traejan's eyes brought her back to only two nights past when she was sure that the elf's eyes had changed color. She had never heard of such a thing, but the Norseman obviously knew something that she did not.

And the Norseman knew her. Knew her well.

His question on whether or not she had taken any meals with Traejan upset her. Ryen was quite aware that she rarely, if ever, ate with her students. She claimed that it was because she did not like to breed familiarity or comfort with her pupils - which was true. More true was that she rarely liked them. She could honestly argue she did not believe Traejan would lose respect for her from a closer acquaintance, but she could not deny that she liked to talk to him.

She cursed the Vikeman inwardly as she stalked between the trees, even as his words echoed in her ears.

The auburn-haired warrior was resolute not to believe the Norseman, and was determined to watch the elfin prince that night to see if he acted unusual in any way.

She never got the chance.

# 26. SAVING A PRINCE

Traejan, watering the horses, was unable to shut his ears to words that no human could have heard at that distance. He tried not to listen but found he could not stop himself. The young prince paled at Ryen's words, his jaw falling open, almost dropping Peg's reins.

That bastard! he thought, mortified. *How dare he!*

Finally, the horses finished and he led them back to the clearing, his ears closed to the present and ringing with what Ryen had said to the Roshan. He knew he should start unpacking their gear but his mind was miles away. Absently, he tethered Peg and the Vikeman's khusar while Coal loomed nearby. The Night Stallion snorted and stomped the ground with a massive hoof. The young elf was so distressed that he did not notice Coal's warning. Nor did he hear the man running into their camp and did not even see him until he burst into the clearing, almost plowing him to the ground.

The prince, surprised but with reflexes that had been honed over a season and a half, caught the man before he could fall. He was human and filthy - sweating profusely and panting for breath. He would have run into Coal if Traejan had not caught hold of him. The man jerked back at first, terrified. Then, seeing that Traejan was an elf, he grasped him by the forearms. The Roshan came into the clearing then, a frown carved into her brow and Ryen at her heels.

"Help us!" the man gasped at Traejan, clutching him. "Please, help us!"

The Roshan, like a wisp of smoke blown by a gust of wind,

was at his side in an instant. "What's wrong?" she asked. "What happened?" The man darted his panicked stare at her and then back to Traejan.

"They're captured!" he told them both, his wild eyes going back and forth, searching. "All of them! Can you help? I escaped when they were tying us! I was on my way to Goldensword for help. Please, my lord is there, and all his men. Please help us!"

Ryen, looming at first like the shadow of a tree, moved close and detached the man from the elf, trying to steady him. "Em, he needs some water," he commanded. The Roshan passed him her waterskin and Ryen gave it to the man, practically holding him up by the shoulder with one of his great hands. "Of course we will help, but you need to tell us what happened."

The man nodded quickly, took a long drink of water and then drew a deep breath, calming himself as much as he could. Traejan saw that, under the sweat and dirt and smears of blood, the man was well dressed, almost courtly. His hair was dark and disheveled but cut smart. He took another long drink and another deep breath and looked at them all again, his eyes were a muddy green in color but more composed than they were only seconds before.

"I, along with my lord and his escort, were two hours north o' the Dagger when we saw a group of men - of what we thought were men. They were very tall, even from a distance, and we thought they were Vikemen. My lord was anxious to meet them and get news of the north." He swallowed nervously under the scrutiny of Ryen's ice blue eyes, knowing by the man's seven-foot frame and ginger hair that he could be nothing but Vikeman.

"They were not Norsemen, though. Were they?" Ryen asked. The man shook his head.

"They were Crommags," he said, his voice a harsh whisper and his tone a curse.

"Crommags?" the Roshan asked. She shot Ryen a glance. "I

know the Norsemen aren't the most attractive creatures, but you could hardly confuse them with Crommags." The man shook his head again.

"They were like none we have ever seen, m' lady. They wore clothes, not skins. Their hair was cut. And they had weapons. Steel weapons."

The Roshan looked at Ryen with raised brows but he only shook his head. He had never heard the like. She looked back at the man as he took another drink of water. "What happened?" she asked.

"They jumped us as soon as we saw that we had been mistaken. They killed four of our men and took the other six, me included, captive. They tied me and Keric to a tree and tied my lord and the other three to another tree. Keric and I were able to work our bonds loose and get away, but they killed him as we escaped. We have to get back. We have to help them!"

"We will," Ryen assured him.

"Where are they?" the Roshan asked.

"In the Bridlewood - not far from where we met them. Across the valley where the ground goes wide and shallow into a rolling meadow before it rises up again and enters the wood."

"They will stay the night there," Ryen said quietly. "And torture their captives for sport." The man paled. He looked at the auburn-haired woman. She was looking into the distance, and far beyond.

"Crommags in the Midlon," she whispered. It took her only seconds to make her plans and decisions. Her eyes darted towards the sinking sun and then to Ryen. "I'll take him with me. Break camp and follow with Traejan. Keep to the low ground." Ryen nodded once and she turned away. "Coal!" she commanded as she snatched up her long sword and buckled it around her waist.

The giant horse materialized by her side and Ryen was throwing the stallion's saddle over its wide back the next instant.

The Roshan cinched the straps quickly around his middle as she looked over her shoulder at the man. "What is your name?" "I am Joshun," he said.

"I am Ember L'chiross," she said, straightening. "Do you know who I am?" He nodded wordlessly, his muddy green eyes even wider than before. "Good. Now let's go." She stuck a boot into the high stirrup and swung up onto Coal. Then she reached down and helped pull Joshun up behind her. She caught a glimpse of Traejan and jerked her head towards the Vikeman as she turned the horse and put her heels to his flanks.

The Night Stallion bore her and Joshun through the woods and down into the valley beyond like a fleeting shadow against the setting sun.

Traejan and Ryen reached the edge of the Bridlewood as the sun disappeared from the land, leaving an orange sky and pink light streaked with shadows. The woods ended at the edge of a hilly ridge that dropped softly into a grassy valley. The valley rose on the other side in the same gentle manner, its top lower than the edge of the forest in which they stood. The oak trees on the far hill were large, with branches spread so wide that they made a canopy over the short and flattened hill.

Traejan spotted Joshun immediately, huddled near the base of a tree only a few yards away, and he jerked his chin at him. Ryen followed the elf's movement and nodded, seeing the man. They both dismounted and led the horses quietly to where the man crouched in fear and desperation.

The elf did not spy Coal, but could feel him close by. Peg was too well trained to whicker for him. Ryen tethered his khusar to a branch and hunkered down next to Joshun. His eyes passed over the oaken woods on the opposite side. Where the Crommags were was obvious. They had already built a large fire at their camp and were not making any attempt at secrecy. What was going on there Ryen could not tell. It took his eyes only a second longer to find what he was looking for; a small, still shadow behind a grassy hillock almost level with the wood, just to the left of the campsite. Traejan tethered Peg with Ryen's mount and hunkered down beside him.

"Do you see her?" Ryen asked. Traejan nodded. "Can you see what they are doing in the camp?" Traejan nodded again.

"They are eating something foul, and drinking something fouler," he said, wrinkling his nose in distaste. "They have prisoners, gagged and bound to a tree. Four, all alive as far as I can tell."

Joshun shifted uncomfortably, moaning softly.

"Stay here," Ryen told the man. "Bring our horses. You'll know when." He rose and motioned for Traejan to follow. Traejan snatched his quiver from Peg's saddle and slung it over his shoulder, then grabbed his bow and followed Ryen in a low crouch.

They descended the slope of the hill by way of a shadowed gully in the hillside. They made their way across the darkening valley and crept up the far slope. They found the Roshan lying on her stomach, raised on her elbows, peering into the Crommag camp less than twenty yards away. The Roshan did not so much as glance at them when they reached her. Ryen got down on his belly and up on his elbows to one side of her and Traejan did the same on her other side.

Traejan had never been this close to a Crommag and stared at the group of them in amazement. He had been told they were large, which was misleading. They were *huge*. Each had to be at least eight feet tall, with rough, hairy skin. Their heads were small in proportion to their bodies, with thick sloping foreheads and close-set eyes. Their bottom lips were thick and protruded out, covering teeth that were all fangs.

He had been told they were the most primitive of the world's creatures – that they wore only animal skins and carried wooden clubs for weapons. These, however, wore rough spun shirts and trousers, carried iron knives and short swords, and were still the most primeval creatures Traejan had ever seen. They sat and squatted about their fire, eating haunches of barely cooked meat, drooling and laughing and talking in a guttural tongue that made Traejan's stomach turn.

The prisoners were tied to a huge oak on the west side of the Crommag's camp. They had been stripped of their boots and were bloodied from their capture. Some had been burned - for sport, Traejan assumed. They did not speak or move. Their eyes had the resigned patience of death. The elf looked at the Roshan. Her eyes went back and forth across the Crommag camp, shrewd and calculating.

"How many?" Ryen asked her, his voice a harsh whisper.

"At least ten," she whispered back. "Possibly more, but I doubt it. Crommags don't usually bother to post guards."

"They don't usually wear clothes and carry steel, either,"

Ryen remarked. "I don't like it."

The Roshan favored him with a grin. "When do you ever?"

Ryen grinned back. "Do you have a plan?"

"I'll circle around, and come in from the north side."

"Alone?" Traejan interrupted her, aghast. She looked at him as if she had not realized he was there.

"Of course."

"Of course?" Traejan was equal amounts horrified and bewildered.

One against ten? Ten that were giants next to her? They would cut her to ribbons.

"One of us should go with you, if not both," he argued.

The Roshan barked short silent, laughter. "Your hands are in no shape to hold a sword, and you are not ready in any case."

"I can take out at least half with my bow," he argued in soft tones. The Roshan simply shook her head.

"At this distance," she whispered, "no arrow would

penetrate their thick skin." She turned to Ryen who was watching their exchange with obvious amusement. Traejan did not give up.

"I can help," he insisted.

"Be still!" she ordered, her voice a hoarse whisper.

"I can..."

"You cannot! You may not!"

"But..."

"Be still!"

"But..."

The mistress of weapons turned on him, her eyes flashing. "If you engage in this fight in any way," she hissed, "I will send you home this night - gagged and bound across the saddle of your horse!"

Traejan sat back, eyes wide, and clamped his mouth shut. The Roshan turned to Ryen once again. "I'll free the men and get them headed in this direction but I'll need you to intercept them and lead them to safety." She pressed her lips together, thinking. "Back the way we came, and then along the woodline until you reach the stream that enters the forest. On the far side of the stream there is a journey rest, and the woods open up and you can see for miles in all directions." Ryen nodded quickly. He knew the spot. "Wait for me there," she told him. "I'll make sure nothing and no one follows."

Traejan made to speak again but a sharp look from the Roshan made him bite his tongue. She laid a hand on his arm and her eyes softened for the barest moment. He finally did go still, his entire being focused on where her hand touched his arm and her eyes on his own. Then she was gone into the deepening dark. Traejan let out a long, quavering breath and glared at Ryen.

"I can't believe you're letting her go in there alone!" he accused softly. Ryen's look of surprise was genuine, and followed by a curious smile.

"Have you ever seen her fight?" he whispered.

"Only with me," Traejan admitted. Ryen snorted softly and turned his attention back to the Crommag camp. He settled down to get comfortable, his expression eager as if awaiting a midsummer play. Traejan pressed his lips together so hard they all but disappeared. He warred internally with indecision for a second, then drew five arrows from his quiver and laid them on the ground in front of him. Ryen looked at him, bemused. Traejan ignored him.

It would be almost unbearable to live with the shame if she banished him, but he felt that if something happened to her, he could not live at all. He thought that realization would weaken him, but he found it only strengthened his resolve. He laid a hand on the fletching of his first arrow and waited. He did not have to wait long.

The shadows grew and bled until darkness stole over the land and the only eerie light was from the Crommag bonfire. The elf watched as a shadow dropped from the tree where the prisoners were tied, as fluid and silent as a drop of oil being spilled on the ground. The Roshan placed a dagger in the hand of one of the men and said two words Ryen could not hear, but Traejan could just make out.

Run south.

The Crommags froze when they saw her, in disbelief rather than fear, their hands clutching bones with bloody meat, drool dripping from their chins. Then one fell, then another. They dropped silently, and with a grace that belied their huge forms. One might have thought they had passed out from the foul grog they were drinking, save for the hilt of a dagger that protruded from the neck of the first and another from the skull of the second.

When the Crommags realized what had happened they roared as one and charged the Roshan, dropping bones and drawing swords and knives.

Another fell to a dagger; his last second spent crossing his close-set eyes as if trying to see what had lodged itself in the bridge of his large and broken nose. Traejan watched in horror as the rest descended on her like a swarm of giant flies. He never even had the chance to nock an arrow to his bowstring.

There was never the need.

Her sword was out now and it flashed, faster than even his eyes could follow. Like lightning it struck again and again, felling the monsters like trees in a cyclone.

"My Gods," Traejan whispered. Ryen only grunted in response.

Her sword caught the light of the Crommag's fire and danced and flashed like a demon unleashed. It moved with such speed that the elfin prince, even with eyes such as his, could hardly track it. *May the Gods be damned*, he thought. *And myself as much. She's fast! Too fast.* Then a thought so quick and fleeting touched his mind and flew off before he could even think about it. *She's not human.*

Traejan marveled at the fluid ease with which she moved. There was no stabbing, or hacking – though the giant foes must have outmatched her as much in strength as they did in size. Speed and skill were the tools she used as she cut through them and her sword seemed to be more a deadly flash of light than a weapon of forged metal.

He watched his Roshan deal agonizing death and spill more blood than he could have imagined coming from any creature, all in a matter of seconds. Part of him clenched with terror at seeing the woman he loved so viciously brutal, but the rest of him was filled with a desire for her that he had never thought possible.

The man with the Roshan's dagger was sawing furiously at his bonds but was getting nowhere fast. The red-haired warrior cursed and, without pausing for even a moment in her attack, turned and severed the ropes that held the prisoners to the tree with a single upswing of her sword. The downswing spun her back around and came down between the shoulder and neck of the nearest Crommag, cleaving him nearly in two.

"South!" she shouted.

The men struggled out of the severed ropes and began running like hell down the slope towards Ryen and Traejan.

"Time to go!" Ryen told Traejan, rising up to meet the men in their path. "This way!" He shouted at the on-comers as they bore down upon them. They saw him and followed as he scuttled down the slope and began cutting across the valley. Traejan swept up his arrows in one hand and looked back at the campsite in time to see the weapon master cut the throats of the last two Crommags in a single swing.

Even across the distance and through the dark, her eyes met his and for a moment he was so consumed with lust and the power of the moment that he could not move. She stood facing him with her blood-covered sword, shoulders drawn back, her lips parted and chest heaving. The fire seemed everywhere - lighting her hair and her blade. Her eyes sparked with the flames and were full of lust as well, but it was bloodlust, and had nothing to do with the elfin prince. The killing was upon her and coursed through her veins like a tempest. Traejan half expected her to lick the blood off her sword.

He watched frozen, afraid to break whatever cord of electricity that held them bound. He felt in that moment that there was nothing else in the world but the two of them, and the distance between them shortened with each heartbeat, drawing them closer and closer. Then she turned away, to survey the scene or check the dead - he did not know which. All he knew was that it broke his paralysis and the rest of the world came flooding back to him. He fled, chasing after Ryen and the freed men.

Up the slope they ran, and along the woodline until it broke apart, emptying upon a ridge that exposed the next valley. The Norseman stopped to catch his breath, the others following suit. Once the Vikeman had regained his wind, he signaled for the others to follow him over the ridgeline and into a large clearing.

The ground in the clearing was well worn. There were cut logs that had been used as seats around a cold ring of ashes that showed a much-used campfire. Traejan came upon the group of men as did Joshun, who clasped each man in turn. Their leader approached Ryen.

He was tall and very young, with green-blue eyes and hair as white as foam. A wound from the melee at his capture had opened up the side of a cheek that he had hardly begun to shave. It was clotting poorly but did not seem to bother him in the slightest.

"I am Tristan Greenwater," he told Ryen, extending his hand. "We are in your debt."

Ryen shook his head even as he shook the young man's hand. "Not mine."

The young man paused, thoughtful. "Was that who I think it was?" he asked after a moment.

"I don't know," Ryen replied, his amusement obvious. "Who do you think it was?"

Tristan's first response was merely a grunt. "Is it safe for a fire?" he asked Ryen.

"I think so," Ryen said.

Tristan instructed his men to start a fire and fetch water while Ryen and Traejan retrieved their horses from Joshun. The man looked at them with such gratitude that they thought he might burst into tears.

"Thank you," he croaked, clasping their hands in his own.

"Not us," Ryen reminded, taking the reins of his horse and leading him to the stream past the trees on the far side of the clearing. Traejan retrieved Peg as well and followed him.

The men in Tristan's party were cleaning and dressing their wounds, exchanging whispers when the Roshan came upon them, her body bloodied and her hair like fire, reining in the

Night Stallion that danced to and fro under her slight form.

His massive hooves spewed up the earth in great chunks and foam dripped from his fangs. She slid off the beast and at once they became silent and bowed to her. She bowed in return and the young lord came up to her, lowering himself to one knee.

"I am Tristan Greenwater," he said. "And I am forever in your debt. My men as well."

The Roshan only bowed again in humble accord. Traejan felt Ryen grasp his elbow.

"This is not for us," the Norseman whispered as he threw the khusar's reins around the horn of Peg's saddle and led the elf away.

27. FIRESIDE TALKS

The Norseman and the elfin prince walked until the party of men and the woman who had saved them was well behind them in the wood. The last thing Traejan glimpsed was all of the men going down on one knee in front of the Roshan. The fire that they had made threw tongues of violent light and shadow upon the entire assembly.

"What are they doing?" he asked Ryen.

"They owe her their lives," he said simply.

"What does that mean?"

Ryen stopped at a cluster of boulders and sat down on one, motioning for Traejan to do the same. "Does that not translate into Elfin?" he asked.

"What does that mean, exactly?"

Ryen shrugged. "Like I said, they owe her their lives – so, they are pledging their lives to her. If she ever has the need, she may call upon them and they will fight for her – to the death if need be." Ryen laughed at the look of wonder on the prince's face. "It is not the first time this has happened, nor will it be the last. She has saved as many men as she has killed. Well, maybe not that many." He laughed again and Traejan found himself smiling and shaking his head at the Vikeman's humor.

"Does this happen often?" Traejan asked.

Ryen shrugged. "Often enough to make her a bit of a legend."

Traejan sat on his boulder at the edge of the woodline,

looking across the valley and the star strewn sky that covered it. They waited in silence for almost half an hour before the elf looked up at the Norseman.

"The men are leaving," he stated. Moments later, the Roshan came upon them. Traejan stood up immediately while Ryen merely favored her with a grin from his seat on his own rock.

Traejan tried not to let his jaw drop when he saw her. Victor she might have been in battle, but the woman that stood before them looked so worn, and small. She was obviously near crippled by exhaustion and swayed as if moved by a strong wind. It seemed only pride kept her on her feet. Traejan wondered how often her pride had done that very thing before. He shot a glance at Ryen, but he only looked at the Roshan in a tenderhearted sort of way.

"Tristan and his men have gone back to recover whatever goods that were theirs," she informed them. "If there are any left at the Crommag camp that are still serviceable. I gave them what supplies I could."

"I will resupply you with anything you might need," Ryen assured her but she waved his words away. There was nothing she could not do without or acquire on her own.

"We should probably stay here for the night," she said, motioning behind her towards the glow of the fire in the woods. Ryen stood up.

"That sounds fine," he said softly. "Stop at the stream and clean up first," he instructed. "We'll get the horses settled and the beds made."

The Roshan looked down her arms and at the blood that was caking there. It started at her fingernail beds and coated her arms up to the shoulders. She seemed surprised to see it, and disappointed that she would have to do something about it, but she nodded her head without argument. She turned and headed for the stream while Traejan and Ryen headed for the fire to set up camp.

They led their horses to where Coal waited and tethered them together. Tristan's men had left extra wood by the fire and Ryen fed it a few thick branches. Traejan unrolled his teacher's bedroll next to the fire and carefully laid his own on the other side. He ignored Ryen's chuckle. When the Roshan entered the clearing they both stood.

Her face and arms were red from being scrubbed in the cold water and her hair was wet as well. She wore only her undershirt, breeches, and boots. She had taken off her jerkin and both washed and wrung it dry. She threw it over the branch of a tree to finish drying and shivered though the summer night was warm. Ryen wrapped his cloak around her.

"Do you want something to eat?" he asked.

She shook her head. "Sleep." Ryen nodded and guided her over to her bedroll. She stopped and looked up at him. "Will you watch?"

"Of course," he said.

"All night?"

"All night." His voice was so quiet that even Traejan could scarcely hear him. The Roshan's shoulders slumped with weariness and relief. The moon had not yet risen but her day, like herself, was spent. She crawled into her bedroll and was asleep a second later. Ryen made sure his cloak was secure around her and tucked it under her chin before he stood and looked at the elf, his blue eyes serious.

"You and I should talk," he told him. Then he sighed and a bit of light danced back into his glacier eyes. "But first, we should eat."

So much had happened so fast that Traejan could hardly believe that the moon was just rising. It felt as if days had gone by, rather than a few hours.

Ryen produced some dried meat and bread from his pack while Traejan cooked two potatoes in the fire. Ryen offered him some wine but the prince waved him off after refilling his water skin at the stream. They ate in silence for a while before Traejan, being younger in everything but years, had to break it.

"What did she mean, when she asked you if you would watch?" he asked.

Ryen poked at the fire with a forked branch. "She doesn't sleep well, if at all, when she is out in the open. When she is away from the safety of her haus, I think she sleeps with one eye open the entire time." Traejan thought of the previous night and how her eyes had flicked open just when he was sure she was asleep. He knew exactly what he meant. "That is of course, unless she is with someone she can trust to keep watch over her the entire time."

"So you will stand guard for her the entire night?"

"Of course," Ryen said. "I love her too, you know."

Traejan chewed a piece of bread, thinking. He knew it would be fruitless to deny his love for her or argue with Ryen. Somehow knowing that Ryen loved her too was oddly comforting.

"How old is she?" he asked.

"I don't know," Ryen answered. "When we met, I was a much younger man. It must have been, oh I don't know, fifteen years ago. That's a much longer time for me than it is to you I'm sure."

Traejan nodded. "I remember fifteen years ago like it was yesterday. I had just begun to look for a weapons master to teach me how to fight. I wore my guardsman out with all those years of searching."

Ryen smile was wry.

"For me, fifteen years is almost half of my life. I was barely a man when I met Ember, and now I have reached the middle of my years. My life is half done."

Traejan looked at him, touched with alarm. The short frailty of the human life struck him for the first time. He knew that the lifespan of a human was but a flash in the life of an elf, but he had never been witness to it before. He had never lived close to or befriended a human. Never watched as they aged before his eyes and withered and fell like a leaf in autumn, all in what would be just one more season of his own life.

Ryen laughed gently, reading his thoughts by the expression on his face. "It's not all bad," he told him. "We actually manage to get a lot done, and our lives are much more full than you think." Traejan nodded but the whole idea put a cloud upon him until he thought about what Ryen had said.

"You have changed since you first met her?" he asked.

Ryen nodded. "Very much."

"And her?"

This time Ryen shook his head. "Not very much at all."

Traejan sat back, contemplating what it all could mean. He knew that he looked practically identical to what he was only fifteen years ago. The Roshan as well had hardly changed, yet Ryen's life was half done. He recalled the fleeting thought he had at the Crommag camp. *She's not human*, he had thought. It seemed that the arrow wasn't far from the mark on that one.

What it all meant, he had no idea. But he did mean to find out as much as he could. He had learned more about the Roshan in one hour from Ryen, than he had learned living with her for over three months. His next question he did not want to ask in her presence, even though she was obviously dead to the world, but felt that he must. He looked over at her, just to make sure. Her face was unlined and bereft of worry as she slept deeply.

"Is she human?" he asked quietly.

Ryen smiled. "I have no idea." He watched Traejan despair over the question that must come next. He spared him the hurt. "No. She is most likely not human, even though she thinks she is."

Traejan sat back again. He would think the shock of the implications would leave him speechless but instead it made his head swim with more questions. He hated to ask, it seemed unseemly to ask, *especially with her laying right there on the other side of the fire*, but he couldn't help himself.

"What do you think she...do you think she is...could she be some sort of elf?"

"I don't know," Ryen admitted. "She does not look much like you, but I could see similarities if I was really looking for them. But I could do the same comparing her to a human. And I have never seen a Sylvan elf, or any other kind of elf for that matter, with hair like hers."

"You've got that right," Traejan whispered. He watched his teacher sleep, her breathing deep and even. Even huddled in her bedroll her could see the light of the fire playing with her hair, playing with his heart.

"Even the women in my land," the Vikeman continued, "have gingerish hair, but it is not that deep red. I have traveled this world, and a few others, and I have never seen or met anyone like her, and I don't just mean someone with her coloring." This time Traejan *was* speechless. Ryen never seemed to be bothered with the same affliction. "That she is the greatest warrior to walk this world is beyond any doubt," he continued. "I have seen her outmatched in size, strength, and numbers – and not once have I ever seen her hesitate or turn from her course once she started. There is nothing that she fears, nothing that I know. I believe it is because her heart has no walls. That is why it does not hold fear. I am afraid however, that in the same manner, it does not hold love either."

Traejan sat quietly, poking at the fire with the toe of his boot as he absorbed the Norseman's words, thoughtful.

"What makes you think so?"

"I've known her a long time, and I've never seen her have more than a passing interest in any man. Or worse, the ones who love her she hates the most. I think she sees love as a weakness."

Your greatest weakness can be your most powerful weapon, Traejan recalled her saying just a few nights ago, but he kept that to himself.

"She doesn't hate *you*," he remarked. Ryen laughed.

"No," he agreed. "And I think she does love me, in her own way. And Aiden as well. Aiden loves her passionately, also in his own way. Maybe she's a Sprite?" Ryen laughed at the absurdity of it.

"Aiden is a Sprite?"

"Worse, he's a Wildboy. Worse than that, he's their leader. All of the Wildboys love Em, but with Aiden it is something more. I think he would leave his calling to be with her, if she would have him."

"Why aren't you with her?"

The Vikeman frowned at the flames for a moment before he answered. "I think we would lose what we have now if we tried to make it something more, something that it could not be." His frown melted into a smile, either at a memory or a fleeting hope for the future.

The elf took a deep breath and plunged ahead. "Does it hurt you, to love her and not be with her?"

Ryen gave a silent chuckle. "Well, lucky for me, I love other women as well. Chastity was never my strongpoint." He gave Traejan a conspiratorial wink. Traejan shook his head and prodded the edge of the fire some more with his boot before he looked back at the Vikeman.

"Why are you telling me all this?"

"Because I like you. You are nothing like your brother."

Traejan jerked as if he had been poked. "You know my brother?"

"Not well, but I have met him."

"When?"

"Not that long ago, in your city. He is not a bad guy. But

very different from you. So stoic! I like you much better."

Traejan smiled. "Thanks."

"No need. But you do need to get some rest. You should turn in." Ryen stood and stretched, his knees and back popping like the branches on the fire. He put his hands to the small of his back and groaned softly.

"I'll take the first watch, if you'd like," Traejan offered. He relished the idea of being able to watch the Roshan as she slept, lost in her dreams while he protected her from the world.

"That's okay. If she woke up and found me asleep she would never trust me again. And I would probably wake up wearing my balls for earbobs." He grimaced and laughed softly at the prospect. "But if you would guard the fortress while I relieve myself, I will be greatly in your debt."

Traejan dipped his head in mock majesty. "At your service." Ryen bowed and strode into the forest. Traejan listened for a few moments and then crept up to where the Roshan lay sleeping. Cautiously, he stretched out a hand and gently moved the cloak from her face. Sleep stole most of the lines from her countenance and she almost looked like a child. Traejan sighed.

Some of her hair had come unbound and wisps of it lay against her cheek. He fought the desire to touch it, although he burned inside to do so. While he knew he could watch her all night, he would not do so without her consent and did not like to feel as if he were spying. He already felt as if he was betraying the trust she had put in Ryen.

He backed away quietly and banked the fire. When Ryen returned, the prince crawled into his bedroll. He thought he would be up half the night thinking about all he had learned, but he was wrong. He was asleep in an instant.

When Traejan awoke the next morning, it was to the smell of cooking food. Ryen had a pot of coffee over the fire as well. The Roshan was sitting in her bedroll, rubbing the sleep out of her gimlet eyes.

"I thought you two were going to sleep the whole day away," Ryen remarked to them. He poured coffee into a metal mug and offered it to Traejan who shook his head. He had coffee only once and, although he enjoyed the smell very much, the taste was too bitter and strong.

"I'll take that," Ember said.

"I didn't think you liked coffee without milk and sugar," Ryen mused aloud, passing her the mug.

"I don't, but today I need it." She looked about but the trees hid too much of the sun to tell much more than it was past dawn. "Is it really so late?"

"Not very late. Not even mid-morn."

"Good, we have much to discuss. And do." She sipped her coffee and winced at the taste.

Ryen smiled and handed her a plate. "What did the Prince of Tides have to say?" He handed Traejan a plate of cooked potatoes and sausage.

"You know him?" the Roshan asked, arching a brow.

The Vikeman shrugged. "I know *of* everyone," he gave by way of an explanation. "Almost."

The Roshan grinned. "He said that the Crommag party I dispatched was smaller than the one that originally attacked them," she said before forking a huge bite of potatoes into her mouth. She had to breathe around them while they cooled, and chew and swallow before she could continue. "The monsters had split into three groups. The one at the encampment was intent on returning home, to the mountains in the north. One party of ten headed east for Kenwood and a larger party headed north for Edin Valley."

"He could understand their speech?" Traejan asked.

The Roshan nodded slowly. "Not completely, but enough. They used a form of Northlon common, combined with their own guttural sounds and gestures. It was not just what he picked up by chance," she said, pausing to measure their eyes, "the Crommags were questioning them."

Ryen sat back hard, his blue eyes lost in the forest as if he searched the trees for a response - but it was the Roshan that he asked aloud, even though he felt he already knew the answer. "What did they want to know?"

The red-haired warrior, though already recovered from her exertions of the night before, sighed heavily. "Numbers."

It was one word, and harmless on its own. It could mean anything or nothing - but to those wise enough to know, it meant everything. The Vikeman closed his blue eyes but held his form steady and did not sag. The Roshan respected that, and stuffed half a potato into her mouth.

Traejan swallowed his own bite, albeit much smaller, his brown eyes flicking from the Roshan to the Norseman and then back again. "What does this mean?" he asked.

"It means that *they mean* war," the Roshan said, simple as day. Her gem-like eyes bore into the elf, and he felt that he could read the answers there – simple as day.

Asking how many men that were in each village was the question of how many men the Crommags must face and kill. How many were farmers, how many were armed? How many sheep or fish to be found would tell how much they could eat without hunting.

"War," Traejan whispered. "Why?"

"Crommags use to always stay in the Mountains of Ice," Ryen mused aloud, "and always kept to themselves. Primitive creatures that wore skins and carried clubs. We thought them hardly more than animals. Now they are wearing clothes and carrying steel. Both are very crude, but they are clothes and steel all the same. What is going on?"

The Roshan chewed thoughtfully. "There is a word for it," she said after a while. "It's called evolution."

"No," the elf said, shaking his thatch of dark blonde curls. "Why would they want war? There is so much land, so much *good* land. They could settle almost anywhere, peacefully."

The Vikeman looked at the young prince with a touch of fondness. "Because they don't just want land," Ryen told him. "They want *our* land. They want *your* land. They want us – to rule over us. There is nothing peaceful about what they want. These groups are not raiding parties, not this far south. These are scouting parties."

"We need to stop them," the Roshan said. She looked at Ryen quizzically, as if there could be no other answer and she dared him to find one.

"All of them?" Ryen asked. "The whole Crommag race? That's quite the undertaking, even for you."

The Roshan frowned at him. "The scouting parties. We need to stop the scouting parties. We have the advantage of being on horse while they are afoot. You can ride east and warn the men of Kenwood and we can ride for Edin Valley."

Ryen nodded. "They will most likely cut through the forest. It is flat and will afford them cover. I can skirt the woods by the east road and still get there a day ahead of them."

"We can follow the short stream north to the Exus Ravine," she mused aloud. Ryen looked at her sternly.

"Do you mean to warn the people of Edin, or do you mean to ambush the Crommags yourself?"

The Roshan gave him a crooked smile. "We shall see," she told him. Ryen sighed. She looked at Traejan. "Are you done with your breakfast?" she asked.

The elf, who had lost his appetite, nodded. She relieved him of his plate and finished it for him. When her hunger was sated she stood and rolled her head on her shoulders, stretching her neck.

"Well," she said, "let's not waste time." She returned to Ryen his cloak and shook out her bedroll.

Traejan saddled their horses and tried to not watch her as she brushed out her still-damp hair. He noticed Ryen watching him with a wry smile and gave him an exasperated look. He turned sharply to see the Roshan twisting her hair to the back of her head, like she did when he first met her. This time, instead of a dagger, she inserted a sharp metal stick, like a knitting needle. Traejan had no idea how it held her hair in place, but it did.

Ryen laid a hand on his shoulder. The elf turned and grasped the other hand of the Vikeman that was already extended to him. "I like you, Traejan," the Norseman said earnestly. "I wish you the best, and will pray to the Gods for you." He leaned close. "Especially to Eros," he whispered.

The elf blushed fiercely, knowing all too well the Norse God that Ryen meant. Nonetheless he pulled the man's tall frame even closer.

"And I shall pray for your chastity," he whispered back.

Ryen roared laughter. "If you love me do not curse me!" he exclaimed and then put his hand on the prince's shoulder and grasped it, the elfin sign of comradeship. Traejan did the same, reaching up to do so.

"May I find you again," Ryen told him. "And may I find you well." The elf nodded in accord and then they both turned to their mounts.

Traejan noticed that he already felt a great bond with Ryen, as if he were a brother. Ryen had probably befriended him more in the last day than his older brother had in the last ten years. Xander was more like a second father to him than a brother. And Zeph was, well, Zeph. Ryen was more like a conspirator, or a brother in arms. Like Dell.

Dell.

Traejan realized with surprise that once again he had not thought of his Praetorian in weeks. He wondered suddenly where he might be and what he might doing. He wondered when he would see him next, and if he would be ready to return with him.

He swung himself into his saddle and turned Peg to face the Roshan, a cold feeling of dread stealing over his heart as he realized he would have to leave her someday.

Someday soon, he thought, feeling a bit of panic grip him by the throat. *Much too soon. It is already past midsummer. How much time is left? A month? A few weeks?*

Caught in a sudden rush of desperation, his heart started racing and he looked at his teacher, wearing her brace of daggers over her black jerkin, the sleeves of her dark undershirt rolled up to the elbows. It was already too warm for a cloak. She was mounted and watching the men with a look of impatience.

"Are you girls ready?" she asked. Ryen laughed again and forced his reticent khusar up next to Coal.

"How about a kiss for luck?" he suggested.

"How about I put a dagger in your ribs and save a Crommag the trouble?"

Ryen only smiled and grasped the front of her jerkin and pulled her close into a quick kiss. The Roshan pushed him away, laughing. Ryen turned his khusar and gave Traejan a wink. The elf narrowed his eyes at him, envious but unable to keep a smile from his own lips.

"I will come see you at harvest, if I do not see you sooner," Ryen told her, his voice oddly somber, his normally merry blue eyes serious. "Kings expect answers."

The Roshan gave him a curt nod to show she understood. "Stay safe," she instructed.

The Vikeman gave her the same nod as he wheeled his horse and galloped away to the east. The Roshan turned to the elf and seemed as if she was unsure of what to say. She looked at his unlined face, bright and still in the morning light. He wore the same look he always had, like calm water reflecting ancient mountains. She had always thought it too old and serious for a face so young, but now thought she might see something different. Or maybe a different meaning in the same look. She couldn't help but smile.

"Are you ready?" she asked.

Traejan nodded as he urged Peg forward to follow the Roshan. Her smile widened into a grin as she turned Coal north and put her heels hard to his flanks.

28. THE WEAPON FOUND

The elfin prince and the master of weapons rode hard, cutting straight north through open grassland that had gone from spring green to summer gold. Peg and Coal ran smoothly, stretching their legs and eating up the miles while the morning warmed, their riders crouched low over their necks.

The Roshan called a halt before the wear on the horses could become too hard. She dismounted and Traejan followed suit. They watered the horses in a small gully that was running despite the summer heat, then found a grove of fruit trees and walked them in the shade for near half an hour to give them a short respite. Then they mounted and kept them at an easy trot, this time angling east.

Traejan thought the Roshan uncharacteristically quiet; whether she was thinking of the night before or the day ahead the elfin prince could not even venture a guess. He was too preoccupied with what Ryen had said about her.

The Roshan, oddly enough, was thinking about Traejan, and what Ryen had said about the elfin prince. Inwardly she cursed the Norseman for putting such thoughts in her head. The training had been going so well, and she did feel very much at ease around the young elf. He was so open, so honest, and had a cautious sense of humor that had begun to endear him to her. He was an excellent student. Dedicated to learning and worked so hard to excel at everything she taught him.

Could he really have feelings for me? she wondered.

The whole idea seemed both preposterous and impossible.

She gave a sidelong glance at him astride his subtle palfrey. His face was as serious and somber as ever, though he kept his chin up, his eyes moving. She considered the past months they had spent together – the training, the talks, they way he would blush. She had always believed it was due to his intense desire to succeed. Even now she believed the same, though recalling the way he would look at her sometimes made her realize that it was also something more.

Is it important?

No. Not if it doesn't interfere with his training.

Most of those that she trained had a deep respect for her before they were done. There were a few who felt more, and even a few she had actually developed a personal relationship with. But those were very few, very fleeting, and very far between.

What *was* important, the Roshan knew, was if she had feelings for him. It would be more than important, it could be dangerous. For the both of them.

She scanned the landscape. From where she sat astride the Night Stallion she could see the Stonefield Road, less than a mile distant. They had a bit of time. Not much.

The Roshan glanced at the elf by her side once again and looked at him for the first time as something other than a student. She noticed how smooth his skin was, and pale, even after spending a season and a half outside every day. The color was not uncomely; it seemed the color and texture of polished alabaster. His hair had changed. It was longer, and thicker, and here the effects of the sun were apparent.

And he is tall, she noted. He was almost the same height as her in the saddle, though Coal's back was a good foot higher than Peg's. *And not just for an elf.*

The Roshan realized with a start that this was not the first time she had noticed these things. The first time she had met him she was aware of those traits, but had pushed them from her mind.

It was a habit she had acquired that had kept her alive these many years. Her attention was for the present and the very near future - what the current situation demanded. She would often catalogue things in her mind and store them away for future use. People, towns, weapons and the like. If she had time later, or the need, she would pull these memories back out and turn them about in her mind, inspecting them like a jeweler turning over a gem he thought lost or forgotten.

It was his height, she remembered. *That was the first thing I noticed about him. How tall he was. It made me feel something. Like I wanted to lean towards him, lean on him even.*

The Roshan's eyes widened at the memory. Her face turned to Traejan, seemingly lost in his own thoughts. She gave her head a shake, her eyes back on the horizon, and held up the memory so that it caught more light.

I noticed he was broad shouldered but light of frame. I think I was surprised to find that I liked his hair. I noticed his features and found they had a fine quality. His cheekbones, his eyes, the line of his jaw.

The Roshan mulled these memories over in a state near disbelief.

How could I notice such things and then push them from my mind?

Because it wasn't important.

Is it now?

Do I have feelings for him?

It seemed impossible.

There was more, Ember thought. *Something I didn't even think about then. The way I felt, that first meeting, when he caught me. My heart beat so fast! At the time I dismissed it. I thought I was merely impressed by his speed. Was it something else? Did something stir inside me? How could I know? I pushed it away before I could even realize what it was. But I felt it again yesterday when we were alone in the glen, just before Ryen came.*

The way he touched me, the way he slipped his arm around me and put his lips to my ear, I felt it again.

The Roshan repressed the shiver that caressed her spine.

Bah! Ryen is full of shit, as always. He just said it to fuck with me. The whole idea is absurd, just like I told him yesterday. Traejan is an elf, and a prince as well. I'm a human mercenary, and worse. The mere notion is outrageous.

The Roshan fixed her eyes on the road as they approached it, searching its length from where it left the Stone Hills in the west and disappeared as it wound northward between the knolls in the east. There was not a soul in sight, not a mote of dust over the road.

What Ryen had mentioned about taking her meals with the elf was what bothered her the most. She was not always training someone, so there was no real routine for mealtimes. But, in truth, she rarely ate with her pupils. Mostly because she rarely ate meals. If there were guests at the haus it was more normal for her to retire to her room after training. Gatha would bring her a bottle of wine and a few slices of cheese.

Ryen had asked if she had eaten any meals with the young prince. The answer was not only yes, but every time. But the real question, she supposed, was why. She knew she liked talking to him, and she rarely found people she enjoyed talking to. She suddenly recalled the sculptor she had once met, and the gunslinger.

Is that it? she asked herself. Is that all?

I liked looking at him, she decided, and then felt something in her heart shift weight. *I always liked the way he looked at me.*

Shit.

Damn that Ryen!

The Roshan jerked the reins in her fist, pulling Coal up short. The beast was slightly put out at the rough handling, yet even he could tell it was a time for silence and shook his mane defiantly. Peg halted obediently for Traejan, the tall grass rising about her legs in waves of gold. Summer sun baked the air around them, still and silent.

One glance at the road told the Roshan what she wanted to know. They had found the Crommags trail. They had come the same way as the woman and the elf, though farther to the west. When the brutes had reached the Stonefield road, whose dirt byway wound its way alternately north and east through the valley towns like a dusty river, they had gone straight up it.

The Roshan dismounted and Traejan did the same, holding Peg's reins with a gentle hand. He turned to the Roshan, his chin up and his unlined face expressionless. But his eyes held everything, and hid nothing. His gaze met hers and in that instant she knew without a doubt that everything Ryen had said was true. He loved her.

The Roshan experienced a moment of consternation that passed through her like a ripple in a pond. What it meant and how things would play out from here on she had no idea, but she knew it would never be the same. She pushed her worries to a corner of her mind and focused on what lay at her feet.

She squinted at Traejan in the bright light. "What do you see?" she asked.

"Tracks. Crommag tracks." *No shit.*

The Roshan pressed her lips together to hold in an acid remark. "Close your eyes and tell me what you see."

Traejan closed his eyes. He saw the Roshan with her hair down, and he saw himself reaching a hand out to touch her face. He decided he would rather bear her wrath than tell her that. He opened his eyes.

"Nothing," he lied.

The Roshan reined in her impatience. "Be still," she said softly. "Remember what I told you about the skills you already possess. Remember who you are and what you are. Now look down the road and tell me what you see."

Traejan took a deep breath and looked down the road, relaxing. His eyes became slightly unfocused. Immediately he knew what she meant.

"There are sixteen," he told her. "All armed and heading for Edin, not quite one mile ahead. They are taking the road. I think they mean to attack the town." He stayed still for a moment, as if caught in a trance, then blinked in surprise like a man awoken suddenly from his sleep. He looked at the Roshan, surprised. "I've never tried to see so far," he admitted. "Or for such a purpose."

The Roshan stared at him, astonished at seeing him use his elfin sight – it was so precise. It left her a touch unsettled. "Can you read my thoughts?" she asked.

"No. Will you share them with me?"

"Yes," she said with a crooked smile. "We can head them off."

Traejan found it impossible not to return that smile. "You think so?"

"I know so. The Crommags took the road, which will take them north for nearly two miles before bending to the east towards Edin. If we ride, and head directly northeast, I know the exact place where we can intercept them, if that's what we choose to do. Or we can ride for town and warn the people."

Traejan watched her and knew that intercepting the Crommags was what she wanted. She looked down the road as the elf had done, but all she saw was an empty dirt lane until it disappeared where it dipped down in the north, a good half mile away. She had to rely on true memory as she gauged distance and time.

"If they are a mile ahead," she deliberated softly, "they will hit Timmer's Box in about an hour and a half. We can make it there in an hour."

Traejan's smile widened as he watched her features harden before she turned and put a black boot in a stirrup. She swung up and into her saddle with an easy grace and the young elf did the same. She looked at the elf, searching his face.

"What are we waiting for?" he asked.

The Roshan grinned and put her heels to Coal. The great beast gave a snort and started off at an easy trot, Peg following quickly until she was by his side, picking her way along. They rode directly northeast, the land gradually sloping upwards. The road fell away to their left and then disappeared altogether. The rise was gentle but the ground was rocky so they kept the horses at an easy pace.

Midday passed and with it the worst of the heat, leaving them with a warm afternoon and a bright blue sky. Spring had brought an abundance of wildflowers to the hills and they had grown tall under the summer sun. Blooms of orange, pink, and yellow nodded at them from tall stalks that sprouted up from between the multitude of rocks that gave Stonefield its name.

Within an hour they reached the place the Roshan was looking for. The land had sloped up and ended in a ridge that ran from east to west. The pair dismounted and crept to the edge. Thirty feet down was the Stonefield Road leading to Edin. On their left the road appeared a quarter mile down at a curve that swung the road from north to east. To their right it disappeared into a small wood with the town just beyond.

The fields on the far side of the road had long been cleared of stones, plowed and planted. Acres of summer wheat undulated softly like an ocean of gold, spotted here and there with huge, spreading oak trees.

The cliff that they were atop was not sheer, but almost. It did, however, have large boulders jutting out from the sides that would provide an easy way down. The Roshan saw two that were flat and wide, like stepping-stones for a giant.

Or landing pads for a killer, she thought, smiling.

Traejan watched her survey the road. "What do you think?" he asked.

"Well, they haven't been here yet, but they will be soon enough."

"Are we going to go to Edin or are we going to take them here?" he asked, though he already knew the answer. The Roshan looked at him in surprise, her smile widening to a grin.

"We?"

"I'm ready," Traejan told her, his voice firm.

Something tugged at her heart at his insistence and she almost laughed even though she cursed herself inwardly.

Damn that Ryen!

The Roshan bit the corner of her lip and her gimlet eyes went to the left where the dusty ribbon of road appeared from around the bend, considering possible outcomes. She thought it too soon, but maybe not for him. After all, his training was damn near complete. He wasn't great with the sword, but passable. Still, that did not make him ready to face over a dozen bloodthirsty monsters that were more than twice his size.

"How are your hands?" she asked.

Traejan held them up for her to see. He had removed the bandages that morning to see the wonders of Gatha's ointment. The pads of flesh where his fingers met his palm were pink but otherwise healed. A single scab remained on his left hand, under his pinky. It was inconsequential as far as he was concerned but the Roshan still looked doubtful.

A quarter mile to the west rose a dusty murmur that grew into a soft clamor. Ten seconds ticked by as she weighed the possibilities and consequences and then the Crommags were coming into view around the bend in the road. Huge and grotesque, the smallest was almost eight feet tall and at least five hundred pounds.

Traejan could see her hesitation. "We can take them!" he whispered hoarsely. The Roshan let out a deep breath in a rush.

What's the worst that could happen? she thought. *If he's freezes I can push him against the cliff and both defend and attack from there, killing them all myself if I have to. It wouldn't be the first time.*

She raised her head a bit, appraising the band of beasts with a look of distaste. They did indeed wear clothes, something she had hardly noticed during her raid on the camp of their fellows, but they were crudely made and ill fitting. She felt Traejan lay a hand on her arm and smiled at his touch.

"We can take them!" he repeated.

The Roshan looked at him. He trembled with excitement, taut as a bowstring. His eyes were a blazing blue and she wondered if he knew it. She gave a quick nod and held up a hand telling him to wait. She motioned towards the two stones she intended to use for her descent. He nodded to show he understood, although he knew he could make the drop without the use of them. First fight or last, he would follow her lead.

The horses waited tensely behind the pair crouched upon the cliff, still and silent.

The Crommags came right down the road, not making any attempt to hide their approach. They walked in twos and threes, as disordered, disorganized, and disheveled as a gang of Ogres.

That's what they are, Traejan thought. *A bunch of Ogres.* He had never seen an Ogre but he couldn't imagine they looked any better than the creatures that were slowly passing beneath him. They were so near, he could see them much better than he did the night before. They were even uglier up close.

Both muscular and fat, their hairy bodies gave off a stench that made his stomach clench. Their eyes were dark and mean, topped by a thick rope of muscle that ran across each brow. Their heads were slightly pointed and covered with hair that sprouted like eyes from a potato. They grunted and growled at each other and occasionally one would honk laughter that sounded like an animal dying in pain.

Nearly the whole troop had passed beneath them. Traejan looked at the Roshan, making sure she hadn't changed her mind. She looked into his eyes, feeling his excitement, and smiled. She gave one curt nod that said it all.

Let's go.

Traejan, his heart thumping like mad in his chest, smiled back.

They dropped from the ridge as one, silent as shadows and quick as the death they brought with them.

The two Crommags bringing up the rear were the first two to go – the Roshan dispatched them so quietly that the next two dropped before the monsters even knew they were under attack. She edged close to Traejan so they were shoulder to shoulder and she could maneuver them easily into fighting back to back, but kept herself at an angle where she could watch him. Her plan was to let him do as much of the fighting as possible so she could judge his ability with the sword.

The plan went to hell in a heartbeat.

The remaining Crommags turned as one, the realization of attack like a splash of acid. They were huge, but not stupid and certainly not slow. The first one was upon Traejan instantly, roaring through jagged teeth and bearing down on him with brute strength. He disarmed the elf with his first blow, sending his sword flying.

The Roshan cursed but Traejan never hesitated. He dropped to the right, ducking the second swing of the monster's sword. He dipped down, rolling over one of the bodies of the already slain Crommags, pulling a pair of hunting knives from the giant's belt as he went. He was up again in less than a breath, and never fell again.

The Roshan held her own breath as she watched him. A Crommag closed in and she killed it effortlessly with her sword, barely giving it a glance. Her eyes instead were fixed on her pupil.

He smashed the face of the first Crommag with the hilt of the knife and cut its throat in the same sweep. He was all movement – graceful and powerful. The next Crommag found both knives buried in his chest and a third was cut from neck to hip as Traejan pulled the knives free. He was elegant and precise and as unwavering - and nearly as quick - as the Roshan. No movement was wasted as he spun and cut, and spun away again, his enemies dropping around him.

Seven Circles, she thought, *he is fast. He could be as fast as me some day, maybe faster. And those blades are as natural to him as his hands.* She watched him whirl like a trumpet flower being carried down a stream. But instead of soft petals and rushing water there was only lean muscle and even leaner metal.

He was all powerful movement. Two of the monsters bore down on him at once and though he might have been able to handle both, the Roshan killed one quickly. The elfin prince shot her a look of reproach as he killed the other, making her smile as he turned away towards the next group of attackers, the knives inward at first, with the blades along his forearms, and smashed one Crommag's jaw and another's nose. Then he flipped them out and two more fell as he turned and cut, ducked away and cut back at his attacker. His movements were so fluid they were almost methodical as he anticipated and brought down each opponent.

She watched him fight with an approval that made her swell with pride.

Only three more Crommags remained. One rushed at the Roshan but she sidestepped it lightly, nearly cutting it in half as it went by. Traejan eluded a blow from the axe of the second Crommag then rose swiftly, driving both blades up under its ribcage. He pulled them out as he turned upon the last. He brought the knives together on each side of the monster's neck and pulled them together and towards himself with all the force he could muster.

The Crommag crashed to its knees, making the ground shake as its life sprayed out the sides of its throat.

Traejan watched it fall to the earth, his breath coming in ragged gasps. He and the Roshan stood alone in a path of carnage, the air full of dust from the road and the stench of blood from over a dozen slain Crommags. Their massive bodies lay in ungainly heaps. The Roshan stood back, her smile crooked and proud. The elfin prince turned to look at her.

"I think you've found your weapon," she told him.

Traejan came at her in response. Faster than she had ever seen him, even in fight, he moved. Like a flash of lightning, he was upon her. His mouth was on her - her face, her chin, just below her jaw. Her eyes widened in shock then closed tightly as her body flooded with emotion.

Some force ran through her like a feral tremor.

She did not know when or where he dropped the knives he had fought with. Now the only weapon he held was her. His hands, bereft of their blades, pulled her close. They gripped her shoulders, the back of her neck, searching. At last they found what they were looking for as he pulled the pin from her hair. His hands lost themselves in her burnished locks as they came pouring over her shoulders and he held her face to his own.

He was whispering something in elfin that she could not understand. She could feel every muscle in his body as it pressed against her. It was like a metal spring, a tense coil exulting in the power of fulfilled motion. Then his lips found hers and, for the first time in her life, Ember donnis L'chiross dropped her sword.

# 29. FIELDS OF GOLD

The sun was a bright and glittering eye as it hung halfway between mid-day and the horizon. The dust had settled on the road and over the humped bodies that still soaked the ground with their congealing blood.

The elfin prince and the auburn-haired warrior sat in the golden wheat, twenty yards from the Stonefield Road under the far-reaching limbs of a gnarled oak. They knelt under the spreading branches, facing each other, her thigh between his. Ember did not remember retrieving her sword, but it lay next to them. The bloody knives Traejan had used in his first battle lay a few feet away.

Their horses, after the battle, had wound their way down the cliff on a trail fifty meters to the north. They stayed there, keeping an eye on their masters but keeping well away from the dead bodies as they nibbled on golden heads of wheat. Elf and woman stared at each other in unabashed astonishment.

"Your eyes are blue," the Roshan told him, her voice full of wonder.

Traejan smiled. "They oughtta be."

Ember reached out a hand and traced the arch of his cheekbone with the tip of her finger, and then the line of his jaw with her hand. He closed his eyes, incredulous.

Traejan pulled her close and buried his face in her hair. She sighed, closing her own eyes.

"It's you," she whispered. "It's always been you."

"Yes," he whispered back. Then, after a pause, "did you

know I loved you?"

Ember smiled as she looked at him. "Yes, but only recently. Ryen told me, and I didn't believe him at first."

Traejan laughed softly. "I know. I wanted to kill him for it at the time, but now I'm glad he did."

The Roshan grinned. "You could hear us?" she asked.

A slight flush crept into the elf's cheeks as he nodded. "I tried not to listen, but I couldn't help it."

Ember chuckled softly and then moved her body so that she could lean back into him. He rested his back against the trunk of the oak and wrapped his arms around her. She let out another deep sigh.

"I cannot even begin to describe how I feel right now," she said, her voice tinged with wonder and confusion.

"You don't have to," the elfin prince whispered. "I know." He put his cheek against the back of her head and watched the fields of wheat undulate around them, full of the same wonder. He closed his eyes and saw their bodies, clasped tightly on a small island in a sea of gold.

"I've never felt so at peace," she told him. "I don't understand it, but I feel so safe. So right."

Traejan inhaled deeply, stroking her hair. It all seemed like a dream. Everything had happened so fast. The fight, his kiss, the way her walls had come down. He never stopped to consider what she might do when he kissed her, he didn't even realize what he was doing until it was already happening.

It was a good thing, he thought. *I never would have had the nerve if I had been in my right mind. And I wouldn't be here right now – touching her hair, feeling her heartbeat.*

Still unable to believe that he held his Roshan in his arms, the elf closed his eyes as he thought back over what had happened.

Once the fight began he had felt like a man caught in a

riptide, unable to impede the force pulling him out to sea, but not wanting it to stop. The current took over and he let it take him. Then he found his center and he had taken the current and began to ride it like a wave. The wave grew and grew until it crashed down with him bearing down upon the Roshan like a rising tide against the rock.

Now he felt like the tide was ebbing back and he could rest with the echo of the ocean in his ears. He brushed his lips against her hair, full of wonder.

How did it come to this? he marveled. He had no idea where it would go, or what would happen from here on out. *What difference does it make? All that matters is right here and right now.*

Ember lay in his arms, feeling uncharacteristically vulnerable and yet not caring. A part of her knew that her world had shattered and fallen apart around her like shards of broken glass. Yet she felt complete, a feeling that she had never experienced though it seemed so familiar. So *comfortable.*

She pressed herself against the elfin prince. She wanted to melt into his body, become a part of him. She felt like she could not get close enough. She wanted to bury herself in him, body and soul. Ember closed her eyes and decided it would be enough for now only to rest against him – dirt and sweat, bloody steel and all - and feel his breath against her cheek. *If life could be perfect,* she thought, *this would be it.*

Is this what love feels like? she speculated suddenly. She felt the rate of her heart quicken the way it would before a battle and smiled at the trepidation that it brought. Then it slowed, and she could feel in beating in time with his. It felt so good that she could hardly believe it.

"Roshan?" he asked and felt her body tremble with silent laughter.

"You can call me Ember."

Traejan smiled into her hair. "I don't think I can."

She shook silently again and he laughed softly with her. "Em?" she suggested.

"Absolutely not. That's what Ryen calls you. 'Ber seems more fitting, since you can be as angry as a real bear."

The Roshan laughed aloud. "Am I so bad?" she asked, craning her head up so she could see his face. She looked at him with a sense of near breathless enchantment, as if almost doubting his very existence, like a child seeing a rainbow for the very first time.

Traejan shook his head and put his lips on her forehead. "Not so bad, but just as frightening at times. Maybe more. I will try Ember," he conceded, tasting her name as his mouth shaped the sound of it.

Ember laughed again. "Very well. You were saying?" She turned her face forward again so that she could lay her head on his chest.

He looked across the golden fields of wheat as they dipped in the gentle wind and put his cheek against her hair. "Where should we go from here?" he asked softly.

The Roshan smiled and brought her hands up to cup the arms that held her. "Do you mean that literally and right now, or figuratively and in the future tense?" she asked.

The young prince kissed the top of her head, his blonde curls falling forward over his face. "Both."

A frown creased Ember's auburn brows. "Crommags in the Midlon," she worried aloud. "I can hardly believe they aim to make war. They are slow, but not entirely stupid. They must be confident they can win, or they would not leave their homelands in the Mountains of Ice."

Traejan shook his head. "The idea of war seems unfathomable to me," he admitted. "Probably because I have never seen one." He remained silent for a moment, and then gazed down at the form in his arms. "Have you?"

The Roshan nodded slowly. "Yes. But not in this world."

Those words only raised more questions but Traejan found that he did not have to ask them, at least not yet. He knew it would be better to be still for the present moment. Answers could come later.

"So what do we do now?"

Ember moved her head slightly from left to right, not to indicate that she did not know, but that she was unsure.

"Get more information," she realized aloud. "The Crommags have been raiding the western Northlon for decades. It is there where we will learn their true numbers and their recent movements."

"Who do you know that we can ask?"

"Gatha," the Roshan said immediately, then chuffed laughter. "Aiden," she said, this time her voice serious.

Traejan remembered Ryen mentioning someone named

Aiden, along with the notion that he loved the Roshan deeply. The young prince made an effort to stay relaxed but he must not have succeeded, for the Roshan cocked her head.

"Are you okay?"

"Yes. I just do not like the thought of war."

Ember wrinkled her nose. "You lie horribly."

"Alright. Who is Aiden?"

The Roshan laughed, arching her back to look at the man she had recently discovered that she loved. "He is the leader of the Wildboys," she said. "Do you know of the Wildboys?" Traejan shook his head.

Ember stroked his forearm with the tip of her finger.

"The Wildboys," she explained, "are what your people call Sprites – a splinter group of Sylvan Elves. Do you know of them?"

"Of course."

The Sprites were a number of the smaller, native elves. They wanted nothing to do with the new elves - the ones that had traveled from the Old World, meaning Traejan and his people.

"The Wildboys are a splinter of a splinter," she explained. "Orphan boys that don't live with the other Sprites. They keep to themselves and wander all throughout the western Northlon, though they normally keep way up in the High Forests. But they hear and see all of what happens in the North, west of the Vale. They can tell us what they know, and I am sure they know much, if not all."

"So for right now?" Traejan asked. The Roshan sighed and closed her eyes.

"Right now," she said softly. "I am afraid to move. Afraid that if I open my eyes, this will all have been a dream."

The elfin prince tightened his grip around her slender body and kissed her hair again. The tips of his fingers rested on the hilt of a long dagger that had been secured to her belt. He closed his eyes and inhaled the scent of warm skin and cold steel.

"But if your arms are still around me when I open my eyes," she continued, "we should clean up, and go back to the haus." She sighed. "Although, first, we should go to Edin. There are happenings in the Midlon that do not bode well for anyone, and people need to be warned. Also, something needs to be done about the bodies in the road and I, for one, have had enough smell of Crommag for one day."

She sighed again, keeping her eyes tightly closed, taking in the feel of the body so close to her own. A warmth spread through her chest, a burning tempered by a frost of trepidation. The Roshan held onto the arms around her, truly fearing that they might disappear like morning mist with the sunrise.

This is what love feels like, she acknowledged with astonishment, not knowing whether she should laugh or cry, or both.

She opened her eyes and, finding herself still wrapped in

his embrace, bent her head to kiss one of the arms that held her. She turned her body and he leaned down and kissed her deeply. Finally he rose, pulling her up with him. Above them, the limbs of the oak moved with a warm breeze. Somewhere in the gentle flutter of its leaves they could hear the song of a nightingale.

Ember smiled and looked up, her eyes of green and brown and gold seeking out the feathered minstrel.

"Do you truly know what the nightingale sings?" Traejan asked, recalling her previous encounters with the bird along with something Ryen had said. "Are there words that you can hear behind the notes?" His sharp eyes spotted the nightingale as he wrapped his arms around her.

"Yes," she said, leaning into him. Her eyes found the bird a moment later, perched on a low branch, dipping and bobbing its head as it sang.

"What does she say?" Traejan asked, his lips against her temple as he watched the bird.

"He," the Roshan corrected smiling. "He says there is a peddler in the woods that we will meet on the road to Edin."

The young prince pulled away from his love to stare at the singer on the branch, but still kept her within the circle of his arms. "Truly?" Then he frowned at her and gave her a dubious look, sure that she was teasing him.

Ember laughed.

"Truly," she swore. "He is always full of advice, warnings, and gossip."

"Does it always come true?"

The Roshan shrugged, a tight smile tucked into the corner of her mouth. "Every time but one."

The young prince smiled knowingly, resting his chin on her head. "He did not know of me, I'll bet."

Ember shrugged again, watching the bird sing. "Not exactly.

He told me that love would find me one day, but that it would be the lord of song." The Roshan chuckled softly and Traejan gently turned her around so she was facing him. "Thank goodness!" she said, laughing. "I thought maybe I was doomed to love some traveling troubadour or..." she trailed off as his expression fell and then tightened. "What?" she asked, a line furrowing her auburn brows. "What is it?"

His eyes, bright and brown, searched her face before answering. "Song is the name of my grandfather's castle," he told her. The Roshan cocked her head and gave it a small shake, not understanding. "It is the castle I will inherit one day," the elf continued, and then continued again when still she did not see. "When I do, I will be the Lord of Song."

Ember's gimlet eyes widened as she looked at the young prince, and then narrowed as she glanced back at the nightingale, still twittering on his branch. "Smug little bastard," she murmured with a smirk.

The elfin prince put a finger under her chin and tipped her head back and kissed her. He didn't know if it was the tenth time or the tenth hundredth time he had done so. He didn't care. Traejanale Royce felt more powerful than he ever had in his life. He had all that he wanted in the world. Nothing would take it from him.

30. CATCHING UP

Only two hours after Traejan had pulled the Roshan to her feet under the spreading oak in the fields of gold, when the sun was low and subsiding on the horizon in a deepening orange, Sir Dellion of the Praetorian Guard stood in the middle of the Stonefield Road.

The Jägers had ridden straight south for ten days. They made haste, without driving their horses too hard, and managed to cross the entire Northlon and most of the Midlon. Each time they stopped to eat or rest, they warned whom they could with what they had seen. Everyone in the Northlon had taken the news with expressions that were either grim or full of fear. Everyone in the Midlon had looked at the Jägers as if they were mad.

The nightingale had been correct. The Roshan and the elfin prince were in luck and had been spared the trip into town. Half a mile into the forest they met a peddler leading a mule on the road from Edin Valley. The Roshan told him of what had happened and pressed a silver coin into his hand to hasten him back with word and warning. That task being done they turned the horses west. Once clear of the forest, they cut straight through the grain pastures to avoid the bodies in the road. Even from a distance, the pair could hear the squawk of carrion birds.

Dell surveyed the landscape with growing dismay and unease. It seemed that every adult and teen from Edin had turned out for the occasion and the villagers had walked up and down and all over the dirt lane before deciding to drag the huge bodies of the Crommags in every which way as well. They had finally settled them into a dry ditch by the Stonefield Road as far as possible from the wheat fields and were preparing to burn them. Wood was hauled in and oil spilled and slopped as it made its way to the nasty heap. The whole place was a bloody, dirty, mess of a mess of a mess.

Nonetheless, Dell could see the battle that was fought only hours ago with a clear eye and the scene played out before him as if he had born witness to it firsthand. The tracked and kicked dirt did not hide from his keen sight the boot prints of his prince, his obvious victory, and where he had faced his Roshan in the road. This was the most disconcerting part of all for Dell. Along with the tracks that led into the golden field.

Seventh Circle, Dell thought. *If we had not stopped to lunch in Lyre we might have come upon everything as it happened.* Seeing what *had* happened with the elfin eyes of a seasoned Jäger, Dell was glad they had not. He hunkered down in the dirt, looking at the boot prints there. They were not toe to toe, but closer. His eyes picked out where the tip of the Roshan's boot scraped back and came down again a step ahead. It meant her right leg was practically wrapped around the left leg of the prince.

Looking away quickly, Dell signaled to the novice Jägers in his party and they began helping the villagers prepare the pyre. Nevin broke from the rest and joined his commander where he squatted on the road. He hunkered down next to him and pointed silently to the boot marks in front of Dell. The ones of fine Elfish make, grouped with ones that were significantly smaller. Dell knew that Nevin's eyes, though older, were just as keen. He suspected the same. The aging Jäger raised his eyebrows at Dell and then his sharp gaze followed the same tracks as they left the field of battle to the spot under the oak tree.

Dell looked at him through squinted eyes and gave the elf a begrudging smile and a grunt of irritation.

I have only myself to blame, Dell thought, *I picked men I thought were the best or had the best aptitude. Even though the other two know to be discreet, at least I have no doubt that wild horses could not get Nevin to repeat what he is looking at right now.*

Then his surety was replaced with a sense of foreboding.

Unless those wild horses were Rowland the Great, a voice warned inside Dell's mind. The Praetorian flinched at the thought of Traejan's father, the King of the Elves, and what he would have to tell him upon his return.

But those thoughts were not for here and now. Sir Dellion jerked his chin towards the others, motioning for the older Jäger to aid the younger ones, and stood up brushing the dust from his pants. Dell's dismay turned to a queasy rise in the pit of his stomach as he followed the tracks off the road.

The lady Roshan and her student had left a single swath edged with Crommag blood through the yellow grass, which meant that one of them had been carried. A quick glance showed the prints of Traejan's boots. Dell walked through the tall and golden stalks, letting the fingers of his left hand trail along the tops of the wheat. The prickly heads tickled the pads of his fingers. He stopped when he reached the oak and stood with his arms crossed over his chest and his tongue in his cheek as he looked down upon where the two had held each other close in an embrace.

Maybe he was tending to a small wound on her, he thought, testing the lie on himself. *That would explain why he carried her.*

The elf almost laughed aloud. He knelt down and touched the crushed summer grass. It felt warm to his hand. Not from the warmth of their bodies – that had long since dissipated. It was the heat of what they had shared. What they must still share. Dell rose back up and pondered the scene under the oak a moment longer then returned to his Jägers. The pyre had been lit and the stench of burning hair and fat and flesh filled the air with a black, oily smoke.

The Praetorian motioned to his men and, as they prepared to leave, the villagers once again thanked them for stopping the attack on their town. Dell did not correct them, as he had already tried, but simply bowed courteously. Any explanation would only baffle these people. As it was, they had not seriously taken the warning the Jägers had given them about the Crommags. The people of the Midlon did not fear the beasts the way the Northlonders did. Not yet.

The Jägers mounted their horses and turned them east. Dell meant to warn the Atlanteans and the people of Trigo before he met up with Traejan at the start of fall. It felt wrong to warn others before he brought the news to his king, but he certainly could not return without the prince and he hoped a stitch in time would save nine. Besides, humans were always dubious of danger and slow to act – a few extra weeks might serve them well.

Nevin gave Dell a questioning look but said nothing. Dell led them around the outcrop of rock the teacher and student had jumped from only hours before as they launched their attack. As the Jägers rode over the rise where Traejan and Ember had crossed only half a day since, Dell shot a look back over his shoulder to the darkened woods across the valley in the northwest.

Traejan, he thought, stilling his horse for a moment of reflection. *What have you gotten yourself into?*

His courser stamped and gigged to the left, wanting to be away. The animal did not like the smell of Crommag, or blood. The combination was worse and made even a well-trained mount skittish. Dell shook his head, hoping for the best, and then let his horse follow its mates. He wished he could send his prince a warning, or at least a word of caution. But he knew he was already too late. Hoping for the best, whatever it could be at this point, was the best he could do.

⁂

It took the Roshan and the elfin prince longer than it should have to get back to the haus since neither of them wanted to ride. They wanted, *they needed*, to be close to each other. Ember took Peg's reins and flipped them around the horn of Coal's saddle and the great dark beast led them all home.

They walked the entire way – sometimes hand in hand, sometimes arm in arm, sometimes so close that no rays of the setting sun or rising moon could find a way between them. They stopped often to kiss, or to just hold each other quietly under the deepening sky as it faded from indigo into black. The stars shone on them, the air magically warm with an occasional caress of cool air, carried down through the valley on a breeze from the north.

The elf and the warrior talked continuously, sometimes in hushed whispers, sometimes laughing hard enough that they had to pause and catch their breath. Each felt they had a lifetime to share with the other. Each wanted to know everything they could about the person by their side.

An hour after moonrise they reached the Backwoods and stopped for a meager dinner. Traejan sat with his back against a tree and Ember sat up against him, her legs draped over his lap. They whispered and laughed in hushed tones, as if they did not want to disturb the forest. They shared a few pieces of dried meat in between childhood stories and then continued on their way.

They walked all night. They rested when they felt they needed it, but mostly they walked and they talked. Time had no meaning for them that night.

Ember told the prince of her life as a Roshan, teaching others how to fight. Traejan told her of his parents, his brothers, but mostly of his grandfather. He told her of his journey to the New World and she told him, to his surprise, about her own.

"You weren't born here?" he asked.

The Roshan shook her head and Traejan marveled at the color of her hair as it shifted on her shoulders, even muted as it was in the moonlight that crept between the leafy canopy of the forest.

"No, I remember the trip well, though I was very young."

"I was young as well," Traejan said, remembering his ride from the ship to the shore, the spray of the sea in his face. "Only twenty-five, but full grown for an elf."

"I don't know how old I was," Ember admitted, "but I was still a child, not even half as tall as anyone around me."

"Do you know when that was? Were my people here yet?"

"I think we might have arrived around the same time, I'm not too sure. I was small then."

"Do you know how old you are now?" Traejan asked. It was something he had always wanted to know, but even two days ago would have bitten off his tongue before venturing such a question. Now, their bodies close and their fingers entwined, he did not hesitate in the slightest.

Ember shook her head. "Not exactly. How long have the Skye Elves been here?"

"We just celebrated a centennial in the spring, so just over a hundred years."

The Roshan nodded, taking a second to consider. "About a hundred plus eight, I would guess. Give or take a year or two."

"What people did you belong to? Are you elfin in any way?"

Ember laughed. "I had no people. Just my Roshan."

The elf turned his face towards hers in surprise. "You had a Roshan?"

Ember laughed again, harder this time. "Of course I did! Did you think I learned everything on my own?"

This time Traejan laughed. "With you, I would believe anything." He stopped and she turned to him and he kissed her.

He meant for it to be quick and innocent, but they stood for minutes, their embrace growing tighter and more passionate until they finally broke apart, breathless. The young prince lost his hands in her hair and pressed his lips to her forehead before they continued on their way once again.

They spoke of the past and relished every second of the present. Neither one mentioned the future. Not because of what it might mean, but simply because it never entered their minds. Their only concern was for each other; they had lifetimes of catching up to do.

At some point before dawn they found the Ravensbrook and stopped for fresh water. The horses splashed in the shallows, drinking their fill before munching on grass that still grew green in the shade of the trees. Traejan sat down to rest with his back against a rock and watched Ember fill her waterskin.

It was enchanting to watch her now that he could do so openly - the way she walked, the way she moved, her every expression. When she was done she came and lay down next to him and put her head in his lap. Traejan stroked her hair.

I always believed that learning to fight was what would complete me, he thought. *I believed it was what was missing in my life, but it was this. This is what was missing. She is what was missing.*

Just as he thought she was drifting off to sleep, she stirred.

"Let's press on," she said.

"Anything you want," he told her, comprehending how true that was. He knew there was nothing he would not do for her. More, he wished there was something he *could* do for her, something he could give her. There was a burning desire inside of him to take care of her and the prince almost laughed aloud at the thought. If there was anyone in this world who would be fine on their own, it was the woman holding his hand. Nevertheless, it did not stop him from feeling the need to protect her.

They reached the haus in the late morning. Gatha was nowhere to be found but together they unsaddled the horses and took time to rub them down before turning them loose. Although Traejan hardly felt hungry, Ember insisted on making a huge meal.

"We should celebrate," she told him.

"What are we celebrating?"

"Your first battle," the Roshan said as she poked around in the icebox to see what they had on hand.

"My first *two* battles," the young prince corrected, slipping his arms around her waist and pulling her close.

Ember smirked him. "Both wins," she remarked. "You are off to quite a start."

Traejan kissed her, wrapping his hand in her hair. He broke the kiss after only a moment, afraid he would not stop if it went any longer.

He built a fire in the oven but left the fireplace empty. The haus was plenty warm. He threw his gear in his room and cleaned up while the Roshan cooked. As the need to be close to her again drew him back into the kitchen, the smells of frying meat and vegetables made him realize how hungry he really was. Thinking back, they hadn't eaten much or slept hardly at all for two days.

He meant to get plates from the cupboard but instead somehow found his hands in her hair and his lips on her brow. Looking over the crown of her head, his eyes fell on her bedroom door at the end of the hall. Despite more than just a spark of interest, even that future was more than he wanted to think about. He buried his face in her hair and kissed her neck. She laughed softly, kissed him, and grabbed plates and utensils.

They sat at one of the tables in the dining room, divided by a table heaped with food. Traejan poured them each a glass of wine.

"You joining me today?"

Traejan smiled and nodded. "You are right. We *should* celebrate."

"There's honey in the pantry," she offered. Both her voice and her eye had a mischievous glint.

"Another time," he told her. "I am drunk enough on you." Ember laughed and began eating. Traejan did the same.

They had fried steaks with peppers and onions (pretty much the only thing the Roshan could cook – all in one pan with a bit of butter), along with an crusty round of bread that Gatha had left for them with creamed butter. When they had stuffed themselves thoroughly, they filled their glasses with the rest of the wine and sipped at them on the huge stuffed couch in front of the empty fireplace, still talking.

The Roshan insisted on pulling off his boots for him as he told her of his trips to the Vikes with his grandfather. She told him about the Gnomin and their lands and their laws as he took off her boots and rubbed her feet, making her laugh. She told him about the time she had spent in the Mountains of Blood, trying to stem the raids of Crommags on the Gnomin. He told her of learning wood lore from Dell and his long forays in the forests with other Jägers. The sun was setting outside in the glen when they drifted off to sleep in each other's arms.

31. THE BEDROOM

Traejan awoke in the morning not wanting to move, but urgently needing to get to the bathroom. He tried to extricate himself from Ember's embrace without waking her but was unsuccessful. She did not seem to mind. She kissed his cheek and rolled over on the sofa they had shared and went back to sleep.

When he returned he lay back down, cradling her as best he could, but was far from tired. He contented himself with watching her slumber. An hour later, she finally stretched and yawned. She kissed his jaw and nuzzled her head under his chin.

"Would you like some breakfast?" she asked.

Traejan shook his head gently.

"You're not hungry at all?"

"Not for food," he whispered, kissing her temple.

The Roshan laughed and pushed his body off of her own and let him pull her to her feet. She looked up into his brown eyes but there was no indecision, no hesitation. She had a peculiar feeling that she had loved him all her life. She stood on her toes to kiss him, then took up his hand and led him past the tables in the dining room and down the hall.

Finally, Traejan got to see what was behind the door there. The door itself was heavy oak with huge iron bands and almost six inches thick. The Roshan turned the handle and swung it open. Then she stood back, waiting, watching the young prince. He glanced at her and then peered inside like a child in a fairytale, following his stocking feet into the space beyond. It felt strange to be walking in the haus without his boots on. He took a few steps past the Roshan and into the room carved into the mountain.

He had often wondered what waited back here – a bunker of weapons with only her bedroll to sleep on? The canopied bed of a warrior queen? A multitude of visions had played through his mind at times, especially as he drifted off to sleep each night, but he was wrong in all his speculations.

It was the room of a scholar.

The bed was huge, layers of burgundy blankets and pillows, with a few worn leather bolsters and small decorative cushions. Though it looked soft and inviting, it was against the back wall of unadorned and chiseled stone - and did not seem to hold the importance of the room.

The room was built around books. On the left side of the chamber was a large rock fireplace, flanked by bookcases that went from the floor to the ceiling. Next to the hearth, tucked into the left corner, was a large, well-worn leather chair guarded by a tall lamp with an electric flambeau.

The entire wall on the right was made of bookcases, save for the center where a slanted table was fixed to the wall by a pair of chains. Next to the table was a huge barrel full of neatly rolled maps. The night tables that flanked the bed also held small, neat stacks of books.

The floor, he thought at first, was a polished stone of some sort. A closer look showed that it was poured mortar – painted and gleaming. It was a map of the New World. Atlantea was directly under his stocking feet.

He looked to his left and saw a narrow opening that led to a hallway, most likely to a washroom.

He took a few tentative steps in that direction and saw that the hallway actually opened up onto a whole other room. It was her bath chamber, obviously, but much more. On the left side, a half-open door gave him a glimpse of a water closet with toilet and a slate tiled shower. On the right, opposite the shower, was a door that opened onto a small room. Another few steps and Traejan could see that it was a large closet, hung with her array of dark clothing and drawers built into the walls. Boots of different styles and heights, though all black, were lined up like sentries against one closet wall.

Also on the left of the bath chamber, preceding the shower, was a large slate-tiled bath, complete with steps. It was from here that came some of the smells that he associated with her – wild rose and lavender. Between the door and the bath, closer to where he stood, was a long padded table.

It was so close to the ground that he could not imagine what it might be for. It was covered in leather that was wiped clean, but bore stains and marks on its surface.

Does she sleep on it?

He doubted it, not with the queenly bed in the other room. He pictured her eating in here, sitting on the floor of the bath chamber, and almost laughed. It had to be for something else. What that was, he could not guess.

Next to the padded table was something he *did* recognize. A small and rectangular ironbound mirror hung on the wall over a small stand with a matching bench.

A woman's vanity.

Though with the Roshan he was sure it was more an item of necessity than of vanity. The table held no face paints or creams. A hairbrush along with a multitude of bands, clips and pins were the only womanly indications of a vanity other than a collection of needles and thread, though the thought of the Roshan sewing made him bite back a laugh once again. The rest of the menagerie included a pair of scissors, tightly rolled strips of linens, the jar of Gatha's salve, and a blunt metal rod.

Traejan cocked his head, trying to discern its use. He did not think she curled her hair, but it looked burnt on one end as if from being held in a fire. He flinched when he figured out what it was for – cauterizing wounds.

His eyes went back to the low, padded table. He did not have to imagine its use any longer, he could see it quite clearly.

It's low for Gatha, he realized. *So she can easily stitch her...* Traejan felt his heart and stomach clench and stepped quickly back into the bedroom. Ember sat on the edge of her bed, watching him. She had taken off her jerkin and tossed it aside. The dark blouse underneath was laced up the front but she had loosed the ties by her neck.

"Well?" she asked.

He pushed the thought of the padded table from his mind as his bright brown eyes traveled over the room, the books and the maps. "You've been so many places," he sighed. He approached where she sat and knelt down in front of her so their eyes were almost level.

She smiled gently. "I'll tell you all about them."

"Later," he said.

She could see his eyes start to change, the blue seeping into them, and her smile widened.

He leaned in and kissed her deeply, pushing her back onto the bed. He climbed up next to her and found that his assumption about the bed was correct in one aspect, it *was* soft. He reached for the laces on her shirt but she caught his wrist and held it tight. Traejan sat up and looked at her.

"What is it?" he asked, his eyes searching her face, wavering between blue and brown with his concern.

She pressed her lips together, as if she didn't want to answer, then shook her head and did so anyway. "I don't have a woman's body," she said softly.

"Do you have a man's body?" he teased, smiling. "A griffin's?" She did not return his smile.

"I have a soldier's body." She swallowed and continued. "A soldier that has seen many battles."

Traejan's smile faded and he brought her hand to his lips. Then he put her hand down gently but firmly and unlaced her shirt. She watched him, unmoving as he opened the ash -colored blouse. She expected him to gasp or recoil, but he did neither and for that she was grateful. Instead he drew a long breath and let it out gradually.

"Where was I, when all this happened?" he asked, his voice low and husky. His eyes moved over her body and his lips pressed together, trying to stem his own flood of emotion.

The Roshan's body looked like a war table in relief, it was so heavily scarred. Some marks were so old they had almost faded away. Others looked like they could not be more than a year or two old, but those ones were small. One of the worst scars ran from her left shoulder to right hip. Another one ran from one hip all the way across her lower stomach to the other side.

Seven Circles, he thought, feeling as if he had been punched in the stomach, *that one almost cleaved her in two.*

Indeed it must have, for he could see the jagged lines on either side of the scar from where she had been sewn up. He thought again of the padded table and again pushed it from his mind in fear he might shudder.

She had a number of marks that were unmistakably from arrows, or from thin daggers. There were a few that might have been from blades, daggers or dirks, but most were most easily recognizable as slash wounds from swords. On her left side were marks from no weapon he could think of. Three perfectly round circles, no bigger than the tip of his little finger, were grouped together just under her ribcage on the right side.

"I wish I could have been there for you," he said softly. "I wish I could have protected you." She smiled for the first time since he had opened her blouse.

"I wouldn't be the person I am now if I had you back then,"

she told him. "Each one of these brought me one step closer to you."

He leaned down and kissed her. She felt then that each scar, each hurt, and every pain that had brought her to this moment, had been worth it.

Traejan ran his hand over her ribcage, feeling the ripple of flesh under his palm before he cupped her breast, feeling the edge of raised skin around her nipple. Ember rose up against him, pressing herself into his hand and against his body.

Her hands found the laces of his trousers and pulled them apart. He tugged at her pants, as eager as she to get out of their clothes. He kissed her neck as he pulled them off, tasting the salt of her sweat from yesterday's journey mingle with the sweet taste of her skin. Stripped to their skin, his mouth found her lips and he filled his hands with her hair as he pushed into her.

They cried out in unison at that first powerful rush. The intensity did not build, it was there immediately. They moved together in the same manner they fought, with sharp awareness and all-consuming fervor.

Forehead to forehead, their eyes locked, they cried out in unison again at the end.

Afterwards, in a tangle of sheets and limbs, they lay together for a long time before either of them spoke.

The Roshan wanted neither to speak or move. She just wanted to be.

She felt so safe within his arms. Protected. It had been so long since she had felt that way. *How long?* she wondered, but only for a second before the thought was pushed from her mind. She did not like to think about time. It came and went and was a concept she could not understand. It was something she could not grasp. It was easier for her to grasp things with her mind if she could grasp them with her hand. Iron and steel, flight and fight. The pounding of her heart and the swing of her blade. They were the only things that made sense.

Traejan kissed her forehead as he lay next to her, tracing the scars on her chest with a finger. "I am amazed that you are still alive after all this," he told her. She laughed, caressing his arm.

"So am I," she said.

"You really are a warrior. Not just a soldier, but a warrior."

Ember smiled at the compliment. "Well, I didn't get them all at the same time. Most of these are very old. I've gotten better over the years."

"I can tell. Which one of these hurt the most?" He expected her to point to one of the long slashes on her torso but instead she held up her right hand and, spreading out her fingers, pointed to a raised sliver of skin no more than half an inch long. "Are you serious?" he asked.

She nodded, her lips curled into a smile but her eyes bore no humor. "I hate getting cut on the hand. The nerves are much shallower and they seem to take forever to heal. When I got this, I couldn't make a fist or hold a sword for three months."

"Really?"

"Really."

"How did it happen?"

"I was trying to fix a chair. My skill with a hammer is quite the opposite of my skill with a sword. It didn't help that I had been drinking. My hammer missed but my swing brought my hand down hard and the nail went right between those two fingers and gouged me pretty deep."

Traejan laughed as if it pained him to do so.

"I know, I know," Ember said. "So careful on the battlefront, so careless on the home front." She held up her left hand. "This one too," she said, showing him a small puncture scar on the underside of her left wrist.

"How did you get that one?"

"I'm not exactly sure, except that it was in a bar fight," she admitted with sheepish look, "and, again, I had enjoyed a glass of wine or two."

Traejan laughed heartily this time. "Or ten! I can't believe someone got the drop on you! You must have been quite drunk."

"Actually, there were four of them. One got in a lucky throw somehow with a steak knife."

"A steak knife?" Traejan laughed harder. "That's not the story I was expecting, but I believe it. Knowing you, you probably had it coming."

"Had it coming?" Ember gave him a poke in the ribs and a reproachful glare. "What happened to wishing you could have been there to protect me?"

"I can't protect you from yourself," he said, kissing her neck. "Although I would like to try."

"I think I'd like that, too," she said, feeling that if her heart did not stop swelling with every moment that it might rupture. "I'd also like a shower," she added. "And something to eat."

"There's food left over from our dinner last night," Traejan told her. "I can heat it up in a fry pan while you clean up, and have it waiting for when you are ready."

Ember kissed him and then traced his lips with a finger. "Why don't we shower together?" she proposed. "Then we can cook together, and eat together."

The young prince smiled. The suggestion of showering with a woman was something that might have never crossed the elf's mind before he met the Roshan. A month ago, the idea of showering with her might have made him faint. Now, it seemed as natural as breathing.

They weren't in the shower but for a few seconds before his hands were on her body and her mouth was on his. Her hands knotted in the wet curls of his hair as she tried to pull him closer, opening her mouth wider for his searching tongue as if starving for him.

He grasped her hair, heavy and drenched like a rope of silk, and pulled her head back, exposing her neck to his mouth, his tongue, his teeth. Her hands ran down his shoulder blades under a torrent of hot water, feeling muscles made hard from months of training.

Ember found herself gasping, trying to catch her breath in the steamy air, then moaning as he pulled her legs up over his hips and held her against the wall.

She might have screamed, she wasn't sure, but some sound still echoed in her mind half an hour later - even after she was wrapped in a towel and sitting at her vanity, brushing out her hair.

Traejan, also wrapped in a towel, came up behind her and knelt on the ground to her right. She stopped when she saw him but he shook his head, motioning for her to keep going. He pushed a damp lock of hair off her shoulder and kissed it before gazing at her reflection in the ironbound looking glass.

"You know," he told her, "your hair was the first thing about you that took my breath away." He smiled. "Other than the fact that you were a woman, of course."

"The first time we met?" she asked.

"Yes. The whole encounter had me under some sort of spell, but it was your hair that drew all the life from me. You had my heart, I think, at that very moment."

Ember's smile was gentle and her eyes distant with the memory. "You know that was next to a miracle that you even saw me that way. I never wear my hair down, but that morning I had climbed up on that rock and found quite the tangle in it along with a number of pine needles. I did not expect you to come until the sun was full up, so I decided to take it down and brush it out."

Traejan grinned and kissed her neck. "Providence," he whispered.

Ember cocked her head and studied him in the reflection of the mirror. "What if I had not taken my hair down? Or what if you had been an hour later, as I had expected?"

The elfin prince put his hand under her chin and turned her face to his. "I don't think it would have mattered at all," he said softly. Ember smiled and kissed him. Then pulled him up next to her on the small bench.

"You loved me, even then?"

Traejan nodded. "Even then. Although I did not know at the time what it really was that I felt. It was very new to me. It still is, though I know now that what I feel and what my whole purpose for living has been. It has been for you. Only for you."

The Roshan sighed. "I feel the same within me," she told him, her gem-like eyes glassy with emotion. "I feel as if I have loved you my whole life, I just didn't know it was you." She looked at his narrow face, damp curls and pointed ears a moment longer and then sighed again, turning back to her mirror. She quickly wrapped her hair into a ball at the base of her head and plucked a few pins from the top of the vanity.

Traejan laughed softly, still perched on the edge of her bench. "The nest, always the nest with you."

"Is that what you call it?"

"That's what it looks like. Here. If you must wear it up." He moved her fingers away and took her hair into his own hands. She sat, delighted, as he made a braid on either side and then crossed them at the back of her neck. He brought each twist up the opposite side, wrapping them over the top of her head, neatly tucking the ends underneath, forming a braided crown. "There – pin it there."

Ember did so and laughed when she saw her reflection. "That's a bit elegant for me, don't you think?"

The young elf shook his head, his eyes fixed on hers. "Not at all. Fit for a queen."

The Roshan laughed again. "Well, this queen is twice as

hungry as she was an hour ago, thanks to you."

"Then by all means," Traejan said, pulling her up with him as he rose from the bench and relieved her of her towel, "let me remedy that."

32. THE ARMORY

The elfin prince awoke to find himself alone in the Roshan's bed. His hand slipped between the sheet where she had lain but it was cool to the touch. She had been up for some time. He knew that she could be quiet but was astounded to find that she could be stealthy beyond his own audible means.

Sometime on the previous day, between meals and lovemaking, he had moved his things to Ember's room without asking or being asked. The Roshan had made room in her closet without a second thought, putting his extra pair of boots next to her own. The two moved with a synchronicity as if in practiced dance.

He yawned and stretched and dressed before leaving the room. He was glad he did, because Gatha was the first person he saw.

She was coming through the door to Ember's room at the same moment he was leaving it and they almost collided.

The Gnomin woman pulled up short, but only from their close encounter. She did not seem surprised at all to see him in the Roshan's room. Instead, she gazed up at him – giving the elf a flat look that was almost reprimanding for a full three seconds – and then brushed past him.

"Good morning, Gatha!" he called to her squat, retreating form. The Gnomin gave no indication to whether she had heard or that she cared. Traejan grinned and went into the kitchen to find Ember sitting at the counter drinking coffee from a heavy mug.

"Good morning," she said, her face lighting up with a smile. He wrapped his arms around her shoulders and leaned down to kiss her.

"Good morning," he returned, looking at her quizzically. Her face was freshly scrubbed and her hair was damp. "You are even more quiet than I thought," he said, his thumb touching her hair. "I can't believe I didn't hear you showering."

Ember smiled. "I used yours. Your old one, I mean. I didn't want to wake you."

"Don't ever worry about waking me," he assured her, "especially if you're naked." He kissed her again as she harrumphed and then rounded the counter and opened the pantry in search of breakfast.

He found a few apricots and put them on a small plate with a slice of crusty bread before joining her. She watched him silently, placing her hand on his knee when he sat down. Her touch was all that it took. His face was under her chin and his hands in her hair, his meager breakfast already forgotten, when Gatha came into the kitchen. If she noticed she gave no suggestion that she found it out of the ordinary.

The Gnomin woman drew a glass of water from the tap and put it in front of Traejan. Then she took the towels that hung from the pegs by the pantry door and replaced them with two fresh ones.

The elfin prince finally relented and sat back far enough that he could see into Ember's eyes. She sighed, looking at him as he picked up an apricot and gestured at her with it.

"So?" he prompted. "You are up, washed and dressed, having your coffee and staring intently at the wall. I know you must be thinking seriously about something. The Crommags?"

Ember nodded, her gimlet eyes flicking to Gatha as they discerned an alteration in her movements. The Gnomin woman had stopped in her tracks, her blue eyes intent on the Roshan. Her stubby fingers were curled around the dishtowels so tight that her knuckles had gone pale. The elf was certain it was the first time he had seen her take a keen interest in anything since he had been there.

The Roshan posed a short question in Gnomin. It was just a few words and the only one Traejan recognized was "Crommag."

Gatha nodded, her face grave.

"What do you know?" Ember asked in Anglicus.

The Gnomin held up a hand and made a few brusque motions in the air. Traejan's bright brown eyes went back and forth between the two women.

"What is it?" he asked, when Gatha finally dropped her hand. The look on Ember's face was grim.

"The Crommags have been raiding the Mountains of Blood again, which is highly unusual this time of year. And instead of killing the Gnomin, like they usually do, they have been taking them."

The young prince was aghast. "Why?" he asked, sitting back in surprise. He looked at Gatha but she only shook her coarse blonde curls in response, indicating that she did not know. He looked at Ember.

"We need to find Aiden," she said, still looking at Gatha. "And we can't wait for the next storm."

"The next storm?"

The Roshan nodded, her face turning to find his. "The Wildboys usually stay high up in the mountains, unless there is a storm. Then they come down, lest they get washed down in a flood."

"That's where you went during that thunderstorm," Traejan said softly. Ember smiled and nodded while his expression, though still loving, hardened. "And came back drunk, and hungover the next day," he added.

The Roshan's brows furrowed, though she was still smiling.

"That sounds a bit accusing," she remarked. "Though I don't recall your training suffering."

The expression on the prince softened a bit. "I was glad for any break you gave me," he admitted. "Though I recall you shredding my shirt upon your return."

Ember laughed. "Don't blame my night of wilding on the fact that you can't keep your elbows down!"

Traejan gave her a sour look and bit into an apricot.

The Roshan laughed again and kissed his shoulder before turning her eyes back to Gatha. "We might be gone awhile," she told the stout woman. "Two good packs?" she asked and the Gnomin nodded stolidly. "Good. And don't forget my wine." Gatha frowned but said nothing, of course. Ember laughed once again and kissed Traejan on the cheek as she stood up. "Clean up and get dressed. Pack fresh clothes, whatever you might need for at least a week. Gatha will see to our provisions. I'll see to our gear."

"Can I help?"

Ember nodded, draping her arms over his shoulders. "But get ready first." She closed her eyes and pressed herself against him yet again, deciding that if she lived for a million years she would not have enough of him.

Traejan came out of the Roshan's bathing chamber, cleaned and dressed, to find her standing next to her bed, surveying weapons. A broadsword, a longsword, and three short swords, along with an assortment of daggers and knives were spread out on a clean piece of sackcloth that had been put down to protect the burgundy coverlet.

The elf whistled in astonishment when he saw the small arsenal.

"I'm just deciding what to take," Ember said as he wrapped his arms around her. "I won't need all of these."

The young prince put his chin on her shoulder. "I've never seen these before," he realized aloud, even as it dawned on him that he never saw her usual array of weaponry unless they were on her person. "Where did they come from?" he asked.

She turned, carefully staying within the circle of his embrace. Her eyes moved over his face and a small smile played on the corners of her lips. "You tell me."

Traejan peered at her for a moment, perplexed, then closed his almond-shaped eyes. He was straight away filled with the smell of her and his first instinct was to bury his face in her neck or her hair. He pushed himself past the smell of her skin, of rosewater and lavender and leather, and concentrated on the other scent that always surrounded her - even from the moment they first met.

Iron.

Forged steel.

Keeping his arms around her waist, he turned his face away. He trailed the scent from the bed to his left. His eyes, brown and bright, popped open to stare at the bookcase behind her reading chair. His face turned back to the Roshan, his expression skeptical, and she smiled.

"Go on," she encouraged.

He let her go and walked towards the shelves of books, circumventing the chair as he went. Now that he was close, the smell of oiled metal was so heavy that he could taste it. Gingerly, he placed his hands on two polished planks of mahogany and pushed.

Nothing.

He could feel the Roshan's smirk upon him but, unlike the past five months, it no longer made him inwardly cringe with discomfort. Now that sardonic smile was a challenge. His bright eyes scoured the books that were lined up or neatly stacked, scanning the titles until they stopped on one, almost by accident.

Drawing the Dragon

Traejan reached up and, using the index finger of his right

hand, carefully tugged at the book from the top of its spine.

It came free easily, falling into his palm, leaving behind a barely audible click - even to his ears. Curious, he opened the book and flipped through the pages. They were all blank. He placed the book on the nightstand between the chair and the bed and again pushed on the shelves. This time it moved, pivoting silently on a center pin, to reveal a corridor beyond. As it did, he could feel the hint of a breeze move past his cheeks as if being pulled out of the dark.

A cross draft, he realized.

Traejan turned his face to follow the current of air as if he could see it. The invisible path led to the bookcase on the other side of the room. He looked at the Roshan, nonplussed, and she leveled her gimlet eyes at him.

One thing at a time, those eyes said. *Stay focused.*

She nodded for him to go ahead and he did so, slowly.

It was dark in the passage but, as he took a few tentative steps, it slowly illuminated in response to his movements. The walls were rounded and the air cold and, for the first time, Traejan had a good mental map of how the haus was built into the hill behind it before its rooms and hallways really delved into the mountain.

There was no façade here - the sides of the tunnel were stone, rough and jagged. The elf touched his fingers to its surface and, though it was past high summer and hot as hell outside, the rock was cold. He went forward and, as he did, he could feel a touch of claustrophobia caress his spine. The crushing mass of the mountain was above him now, growing more oppressive with every step.

A shiver stole through his body and he was only slightly placated by the feel of Ember's presence as she followed him into the passage. A few paces more brought the elf to an opening and the prince sucked in a breath of the cold air as he walked through it, thunderstruck.

Like the tunnel, it lit up at his presence – a glow that spread along the tops and bottoms of the hewn rock walls.

Like the Roshan, it was one answer that led to a thousand more questions.

It was a cavern, undoubtedly. But the elf was unsure if it were also an armory or a museum.

Both, he decided.

In a space that could easily fit twenty horses or a hundred men, were implements of death beyond measure. Some ornamental, many displayed, and even more stored or stacked carefully for future use.

The natural curve of the chamber had been chiseled, making the vast area roughly the shape of a rectangle. Artificial light ran along the tops and bottoms of the walls and flambeaux were set into the stone ceiling. Everywhere the prince looked, the ersatz illumination gleamed on more weapons than he could count.

In the center of the room were a series of shelves made of polished cherry wood displaying a myriad of swords and knives and weapons that Traejan did not know or recognize, even from books. Some had hilts of bone, some of worked gold with elaborate and intricate designs, and a few were inset with precious gems. All shone and sparkled.

Slowly, he walked around the exposition of weaponry. Most had the name of the weapon carved into a corresponding tag made of wood, leather, or brass. The names were all foreign to Traejan, so he formed the words on his lips as if sounding them out in soft Anglicus.

Hrunting

Kladenets

Shamshir

Chandrahas

One shelf bore a small, chiseled plate of brass that read

Excalibur - but the shelf was otherwise empty. The young prince looked at the auburn-haired warrior questioningly and she shrugged, her sardonic smile almost an answer in itself.

"I have yet to find that one," she explained. "But his sisters are there," she said, motioning with her head.

Traejan's face turned back to the display and he looked at the bottom shelf under the empty plank still waiting its prize. Two swords were crossed there; held by knobs of brass and labeled *Caliburn* and *Clarent*.

A few steps took him to the next set of shelves. They were identical to the first, made of the same polished cherry wood, but held swords that were as different as apples from pears.

On the highest shelf were two crossed swords; *Tizona* and *Kusanagi*. The second shelf displayed *Joyeuse* and *Fragarach*. A single sword, short and carved with runes, lay on the bottom shelf. Its name, *Sting*, was carved into a small and simple plate of hammered silver.

A third set of shelves held knives and daggers though two staffs rested on the highest plank and were labeled *Ruyi* and *Jem Kukulkan*.

The elfin prince walked between the ledges of polished wood and treasures like a child in a fairytale forest. His almond eyes noted an ancient trident from Atlantea next to the dagger that Ryen had given Ember only a few days past, held in a brass cradle.

A menagerie of steel in all shapes and sizes graced the last stand of cherry wood. There was one enormous shining thing that took up almost an entire shelf. It looked to Traejan like a silver anvil with a colossal handle wrapped with strips of leather. It was so huge that it could only be wielded by someone the size of a Vikeman, or larger. It was inscribed with eight letters - MJOLNIR.

The young prince walked past the collection of death delivering art and artifacts.

To his left, shirts of chain mail and leather armor replete with nickel studs hung on crossed beams of wood. They were guarded by plate mail on one side - breastplates and pauldrons, greaves, vambraces and lobstered gauntlets. Shields of all shapes and sizes guarded the other.

Hooks had been driven into the stone of the walls and from them hung braces of daggers and dirks. Wooden racks held dozens of swords, and dozens more had been thrust point first into barrels of sand. In the corners of the chamber, more barrels held rolls of parchment that Traejan guessed must be lists and maps.

A line of pikes and spears leaned together along the back wall, most too tall to stand upright in the cavern. They gave way to an area dedicated to maces, morningstars, and battleaxes. There was a single yet enormous cudgel – undoubtedly gleaned from a Crommag or something just as large and gruesome.

There were racks upon racks of bows – longbows and recurve bows, reflex bows, and self bows. Bows of ash and elm and yew. Some were strung and some were not. Next to the racks of bows were orderly piles of quivers and crates of arrows.

To Traejan's right, where he stood by the polished displays that held the rare and shining weapons, were tiered ledges of oak that had been driven into the stone walls. They were laden with tightly rolled belts, scabbards, and sheaths. Next to the ledges, hung from pegs that had also been driven into the rock, were more sets of belts and scabbards - these with the weapons already nestled inside.

Ironbound trunks of wood filled the spaces against the walls like chests of treasure. What they held Traejan could only guess. He turned to find the Roshan at the cavern's entrance, watching him. One of her hands clutched two of the dirks and the dagger that had been on her bed. The other hand held the pommel of the broadsword, its tip resting on the toe of her boot.

He stared at her, speechless, as she replaced the items she had taken but decided she would not need.

"How?" he asked, dumbfounded. "How did you get all of these?"

"A lifetime of collecting." She smiled crookedly. "Well, not an entire lifetime," she corrected. "But a good part of it."

"But this is enough to outfit an army!"

Ember laughed. "A small army, maybe."

His bright brown eyes scoured the walls and shelves, the barrels and racks. "You could not possibly have collected all of this," he argued softly. "Was it, I mean, did some of it belong to your Roshan?"

Ember shook her head gently, her auburn hair lambent in the dim light and her face rigid with memory. "My Roshan did not use weapons."

Traejan's almond-shaped eyes were near round with wonder. They left her face to travel over the vast armory once more.

"Your Roshan did not..." he whispered. "You...all this..." His soft brown eyes stopped again at the display in the center of the room, transfixed by yet another blade held by a brass cradle. It was forged from no metal he had ever seen – greenish silver that almost disappeared from sight if he moved his head the slightest bit. On another shelf was a smaller weapon that appeared to be carved out of pearlescent bone. He knew that he had not traveled as far as Ember, but something about those two weapons...

His eyes picked out two more oddities before he turned to her.

"These are not all of this world," he said.

The Roshan shook her head slowly again, walking towards him in the same manner, almost hesitant as she watched him puzzle it together.

"The draft," he ventured. "There is another passage, behind the opposite bookcase, isn't there?" Ember nodded. "Where does it go?" he breathed.

"Other worlds," she returned, her voice barely above a whisper. "For another time." She lifted her chin. "For now," she said, her voice rising, becoming firm, "we are needed here."

Traejan nodded, feeling himself filled with the same determination - the responsibility brought on by his training. He straightened. "You are right," he said. "We should make haste."

Ember smiled at him and returned the pair of dirks she did not currently need to their designated places. "We should," she agreed. She took a leather-wrapped bundle from a shelf and handed it to Traejan. "I will bring a sword for you, but I think you should wear these."

The young prince took the bundle from her grasp – two blades sheathed and wrapped with a leather thong. He grasped one by the hilt, six inches of carved and polished bone capped with gold, and pulled it free of the scabbard. The blade itself was another fourteen inches of honed steel that curved back slightly.

"We can secure them to either side of your quiver," she told him. "I think they will serve you well."

Traejan beamed at her as he returned the blade to its sheath. "Thank you," he whispered before kissing her. It was some time before she broke away.

"We should get going," she murmured, breathless.

The young prince nodded.

33. WILDBOYS

"Look," the Roshan said, pointing. "There."

The mountain was a triangle of shadow against shadow, reaching up into the darkening sky. Halfway down, bouncing along at a downward angle, were sparks of dancing fire - red and gold against the shadows and throwing shadows of their own.

The elfin prince and the woman warrior had spent a week threading through the mountains, looking for some sign of the Wildboys. They had pressed ahead diligently, but without any fervor.

They stopped three times a day to rest the horses, Ember taking the time to continue Traejan's training, though it often ended with them making love on the ground or against a tree. They slept at night in each other's arms, wrapped in his bedroll.

"Do you sleep well out here?" Traejan asked one morning, remembering what Ryen had told him.

The Roshan shrugged. "I doze well enough. Coal will alert me if anything is about. I'm careful not to have more than a cup of wine, if I have any at all."

Up and up they went, deeper into the forests and higher into the mountain passes. They were about to call it a day once again when the elf dismounted and then stood stock still as dusk settled though the trees, looking around. Ember froze, her eyes of green and brown and gold darting about. When she did not see or sense danger, her gaze went to Traejan.

"They were here," he said.

"They were?" The Roshan looked around but she could see no evidence of anyone having been there, and the Wildboys never made an attempt to hide their passage. Besides, the clearing was too small for the band of miscreant Sprites to have stopped and stayed.

"A woodland elf was here," he said, cocking his head as he examined the ground. "A small one." His almond-shaped eyes rose from the ground and traveled around some small ground brush and through the trees. He started walking in the same direction as his gaze, leading Peg with a grasp on her reins so gentle that he might have forgotten he still held them.

Ember shook her head. "They don't travel alone," she said, though she followed him, silently leading Coal.

Traejan grunted quietly, as if amused by her declaration, and continued walking. "But I am sure," he remarked softly over his shoulder as he led them uphill, "that they break away to relieve themselves in private."

He stopped in his tracks and in a few seconds the Roshan stood beside him. They were in a flat clearing that had obviously been occupied recently. Low branches on the bushes had been bent or broken haphazardly and what grass that was growing this high was crushed. In the center of the clearing a pile of ashes and blacked wood remained from a small fire. In the ashy mix was a large assortment of tiny bones.

The Roshan's eyes shone as she looked at him, full of pride and admiration. The young elf smiled at her. He did not have to touch the ground or check the ashes for heat to tell her what he already knew.

"They were here last night."

In turn, she did not have to judge the growing dusk or see the direction of their trail to tell him what she already knew.

"We can catch them by moonrise."

The pair remounted and put their heels to the horses, keeping at a safe yet steady trot through the forest while they still had some light. They slowed in the darkness, but the trail was flat now, and wide. An hour later they reached the broad ledge where they spotted the flickering lights heading down the mountain.

The prince and the Roshan descended the path towards a ridge in the mountain passes, losing sight of the flickering lights for a while. When they found them again they had converged from individual lights into an enormous campfire that was visible even from a distance. As they closed in, it seemed to become a live animal - bursting with heat and light and surrounded by small filthy bodies.

Traejan was shocked beyond speech to see them. They looked like very young boys, varying in age from ten to twenty years, had they been human. Their tall, pointed ears and high arched brows over their almond-shaped eyes, however, gave no doubt to the fact that they were elves and therefore could be any age at all – from five to five hundred, though the prince was guessing much less.

They were certainly Sylvan, not one of them much more than four and a half feet tall, with dark eyes that sparkled with mischief. Their dark hair, kept reasonably short from dreadful looking cuts from a knife, were once curls that had run now wild into shaggy halos, some complete with dead leaves and broken twigs.

There had to be at least thirty of them, and not a single shirt to be had among the lot. They wore shorts or breeches that were horribly tattered, some only loincloths, as well as feathers and paint. Most had a knife of sorts attached to a belt, others had spears made of sharpened sticks that had been hardened by fire. A few had beads or knots tied in their hair. The tallest one, who was obviously the leader, wore a crown of woven laurel leaves on his head. He grasped a real spear that was short, but tipped with forged iron.

The only thing in the rag tag band of wildlings that was common to all among them, other than their race, was dirt.

Traejan watched as they chatted and laughed as easy as the summer. A few banged intermittently on drums of animal skin and a few held flutes at the ready as they passed around a wineskin. Rabbits, squirrels, voles, and even a few plucked birds were spitted over the fire. He looked at Ember with his brows raised, awaiting her move.

The Roshan gave him a wink before she stepped into the circle of light cast by the fire and was hit with a wave of silence as every boy crouched defensively at the sudden intrusion, a hand at his belt.

The tension broke instantaneously as she was recognized and greeted with great whoops and bellows as nearly three dozen boys tried to pounce on her.

Some ran to jump on her, some to hug and others only to touch. A few others, the youngest ones, eyed her fearfully, knowing who she was without having to be told. She was known to the Wildboys by many names. She was the Lady of Night, the Roshan Simorgh, Master of Weapons, Mistress of Death. The youngest ones watched her with awe, the older ones chatted away at her, relentless in their questions.

The tall leader, who came barely eye level to Ember, shooed the other boys away and wrapped skinny arms around her in an enthusiastic embrace.

"Aiden!" Ember greeted wholeheartedly, hugging him.

He took her hands eagerly in his own and looked at her with unabashed adoration in his eyes.

"I'm so glad that you came!" he exclaimed. His face betrayed the obvious love he had for her. "I was hoping to see you but I did not know if you would travel to the Mountain this summer, or find us if you did. I know you told me at the Stormdance, but I was too drunk to remember!"

"Good, because I was too drunk to remember what I told you!" she said as the smaller boys closed back in on her.

He laughed and began to lead her to a seat by the fire when

he saw Traejan, standing tall at the edge of the light, his arms crossed over his chest, watching. The horses waited silently behind him. Aiden froze and looked at Ember. He motioned towards the tall visitor with his short spear.

"And who is this?" he asked, his voice more stern than curious. The other boys who had begun to return to their seats stood up, taking notice of the newcomer as well. The Roshan shook off two boys that still clung to her limbs. Ember smiled wickedly.

"This," she exclaimed with a flourish, "is Traejanale Royce! Son of Rowland! *Prince* of the Elves!"

The boys froze, their eyes growing wider and wider. Traejan, who had taken a step into the circle of light at her introduction, now kept still even though he wanted to shift under the uncomfortable stare of the entire group, hushed with awe. He was about to tell them it was nothing when every one of the Wildboys burst out laughing.

They laughed and laughed and laughed.

Their combined laughter echoed through the woods and back again. They laughed until tears streamed down their faces. Some fell to their knees and a few even rolled on the ground, clutching their sides. Aiden had dropped his spear and bent double, his hands holding his stomach.

Traejan looked at Ember, puzzled. She only smiled with her tongue in her cheek, obviously amused by the show.

"An elf," one cried. "An elf!"

"The Prince of the Elves!" another shouted. That sent them howling.

Traejan went from amused to annoyed. "Do they doubt my lineage," he asked Ember, incredulous, "or that I am an elf?"

His query sent them off into fresh gales of laughter. They were all on the ground now, overcome with hilarity. He glared at them, asking them the same question when the Roshan did not answer.

"You doubt my lineage?" he demanded. "You certainly know that I am an elf!"

"Stop it!" one boy gasped. "You're killing me!"

Traejan looked at Ember again but she only shook her head and looked ready to laugh as well. He crossed his arms over his chest again and waited impatiently for the boys to regain control of themselves. His dark brows knitted together, his brown eyes reflecting sparks from the fire.

After a while the wild tribe of miscreants calmed, lying together in one panting heap that still tittered and giggled. Their dusty faces were streaked with tears.

Finally, Aiden disentangled himself from his pack and stood up.

"I am Aiden," he told Traejan, offering his hand in the manner of humans. The elfin prince eyed him dubiously, but grasped the proffered hand firmly.

"It's a pleasure to meet you, Aiden," he said, taking a measure of him.

The young Sylvan was more of a height with Ember, and barely came up to Traejan's chin. His brown hair was knife-cut and soft dusty curls fell about his face but not as far as his neck. His eyes were much like Traejan's - a light brown that caught the light and sparkled. He was dirty, but not quite as filthy as the rest.

Aiden turned to Ember and took her hand.

"Dark Lady," he said, bowing. She laughed and pulled his small frame to her own and hugged him tight. The other boys watched, envious. Aiden's grin looked wide enough to split his head. "Thank you," he told her. "I haven't laughed that hard since the last time we ambushed Ryen."

He took her hand again and led her closer to the fire. Traejan followed, perturbed.

"Just what was so funny?" he asked Aiden. "Is humor so different between elves?"

Aiden turned to him, holding up a hand. "Please," he said, "no more. My sides feel like they have been kicked by donkeys." The young prince looked at Ember for help.

"They don't believe your people are real elves," she informed him. Traejan stopped in his tracks. He knew that Sylvan Sprites did not like the Skye Elves, but he had no idea that they did not consider his race to be elves at all. The notion was ridiculous.

"Are you serious?"

Ember nodded. "Your people came from across the Ocean of Stars, a whole other world away. They do not trust people from so far."

"You must be a good man, for my lady to escort you," Aiden assured him, "though I am sure you are merely a student. Yet, you are a man. A man with pointed ears, but still a man."

Traejan could only gape at him in disbelief.

The boys had begun to disengage themselves from one another and seat themselves around the fire.

"The lady is more elf than you," one assured him.

The band of boys all hooted soft laughter at this.

"Ryen is more elf than you!" another chirped. Now they howled.

Aiden held up a hand, silencing them.

"Sea Elves swim," he told Traejan, explaining. "Black Elves own the night. But I have never seen a Skye Elf fly. What do you do?"

"What do *you* do?" Traejan retorted.

"I fight!" Aiden told him, holding his chin high. "I am a real elf, a true elf!"

The prince, tired of being goaded, provoked in return. "*I* am a true elf," he told Aiden. "You are a Sprite."

It was a step above being called a Faerie, but a small step. More of a slap.

The Wildboy's good nature dissolved into constrained fury.

"How dare you!" he hissed. "I fight! As do all my pack. We are the keepers of the forest and live by no law except for what nature decrees. *You* are a man with pointed ears. Full of fat and full of fear."

Traejan bit his tongue to keep from smiling but Aiden was not fooled. His anger only grew. The young prince looked again at Ember but her look of amusement only told him that he was on his own. He was baffled by the entire situation. He finally sighed.

"Look here, my boy," Traejan said, laying a fatherly hand on Aiden's shoulder. The small elf shook it off, vehement.

"I am not a boy, nor yours neither! We are neither kine nor kin. I am a true elf, a defender of the woods and the land, brave and true!" He looked at Traejan with disgust. "You are a man with pointed ears!"

"I am not!" the young prince argued, hating the petulant rise of his voice.

Aiden did not try to hide his smile. "You are!" he scoffed.

"I am not!" Traejan said firmly.

The other Wildboys still sat in disentangled heaps, watching the exchange between the two like it was the best thing they had ever witnessed.

"You are soft and shallow," Aiden taunted. "You are not brave! A true elf is brave!"

"I am so!" Traejan defended.

He knew that Aiden was taunting him and that he should take the higher ground but he could not seem to find it. He despised the way it made him sound like a child but could not seem to help himself. Just as bad, he knew that most of it stemmed from the fact that the dirty boy in front of him, who could be no more than twenty years old, loved his woman. He could see Ember from the corner of his eye and knew there was still no help from that quarter.

"Are not!" Aiden declared, sticking out his chin and taking a defiant step closer to the young prince, his spear held tightly by a grubby fist.

He means to fight me, Traejan thought, amazed. *He* wants *to fight me.*

Then Aiden took another step - not just towards Traejan but a bit to the side as well – putting his small frame between the elfin prince and his love.

"Am so!" Traejan argued, growing more heated by the second.

"Then show me you have no fear!" the Wildboy taunted. Traejan bristled at the challenge.

"I will!" he nearly shouted at Aiden, leaning towards him. He threw the Wildboy the fiercest look he could muster and sidestepped him.

Silence fell over the entire pack as they watched him advance upon the Lady of Night, the Master of Weapons, the Mistress of Death. Their wide eyes were like full moons in fields of dust and even Aiden was aghast, seeing he meant to take on the Lady herself.

Traejan stopped brusquely in front of the Roshan and seized her around the waist. His other hand grasped the back of her neck and pulled her to him, kissing her hard upon the mouth.

There was a great collective sucking of air as every boy in the pack gasped and stared open-mouthed at the boldness of the tall man with pointed ears. It was soon followed by a hush, heavy with anticipation of what the Lady would do. There was not one among them that did not expect the man-elf's face to be crushed with the hilt of a dagger or his throat to be slit.

Instead, the tall elf pulled the Roshan even closer, opening her mouth with his own, kissing her deeper. The Wildboys waited with bated breath for the punishment for such unprecedented boldness... but it did not come. The Dark Lady was bent backwards, her spine curved and supported by the man with pointed ears. The kiss went on.

"Ohhhooooooooooooooo!" they cried as one, their single sound of astonishment slowly turning into hoots and howls of delight and encouragement. They clapped and cheered. Even Aiden, who stood with his jaw so far open that it seemed to be unhinged, showed plain his surprise flash to fury then to shock and then to astounded glee. Finally, he laughed and clapped with the others.

Traejan broke the kiss but held his love close, looking into her gimlet eyes.

"You knew exactly what was going to happen here," he whispered accusingly. The Roshan's smile was as wicked as it ever was.

"No," she said, "I could only hope."

Traejan could not help but smile back. He was never able to do less. He pulled Ember upright then turned to see his newfound brethren on their feet and cheering for him. Aiden shook his fists at the sky as he howled then slapped Traejan on the back.

"You *are* brave!" he conceded with a shout. "Braver than me, even!" He laughed heartily, eyeing the tall elf with respect and envy. "Come! Share meat and mead with us!"

Traejan followed the small elf as he led him to the fire. He threw a grin at his warrior love. She grinned back, helpless to do less.

Boldness has genius, power, and magic, she thought. *Where have I heard that?* It didn't matter. She knew it was true. She watched the Wildboys flock around Traejan. Some shook his hand, some clapped him on the back – some just reached out a tentative hand to touch his clothing. All were full of awe and admiration.

Ember rolled her eyes and sat herself on a log, a small swarm of bodies around her own. A young boy offered her a horn of mead, which she gladly took.

"Will you tend to our horses?" she asked. She jerked her chin to the right, where the light of the fire disappeared into the trees. "Take off their bridles but leave them saddled?"

A dozen boys, streaked with paint and dirt, nodded eagerly and raced away. Ember hoped that they were tall enough and strong enough to manage Coal. Though the beast had not been fond of the wildlings at first, he had grown quite accustomed to them over the years. Still, he seemed to delight in giving them a scare now and then. She sighed and took a long pull from the horn. It was heavy and sweet.

She turned her face to see Aiden pushing boys out of the way so that he and Traejan could sit near Ember. She handed the young prince the horn and he gave her an amused look as he passed it along to Aiden. The leader of the Wildboys drank deeply and handed the horn to his second in command, a stick of a boy with unruly black hair named Simon.

"Did you come upon us by accident?" Simon asked the Roshan. "Or were you seeking us?"

"We were seeking you," Ember confirmed. Her eyes went to Aiden. "Have you had any problems with the Crommags? More than usual?"

His dark eyes glanced left and met Simon's. Small hands reached for the horn but he pushed them away. There were disgruntled murmurs but Simon shushed them.

"Find another horn," he scolded, "and hush now. Serious talk."

"Serious talk...serious talk..." was repeated throughout the tribe in muted tones. Some of the older boys edged close so they could listen silently, squatting down on their hams and rocking back on their heels. Other, younger boys, drifted away to find food and drink but knew well enough to keep quiet during serious talk.

Aiden looked at the auburn-haired warrior and the elfin

prince and told them what he knew, what Dell and his party had learned quite recently. The Crommags were coming down from the Mountains of Ice and massing at the steppes.

"How many?" Ember asked.

Aiden chuffed out a short breath that might have been a laugh, had there been any sound or humor to it. "All of them," he said.

The prince and the Roshan stared at him in surprise for a long moment before their eyes found each other.

"Are they moving as one?" Ember finally asked.

Aiden shook his head. "Many are massing north of the Ice Floe, but they are joined by more every day. A few large bands spent some time raiding the Gnomin Vale, then massacring the Northlon Farms. Now, raiding parties have been spotted in the Midlon."

Traejan nodded. "We came across two such parties," he said. "More than a score of them won't be going back."

Simon grinned at him. "That is good, but they will send more. They are after something. Something big enough to bring them all down from the Bite."

"Ryen believes they mean to make war," Ember told them. "I think so too."

Aiden shrugged. "If they are after warmer lands, most likely yes, but it doesn't matter. They will take, not ask or barter. They will kill everyone where they decide to settle, and everyone along the way."

"Is it possible that they won't go far?" Traejan asked. "That they will settle the lands of the Northlon and stay there?"

"Anything is possible," Simon remarked, "but why would they send scouts all the way into the Midlon?"

"And," the Roshan added, "if they are tired of scratching a life out of the snow, why would they want to try to scrape a life out of the Siber Massif?"

"Aye," Aiden agreed. "A little more trekking will yield them rich farmland, already ploughed."

"And the river, and the sea," Simon added.

A quiet followed and the Roshan and the prince looked at each other once more, the enormity of the situation sinking into them with claws that dug deep. If the Crommags were after warmer lands there was only one thing in their way – people. Humans and elves.

The lingering silence was broken only by the snap of a branch as a knot popped in the fire. It was more gravity than the Wildboys could bear.

Incapable of being somber for long, Aiden clapped Traejan on the back. "Do not fret so!" he commanded. "It won't be tonight! Tonight, we celebrate!"

The elfin prince managed a smile. "What are we celebrating?"

"That it is time to eat!" Aiden returned loudly and was cheered by all with hoots and yells. It signaled the end of serious talk, to the great relief of all.

"Food!" Simon called out, loudly.

"Mead!" Aiden shouted, louder.

The band of Wildboys whooped and hollered in return, the noise of the group rising to a cacophony, as they set about their nightly celebration, moving as riotous as their name implied.

34. LOVE AND LEAF

The young prince and his teacher had gotten the information they had come for, but to just up and leave would go against all good manners of any race. So Ember drank more mead, shared a squirrel with Aiden, and glanced often at Traejan. She wanted badly to talk to him, to be alone with him, but knew it prudent to wait. There was more Aiden could tell her, and it would be better to break the tension of his news with the party atmosphere the Wildboys took with them everywhere they went.

The elfin prince was offered a horn of the honey-ale quite often, but always declined.

"I'm half-drunk from the smell alone!" he told the boys each time, making them howl with laughter. Each time they chided him in good nature. They had found him brave beyond measure and, for them, it was enough to make him a brother.

"Naught to worry!" Ember shouted each time it came his way. "I'll have his share!" The boys roared with approval every time, cheering her on as she took large gulps from the horn.

When the night's fare began to dwindle, leaving only greasy fingers and faces and small animal bones as evidence of the meal, more instruments appeared. The sound of reed pipes, wooden flutes, and skin drums first teased the dark air, tasting it, before rising and falling into a rhythm.

More wood was thrown on the fire, sending up a shower of sparks and the Wildboys took to their bare feet, stomping and dancing in a manner that gave testimony to their name.

Aiden swayed on his feet and pounded his thin chest before tipping his head back to bellow lyrics with the rising music. "When I get to 'evan!" he belted out.

"When I get to 'evan!" the rest of the boys shouted back in the same tune.

"Faith is gonna say!" Aiden sang in a deep baritone. The other boys mimicked him, repeating his song. "How'd you earn your livin'?" he yelled and then paused for the echo before continuing, "how'd you earn your way?" The boys duplicated his lyrics and tone and Aiden cupped his hands around his mouth to bellow out the last few lines.

"By takin' mead and maidens!" he shouted, "and fightin' in the fray!"

The boys not rolling with laughter echoed their leader while Ember and the elfin prince clapped their hands and stomped their feet, singing and hooting along with the bunch.

The half full moon, known as the Reaper's Choke, rose in the star-studded black while the antics around the bonfire continued. When it had passed its zenith, the Lady of Night and the elf-man-prince took their leave. Most of the younger boys had already fallen asleep, curled up or sprawled on one another like a pack of wolves. The older ones embraced the Roshan who promised to see them at the next Stormdance. They gathered round Traejan as well, shaking his hand and patting him on the back, some pantomiming his kiss to the applause and cheer of others.

The pair bade goodbye to Aiden last. Traejan watched the Sprite's thin chest swell as he looked at the Roshan, then empty in a sigh. Ember embraced him, making his dirty face split into a grin.

"Stay away from those Crommags," she warned him as she let him go. Traejan thought it good advice – the leader of the Wildboys would barely be waist high to a Crommag, and he was the tallest of the lot.

"Don't worry," Aiden assured her. "Their women are too hairy and their mead is too sour," he said with a mischievous glint in his eyes, "I know because I've had them both!"

The other boys roared laughter. The Roshan chortled and shook her head in wry amusement.

Traejan himself could not help but laugh as the young leader approached him and held out his hand. The elfin prince grasped it tightly and though Aiden only came up to his chest, his grip was strong.

"I still think you are a man with pointed ears," he told Traejan, "but you are certainly brave." He paused, undecided for a moment, then continued. "I know my Lady can take care of herself, but watch over her anyway."

Traejan felt more than just a smile at the corner of his lips. It was as if Aiden was entrusting him. Entrusting him to do something that the leader of the Wildboys wished he could do himself, something the elfin prince would willingly give his own life to do.

"I will," Traejan promised.

With parting waves and hoots, the boys returned to the bonfire. The half moon smiled on their antics as it made a lingering descent towards the tops of the pines. The elfin prince and the Roshan could hear the cacophony start up again as they turned their mounts away and led them through the trees and down the mountain.

"We can make it to the bottom by moonset," Ember said, "and camp there by the Rivulet. We can be back at the haus late tomorrow afternoon."

She went to stick a boot in a stirrup and swayed, keeping her feet by holding onto the girth of Coal's saddle.

"Whoa!" Traejan exclaimed quietly, catching her by the shoulders until she was steady. "I knew you were hitting that mead awfully hard," he muttered. The Roshan chuckled, her boot finding the stirrup this time as she hauled herself up.

"Can you ride?" he asked.

"Of course I can ride," she told him. "I'm hardly drunk. I've ridden much drunker than this."

"I'm sure you have."

The Roshan chuckled again. "But why don't you ride pillion?" she suggested. "You can keep me warm, and it will be easier for us to talk."

Traejan looped Peg's reins loosely over the horn of the Roshan's saddle and then pulled himself up – seating himself on Coal's back, just behind Ember. He gave a low whistle, peering around from his vantage point on top of the huge beast.

The Night Stallion twisted his neck to look at the effrontery of the elf, gave a reproachful snort and twitched his tail at the added burden, and then turned his face back front and started down the mountain. Traejan wrapped his arms around Ember and kissed the side of her neck. She leaned her body back into his with a contented sigh.

"I don't know why we haven't done this before," he murmured into her hair, closing his eyes.

"Me neither," she agreed. "Except that it's been so hot during the day."

Traejan nodded. "The nights are getting cooler. And did you see the moon tonight? Humans call it 'the Reaper's Choke.' The next time it rises full it will be the Scream - Harvest Moon. Summer is almost over."

His remark had been just that – a remark. But the Roshan, who had been feeling more than a bit loopy from all the mead, sobered instantly. She felt as if the icy waters of the Floe had just been splashed full upon her face. It was shocking, and not pleasant.

Summer was indeed almost over. The cooler nights were not the first sign. She thought of the golden fields of wheat, where Traejan had kissed her for the first time. She thought of his training, almost done.

And the nightingale.

The nightingale had been singing those words for week, sweet as you please.

Summer is ending, summer is ending.

Then why had the thought not occurred to her?

It did occur to me, she thought, *but I pushed it away.*

The end of summer, she knew, would mark the time for the elfin prince to return home.

She suddenly found it hard to breathe.

When the pair reached the bottom of the mountain they unsaddled the horses. They forwent a fire and simply wrapped themselves together in Traejan's bedroll to sleep the few hours before dawn. The Roshan, however, was far from sleepy.

She lay with her head on his chest, feeling the beat of his heart. It was not in sync with her own this time. Hers was going too fast.

Is this what love feels like? she wondered. Something was gripping her heart, but it did not feel good. It was squeezing her, flooding her with an emotion she had never known. It wasn't until the unseen sun was rising in the east, painting the Low Forest in hues of pink and orange, that she identified the feeling. It was fear.

Part of her wanted to feel sorry for herself - but that, too, was a foreign emotion.

It is unfair that I should find love now, she thought, *and that it be taken from me so soon.*

She closed her eyes and listened to the sound of his heart, the sound of each breath that she felt warm her cheek.

But I found it. Is that enough?

She did not want to wake him, but she could feel her arms constricting around his body, as if by tightening her grip she could somehow hold onto him.

I have loved. I am loved. I know his face and his smell and the feel of his body. I know he lives. Maybe that is enough.

The world grew bright around them and the young elf blinked the sleep from his eyes. He closed them again and kissed the top of her head.

"Awake already?" he asked.

Ember marveled at how he knew she was alert without seeing her face. "Awake all night with you snoring!" she teased, lifting her face to gaze at him. He buried his face in her hair, his hand traveling up her side, under her shirt. The Roshan laughed softly. "We need to get home," she whispered.

"We will," he whispered back, unlacing her jerkin as he kissed the corner of her jaw. Then his lips found hers and she forgot all else.

Later, he saddled the horses as she packed their bedroll and found a few hard apples for their breakfast.

"Should we ride together again?" Traejan asked, putting his arms around the Roshan and kissing her cheek softly.

She gave him a wan smile. "Coal says you're too fat."

Traejan laughed. "Why do I suddenly feel like we have been married for a hundred years! I snore, I'm too fat..."

Ember's soft laughter joined his and she put her cheek against his chest. "I feel that too," she agreed. "But in a good way."

"Besides," Traejan said as he let go of Ember and took a proffered apple, "that beast could carry a family of Crommags!"

The Roshan's smile brightened. She found it impossible not to smile when she was looking at the elfin prince.

My love, she thought. *My love.*

"You are probably right about that, but we can press harder if we ride separately. I'm anxious to look at my maps."

"The Crommags," he said.

The Roshan nodded, her smile dissolving. It was true. It gnawed at her mind almost as much as the thought of him leaving.

"There is so much to do," she said, a frown creasing her auburn brows. "I have never felt pressured by tasks before," she admitted, "but I feel overwhelmed by this, though we have some time. Maybe *because* we have some time." She shook her head, her red locks chasing one another. "I feel that, if I am home, I will be able to organize my thoughts better." She pulled herself up high and was astride Coal a single fluid motion. "Plan better," she added.

Traejan nodded as he swung up gracefully into his own saddle.

Ember turned Coal's head and put her heels to him before the prince could answer more.

They pressed the horses to a steady trot all through the morning.

When they stopped for lunch Traejan sat with his back against the gnarled trunk of an old oak and Ember sat across his lap, her head on his chest.

"You're so quiet," he said, brushing a strand of hair away from her face.

"I'm just tired from last night," she lied.

"Then eat something and we can press on."

Her head gave the slightest shake. "I'm not hungry." Which was true.

Traejan put a finger under her chin and lifted her face so he could look into her eyes. "I hate to see you so worried," he told her, a frown creasing his smooth brow.

Ember smiled at him. "I love you," she said.

The crease in his brow disappeared and the bright brown of his eyes melted into dark blue. "I love you, too."

"Then that is all that matters," she said, putting her hand behind his neck and pulling his lips down to her own.

I'm not going to think about it now, she decided. *I have to think about what we are going to do about the Crommags.*

Besides, autumn is coming – but it is not here yet. I will not ruin what time I have in the present by agonizing over the future.

Relieved by her decision, the Roshan was much more animated for the rest of the afternoon as they rode to the haus. She asked Traejan about all he knew of the Northlon, including the Vikes. Ember was impressed by his knowledge of its history and how much he had seen firsthand. She was eager to get home and get out her maps so they could go over them together.

The sun was beginning its descent, but still above the treetops, when they entered the glen. Traejan cocked his head, looking at the haus as the horses picked up the pace on their own, also eager to be home.

"Gatha's there," he announced.

"Good," Ember said with a smile. "I hope she's cooking."

"She is."

The Roshan slid off the back of her great black beast and stretched. She did not see the elf dismount but suddenly he was there, one hand supporting her back as it arched under his weight, his lips on her neck.

"What do you want more," she asked, letting him hold her and kiss her, "food or a shower?"

"You," he whispered.

Ember laughed. "Then I need to shower first. I hate being grimy, and I'm sure I smell like the Seventh Circle."

Traejan kissed her on the corner of her jaw and pulled her upright. "I like the way you smell," he said. "But I'll take a shower before food as well."

They unsaddled the horses, removed their packs and rubbed them down before turning them loose.

The elf and the warrior each shouldered their weapons and lumbered inside. The smell of Gatha's cooking made both of their mouths water. The two looked at each other.

"Food first," they said in unison.

They threw down their gear in the mudroom and greeted Gatha warmly. She eyed them with suspicion but fed them roasted capon and buttered peas along with fresh bread, still steaming from the oven.

The young prince and the Roshan feasted together and showered together before they ended the day in bed together. As Traejan fell asleep, he decided life could not be more perfect. Ember was resolved that the maps could wait until morning. Instead, she held onto the moment as tightly as she could.

The next day, Ember pulled out her largest and most detailed maps of the Northlon. She spread them out on the tables in the dining area and weighted the corners to keep them from rolling.

"Here," Traejan said, tapping the map with a finger, "is where Aiden says they are gathering."

The Roshan frowned at the map. "The Ice Floe is keeping them there, isn't it?"

Traejan nodded. "I would think so. It thaws in the spring and the summer melts the snowcaps in the Bite, turning the river into a torrent. It dwindles in the fall and freezes over in the winter, which will make it easy for them to cross. If they bide their time, and wait till the mid of winter, they can cross before the next melt. They will have to have enough provisions, however, to last them until the passes in the Siber Massif are clear of snow."

"May the First Circle help the farmers there," the Roshan murmured.

Traejan nodded his agreement. "Once the passes are clear, the Crommags can travel through the Veldt as spring begins."

"That way they can live off the land as they go," Ember remarked, her eyes of green and brown and gold tracing a course over the map. "They can't farm the Echo Sea, nothing will grow there. They can skirt Tuar Ceath, but it is unlikely. I expect they would take the pass between the Mountains of the Moon and the Mountains of the Sun." Her gaze lifted. "How well is the elfin city defended?"

"Unless you count the Mountains," Traejan said, his voice barely above a whisper, "not at all." His soft brown eyes remained on the map.

The Roshan nodded as if she had expected such an answer. "The elves need to be warned. And the Atlanteans."

"I am to meet Dell under the Harvest Moon in Amherst. I'm sure he will be there the first night, maybe sooner, but he will wait till it is half gone before he comes looking for me. We can warn him there, and then you and I should continue on to Atlantea."

Ember was silent until he looked up and met her eyes.

What will you do? she wondered, but asked aloud, "What will your people do?"

Traejan shook his head, his thick blonde curls moving slightly. "I really have no idea. This will be devastating to all. We came to this land to avoid war, and here it is, thrust upon us anyway. Elves are notoriously slow to act when it comes to war. How long do you think it will take the Crommags to reach Tuar Ceath?"

The Roshan's green and brown eyes went back to the map. "If the beasts are stuck until spring, it will take them the whole season to reach the Mountains of the Moon. They are on foot, with women and children and – according to Aiden - all that they own. The elves would have until Dia Prima at the least, Midsummer at most." She looked back up at her love. "Nine months, roughly. Will that be enough time?"

Traejan put both hands on the map, a crease between his brows as he pored over each mountain and pass that guarded what he thought of as his homeland. "It will have to be," he said softly. "When do we leave?"

Ember gave him a sad smile, glad that he was still contemplating the map. "I was told I have you until the first sign of Autumn."

The young prince looked up and a real smile changed his features, making them bright and making her heart skip.

"You have me forever," he said, wrapping his arms around her and pulling her close. He kissed the top of her head.

Ember pressed her face against his chest, squeezing her eyes shut until the tears that threatened had subsided. "Then get your sword," she instructed, breaking away from him and giving him a ghost of a smile, "we still have work to do."

The elf was more than happy to acquiesce and gave her a parting kiss before hurrying off to retrieve his swordbelt.

The Roshan upended her mug of coffee and saw that Gatha was watching her from the kitchen, her blue eyes flat yet full of meaning.

"Don't look at me like that," Ember said testily, her auburn brows drawing together.

Gatha continued her stare for another two seconds and then turned to finish putting away the breakfast dishes.

The Roshan and the prince took to the glen where she worked on honing his swordsmanship.

They did the same routine for four days – scanning maps, planning their journey, and swordfighting. Everything they did always ended the same, both of them naked and exhausted and ecstatic.

Neither one of them had ever known that they would feel such a deep sense of love and belonging. They cherished each second - fighting, loving, laughing - and cherished each other. Ember let herself forget, made herself forget, about the time and the tide.

The summer was undoubtedly ending, but it was not over yet. For the moment, the world was made of nothing but warm skin, half-lidded eyes, and parted lips.

The song of steel filled their days, the sound of heartbeats filled their nights.

The Roshan held onto the prince every night, her eyes closed against the world. That a single form of muscle and bone and breath could hold so much fulfillment for her filled her with wonder.

She spent every moment immersed in the present, living in every movement he made – from pouring her wine to the slightest change in his facial expressions – her own life infused with every breath of air he drew into his lungs. Their heartbeats were again the smooth rhythm of summer.

Five days later, Ember saw the leaf.

The future, which she never allowed to be more than a fleeting thought - a silent promise that whispered on the wind - was now a looming presence. She had to force it from her mind but it was like trying to shoulder an oversized and disgruntled ogre out the tavern door.

The prince had run back into the haus to exchange their long swords for short swords and the Roshan had walked in the other direction to get under the shade of the trees. She had been laughing at something Traejan had said, but it died on her lips as if stolen by the cooling breeze. Standing frozen in time, rooted to the forest floor, she did not know if the world had gone silent around her or if her ears had gone deaf. Her lungs had certainly stopped drawing air. She stood wordless and motionless, feeling as if maybe even her heart had stopped as well.

After long seconds, the Roshan forced herself to take a slow deep breath to steady herself. The air came in a deliberate yet shaky stream of warm air. Warm air, yes, but threaded with a current that was decidedly cooler. It was summer air no longer, but it was not the air that had stolen her breath.

Two feet away from her face was a single leaf. It was a verdant green, like its millions of brothers that covered the tree in front of her. Green and full of life, but along its top edge crept a vein of brilliant orange-red.

One of the simple miracles of nature. The days were still warm, but the nights were getting cooler. The sugar made inside the leaf during the day found itself unable to move its nourishment to the tree at night because of the drop in temperature. The trapped sugar produced a red pigment and, lo and behold, nature began to change her dress for the season. Simple as that. Autumn had come.

The first sign of autumn.

Ember had no idea how many battles she had seen. Hundreds? How many times had she been wounded? Half that? Twice that? She could recall being stabbed with knives and swords. Pierced and run through with weapons from worlds beyond count. She remembered the one time she was sure she would die.

She recalled one time, with perfect clarity, laying with her cheekbone pressed into hard-packed dirt. Bodies, broken and hewn, lay heaped and sprawled all around her. The one closest was the bastard of the bunch. He had borne down on her with more strength and speed than she had expected and she had paid the price. Her only satisfaction was that his head lay ten feet away from his body. She would have spit on him if she could.

Her own head had felt thick and dull. Her forearm lay tight against her lower belly where the bastard had cut her. Her palm pressed tight against a hard slimy tube of what had to be an intestine. One that seemed determined to take a peek at the outside world. The more she tried to keep it inside the more it seemed to slither out. A groan slipped from somewhere deep in her throat. Before her eyes glazed over she found herself mesmerized by the puffs of dust her breath roused from the ground every few seconds.

The Roshan's eyes, green and brown with glints of gold, were glazed over now. She knew there was no wound she had ever suffered, not even laying almost cut in half and watching her tiny puffs of breath stir the dirt of a foreign land's soil, that had made her feel what she felt now. This hurt was so sharp that it was surreal. Real pain was not as bad, as horribly *deep*, as what now cut through her heart and soul. She felt her knees turn to water but she held her feet, reflexively tensing the muscles in her legs and back.

She reached out and pulled the leaf from the tree with a violent snap. Not satisfied, she threw it to the ground and stamped it with a boot. She ground it with her heel even as she tried to stem the tide of emotions that now flooded her body. Her knees finally gave and she sat down, helpless on the forest floor.

You have been hiding, she thought, chiding herself.

Worse, was that she wanted to keep hiding. Hiding in his hair and his eyes and his arms.

Ember drew a shaky breath and thought back to the day they had dropped as one onto the Stonefield Road. They had ambushed a band of Crommags and her love had kissed her for the first time.

That kiss had shattered the world she had known and she felt that world now, drawing back in and closing around her. The jagged pieces fit themselves back together in a ragged jumble, like a broken toy repaired by rough and desperate hands.

How long? she questioned, trying to add the days together. *How long did we have? Two weeks? Three? No, not quite that long. Not that long by far.*

Such a short amount of time.

Her head snapped sharply to the right as she heard something. It was the nightingale, on the branch of a branderbush.

"Summer has ended..." it sang, the notes clear and sweet, "...has ended, has ended! Harvest, harvest, harvest!"

Ember listened, her gimlet eyes wide, and wondered how

long it had been singing that song. She looked down and was surprised to see she had picked up the crushed leaf with the crimson edge. Such a bearer of bad tidings there never was.

Then she heard the door to the haus open and the Roshan was on her feet in an instant, steeling herself against the song of the nightingale. It was not in her character to hide. It was in her to fight. She watched the newly made warrior walk towards her, her chest filling with air and her heart rushing at the way he moved.

Two weeks, she thought – not with bitterness but with a gratitude that warmed her to her very soul. *Two weeks to know my love and listen to his heart beat with mine. I have loved. I am loved. I know his face and his smell and the feel of his body. I know he lives. Will it be enough to know that I found love, and that he is out there somewhere, and that I will always love him? It must.*

Then he was there before her, filling her eyes and her nose and her heart. The elfin prince kissed her and pressed the hilt of a short sword into her hand.

Before sitting down to dinner, the Roshan found the biggest wine glass in her cupboard and filled it to the top. It took half the bottle. She sat with the young prince in her favorite spot, the two chairs with the low table by the long fireplace in the living room. The nights were cool enough again for a small fire and the light danced in his hair, now bleached by the sun, turning it a burnished gold.

When the wine in her glass was gone, along with half of their dinner, she refilled it. Traejan was telling her about his first hunting trip. She hardly heard what he was saying but was listening as well as she could. He must have said something to make him expect a response, maybe even a laugh, because he looked at her, puzzled.

"What is it?" he asked.

She forced a smile and reached a hand into the belt on her tunic. Then she laid the leaf she had found and torn from its branch on the table by his plate. "The first sign of autumn," she said simply. She expected dismay, alarm, fear – hopefully nothing akin to what she felt but *something* other than what she saw.

Traejan closed his teeth around the bit of meat on his fork and pulled it off without appearing to feel anything. His eyebrows rose for a moment then he sat back in his chair, chewing thoughtfully.

"It's about time," he said when he was done. "You were right about the mad season here – I've seen over a hundred summers and can't recall one that was longer." He smiled and put his hand over hers. "Or better."

Ember forced herself to be still. "It will be time for you to go home," she said, making an effort to keep her voice even. Traejan swallowed a drink of water.

"Time for us to go home," he corrected.

"Excuse me?"

"Time for us to go home." He looked at her with her mouth half open and seemed startled by her shock and then shook his head. "Of course it doesn't have to be *my* home, we can go wherever you want." He put his fork down and covered both of her hands with his own. "If we still plan to warn the Atlanteans ourselves, we can stay there. Or go south. Home will be wherever we are together. As long as I am with you, I don't care where we are."

Ember felt her eyes well up with tears and swallowed against the hot lump her throat. "You will need to go home. You will need to help your people prepare for what is coming. You have a warrior's responsibility now."

The elf nodded slowly, looking into the fire. "I remember you saying that when I first started. It seems like such a long time ago." He looked up, seeing the fire reflected in her eyes. "But you are right. We will warn the Atlanteans, then go home to Tuar Ceath. They will need us."

When the Roshan spoke it was almost a laugh. "Traejan, you cannot take me home. Not to Tuar Ceath."

Traejan did laugh, but it was short and confused. "What do you mean?"

This time it was Ember who was perplexed.

How could he not see? How did one explain something that should be as plain as day?

She put down her wine and sat back, rubbing her face with her hands. Then she sighed and looked at the one she loved, the only one she knew she would ever love.

"Traejan," she said at last, "these past four days I have purposefully not thought of the future, other than the Crommags and what we must do. I have deliberately not thought of what the future might hold for you and me. Have you?"

"Of course, and I can't wait! I want you to meet my family and see our land. I would love to live there, but not yet – not until we are ready for a family of our own. Our first obstacle, of course, is an impending war with invading Crommags." He laughed again. "Do all of those in love face such hindrances?"

The Roshan would have chortled if she had the breath to do so. "Our first *hindrance* is us," she whispered. Traejan frowned, clearly not understanding, so she went on. "How do you think your family would feel about me?"

He shook the question off as if it were a gnat. "What do I care?"

"Because they are your family," she said softly. "They are your people."

"And?"

She shook her head slowly and let out a deep breath. "I am not your people." She made no mention of the snobbery the Skye Elves were known for, she was quite sure he knew, but still he kept silent. She sighed again, impatiently this time. "I am not an elf."

Traejan clenched his jaw, visibly upset for the first time. "Are you sure of that?"

Ember was almost too shocked to speak. Almost. "Trae, I know I am not like most humans, but I'm not like any elf, either. Even if I was, I would be an outsider."

The elf shook his head. "Plenty of elves from the Old World have begun to marry Sylvan elves…"

"You are not some merchant elf!" the Roshan interrupted, cutting him off. "And I am not a Sylvan! You are the Prince of the Skye Elves and I am a mercenary! They would not accept me as part of their society, much less as some sort of royal mistress!"

"Don't ever say that!" Traejan blurted, his voice near shouting. The Roshan sat back, surprised, and his shoulders slumped. The elfin prince reached out and wrapped his fingers around her wrist and she saw the soft brown of his irises bleed out to blue.

"They will accept you," he told her, his voice low. "And you will not be my mistress but my wife. You will be the Lady of Song."

Ember held his gaze for long moments and then sighed. "Would that I could," she whispered. "I will always be no more than the Lady of Steel, the Lady of Death. The elfin people will not accept me, your family even less."

"They will accept you," Traejan told her, "or I will be gone to their line forever."

Ember sat back, harder this time, her mouth open. This scared her as much as the thought of being away from him.

No, she decided, more. Much more. Yet when he spoke of her as his wife, it broke the places of her heart that had still been whole. Her eyes squeezed shut, trying to stem the flood of feelings and her newly discovered emotion of fear.

Traejan moved around the table to kneel in front of her and brought her hand to his lips. "It's okay," he assured her.

"Everything will be alright. I promise. I will not let anything happen to you. And I will not be parted from you."

Ember embraced him and gave way to the tears that she had been holding. He kissed them from her face and she knew that what the future held was going to be harder than she thought. Much harder.

Just when she had found resolve, his determination and tenderness took it from her. Ember was finally flooded with self-pity. It made her sick to her stomach but she could not seem to stop it.

Two weeks! her heart cried. *Two weeks! So little time! So unjust!*

The young prince was wiping her face dry with his hands, kissing her and whispering words of love in elfin while Ember racked her brain for a solution.

What am I going to do? she thought, despairing. Deep inside she could hear the soft whisper of her Roshan.

You know what you must do, he told her. *You have a warrior's responsibility.*

The bitterness that filled her was so great that she could taste it. Like blood and dirt and ersatz steel.

What would you *do?* she asked back. *What* did *you do?*

But for this there came no answer.

35. WATERFALLS

"Where are you going?" Traejan asked sleepily. "It's not even dawn."

Ember had turned on the flambeau by her bed and was sitting up, stretching her arms high above her head as she yawned mightily before she turned her face to him. The prince was happy to see her wicked smile had returned. The glint in it was enough to make him want to pull her back into bed. She recognized the look and laughed.

"*I'm* not going anywhere. *We* are going for a hike." Traejan wrapped his arms around her and kissed the skin over her spine.

"Let's go for a hike around here," he said, indicating the bedroom. "I want to show you my version of returning the gift."

Ember laughed and pushed him away. "Get dressed! I'm going to pack our lunch. I want to be out of here in half of an hour."

Traejan groaned but did as he was bid, getting dressed and scrubbing his face and quickly cleaning his teeth over her bathroom sink and then pulling on his boots.

When he came out of the room, the Roshan was talking quietly to Gatha. The Gnomin woman's face was somber as she nodded in understanding. Ember grasped the smaller woman's shoulder, giving it a squeeze, and then turned to Traejan.

"Gatha is leaving," she announced. "We probably won't see her again before we leave ourselves."

The elfin prince held out his arms to the small woman. She

already had a pack slung over the shoulder of her blue-checked blouse, a small leather purse clutched in one stubby-fingered hand, and a fold of parchment in the other.

"A goodbye kiss?" Traejan suggested.

Gatha snorted and turned and headed for the front door, but gave him a wisp of a smile as she did so.

"I'll miss you!" the young prince called to her retreating form. Gatha snorted again as Ember tossed him a leftover biscuit for breakfast.

The Roshan picked up a heavy pack from the kitchen counter and began to slip her arm through the strap but the young elf took it from her and slung it over one of his broad shoulders.

"Is there wine in here?" he asked, his voice full of mock suspicion as he bit into the hard roll of bread.

Ember smiled at her love and kissed him, standing on her toes, her red hair falling down her back. "Maybe," she said sweetly.

They left the haus in time to see Gatha trotting away on her donkey. The Roshan watched the Gnomin ride away for a moment, then went the other way, north - towards the stream. Coal and Peg stood companionably on the other side of the water on the edge of the forest, munching on golden grass.

Dawn was bright but the early morning air was crisp enough that they could see their breath as they crossed the stream next to the water wheel and followed it up into the hills.

Traejan walked behind Ember, watching her move with the fluid grace he loved so well. He watched her hair, which she now almost always wore down, pendulum back and forth across her back.

As if the color alone was not hypnotic enough, he thought with wry admiration.

Within an hour the forested hills became mountain and they paused to look back into the vale of the Backwoods that she called home. The morning sun had not yet broken over the forest and the iron sentinels threw long shadows into the clearing. The once green patchwork of the clearing floor was gold, ripening here and there into tones of rust.

They left the stream and took a switchback path that cut up into the mountains. The path, if it could be called that, was not worn down nor did it bear the appearance of ever having been a walkway. It was merely a relatively flat strip where the footing was less rocky and that the Roshan's eyes seemed to pick out with ease.

The iron sentinels began to give way to soldier pines and moss, ferns were replaced with small bushes and pine needles. Before they started to climb again, Ember led him though a copse of trees to show him the springs of hot water that supplied the haus. A dozen miniature tarns pooled between rocks at varying heights, many spilling into others. Some were no more than a few feet across while others were big enough to swim in. All of them had steam rising from their surfaces.

Traejan dipped a handed into the closest one and pulled it back quickly. It was near boiling. He smelled his fingers.

"It's fresh!"

"I hope so!" Ember said. "It's what we bathe with!"

Traejan was surprised. "I always thought it was heated water from the stream. Usually, natural hot ponds are full of sulfur."

"I know. I'm very lucky. It has something to do with the water coming up through the rock, instead of through clay. And the temperatures vary from pool to pool." She pointed to one of the ponds higher up. "That one is cool enough to soak in."

"Which ones lead to the haus? How does it work?"

Ember laughed. "I have no idea."

"Aren't you curious?"

"I was at first. Now I just take it for granted. Like the way the lights turn on when I touch the switch. Many things are that way, I think, when you see them work for the first time. At first it seems miraculous, then a blessing, then it becomes ordinary. You don't even think about it until it breaks or isn't there any more. Then you're angry."

Traejan drew her close and put his arms around her. "I will always think of our love as miraculous, and a blessing. And *you* will never be ordinary."

Ember smiled and laid her cheek on his chest. "Good. That ties in with my lesson for today, so let's press on."

"Today is a lesson?"

"Every day is a lesson," she told him.

More than you know, Traejan thought.

His body began to warm with the day and the exertion of the climb. As it did he could smell her scent lingering on his own skin. He breathed deep the soft bouquet of leather and iron and morning roses that he knew, now, was from Gatha washing her clothes with rosewater.

They returned to the route Ember had chosen and began to follow its zigzag course up, over, and up again. Each time they switched direction the trees would open up and Traejan would look back over the valley. The view was enough to take his breath away. It became even more so the higher they climbed.

Ember regarded the landscape with a sort of beaming pride and deep sense of satisfaction. An hour before noon, their direction turned from the valley side of the slope and wound around to the other side where it met another mountain. The meager path opened up into a meadow and this time Traejan did feel his breath stolen away.

A crystal clear lake spread out before them, fed by twin waterfalls that cast rainbows like toys in their swirling mists. On the far side of the water, to the right of the twin falls, another set of waterfalls broke off from the lake - spilling their liquid treasure into a gorge that fed the rivers and streams of the high forests. The source of the twin falls was a lake high above them, where Traejan could hear the roar of more waterfalls. He turned to Ember, his almond-shaped eyes wide with surprise and delight.

"I had no idea this was up here," he told her.

She smiled at his child-like enthusiasm and he found that her smile was enough to break his heart and mend it again in the same breath.

"We can have lunch here," she suggested, "and hike up to the other falls afterward." She helped Traejan shrug off the pack they had brought. A thin blanket had been rolled and tied to it. She shook it out and spread it on the ground. Traejan knelt on its edge and pulled out the lunch she had packed for them. It was a small feast of meat, cheeses, and bread. She had nuts and fruits as well as a dark green bottle full of wine. Traejan was surprised to see beads of moisture on it from being chilled. He looked closer, squinting at the liquid inside.

"White wine?" he asked. Ember grinned broadly.

"It's more appropriate for a picnic."

"Pick-nick? What's a pick-nick?"

Ember laughed. "It's what we are having right now."

"Is that a Gnomin word?"

Ember sat on the edge of the blanket, folding her feet under her legs. "No," she said slowly, thinking. "I'm not sure where I got that one." Her eyes were far away for a moment, and then returned to him. "Whatever the origin of the word, it means a leisurely lunch outdoors. And that is what we will have."

"Did you bring anything to drink this out of, or do you plan on upending the bottle into your mouth like a sailor?" Traejan asked.

In response, Ember produced two small silver cups from her pack.

"You thought of everything," he conceded.

"That's not all," Ember confessed with a mischievous smile.

She dug into the pack and pulled out a small square of waxed paper. She unfolded it carefully, revealing the golden gem inside - a piece of fresh honeycomb. Traejan laughed.

"What are you up to?" he asked, moving closer to her.

"I thought we might honey the wine," she suggested. Traejan laughed again and the sound of it was honey in her own ears.

"I've never tried it with white wine, though many elves do. Women especially – they seem to favor the sweeter drinks."

Ember was almost crestfallen but found it easier to feign offense. "Do you mean you think it is effeminate to drink white wine?" she asked, her tone more teasing than accusatory. Traejan held up his hands in surrender.

"Absolutely not!" he laughed. "It's just not for me. I think it would be too sweet for me, and you are more sweetness than I can take."

"Ugh! That is more than I can take!" Ember said, laughing. Though, truth be told, any flattery from her love was warmth to her heart, even in jest. The young prince, seeing her veiled disappointment, sat up straight, suddenly serious.

"I have a better idea," he told her. He picked up the piece of honeycomb and held it to her lips. She took an experimental bite, the wax crushing slowing between her small teeth, causing the honey to flow unto her lips and tongue. Traejan pulled it away and kissed her deeply.

Immediately his head began to swim and his breath left his lungs, leaving him gasping. It was not air that he wanted, that he *needed*, but her. His love, his joy, his life. He could not get enough, could never get enough. He kissed her again and again, drunk with love much more than the honey. The power of it all was enough the make his eyes water and his chest heave. He felt overcome again and again as the waves of emotion swelled and grew with each beat of his heart.

He could see the gold in her hair and taste the gold on

her lips and felt it was the sweetest moment of his life. Truth be told, the honeyed hair and honeyed kisses of Ember that day would be foremost in his mind when Traejanale Royce breathed his last.

Finally, they did indeed have a leisurely lunch and spent most of the afternoon lying cradled in each other's arms. As the sun passed the mark of three-quarter's day, Ember returned everything that was left into the pack and Traejan hung it on the shady branch of a nearby pine. Ember picked up his hand.

"Let's go higher," she said.

Traejan looked at her. The sun shone in her eyes and her hair. He felt his heart swell to the point he thought it might burst and a hard lump formed in his throat. He nodded, unable to form the words he could not find.

They climbed the rest of the way, hand in hand, in the shade of trees that overlooked the lake and the meadow. Traejan could hear the sound of the falls grow from a faint whisper to a turbulent melody. They reached the higher lake, which was just as clear and beautiful as the one they left below, and almost three times as large. Here there was no meadow, only huge rocks and boulders that bordered the lake and jutted out into its crystal surface. Fed by seven falls instead of two, the vista on the surface was all mist and rainbow.

"It's almost like home," the prince whispered. "There are waterfalls everywhere, and colors from the spray. You will love it," he assured her.

Instead of answering, Ember led him to the group of boulders that protruded out into the lake. She nimbly climbed the first and then jumped from one to the other. Traejan followed her to where the rocks ended their voyage into the lake, less than a quarter of the way in. The falls were now a soft roar. The last rock where they now stood was low, wide, and flat. Large enough for another picnic if they chose. Ember searched out his hand again with her own and entwined her fingers in his.

"Water is very special," she told him, and he knew his lesson was at hand. "It was revered among my people," she said, "or my father's people, rather. Even though he said I was a fire sign and thus named me as such." Traejan nodded and brushed a fiery strand of hair from her face. Her father had done well.

"I think all people venerate water," he said. "It brings life and nourishment to men, animals and plants. None could survive without it."

Ember gave a small shake of her head, making her hair sway and dance. "But it is more than that. Not just what it gives us, but what it teaches us." She turned to him fully and his arms slipped around her waist. She put her hands on his chest, feeling the soft weave of his shirt with her palms. "Water signifies the purest way of life. It is humble, always seeking the lowest ground, yet it is strong, wearing down rocks and mountains with its persistence and perseverance." Ember touched his face, marveling at his hard features and soft skin. Unmarked and unlined. She cupped his jaw in her hand. "For the first time, I now see water as even more. I see it as our love. I want you to be able to see it the same way."

Traejan drew a deep breath. He felt like he was breathing in her very essence, and then breathing it out. "Tell me what you see."

She drew her thumb across the high, arched bone of his cheek and sighed, a smile playing on her lips. "Our love is like the water," she told him. "It is clear and pure and yet does not fear the dirt and filth of any world. It will plunge from the greatest of heights, unafraid and unhurt."

Traejan put a hand under her chin and kissed her. She

kissed his lips, then his cheek and then pressed her face against his.

"Its beauty is in its clarity. Its fearlessness. It can be touched and taken, but never destroyed. It does not fear being divided, for it knows that it will be joined again someday. Does that make any sense?" She leaned back and looked into his face, searching.

"More sense than you know," he assured her. He buried his face in her neck and her hair. "Yet, I do not intend to be separated from you, not ever," he confessed, kissing her. Ember kissed him briefly then pulled away, her eyes dreamy and intense all at once.

"But you do know that our love is indestructible? That it will endure anything and everything?"

"Yes," he said, and meant it. "I do."

"Good. And you know that drops of water, when alone, may seem inconsequential, but when joined become rivulets, streams, and rivers - and change the face of the earth for all time."

"Like our love," he breathed. "Our love will change this world." She closed her eyes and he kissed her again. Again her response was brief.

"And when storms churn the river, throw it from its bed and fill it with mud?" she asked, pushing him back half the length of her arm. Her gaze neared a glare with its intensity.

His arms held her motionless, his eyes steady and clear and as blue as the sky. "Then I will be still and wait for the mud to settle." He held her eyes with his for a moment of eternity, and then gave in to his passion and kissed her again. This time she did not pull away.

The day began to cool around them and they left the high falls and reclaimed their pack from the edge of the low meadow. They returned down the mountain before the sun began its final descent into night.

A slight chill crept into the air once they reentered the forest and as they walked hand in hand the Roshan noticed with a sinking heart how many other leaves had begun to change their color. Autumn had always been a season she had enjoyed. The crisp mornings and evenings were a welcome change after a long hot summer on the valley's edge and the many colors of the trees had filled her with a love of the outdoors she only found in the fall. She knew now that the magic and wonder of this season was gone to her.

Not forever, a voice promised. *Not forever.* Her heart either did not listen or did not care. It was petulant and angry for the time being. Maybe not forever, but for long enough. Her eyes caught a sudden movement as a nightingale whipped past and lit on the branch of a branderbush.

"Love the fall again one day, one day," he promised with his song. Then he tittered with the unmistakable sound of laughter. It meant he was keeping a secret. Ember walked past him without slowing.

By the time they got back to the haus she was tired but composed. "Tomorrow we can start getting ready for the journey home," she told Traejan. "Our journey."

His excitement was palpable. "I'm glad," he told her. "Will we make it to Amherst by the full Harvest Moon?"

The Roshan nodded absently, marking out the route in her mind's eye. "We have at least a week. It's a three-day ride to Trigo, and we will most likely meet someone there who can relay the message to the right people and save us the trip to Atlantea. From there it will only take us two days to get to Amherst."

"I can't wait for you to see Tuar Ceath," the young elf exclaimed, his hands caressing her shoulders. "And Song, I can't wait for you to see Castle Song. It's funny because even though I always knew it would be mine someday, I never cared in the slightest. Now all I can think of is where we will put our bed! And I know you have doubts of my family but I want so badly for you to meet them. And Dell!" The prince laughed at the thought of his guardsman. "I can't wait for you to meet Dell!"

Ember watched him with a small smile playing on her lips. She shook her head a little in amazement. *Ryen was right,* she thought. *He really is still a child in some ways.* Yet she could not help but feel a warmth fill her body at his childlike excitement. *Oh how I love him. I love him so much. Who would have ever thought that possible?*

"Tomorrow we can start packing," she said. "And I will need to prepare the haus for my absence. Gatha will be back to take care of the perishables we don't take with us, but I will have to store my weapons properly."

Traejan stopped, surprised. "I hadn't thought of your weapons," he admitted. "What will you take with you?"

Ember smiled. "I will take my regular clutch. There is no need to burden Coal with more than what I may need. He'll also be carrying clothes and supplies as well as myself."

Traejan nodded, understanding, then took her hands into his own.

"What about me?" he asked. "Do you think I am ready? Have I really learned enough?"

Ember smiled. "You tell me. Can you be beaten or bested?"

The elf smiled slowly, his face lighting up. "Only by you."

Her smile widened. "Then my work is done."

"Besides," he said, bringing her hand to his mouth and kissing the tips of her fingers, "I'm sure you will keep teaching me. We have nothing but time ahead of us."

Ember bit her lip, her smile gone. "Anyway," she continued, "let's not start until tomorrow. I'm beat."

Traejan pulled her close. "That's fine with me," he told her. Ember put her head on his shoulder with her forehead under his chin. She loved the smell of his warm skin and the feel of his pulse against her cheek. She nuzzled his earlobe and kissed the corner of his jaw.

"Let's heat up some dinner," she suggested, "and go to bed."

"That sounds even finer."

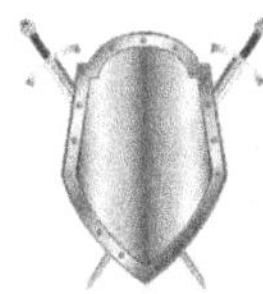

36. GATHA DELIVERS A MESSAGE

Gatha bounced up and down, a jarring ride for most on the back of a trotting donkey. The Gnomin woman, however, did not mind. She always found the ride extraordinarily soothing. It was running she hated, and not because her legs were short.

Gatha had been fifteen years old when her parents were murdered by a band of Crommags.

They, along with their mute daughter, had been part of a mining outpost. The mine, including the housing (the Gnomin always slept underground when possible, for obvious security and safety reasons) had just been started. The Gnomin who had been sent to set up the outpost were living in wooden shelters next to the mountain. The shelters were roomy, sturdy, and well built – most things were that were made by Gnomin hands – but they were no match for the Crommag maces and cudgels that came smashing into them one night.

The Gnomin scattered, screaming, as they were hunted down for sport. One old miner and his twin brother managed to get away, dragging Gatha with them. She would have been dragged screaming, had she been able to scream. She had seen her father cover her mother with his own body to protect her, but six feet of nicked and pitted metal came down upon him, cleaving the Gnomin miner and his wife in two.

Blood-spattered and terrified, the mute Gnomin girl regained enough sense to know that the old miner and his brother could not drag her all the way back to the Coil. She shook them off and ran alongside them. Others were running, and being chased.

The Crommags would let out a great bellow when they downed one of their fleeing prey. It was not long before one of the old twins fell behind, gasping for air. His brother slowed to help and soon Gatha heard the bellow of a Crommag behind her, less than a minute later. Running with terror, young Gatha pressed on.

In the light before dawn she made it to the Coil, along with another girl that was almost her age. Shaking with exhaustion and shivering with fear, they collapsed together by Main Breach, the largest entrance to the Coil, the city under the mountain that housed the bulk of the Gnomin population.

They were the only survivors.

The two girls were brought inside, wrapped in woolens, and fed hot potato soup before taken to the Big Bosses.

The Big Bosses had just begun their first meeting of the day, but broke off immediately as the girls were ushered inside. They listened intently to the one who was able to tell the horrid tale of the Crommag attack.

Gatha, wrapped in a woolen, wept silently as the tale was told. Next to her was the person the Big Bosses were supposed to meet with – a human woman with red hair and dressed all in black. She did not speak Gnomin well, but she grasped the situation with perfect clarity.

When the girl had finished delivering the story, the Big Bosses were full of questions, mostly for each other.

"Crommags?"

"At this time of year?"

"Too early!"

"Much too early!"

"Too early or too late?"

"Maybe they were trapped by the Floe…"

"Could things have changed?"

Then the woman in black stood, Gatha's large and tear-filled blue eyes following her as she took two steps forward and asked one question in Gnomin.

"Where?"

Within minutes the auburn-haired warrior was mounting a great, black Night Stallion. She hunted down the Crommags and killed them, almost getting herself killed in the process. When she went home, six months later, Gatha went with her.

Though the woman warrior had tried to protest, the Gnomin people insisted, none more than Gatha herself.

The Roshan was not completely healed, and the young female had been training to be a nurse. Being mute, it was one of the few professions open to her. The inability to shout *Komm zurück!* - the Gnomin's first line of defense - limited her from more than ninety percent of Gnomin careers, activities, and pursuits.

So when the auburn-haired warrior left, still tightly bandaged around her middle, the mute orphan girl who had thought her life was over went with her – trotting happily along on a donkey.

Now Gatha bounced along, headed for the village of Trimpe at the bottom of the Backwoods. The Gnomin woman was quite familiar with Trimpe, which was both a fishing village and a trading outpost on the Eastly side of the Midlon. She often went there for supplies for the Roshan, including food and wine. This time, however, the Roshan had instructed her to hire a rider to deliver a message. Two messages, actually.

Gatha would have delivered the messages herself, riding the donkey all the way to Amherst or even Atlantea if need be. Despite all her silent grumblings and even after all these years, there was nothing that she would not do for the Roshan.

Ember, however, would not hear of it – even if Gatha could have summoned the words. It was too far and too dangerous for a woman to travel alone, even during the safest of times. And despite all her own grumblings and even after all these years, the Roshan would never risk Gatha's safety.

The Gnomin woman bounced along, carrying a fair amount of gold even though she was not going to purchase any supplies. The Roshan would not be needing any. She was to be gone for a year or more. Gatha would miss her though she never would admit it, even if she were able.

The gold was to pay a rider to carry two messages, written carefully in the Roshan's meticulous script. There was even a bit more for Gatha to have a hearty fish dinner and for her and the donkey to stay the night. Tomorrow she would return to the haus, make sure it was clean and ready for a long spell of vacancy, lock it up tight and return to the Coil. She had not seen her kin since the spring and she was looking forward to some relaxation and gossip.

She stopped to rest and water the donkey in the very same clearing where the elfin prince and the Roshan had taken rest on their unfinished journey to Goldensword. She chewed a roll of bread she had made the night before and then continued on her way.

Sometime between noon and sunset, while Traejan and Ember lay in each other's arms next to a crystal mountain lake, the Gnomin woman and her donkey went bouncing down the main road in the village of Trimpe.

Gatha had been to Trimpe many times. She was well known and the fact that she could not speak was hardly an obstacle. She tied up the donkey in front of the Reel Inn, a saloon in the middle of town that was her favorite place to eat and stay.

There was a leather pouch fastened to the saddle that contained her most important items: the gold and the messages from the Roshan, along with her own pencil and a few small rolls of parchment paper. Gatha took the purse from the saddle, took the two wooden steps up to the plank sidewalk, and pushed through the batwing doors of the saloon. She was greeted with the familiar sound of the piano and tipsy laughter along with the familiar smells of sawdust and fried fish. She made her way past the few patrons sitting at tables having either a late lunch or an early dinner, to the bar that held even fewer patrons and clambered up onto a barstool. Four men in the corner sat a table playing spades.

"Gatha!"

The Gnomin woman turned her head towards the enthusiastic greeting to find Emos, her favorite bartender, holding his arms up in warm welcome. Emos was a short human man that was mostly bald with a waxed moustache that curled up on the ends. He wore a starched white shirt under his long, black, barkeep apron.

The other bartender, Amos, was not there. He was younger than his brother Emos, but Gatha did not like him as much. He was always polite to Gatha, like all of the town's other residents. She may be a Gnomin and a woman and a mute, but everyone knew who she was. It was one of the reasons she did not fear traveling alone. The Roshan was very respected and a bit feared by those in the Midlon.

Emos, however, genuinely seemed to like the silent Gnomin. Gatha held out a hand and Emos grasped it between both of his.

"How are you dear Gatha?" he exclaimed. "Are you hungry? Do you have an order for the General?"

Gatha had long since stopped going to the Trimpe General Stock for groceries and supplies. Emos would simply send her list with the barboy who would purchase what she needed and then load them on her donkey while she had lunch.

Gatha shook her curls and dipped her blonde head to search through her purse, pulling out her pencil and a roll of parchment. Emos waited while she wrote and then turned the paper so he could read it.

I need a rider. To Amherst.

Emos read the note and then leveled his hazel eyes at the Gnomin woman for a moment before they rose up to travel across the saloon. There were riders to be had, the Reel Inn was where most hung out, waiting for employment. His scrutiny stopped on the table of men playing spades.

"Abel!" Emos hollered at them, then turned his head and called over his shoulder, "Amos!" One of the men playing spades looked up at the summons while the younger barkeep came out from behind a pair of swinging doors that led to the kitchen. Emos looked at the card player, a bright-eyed boy with hair the color of golden hay, and pointed to an empty table. Then he jerked his head at his younger brother in a silent command to take over the bar.

"Come, Gatha," he said, walking around the bar to help her down from her stool. He escorted her to a table and held out a chair where a very young man was sitting down with a curious look at the barkeep. Once Gatha was seated, Emos joined her and the youth - who looked to the Gnomin like he was barely old enough to shave.

"Gatha," he said, "this is Abel." He looked at the lean young man. "Abel, this is Gatha." Gatha gave him a curt nod in greeting while he looked at her with a good deal of apprehension. Emos looked back at the youth dressed in duncolored riding leathers and vest. A flat, round hat hung on the back of his neck secured by a knotted brown string. The barkeep arched a brow at him. "Do you know who Gatha is?" he asked.

The young man nodded vigorously. He was a local, of course he knew who Gatha was – which was why Emos had singled him out.

"It's a pleasure to meet you," Abel stammered. Gatha gave him a slow nod to show that she felt the same. Then she wrote on her paper and slid it across the table to him.

Emos looked askance at the note. "Two messages," he read softly, keeping his voice low, "to two different men. Both in Amherst. By sundown tomorrow." He glanced up at Gatha and she nodded. "That's a long ride," he told her. "And hard."

"I can do it," Abel affirmed, drawing both their eyes.

Emos arched a brow at him and Gatha smiled. She took another piece of parchment from her purse and passed it to him. This note had been written by the Roshan, the names and descriptions of the men he was to find. Emos read the note as well, silently this time, before he looked at the young rider. Abel gave him a nod, and another to Gatha.

"I can do it," he repeated, even more confident than before.

Gatha's smile widened and she reached back into her purse. She withdrew two gold coins and pushed them across the table to the messenger. She held up two fingers and then pointed first to him, and then at Emos.

Two more when you get back, the gesture said, *and two for the man that vouched for you.*

Both men nodded. They understood.

Gatha reached back into her purse and withdrew the two messages, tightly rolled parchment tied with short black string. She pushed these across the table to the messenger. He glanced at them and saw they were marked. One had a name followed by 'elf,' and the other a name followed by 'Vikeman.'

The messenger gathered both rolls of parchment and both gold coins in a single sweep as he stood, tucking it all into a leather satchel that hung from one of his narrow hips. He gave his head a smart shake, clearing his golden locks from his face as he pulled his hat forward and secured it, his fingertips on the brim as he nodded a quick and respectful goodbye to Gatha. Then he was gone.

Gatha sighed and Emos stood, his hands resting on the back of his chair.

"Supper, then?" he queried.

Gatha nodded then scribbled on the one parchment still on the table and pushed it to him. He turned his head so he could read it without taking it.

"And a room?" he read aloud to confirm. Gatha nodded. She almost reached for the paper again but Emos knew what she was about.

"I will have your donkey stabled," he assured her before giving her a wink. "And send out a stout, on the house, with your supper."

Gatha touched her fingers to her lips and blew Emos an exaggerated kiss, making him laugh. He bowed and hurried off. The Gnomin woman sighed, looking around absently as more patrons trickled in as it neared dinnertime. She was looking forward to her own dinner of fried fish and the fried potatoes that Emos called 'chips.'

She worried a bit about the messages she had just sent.

More than those, she worried about the Roshan.

38. OVER THE RIVERS

Trigo was a sprawling city-town made of many small villages where the three large rivers of the Midlon met and joined forces, creating a hammering tributary that rushed three more miles before emptying out into the Sabado Sea.

Each village had an epicenter that sprang from its docks and then spread out like a fan. The villages were linked by bridges, ferries, and an occasional tunnel. The towns, depending on age and location, ranged from clean and bustling to tawdry and rundown.

The Roshan chose one of the latter. On the most westerly side of Trigo, Tannery Village was dirty, smelly, and all but deserted except for the long-time denizens that had dug in like stubborn ticks.

The warrior and the elfin prince stopped at the first stable they found since Ember was quite aware that Coal spooked other animals, people too. Besides, she was hoping to come and go as quickly and as quietly as possible. With the horses stabled, the Roshan and the elf skirted what passed for the busy part of town and wound their way through alleyways and byways used mostly by locals, and even those were few.

Hand in hand, they made their way to the waterfront – keeping to the shadows. The Slag, the southernmost river of Trigo, sloshed its waters against a wharf crusted with barnacles on the bottom and guano on the top. Old warehouses with faded and peeling paint formed a backdrop to the docks where fishing boats coming in with the morning catch were tying up and unloading crates of shellfish. The place smelled of old wood, old fish, and tar. Birds cried in the morning air as they swooped in for bits of food, mostly stolen, leaving spatterings and squawking in their wake.

A Sylvan elf, four feet tall and as chipper as a finch, was tying off a small skiff and yelling at the two still aboard when he looked up to see the black-clad woman and tall elf beside her. A nimble step brought him into a quick embrace with the Roshan.

"Dylon!" she exclaimed, pulling him close and then letting him go just as quick. The small elf was fair and freckled. He wore a long-sleeved shirt that was the color of the sky, covered with a vest that was the same dark blue of the river. Boots that came to his knees were crusted with fish scales.

"My lady," he replied with a bow.

She gently grasped the Sylvan elf by the elbow and pulled him aside. "Do you have a few minutes to talk?" she asked.

"Of course," he asserted, waving off his skiffmates as Ember took a quick look around and then led him into a watering mill that had seen better days. The sign over the door was battered by weather and bleached by the sun but the name, *The Salmon Moose*, was still readable. The piece of wood, swinging gently in the breeze by a pair of rusted chains, bore a faded painting of a leaping fish with a pair of antlers sprouting from its head.

The small elf was not put out in the slightest by the dingy bar. He ushered the taller elf and the auburn-haired warrior to a booth and signaled the barman right away. "A glass of your finest red for da lady," he instructed in a deep Sylvan accent, showing Traejan that he knew the Roshan well enough. Then he turned to the prince and held out a hand. "And for you, Your Highness?" he inquired softly, showing that he knew who Traejan was, well enough.

"Just a glass of water, please," Traejan told the keep who rubbed his dirty hands on his even dirtier apron before raising a brow at the smaller elf.

"Watered mead, if ya please," Dylon instructed. The man grunted and lumbered away. "As if it not be watered enough to the ready," he muttered at the man's retreating bulk. He glanced back at the Roshan, his normal good cheer returning in an instant.

"So!" he exclaimed. "To what do I owe dis honor?"

"Crommags are invading the Midlon," Ember confided without any preamble.

Dylon's high arched brows drew together over his almond-shaped eyes and his small mouth pulled down in a frown. "Raiding parties? Can't imagine such. Ida heard."

The Roshan shook her head. "Not raiding parties," she corrected. "They are all coming, or enough of them to seem like all." She paused as her words sank in and then took a deep breath before she continued. "They mean to make war."

Dylon sat back hard in the booth as the bartender returned and drinks were clunked down onto the table in front of them, sloshing over the sides of the none-too-clean glasses. The Sylvan, still stunned, picked up his glass and absently touched the rim of it to the Roshan's and then Traejan's.

"War," he said softly, taking a sip of the watered mead and not tasting it. "We've never had war."

The Roshan sipped her wine and winced at the sour taste. "We think the Crommags will make for Tuar Ceath, or go straight to Atlantea. Either way, we need to warn both kingdoms. They need to prepare."

"How long dey have?" Dylon asked.

"Six months, maybe nine."

The Sylvan gave a low whistle. "Where you going first?"

"Tuar Ceath," Traejan said. Dylon looked at the Roshan who nodded in agreement.

"I need you to warn the Triumvirate here in Trigo," she said, "then go on to Atlantea. Can you find Prince Tristan?"

"I'll hava eno trouble finding him," he assured the Roshan, "the trouble is getting ta speak wit em."

"No trouble there," the Roshan assured him. "Find his man Joshun, and tell him you bear a message from the Roshan Simorgh. He will listen, and he will believe. His scars are still fresh. Very fresh."

The small elf nodded. "I will take your word."

"Joshun?" Traejan asked. "*Prince* Tristan?" He was quiet for just a moment as he put the pieces together. "The men from the Bridlewood that you rescued from the Crommags?"

The Roshan nodded before taking a drink of her wine and holding it up to the dusty light that streamed in from the dirty windows and contemplated its contents. "Yes," she agreed.

"Tristan *Greenwater*," the elfin prince murmured. "So much was going on, I did not realize who he was."

The Roshan smiled, the lip of her glass now hovering about her mouth. "The son of Triton, King of Atlantea. Ryen calls him 'the prince of tides.' Don't you know of him?"

Traejan sighed, sinking back into his chair. "Of course I do. I met him once. It seems like just a few years ago, but he was quite small then. Still holding his mother's hand."

"Time and tide," the Roshan said, her voice faint.

"How many princes do you have under your thrall?" Traejan asked with a sly smile but it was Dylon who answered.

"How many are dere?" he asked.

The Roshan took a long drink of wine and made a face. "This is terrible," she decided aloud, putting down the glass and pushing it away.

"You picked da place!" Dylon accused in good cheer, swilling his watered-down honey-ale.

"I know, I know," she agreed, reaching into a leather bag. She pulled out four gold coins and pushed them across the wooden table. "If you need help, find Ryen. He will probably be..."

"Keep yer coins," the Sylvan interrupted with a scowl, pushing them back across the dirty planks. "And I know where ta find Ryen," he muttered, rolling his eyes before he quaffed the remainder of his mead. "But ya ken pay for my drink if ya must."

The Roshan left a copper coin on the table as Dylon wiped his mouth with the cuff of his sleeve. Traejan followed them from the table, his water untouched. He didn't need the eyesight of an elf to see there were things floating in it.

Outside, Ember gripped the Sylvan's hand in her own and then embraced him. His boyish face was somber when they broke apart. The day was bright but their mood was obviously clouded.

"We have dark times ahead," he said softly, "don't we?"

"I'm afraid we do," the Roshan agreed, her voice cracking on the last word. Traejan cocked his head at her, his brow furrowed.

She must be more worried than I realized, he thought, laying a hand on her shoulder.

Dylon gave him a short bow. "Prince," he said by way of farewell. Traejan bowed in return then the Sylvan was gone.

The docks were quiet this far up on the outskirts. The Roshan looked one way and then the other, her face pinched with indecision.

"Are you okay?" Traejan asked, placing his hands on her shoulders. She nodded quickly.

"Of course," she assured him, "just planning our next move." She bit the corner of her lip and frowned as her eyes traveled over the small shops of butchers, bakers and fishmongers that still coaxed a living from this lonely quarter. Then her gaze landed and her face lit up. Traejan followed her line of sight to a storefront on the waterway and almost laughed.

"The WineBank," he said, reading the title that adorned the

shop in a flowy, washed-out script. He looked down at Ember, who was beaming up at him. "Afraid you'll run out?" he asked. Her smile widened into a grin and he kissed the tip of her nose. "There is wine in Tuar Ceath, you know."

"I want something for tonight," she told him. She thought he might tell her that she already had plenty for tonight but his eyes were busy searching out the building fronts as well.

"Actually," he said his hands moving from her shoulders to her elbows and then back up again, "there is a barber next to the wine shop."

"You still after that haircut?" she asked, smiling.

Traejan stuck a hand into his mass of dark gold locks and laughed. "Don't you think so? I feel like a rogue sheep after a mad winter. I've never had it so long!"

"I like it," she told him, standing on her toes to kiss him. "But I would like it any way you chose to wear it."

"Haircut it is, then," he affirmed.

They turned as one, fingers entwined, and headed for the wine shop. She felt a pang of discomfort, worrying that someone might witness their intimacy, then pushed it from her mind and leaned on the young elf as they walked. She would savor every moment and be damned if she worried about who saw.

But when they reached the barber she held him back, suddenly wary.

"What is it?" he asked.

"I don't know," she answered, peering through the grimy window. Both chairs reserved for patrons were empty. The proprietor, who only had a few wisps of his own graying hair left, sat on a high-backed stool reading a small book with worn out corners.

The elfin prince chortled laughter as he peered with her, then feigned a deep seriousness. "Do you think there might be a Crommag hiding behind the old man?" he asked softly, his voice grave. "Or is it the old man himself that worries you?"

The Roshan frowned at him. "I just don't feel right leaving you alone."

Traejan tried to hide his smirk but found he was unable. "Then you haven't done your job if, after all that training, I can't handle an aging human barber."

"Fine then!" Ember admonished with a mock frown and a playful shove. "I hope he nicks an ear!"

The young elf kissed her cheek and turned, pushing open the door to the barbershop before he went inside, still smiling at her.

The Roshan watched him for a few moments, and then hurried next door to the wineshop to conduct her business. When she rejoined the prince once again, he was still in the chair, though almost ready. She laughed and teased him until the barber was done. They paid the man, retrieved their horses, and took the Ha'Penny Bridge to the other side of the Slag.

From there it was a short ride through Maycomb Village, where they found a ferry to carry them to the other side over the High Calm, the wide waterway where the Basalt River joined the Boreal.

The pair reached the Riverwood by sunset and Ember suggested that, since they were ahead of schedule, they stop for the night. Traejan agreed and the Roshan found a clearing with a nearby brook that was small but looked well worn by travelers. The black-clad warrior slid from the back of the Night Stallion and stretched mightily, then put her arms around her love, holding him tightly. He buried his face in her hair, delighted.

"Get wood for a fire, would you?" she whispered, her lips tickling his neck. "I'll take care of the horses."

"Of course." He kissed her and started gathering dried sticks and branches as she pulled the bedrolls from the horses.

Twice he needed to venture quite a ways from the site, more proof that it had been well used, but finally returning with enough wood to last them the night. When he came back the second time he could see her through the trees, watering the horses at the brook. Their bedrolls were still tied, leaning against a nest of small boulders.

Traejan built the fire as darkness took the land and rolled two large rocks closer to the flames so that they could recline against them. The Roshan returned with the horses and rummaged through their packs for dinner.

"Your timing is impeccable," he told her, nodding towards the fat moon that could be glimpsed between the trees as it rose. "The Harvest Moon will be full tomorrow, when we get to Amherst."

"This isn't my first Harvest," she assured him with a smirk. She threw more branches on the fire, building it up with a knowing smile while the elfin prince pulled hard bread and a small wheel of cheese from his pack.

"What does that smile mean?" he asked, biting into the bread and tearing off a small chunk. "That you want me to unsaddle the horses? Don't think I didn't notice."

The Roshan laughed. "I'll take care of them in a minute. First, I'm in the mood for something special."

"What did you have in mind?" he asked, thoughts of the horses already far away. Her suggestion, though harmless, was arousing to him. As always, everything about her was. Nevertheless, he kept still as she pulled a bottle from her bedroll and favored him with her most wicked smile.

"This," she announced.

"And what might be in there?" he asked.

"Red," she assured him, "*Honeyed* Red."

Traejan laughed. "You are bound and determined to get me drunk, aren't you?" Ember answered by pulling out two cups, golden this time, from her pack. Traejan watched with what felt like unending joy and laughed again. "Well, since you went to the trouble, and we do have cause to celebrate...may I?" he asked, reaching for the bottle.

"Of course." Ember handed him the bottle and held out the first cup for him to fill. It was wide and round and simple, gold without any adornment save a ring of silver around the middle. Traejan poured the wine from the bottle to the cup, mesmerized. The red and gold, made even more intense by the firelight, matched her hair perfectly.

I knew it would, he thought as he filled the second cup. *I always knew it would.* He looked at her and his breath caught in his throat as he saw her eyes, sparkling in the light of the fire. He raised his glass in a toast.

"To unending love," he told her.

"To our love," she said, her voice soft.

Traejan raised the simple chalice a tad higher to her toast, and then drained half of it as she watched.

"How is it?" she asked.

"Terrible!" he answered, grimacing.

A laugh burst from her lips. "You can't hold it against me!" she defended lightly. "I'd never bought it before." Traejan took another sip, as if to make sure his first judgment was correct.

It was. He stuck out his tongue, making Ember laugh harder.

"What is it?" she asked. "Is it too much honey?"

Traejan took another sip, smaller this time, and savored the taste experimentally, smacking his lips. He could already feel his head beginning to swim a bit from the first huge gulp he took. He could feel the warmth of the drink traveling down his throat to where it blossomed like fire in his belly – it was not entirely unpleasant. He was even already beginning to feel a bit giddy.

"There *is* a lot of honey," he agreed, "but that's not it." He took another experimental taste and shook his head. "Maybe it's the wine. Maybe the wine is bad."

Ember was suddenly all mock seriousness. "I am sure it is *not* the wine," she assured. "It better not be, not for the price I paid!" She took a sip herself and made a face before she did her best to hold back a shudder.

"Is this what you bought at the wine shop in Tannery Village?" he asked.

The Roshan nodded, looking none too pleased. She took another small sip. "That bastard of a wine monger!" she cursed.

Traejan burst out laughing, and then drained the last of his cup. He watched his love and felt his heart beat in time with hers and decided that they should celebrate indeed. He had never felt such happiness. The same could not be said for Ember, who was clearly disappointed.

"I'm sorry," she apologized, disconsolate. "He really told me that this was a good vintage, honeyed in the elfin way."

"It is," the young prince told the Roshan. The look she gave him said she knew he was patronizing her. "Pour me another glass," he insisted. Ember gave him a dubious look but refilled his glass.

He took a huge draught of the wine and smacked his lips in mock appreciation.

"Mmm mmm!"

The Roshan took another experimental sip and gave him a real smack, though not hard, with the back of her hand across his chest as she laughed.

"Stop lying! This is terrible!"

Traejan laughed with her. "It is," he agreed, falling forward, laughing. "It's horrible!" He laughed harder and sat back, upright, and swayed a bit.

"Whoa!" she exclaimed, grabbing his shoulder to steady

him. "I think you've had enough!"

"Mmmm," he said, this time leaning a bit to the side. He upended his cup into his mouth and Ember clutched his sleeve to help keep him erect. "It's not the wine, though" he corrected. "It's something else."

"The honey?" she asked.

Traejan shook his head, his newly shorn locks going back and forth in an exaggerated motion.

"Not the honey," he said, mesmerized as he always was by the glints of gold in her eyes and her hair.

He watched her shimmering eyes and shimmering hair as he thought about the wine and something suddenly leapt to his mind - two things, actually – which made it hard for him to concentrate.

The first was that he believed he recognized the taste he had been thus far unable to identify in the wine.

The second thought was more powerful, distracting him. It was of the time he had first seen her.

The thoughts mixed and became a blur and he was ready to shrug them both off and pour another glass of wine, yet some force inside of him fought against it. The warrior that now lived within grasped him and gave him a shake.

She's fooled you before, a voice whispered inside his mind. It was that whisper that made him afraid, enough to make his boiling blood run cold. Traejan knew immediately what the voice spoke of, warning him.

He thought back to that day, that chill spring morning on the banks of Ravensbrook. He had felt caught in a spell by the woman clad all in black, mesmerized by her hair and her eyes. The young prince had thought that the eyes of the Roshan sparkled that first day, that but only moments later he had realized that they glittered. With death. And now, they neither sparkled nor glittered. They shimmered. With tears.

Quizzically, Traejan looked at her and saw that behind

those tears she was watching him intently. All of the giddiness drained from his heart in perfect unison with the strength that drained from his limbs. His arms felt as if they were filling with lead as they dropped to his sides. His tongue felt thick and furry. Now tears filled his eyes as well.

"Absinthe," he tried to say, but his tongue was as numb as the rest of him. "Why?" he tried to ask, but he could not form even a single word.

Why? he wailed in his mind. But he knew why. The warrior inside him answered, his voice like a feather across his psyche.

Because she is going, the warrior whispered. *And you may not follow.*

The Roshan leaned forward, kneeling before him, and grasped his arms. "Does it hurt?" she asked, terrified that the drug would pain him somehow. She had battled mentally with the choice, not knowing exactly what the absinthe might do.

"Is there any chance he could die?" she had asked the winemonger who had sold her the liquor that morning. "What if I give him too much?"

"Nay," the man had assured her. "Even if he drinks this whole vial he will be fine. He would have to drink gallons of the stuff to kill him, but he would pass out long before that could happen."

"But this will be enough to incapacitate him?" she pressed, holding up the small vial he had given her.

"And then some. Elves take this just by the drop, and that is usually in a pitcher of lemon water. If you mix this in a small amount of wine, just one sip will take his strength, and another his ability to move even at all. But it is perfectly safe. No elf has ever died from absinthe."

All the same, the last few minutes by the fire had been the most tense of the Roshan's entire life. She exhaled sharply in relief when she saw that he was not in pain, but she asked again to make sure.

"It doesn't hurt, does it?" she queried softly. Traejan struggled motionlessly but Ember could see the turmoil in his eyes.

Yes, it hurts! he wanted to shout. *You can't do this! You CANNOT!*

But all that came out was a muffled, "hup."

Ember relaxed, her hands sliding down his arms.

"Aye," she told him. "The pain in your heart. I know it, for I have carried it myself for this past week."

This past week? You have known this - you have planned this all week?

Traejan thrashed inwardly as a new pain seared through his immobile form. Not for anything his love had done, but for how hard it must have been for her. How much it must have hurt her, and to have borne the pain alone. It was terrible.

She leaned forward and brushed his cheek. "Your training is done, Traejan. I have taught you all that I can. The rest you must learn on your own." She shook her head in response to the question in his eyes. "No. This is not a lesson. I wish it could be that easy too. You must know in your heart that if you were to bring me home I would not be accepted by your people, and worse, you might not be either."

Traejan tried to shake his head but he could not get it to move in the slightest. He might as well been cast in stone. All he could do was blink, his eyes as blue as the sea as they filled with tears and spilled over. Ember picked up one of his limp hands and held it between her own.

"I know you don't care about that. Not now. And you know I could not care less about what anyone thought of me – but what they think of you, what they *would* think of you – I could not bear." She felt a lump grow in her throat and swallowed it down with the pain.

For you I would leave everything, he wanted to tell her. *For us.* He also realized that she already knew that. That was why she was leaving him this way.

"I know nothing of fate, or destiny. But my heart tells me that this is not forever. You have much to do and learn before the world brings us together again, but that will come. For now, we have a warrior's responsibility. Can you feel it within you?"

The elfin prince closed his eyes. Yes. Death was coming to his people, all people. He now had to fight to protect them.

He opened his eyes and the pain she saw there was all the answer she needed.

"Do you remember the waterfalls?" she asked.

Traejan could only close his eyes again in response, pressing fresh tears from his lids and sending them down his cheeks. Ember nodded.

"Remember the lesson there."

She stood and retrieved her bedroll, which Traejan saw now that she had never unrolled. She fastened it to a horse that had not been unsaddled. She pulled her cloak from where it was tied to her mount, swept it over her shoulders, and fastened it at the side of her neck.

He looked at the rest of her gear and weapons, secured to Coal's saddle. He thought of the way she had packed up the haus.

She does not intend to return there, he realized. *Not anytime soon. For now, she is going where I cannot follow.* He closed his eyes again, more tears freshening the tracks that threatened to dry on his cheeks. When he opened them she was in front of him again, kneeling before him, sitting back on her heels.

He could see that she was struggling for words. The ones she wanted to say, and the ones she would not let herself speak. In the end she decided it was best to say nothing at all.

Traejan felt her soul slip away and pull back from him - going cold and dark, as if encasing itself in iron. Her eyes never left his and her expression never changed. His own soul drew back, screaming silently in pain.

Ember nodded once, just a slight dip of her head, and rose to leave. Then Traejan reached up and grabbed her arm. Her eyes, wide with disbelief, went from his face to the hand that held her fast and then back to his face.

Seven Circles! she thought, staring at him. *How can he do that?*

She had been assured that paralysis would be complete with the dose she had given him, and it would last an hour or more. Possibly the whole night.

It must be taking everything he has, she marveled, glancing again at the hand around her elbow then back into the eyes of her love.

It was.

Everything he could muster, he did, just to hold her.

Just a few seconds more.

He thought at first that it was because he could not bear to let her go. He knew there were no words that would hold her, but he knew what he had to say, what she had to hear before she rode into the dark. He swallowed, willing his mouth to obey, and then cleared his throat, fighting for control. He did not want to sound foolish or drunk. His control won out in the end.

"From this day forth," he told her, "the sun will bring me neither light nor warmth. The night will bring no rest. Food will not stave my hunger nor water quench my thirst." His words did not slur and his voice was clear and true.

Ember watched him, amazed at what he was able to manage and the strength she knew it was taking.

A hundred yards into the forest, Dell sat with his back against a tree, his eyes growing wide at the words being spoken by his prince. He turned his face away, blushing, trying not to hear.

Traejan continued, his voice even and sure. "I will not be whole until I hold you in my arms again. You are my love, my life, my passion, my way. I will live and die this day forth only to be with you." He gripped her arm as tightly as he could but it barely lasted a second before it slipped lifelessly to the ground.

Ember ignored every promise she had made to herself on how she would leave. She knelt again quickly, close to him, and picked up his hand in her own. "Find a way," she whispered fiercely. "I will be there when you do." She kissed him. He tried to put his arms around her, to pull her down, but his body would not respond. She pulled away and he felt his soul scream out again.

She stood and backed away from him. Her eyes – green and brown with glints of gold that the firelight turned red – were as cold and as hard as iron.

"Now tell me what I want to hear," she said. Her voice was edged with steel. His heart ached miserably but he was amazed to feel everything else harden inside him.

"I cannot be beaten," he said evenly. He was not surprised to hear the iron in his own voice.

He saw her slight nod one last time, and the fire flare within her eyes. Then with a sudden turn he caught nothing but a glimpse of her hair and the whip of her cloak.

She was gone.

Traejan let his head fall back. He let the tears come, and there seemed no end to them, but he tried not to weep. Not because he could now sense his Praetorian nearby, but because he felt that if he gave in to the pain he would not be able to recover from it.

He closed his eyes and saw waterfalls. He tried not to think of that day, of his love - the light in her hair or the plan that had been in her heart - for that was too painful. Instead he thought of the lesson, and what she had taught him.

Our love is like the water, she had told him. *It is clear and pure and yet does fear the dirt or filth of any world. It will plunge from the greatest of heights, unafraid and unhurt. It can be touched and taken, but never destroyed. It does not fear being divided, for it knows that it will be joined again someday.*

He took a deep breath, cursing his useless body and trying to assess it. His chest felt as if it had been crushed, and his arms and legs were still dead and lifeless. But he knew that the pain in his heart would subside, and when the feeling returned to his limbs he would have more strength than he ever had before. He had a feeling of determination that he had never known.

Peg came slowly up to him. She, too, was still saddled and looked as sad as he felt. She dropped her head and nuzzled his cropped hair.

"Did you know what they were up to?" he asked her. She whickered softly. Traejan was not sure but he thought it might have been a yes. "Traitor," he said, accusingly but without malice.

Peg only looked at him as if to say, *what was I supposed to do about it?*

Minutes passed and the fire crackled and fell. As the feeling and strength returned to his body he could feel the strength and resolve return to his heart. The tears dried on his face and eventually he was able to raise a clumsy hand and wipe away their ghostly tracks.

Dell entered the clearing almost an hour later, looking shy and uncomfortable. "It's good to see you," he said, hardly looking at his charge.

"You too," Traejan said. He tried to rise and only managed to fall over. Dell was there, helping him back into a sitting position. "I might need a few more minutes," the young prince admitted.

"Take all the time you need," Dell assured him. There were many questions that the guardsman wanted to ask the prince, but he felt that the closeness they had shared over the past few decades had dissolved with the summer, and now he did not dare. Instead, he fed a few branches to the fire, waiting patiently. The silence drew out for minutes, then an hour.

"You have been north?" Traejan finally asked.

Dell looked up, the light of the fire glinting off of his dark eyes. "I have."

"You know of the Crommags?"

Dell nodded, his eyes grave. "I do." Then a ghost of a smile touched his lips. "And it seems that you have fought a few."

Traejan did not ask Dell how he knew - the elf was a Jäger. The prince just nodded and smiled as well - yet his smile was small, forced. It had been his first fight, his first victory, and the first time he kissed her. Tears threatened his eyes so he tried once again to stand. He managed to get to his knees, and then staggered to his feet.

Dell offered the young elf a hand, grasping his arm tightly as he regained his footing. Traejan embraced his Praetorian on unsteady legs and clapped his guardsman on the back, lost for words. He turned, careful not to topple over, and reached for Peg.

"I can help you up..." Dell offered, "or if you would rather stay and rest some more..."

Traejan shook his head. Holding onto his mount, he attempted to stick the toe of his boot in the stirrup and missed. Tried and missed again. Dell reached out and held the stirrup steady, making sure the prince found his mark on the next try. Traejan then reached up and grabbed a handful of Peg's mane in one hand and the saddle horn in the other and hauled himself up. He took a deep breath and turned the white palfrey and urged her on, headed for home. He did not look to see if Dell followed. His heart was so heavy that it pulled his shoulders down with it. But determination kept it going, as it always had.

He would find a way.

Dell followed silently. He watched the young prince riding a few paces ahead of him, and knew he was a different elf from the one he had known for more than a hundred years. He could feel a great pain from him, but there was so much more. There was an intensity about him, so strong that he practically glowed with it.

Three miles later, at the edge of Amherst, the rest of the Jägers joined them, falling in and following without a word. Dell was relieved that he had them wait for them out of elfin earshot. The message he had been given by a golden-haired rider from Trimpe had told him of the new meeting place, and that it should be as private as possible. He had no idea to what extent.

As they neared the human town, a number of sharp snaps could be heard from firepops being set off by children. The Jägers heads turned as one toward the sound, and then swiveled back to the path ahead. The way was well worn and the light of the moon shone down through the trees, giving them a silver ribbon to ride upon.

Soon, more sounds drifted through the air, carried on a warm breeze laced with cool fingers. Autumn had come to the land and the people were celebrating harvest. The elves rode silently, but they could hear the notes of music and people laughing and children shouting as they ran and played. The nearby town was full of bonfires, dancing, games, and the smell of roasting meats and maize.

The group of elfin Jägers skirted the settlement as they made their way for home, silent and unnoticed.

Dell watched the young prince sway slightly in his saddle, stiff and proud and fierce, and wondered to all the gods and demons of every circle what would come of all this.

The Praetorian still could not believe what he had heard and wished that he had not. The words that Traejanale Royce, the Prince of the Elves and second son to Rowland the Great, had spoken when he had grabbed the woman's arm, had been elfin vows of marriage.

Irrevocable, even by death.

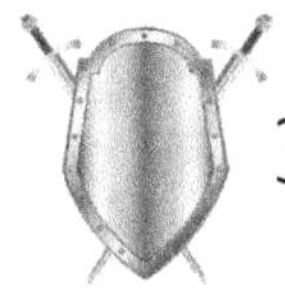

38. ROSHAN AND CROMMAGS

The Roshan rode like the Seventh Circle and as if all the hell that it contained were after her.

Never before had she pressed the Night Stallion to such a full and hard gallop or for so long. The giant horse did not seem to mind. Massive muscles stretched and flexed under his smooth black skin and his red-ringed eyes were as intense as her own as they pushed hard for the south. Foam flew from his fangs and his great hooves beat the ground as he ran, leaving clods of earth and wind in their wake.

The wind of the ride pushed her leaking tears back towards her ears, even as they dried. Coal's black mane whipped in her face and her black cloak snapped behind her as if they were being chased by a storm.

She put her head down as the landscape slid by, forests and hills and grasslands shaded grey in the darkness made twilight, the night illuminated by the swollen Harvest Moon. Coal put his head down as well, his powerful legs stretching and contracting as they ate up the terrain. Together the horse and rider were a black streak in the night.

Had she been wrong? Had she made the wrong choice?

Yes! her heart screamed.

Her mind said, *no.*

Go after him, her heart cried, *it's not too late!*

Coal raced for the end of the valley and the Roshan released the pressure of her heels in his flanks. She realized that she was trying to put as much distance as she could between herself and her love, lest she change her mind. The great stallion slowed, but not much. He had not yet had his fill and ran on for near another mile.

Traejanale Royce is a warrior now, Ember told herself, clinging to the back the enormous charger as he plunged ahead. *With what you've instilled in him, he need not fear neither death nor defeat. He is safe, and will only be made stronger by the trials ahead of him.*

She could feel her shoulders, as well as her heart, slump. Coal, sensing this, finally pulled out of his wild gallop and danced sideways, snorting and tossing his mane while his fangs chomped his bit, dripping foam. Then, to the Roshan's surprise, he reared. Ember held tight, no easy task with his monstrous size, as he pawed the air with his great hooves and let out a mighty scream.

He came down with a crash that made the trees on the edge of the valley tremble and, feeling his turmoil, the Roshan did not rebuke him. Instead, she reached down and gave him a number of rough pats on his neck.

"I know," she soothed. "I know."

Fresh tears painted her cheeks and she wiped them off with the back of her arm. For some reason Coal's outburst had calmed her.

Is it enough? the voice whispered inside her mind. *Is it enough to know you've found love, and that he is out there?*

"It has to be," she whispered back. "For now."

Sobered, the Roshan's eyes flicked about their surroundings. Coal had managed to dance sideways enough times to turn a half-circle, so they were facing back the way they had come.

"Nice try," the Roshan said, her tone wry.

She clucked her tongue and pulled on the right rein, turning him south again before she put her heels to his sides and urged him forward. She would be crossing the rivers again before moonset. Coal tossed his mane in her face but did as he was bid.

"He has a king to report to," the Roshan told the great beast. "And so do we."

⚮

Ayala, a mountain of a man, shifted the skin of the snow leopard so that it fell tighter around his shoulders. The lands to the south might be celebrating the joys of autumn but, in the Northlon, winter was already nipping about the place, tasting it. Soon, she would sink her fangs into the land and its people. The first snow was still a few weeks away but the clans, encamped at the foot of the Steppes from one end of the valley to the other, had awoken for the past six mornings with a dusting of frost on the ground and more on the tents. They looked at it without surprise or dismay. They were a people of ice and cold – the thin veil of crystals meant nothing.

The meetings with the tribes had gone well, just as Noga had said they would. Not that Ayala had doubted him. He knew that his brother was wise beyond size, and years. He had never known Noga to be wrong. Only one clan of the Great Men had declined to join them – the Mammoth Hunters.

It was the same clan that Noga had predicted would decline. When the leader of the Mammoth Hunters had told Ayala that he was sorry but his clan would be returning to the Frozen Waste, Ayala had grunted and smiled. Not because he did not want the clan, but because Noga had been right once again. The leader of the Mammoth Hunters had paused with a frown, wondering if the Chief of the Bite, now Chief of all Great Men save for his own, knew something that he did not.

Ayala adjusted the skin once again as he left his tent and walked south between the shelters and campfires. Four men fell in around him, each from a different tribe, huge and silent.

Ayala had not wanted a guard but Noga had insisted.

"I can protect myself well enough," Ayala had grumbled. "And certainly I will not be attacked within the camp." Noga had rolled his pale eyes.

"They are not there to protect you," the smaller Crommag explained. "Though you probably need it, weak and small as you are." Ayala had grunted in amusement and swung a colossal fist at his little brother. Noga had ducked easily and continued. "They are there to show the others how *important* you are."

Ayala had grunted again as he considered his brother's words, then frowned. "But there are eight tribes," he speculated aloud. "Won't the tribes that are not chosen to have a guard for me be offended?" Noga had been schooling his older brother on politics for the better part of a year.

The younger Crommag had grinned. "I see the chipmunks that serve as your brain are still fucking," he commented. Ayala, who could recognize a backhanded compliment from his brother well enough, took another swing at him and this time managed to cuff him across his untiring mouth.

Noga had laughed as he gave his head a hard shake, recovering quickly from a hit that would have knocked a human unconscious. "They will," he agreed jovially, "which is why you need to take them aside afterwards and say that you need members from their tribes for something special." Ayala had nodded, listening carefully. "You must tell them it is because their tribes are the most cunning, and you must say it quietly so they think they are being told something serious and in secret."

Ayala had nodded. His brother was smarter by far, but that did not mean that Ayala could not comprehend his strategy and tactics. Once the brothers had begun to plan their quest in earnest, he had been an apt pupil.

The breeze picked up as the sky darkened, turning into an

icy wind as it blew through the glacial pass. The leader of the Great Men pulled the snow leopard skin tighter around his shoulders. Two men walked before him, off to either side. The one from the Cave Bear Tribe was as large as Ayala himself, the one from the Polar Bear Tribe was even larger. His rear guard consisted of a man from the Snow Leopard Clan and a brute from the clan of the Ice Walkers.

The leader of the Great Men had to admit, an escort did make him feel as important as he looked. Women and men and children, gathering around their night fires for the evening, nodded at him as he passed. Looking into their eyes, Ayala saw something for the first time.

They don't just give me pride, he realized. *I give them pride as well.*

Unification was the word that Noga had used and Ayala had heard it and understood it well enough, but only in the simplest of terms. He knew that it meant it would bring the many tribes together into one.

But now it was more.

Together, they had purpose.

They had *meaning.*

The humans and elves thought of the Great Men as having no more thought, substance, or meaning than animals. Less, even. Humans and elves alike held some animals, from their horses even to their dogs and cats, in high regard – almost members of their families. The Great Men were spat upon, scorned and killed.

No more.

That debasement was at its end. Ayala would see to that end.

Men gave him discreet smiles of pride as he passed by them. Women looked up from their cooking pots over their fires to give him a nod of appreciation. They knew that what he did spoke for their past, present, and would change their future.

Children cheered as he walked by and many followed.

Ayala's chest swelled as he made his way to the Floe.

Finally, the leader of the Great Men, the *unified* Great Men, stood at the river's edge.

The river itself was becoming sluggish, lazy as its freezing waters began to turn to a slush that would gradually fuse into a solid mass of winter ice.

Noga, his brother – both a runt and a sage among the Great Men – stood waiting a hundred yards away, across the slothful and erratic lurch of the icy waters. The head on the pelt of the snow leopard that he wore around his shoulders was thrown back, exposing his unnaturally fair hair.

The Ice Floe, still wide enough to rage and yet cold enough to have small bergs smash and grind together, would keep their voices from being heard. Having foreseen the need, the two brothers signaled each other.

Noga held up two fingers and then drew one across his throat. Ayala nodded. His brother had told him before that, like than naught, two scouting troops would be taken. Then Noga hitched a thumb over his right shoulder and nodded. The chief of the Great Men dipped his own head again to acknowledge. The signal meant that all was going according to plan on the south side of the river. Noga had secured a number of Gnomin and was putting them to work. Soon, the Great Men would have weapons.

Weapons of steel.

The weapons of an army.

Ayala held up seven fingers and Noga, from across the wide and icy river, gave his brother a quick nod – he had expected as much. He knew the Mammoth Hunters would refuse to join, at first.

The Great Men of the arctic passes did not have the need that the other clans did. The enormous beasts that they hunted gave them nearly everything they needed to survive, mainly food and warmth.

The Walrus Men were also favored with a surplus of food in good years, but they lost many husbands and wives and sons and daughters to the sea. If offered a better life, they would take it, and they did.

Still, Noga thought, the Mammoth Hunters might come back. *If they have any sense of pride, they will come back.* He had a feeling they would.

But, even without the Mammoth Hunters, the small Crommag was fairly sure that they would outnumber the elves.

Such numbers had been hard to discover.

Noga had spent six months with the parties of Crommags that had raided the Northlon farms. Along with their intent to drive the humans out, he had the self-appointed task of finding a human that spoke Gnomin. It was a task neither easy nor expeditious.

The smaller Crommag knew but a little of the language the humans used, and most encounters with them resulted in panic. Humans, he had found, only had two reactions to panic – fight or flight. Both responses usually ended equally quick and fatal. It had been a time-consuming and trying time for Noga. He had finally discovered he needed to hold back the raiding party from an all-out attack long enough for him to blurt out *"talks Gnomin?"*

Most encounters were followed by the usual fight or flight, though Noga had gotten an occasional blank look or one of surprise. Late this summer, he had gotten an actual response. A young human male on the westerly edge of the Veldt had spoken, brokenly, with Noga. In the end, he let himself be taken in order to spare his younger sisters.

In the few months that ensued, Noga kept the man alive the best he could, yet as the terror in the youth dwindled, a dejected sullenness set in that the Crommag feared was a sickness. The raid and capture of the Gnomin had been a success and the young man had become a bit more animated for while, having someone else to talk to besides the stunted yet fearsome Crommag.

Still huge compared to the human, Noga spoke with him every day. Every chance he was afforded, he honed his skill with the human language. The human knew little of elves, but held a disdain for them that surprised Noga. He told the Crommag that the elves were weak, and few. It was something Noga was glad to hear, but did not trust the youth any more than the youth trusted the runty Crommag.

Noga listened intently whenever the human communicated with the new captives and slowly he began to learn some Gnomin as well. He itched to get his great hands on a Vikeman.

He would learn a new dialect, and get more information on the Skye Elves. He wished he could tell his brother in more detail about what he was learning. He knew that one of the Walrus Men could probably snag a Vikeman for him, but he had no way to ask. For now, all the brothers had were the signals they had decided on and practiced until the end of last winter.

So Noga signaled.

Ayala, on the far side of the sluggish Floe that surged with chunks of ice, nodded. His eyes were beady and small, but that did not keep him from seeing far across the freezing waters and noting the bulge at Noga's hip. He could even see the hardened leather tip of the bladder that served as a spout, poking out from the snow leopard skin that he wore. He knew that the bladder was full of a very strong grog. Noga was small for a Crommag, yet he would drink it all tonight – quaffing it down quickly – and soon. Ayala hoped it would be enough. He did not envy his brother this night. Noga was small, he was cunning, and he was very brave.

Maybe a little crazy even, Ayala thought. He gnashed his fangs together in aggravation and Noga smiled at him from across the river.

Ayala, a mountain of a man and the leader of the Great

Men, turned from the river and headed back to his tent. His guard, a squad of brutes that were terrifying in both size and ugliness, followed without a word. Their massive heads would occasionally swing to the side and beady eyes would dart suspiciously about as they looked for any threat to the Great Chief. Their brains were small and slow, and they knew that no threat would come from inside the camp, but they were filled with pride by their appointment as his personal guards.

Noga turned as well and pulled the bladder full of grog from where it hung on his hip and took a long series of gulps. His own personal guards watched him. They were only two but handpicked by the younger brother since they were almost as smart as Noga himself.

The small Crommag finally paused and drew a large hand across his mouth, and started for his tent. When he reached the entrance he stopped and upended the bladder, slugging down the rest of the grog in three long swallows. His guards pulled back the flaps of the tent, spilling the bright light inside out into the darkness.

The tent was large, befitting a leader, and Noga was second to the Great Chief. Two great braziers held newly built fires that lit and heat the structure as if it were high-noon at midsummer. There were tables with maps, a few chairs, and a number of weapons stacked in one corner. A low bed skulked in the back.

Also inside, waited the human prisoner and a pair of nervous looking Gnomin. The guards looked at Noga but he frowned and shook his head, much to their relief. Both guards, like most Crommags, were sadistic and cruel. But even they did not want to watch what was going to happen. Noga handed one the empty bladder to refill with the same, strong grog.

He would need it tonight.

Tomorrow too, most likely.

Noga shouldered the partitions aside and lumbered into his tent, letting the flaps drop close behind him.

 AUTHOR'S NOTE

Of course the natural thing to do is to end with a quote about love, but there are just so damn many. Love is patient, love is kind, love is all you need, hurts, wounds, scars...fill in your favorite poem or song or movie. My favorite romantic movie is *The Terminator* – and if you do not think of it as a love story then you need to watch it again. The story alone is so all encompassing and awesome, plus I think it has the most poignant love scene ever captured on film. Songs of love, and war, predate the Greek ballads so you have plenty to choose from.

Speaking of love and war, isn't it funny how the two of those often go hand in hand? Even in this simple story, love finds a way and war is destined. Let me interject here that, for me, this story was anything but simple. My mother read *The Hobbit* to me when I was six years old and I spent the next twelve years devouring every novel on magic and fantasy that I could get my hands on. After writing four science-fiction novels I thought that writing a book about fantasy would be easier than riding a bike. It wasn't. More like learning to ride a unicycle... while juggling - two things I have never been able to master. Nonetheless, I think it turned out just fine.

So, dear reader, am I to guess you want to know how this ties into the GwenSeven Saga? Well, for the most astute readers, you already know. I left enough clues for you to know who Ember is, just not how she got there. Not to worry though, the next book (The Rings of Saturn Part Two) will bring it all together with startling clarity.

So for now, consider what love is to you. Music? A cheeseburger? Sunday brunch with your closest friends? Your cat? It really doesn't matter. The one thing I can tell you for sure is that love is the highest frequency in which we can live and it doesn't have to be with another person – though that can be nice. First learn to love yourself, which is hard for most of us. Then learn to love life. Then let that feeling expand and fill the world. Sound impossible? It isn't.

I'll be back.